THE SILVER TOKEN

a novel

ALAN R. MARBLE

The Silver Token
2012
Relic Books
www.relic-books.com
ISBN-13: 978-0-9886239-0-3

Cover illustration by Maarta Laiho | www.pencilcat.net

ACKNOWLEDGMENTS

Books do not write themselves. They require inspiration, encouragement, long hours at the keyboard, and a whole lot of time and other investments to get off the ground. This is not a task I could have accomplished on my own, and I would be remiss were I to fail to mention their contributions, direct or indirect. I have neither the time nor the ability to mention them all by name, but let me at least offer my profound gratitude to:

Dawn, for getting me off my behind and making me do it;
Mom, for being a fan before I deserved any;
Derek, for showing me that it could be done;
Nathaniel, for cheering me up.

I must also take an opportunity to personally thank the following, whose generous contributions and confidence have made this endeavor a reality:

Greg and Kelly Marble
Cmdr and Mrs Robert C Alexander (USN Retired)
Virginia Brough
Waylon and Erin, the young Marbles
Luke Mezera (Fielious)
Soreth
Justin Freeman (Shadowsedge)
Francis Barbeau
Goldkin
BlackfootFerret
t'sChillin t'soulntai
Jak Forster
Taylor

For all the dragons out there

PROLOGUE

Jonah rolled over reluctantly in his bed at the behest of the alarm clock buzzing angrily at his side, reaching over to smack at the snooze button and silence the unwelcome sound. The big LED digits burned an insistent 6:18 into his retinas. Third time he'd hit the snooze button, he realized. Sighing heavily at the conclusion that he couldn't put his day off any longer, he finally pushed the blanket off and stumbled out of bed and toward the bathroom.

Sunlight was already filtering in through the heavy blinds over the windows but it was still dark enough in his room that when he turned the lights on he flinched, squinting a bit to adjust. Turning on the faucet and running his hands beneath the cold water, he splashed some on his face and ran his palms back over his brown hair, coaxing the tousled mess into something vaguely resembling order. It'd be sufficient, just as it always had.

Peering back briefly at the reflection of his tired blue-gray eyes in the mirror, he ran a finger along his jawline right down to his chin, frowning at the complete lack of stubble. He had been trying to grow a goatee of late - or, at least, hoping that if he thought about it hard enough at least some facial hair might spring into existence. He'd recently turned 27 but didn't look a day over 21, and while the good-natured "babyface" jokes he could tolerate, looking like a college student had its disadvantages when he was hoping to be taken more seriously. His utter inability to grow facial hair didn't help.

Shrugging it off with a slightly disinterested sigh, he turned back to his room and made his way across the landscape of dirty laundry that had failed to make its way to the hamper, pulling open the door to the closet and snagging a pair of blue jeans to pull on. The closest tee-shirt was then grabbed and pulled over his head, once again smoothing his hair down to some extent. He didn't really care which shirt it was, since no one else seemed to, either.

His bedroom, just as his attire, was the image of consummate bachelorhood. More than just the untidy piles of clothing strewn about was the otherwise generic flavor of the room. A full sized bed with a generic bedspread that was almost never made, a plain looking nightstand that sported only an alarm clock and a fashionable if predictable lamp, and a few posters from bands that had been all the rage just after graduating from college that he had not bothered to replace were the products of his lackluster home decorating skills.

Jonah had lived in the same one bedroom apartment in Fort Lauderdale since graduating from college some five years ago. Before college he had grown up in various cities in Florida, mostly on the Gulf Coast : Pensacola, Tallahassee, Orlando, Tampa, and finally in the relatively sleepy Port Charlotte. His parents had never been the type to feel settled down and connected to one place, much to the chagrin of a growing boy who had to constantly make new friends and bid farewell to old ones. Perhaps it was part of the reason that he'd let himself get so tied down since graduation.

He'd gone to the University of Miami to study computer science. Bright but somewhat unmotivated, he'd graduated with good grades and had gotten job offers from companies on the West Coast but turned them down. Most of his classmates and friends had taken the offers and fled the state for newer opportunities but he was satisfied with the offer to work as a junior database administrator for Miami-Dade County.

The brand new apartment complex in nearby Fort Lauderdale promised all the amenities of a cosmopolitan lifestyle at half the price and the commute was something he could live with. Yet in the five years that he'd lived there, Jonah had failed to take much advantage of the promised lifestyle. Nearby clubs advertised heavily, tacking fliers up on the communal noticeboard at the apartment offices, but they'd never really panned out for him. It probably didn't help that he looked so young, either; he'd grown rather tired of the single women responding to his advances with jokes about an imagined skill in forging identification documents.

With few local friends - all of the acquaintances he had made in school had left the state and he'd lost contact with them soon enough - it didn't take long for work to become his only real social outlet. He'd made a few decent friends there, though most were older than him. Their invitations to things like sports bars and NASCAR events down in Homestead, while generally accepted, failed to ignite much interest in him. When such invitations didn't materialize, his weekends were often spent halfheartedly perusing movie channels or plodding his way through the latest video game that he'd picked up.

Even his job itself failed to motivate him. It was a decent place to work and the pay was good, allowing him to outfit his small apartment with all the latest in terms of gadgets and gizmos, but even then he found it less than challenging and motivating. He performed well - the "junior" had been dropped from his title within a year - but it was more out of a sense of duty than any specific desire to excel or make a name for himself. His supervisor had told him that if he showed a little more motivation that he'd be going places. He just wasn't sure where he wanted to be going – or if he cared to go anywhere, at all.

His life had become routine, predictable, even boring, but Jonah didn't much care. He had enough money to buy the things that he needed and wanted, he was comfortable in his position, and felt no real ambition to change the status quo. Years on the move had taught him to be self-sufficient, to not have to rely on anyone else to fulfill his needs or make him happy. He didn't need the accolades of others or the promise of charging his way on up the corporate ladder.

Wandering out of the bedroom and into the small living quarters of his apartment, he made his way over to the futon that sat in front of a medium sized plasma television, finding the remote and flicking it on to the morning news. The weatherman was predicting another sunny day, engaging in some useless banter with the anchorman. Not that Jonah really paid attention to what was being said - he had it on more for the background noise, as well as the traffic report whenever it came up.

A detour was made to the kitchen, small but functional. The counter was decorated with a half-finished can of soda and a plastic bag with a few empty Chinese takeout containers, the remnants of kung-pao chicken and fried rice lending their aromas to the slightly stale ambiance of the room. Briefly he considered cleaning them up, but he told himself that he'd have plenty of time to do it later.

Opening the refrigerator, he was a little dismayed - but not surprised - to see it all but devoid of groceries. Some cans of soda and a few bottles of beer rattled on one of the shelves. Jonah reached for a Ziploc bag with half a dozen peeled, hard boiled eggs, which represented the peak of his culinary abilities. Pulling two of them out, he popped one in his mouth and started to chew on it absently, making his way back out into the living room to catch the traffic report.

Instead he caught the tail end of a brief news story on how one of the local police departments or something to that effect was gearing up for a Memorial Day event to take place later that day. It was Memorial Day. He could have been sleeping in, but he had completely forgotten about it when he had set his alarm clock the night before. Now it wasn't even seven in the morning and he was wide awake.

With a heavy, dejected sigh, Jonah slumped down on the futon and shook his head. Looking down at the egg that he had in his hand, he asked the question aloud : "Well. What am I supposed to do with today, then?"

He had made no plans. His boss had invited him, along with the rest of his department, out for a day of fishing on what he playfully referred to as his "yacht", but fishing was not the sort of thing that Jonah had cared for. He had politely declined. His parents had also dutifully invited him to their home, as they did every year since he had moved out, to enjoy some barbecue with the rest of the family. While he had not outright declined he had left them with a "we'll see" sort of answer, as he did every year. He didn't expect to make it out there, either; the three hour trip across the Everglades didn't much appeal to him.

Somewhat reflexively he scooped up a video game controller that sat on the futon next to him, sliding his thumb over one of the buttons as he nibbled on the egg in his other hand. He did have a few games that he'd acquired lately and not really played much, some battle simulation game that was supposed to be all the rage that everyone was playing. It'd be a chance to finally pick it up, polish his skills and see what the fuss was all about.

Yet even things like video games had lost their luster over time. Back in his college days, or even shortly thereafter, he would have stayed up an entire night after picking up a hot title like that, fortified with Mountain Dew and Doritos, working to become a veritable guru at the game overnight. Now, in spite of the fact that he'd paid the money for the damned thing, he had barely mustered enough interest to fire the game up and give it a go. It was just hard to care about it.

Jonah let the controller slip from his hand again and tumble forgotten to the floor. He just couldn't get worked up about spending an entire day in front of the television screen, game or no game.

Glancing around, his eyes lit upon his motorcycle helmet resting on the ground near the door, brightly colored with a sort of stylized dragon motif done up in black, vaguely reminiscent of a tribal tattoo design. It was going to be a beautiful, sunny day by all accounts, the perfect sort of weather for a ride. Perhaps he could cruise down the seaside and hit up South Beach.

In what had been a life full of otherwise carefully crafted safety, his motorcycle had been Jonah's only risk outlet. He'd bought it within a year of his graduation, nearly ten thousand dollars' worth of shiny green Japanese engineering. It was supposed to have been the embodiment of everything a young guy like himself should embrace : power, speed, recklessness, and a certain carefree disregard for expectations.

Four years later it was still Jonah's primary mode of transportation and still served as a sort of id to the ego of his life, but otherwise failed to change him on a fundamental level. It had done little to garner attention from the fairer sex, and in the few cases it had, had not been able to overcome his overly youthful looks and reserved, risk-averse nature. Some of the local riders he had come to know still teased him mercilessly about the size of his chicken strips, biker lingo for the unworn outer edges of his tires and proof positive of his unwillingness to lean hard into corners at high speeds.

It reminded him of another invite he had gotten for the holiday. A coworker who was also a sport bike enthusiast had introduced him to a small group in the area who got together for occasional weekend rides or other events. They had all taken off for Key West the day before, where they would be attending some sort of party or other event that was supposed to be rife with single young ladies. They were going to be staying overnight - a fact that was mentioned replete with sly winks and nudges implying ulterior motives - and heading back sometime later that afternoon.

That, too, he had declined. Something about the thought of riding such a long distance and over large stretches of water left him feeling unsettled. He also knew that he'd be ultimately unsuccessful with the single young ladies and be spending the night alone. The fear of being the only one to strike out was enough to get him to pass on the invitation and stay at home.

His inability to drag his knees in corners or entice any buxom passengers aside, he did still enjoy the bike and did enjoy the rides, the sense of freedom that it gave him. He didn't need the company of others to enjoy a languid ride down the beachfront highway, after all. Finishing off what remained of his egg, he licked his fingers clean and started to pull on his shoes. He'd have something to keep his day from being completely dull, after all.

ONE

The little chime of the bell that hung over the door was a friendly, pleasant sound, a welcome contrast to the harsh, clattering buzz of the door being unlocked. A simple sign of the times, thought Jonah, no longer the sort of thing that most people would take the time to ponder. It wouldn't do to have a coin shop loaded with gold and silver coins with the door just hanging open to the public, after all.

Letting the door close behind him, chiming the bell once again, the young man turned his attention briefly to the interior of the coin shop. It was a small, cramped affair, crowded with glass jewelry cases wedged in as tight as they would fit. There was a pervasive musty odor that refused to be overpowered by the fresher air that rushed in from the door, lending the shop an old and slightly dilapidated quality to it. The staticky warble of big band music playing over an old AM radio did nothing to alleviate the sense that the store existed in some kind of time warp, none of which seemed to bother Jonah in the least, and all seemed to suit the owner just fine.

"Ah, Jonah. Good to see you!" The elderly shop owner, offering an amiable wave from behind the counter, was a caricature to match the ambiance: dressed in a tweed jacket with a flat cap to match, gazing out through a thick pair of horn-rimmed glasses with friendly, rheumy eyes. "What can I do for you today, sir?"

"Sammy!" Jonah smiled brightly and stepped up to the counter, reaching over to shake the old man's hand, surprised as always at the strength that those big old fingers still held. "Can't I stop by and just check in on a good friend?"

Sam, the shop owner, chuckled heartily. "Ah, a social call is it? Why, that's all fine and dandy but it's business hours, and I've a business to run, don't you know? Customers to tend to, money to earn!"

The shop was, in fact, quite abandoned save for the two men, a fact that was punctuated by the brief lull in the conversation. Jonah paused, looking around the shop in an exaggerated fashion, scanning with his dusky blue eyes, listening to the slightly distorted music filtering through the room. "Customers! Looks like it's just you and Glenn Miller, and I'm not sure he's interested in buying anything ..."

"Psh! Middle of the day and all, you know. I'll have you know that on weekends there's a line outside, people just waiting to get in!" Sam smiled crookedly, a set of brilliant white dentures looking a bit out of place on his otherwise well-worn face. "Say, speaking of the middle of the day, what are you doing here? Shouldn't you be at work, or something?"

"Come on, Sam, it's Memorial Day. Got the day off. Decided to go for a ride and wouldn't you know it, I found myself passing right by your place. Figured I'd stop in and see what's new. What're you doing open today, anyway? Shouldn't you have the day off?"

"Day off?" The old man waved his hand around dismissively at the thought. "A day off is a day when I can't make any money."

"Right," Jonah said with a nod, leaning over and peering into one of the display cases while thoughtfully stroking his chin.

The old man sputtered with a little laugh. "So you say you're here to see what's new? Not just here for the company after all!"

Jonah leaned in and faked a conspiratory little smile. Escaping his apartment for a morning ride along the seaside had done much to invigorate him, lifting his spirits. The thought of indulging in another one of his precious few interests had left him feeling practically giddy by comparison. "I suppose you've got me there, Sam. Money's practically burning in my pocket."

Collecting coins was, in fact, one of the few real passions in Jonah's life. Ever since the day his father had given him a US Mint silver poof set for his 8th birthday, he had become fascinated by coins. He had demanded that his allowance be paid in quarters so that he could sift through them, meticulously sorting them by date and mint mark, storing the new finds away and spending much of the rest at local coins shops when he could convince his parents to take him. When he'd gotten a little older and began to understand the value in certain rarer finds, he had started saving his money. Where other children saved theirs for trading cards or the latest video game, he'd save his for a buffalo nickel.

Over time he'd developed an especial affinity for silver. Since graduating college and getting a fairly good paycheck he'd been able to graduate from a coin here and there to somewhat regular purchases, filling in gaps in his collection, growing from hundreds of dollars to several thousands of dollars in value. Sam, who had gotten to know him quite well over many visits during the years, often joked that the value of his collection hidden away under his bed probably rivaled the stock in the shop.

"Don't want to singe yourself too badly, best hand those burning bills on over," the older man said with a jovial chuckle, before reaching his hands underneath the counter. "You've got some pretty good timing, too. Just finished going through some recent acquisitions, got a whole boxful of new stuff from an estate sale. Some real gems here, and it looks like you've got first dibs."

Jonah watched as he pulled a tray out from beneath the counter and set it on top, waving a wrinkled hand over it with a flourish. There were rows of coins, some encapsulated in plastic containers and professionally graded, others loose but propped up in little slots in the felt tray. Several gold coins glimmered in neat rows on one side of the tray, just begging for attention, but gold was a little too rich for his blood. "New stuff, eh?"

"Oh yes. He was a collector, had a lot of good stuff. Look, here, a 1921 standing liberty quarter. You've been looking for one of these for a while, haven't you?" The old man continued yammering on about the particular little gems and surprises in the lot, carefully pulling a few coins out of their spot and laying them out flat on the top of the counter. Jonah paid them a passing glance - he had, indeed, been looking out for that particular quarter - but found that he could not help but to keep looking back the tray, scanning the little rows of loose coins. One in particular, something dull and easy to overlook among the shinier selections, kept catching his attention.

Reaching in, he pointed at the little dull coin. "What about this one? What's this?"

"Hmm? Oh, well, let's see here," Sam said, sounding briefly disoriented as he'd been interrupted in the middle of his spiel. Thick, shaky fingers pulled the coin out of its slot and laid it flat on an unoccupied piece of the felt. "Well now isn't that odd, I don't remember seeing this one in the collection, how did it get here?"

"Where did it come from?" Jonah asked the question without looking up, his eyes fixated on the coin. It was small, about the size of a penny, silver in color, well-worn and tarnished. There looked to have been some lettering but it had been worn smooth, and in the center some kind of intricate weave pattern. "What can you tell me about it?"

Sam picked the coin up again, turning it in his fingers. "I'm ... I'm not quite sure to tell you the truth, I've never seen this coin before. I'm positive it wasn't in this collection before, I would have remembered seeing something like this."

Jonah grinned a little, briefly looking away from the coin. "Sure this one didn't just slip through the cracks?"

"Psh." The shopkeeper's voice sounded ever so slightly irritated, but his gaze was fixed on the little coin as he turned it around in his fingers. "Not even sure what it is. Feels about right for a silver coin, and it's about the right size for a Roman denarius. Definitely looks old," he continued, muttering, fumbling with his free hand for a loupe sitting next to the register to give it a closer look. "Well-worn but not in terrible shape. But these markings … makes no sense."

Watching with rapt attention, Jonah did not realize he was leaning so heavily over the counter until he nearly bumped into Sam's head, pulling back at the last second with a little blink. "Wrong?"

"Roman coins always had some kind of bust on one side, usually the emperor at the time the coin was minted. Some god or goddess on the other side. This," he said, setting down the loupe and resting the coin in the palm of his hand. "This is a Celtic knot. Inspired by Roman artwork but definitely not Roman. And the inscription … it's pretty worn out but doesn't look Latin to me."

Jonah found himself strangely deflated at the news, but continued to pay attention while Sam turned the coin over. The other side, which he hadn't seen before, looked to be some kind of stylized dragon, like something one might see on an old family crest. "Now, this … this doesn't look right at all. Style isn't Roman at all, and once again this lettering doesn't appear to be Latin."

"So. You know what it isn't … but can't say what it is?"

Sam huffed a little and then sighed. "Afraid not. It's definitely old, and the right size, but the markings just aren't right for a denarius. I suppose the designs are more classically British, so maybe it's some kind of token, maybe an old denarius that someone repurposed, but it's nothing like I've seen before."

Without stopping to think about it, Jonah reached into his pocket and fished out his wallet. "How much do you want for it?"

"What? You want to buy this thing?"

"Fifty dollars." As if to punctuate his offer, he pulled out a crisp $50 bill and laid it out on the counter.

The old man looked from the bill, to the coin, and then back up at Jonah. "Fifty bucks? Look, I'm all for making a buck but this thing is worth maybe three dollars in silver. Hell, even a denarius in this condition might not bring that much, just depending on whose mug is on the damned thing."

"Or it could be the first ever coin discovered that was minted by one of the first kings of England, and might be worth millions." Jonah smirked a little bit, pushing the bill in Sam's direction. "Fifty bucks."

"Well, that's a bit of a stretch of the imagination. Likely as not I'm still getting the better end of this bargain," the old man said, peering down at the fifty and then sighing. "All right, fifty bucks it is. But if you turn around and get rich of this thing …"

With a little more haste than he intended, Jonah snatched the coin off the counter, gave it a cursory look before stuffing it into his pocket. "Uh, yeah. Don't worry, Sam, I'll take you out to dinner if it comes to that," he added, a little meekly.

"Steak dinner," Sam said, waving the fifty in the air and making his way over to his cash register, ringing the sale up. "Make that steak and lobster. Surf and turf." Jonah smiled, and opened his mouth, about to respond to the demand when a loud buzzing from behind him caught him off guard, and he found himself whirling about. "Looks like we got another customer," the shopkeeper muttered, also turning to look in the direction of the door.

The heavy tinting of the glass windows made it so that Sam could see the customers ringing the doorbell even if they could not see him. Standing in front of the door was what Jonah could only describe as a small mountain of a man - barrel shaped chest, broad shoulders, thick upper arms and a head that seemed to sit right on top of them, his neck was so thick. Close-set eyes and a thick brow seemed to give the man a permanent scowl, peering at the door from beneath short-cropped, raven black hair.

"Hmm. Don't know this fellow. What do you think, Jonah?"

Jonah was surprised by the question, turning to Sam with a confused little stare. "What? What do you mean?"

"Not sure if I want to let this fellow in." The sound of another buzz punctuated the big band music still warbling quietly in the background, the big man holding the doorbell longer than was necessary. "Don't like the look of him."

"He gives me the creeps." It was more than that, actually. Something about the man set off alarm bells deep inside of Jonah's mind, enough to make him feel a little knot forming up in the pit of his stomach. Something about the man standing on the other side of the door was inherently wrong. Instinctively he knew that the small mountain of a man standing on the other side of the doorway was trouble.

Sam nodded grimly, waving Jonah behind the counter with him, when the man again depressed the button longer than was necessary. The buzzing sound was suddenly grating on Jonah's nerves, and make his skin prickle. "Yeah, me too. Don't think I'm gonna let this one in." Sam pressed another button on the side of the counter, leaning in to speak into what must have been a microphone, elevating his voice. "I'm sorry, we're closing for the day."

It was hard to read the man's reaction through the tinted glass, but when he reached forward to ring the buzzer once again, it made it clear he had no intention of backing down. Sam turned to look at Jonah a little apologetically. "Look, if this creep doesn't beat it I'm gonna have to call the cops. Don't want you getting mixed up in all that, so, why don't you go ahead and make your way out the back," he said, thumbing in the direction of a door behind the counter. "Last door on the end, don't go in the first one. It's just the toilet."

Jonah opened his mouth to protest, but yet another insistent buzz sounded while the man leaned against the doorbell. With an irritated harrumph, Sam mashed down the intercom button and leaned in to yell into the microphone. "I said we're closed! Go away!"

For a brief moment it looked as if the man was going to take the advice. His arms dropped to his sides and he took a step back, gazing blankly at the darkened glass in front of him before balling his hands into fists. With a grimace and a sudden flash of movement, the man made his intentions crystal clear when he slung his fist at the door, knuckles smashing into the glass, which responded with a dull thud and a crunching sound.

"Holy shit!" Jonah took a step back in the direction of the back exit, turning to throw an incredulous look in Sam's direction, the older man standing with a bewildered expression and a hand over his chest. "Did he really just punch the door?"

The answer came in the form of another fist slamming into the glass, in precisely the same spot. The glass bulged momentarily under the force of the blow, bending into the shop, snapping back into place with a series of spiderweb cracks and little concentric fissures forming around the shape of the man's fist before he drew it back, presumably to strike again.

Again Jonah could only stare in shock. It shouldn't be possible, he thought. "Isn't that glass bulletproof?"

The old man did not answer, but the mention of bullets seemed to galvanize him. The look of shock on Sam's face faded and was replaced with a grim sort of determination, and once again he reached under the counter. "So he wants to play rough, does he? Ain't the first punk come try to make a quick dollar off an old man," he said, grumbling, pulling out a slightly dusty pump-action shotgun. Peering at the weapon, presumably to make sure that it was loaded, he muttered "Time for you to get out of here, Jonah. Back door."

"I can't just leave you here," Jonah protested, another loud crack sounding from the doorway as the man slammed his fist in to it again, the cracks widening and spreading.

"I've handled these bozos before," Sam said with a sort of grim determination, looking over at him and nodding once. "I can't have you just standing there, in the way. Please. I'll have this clown on his way before you can count to ten ..."

His mind raced, looking for some kind of protest that he could offer, something he could say to convince the old man to let him stay, let him help, but he realized that Sam had a good point. He certainly wasn't proficient in weapons of any kind - not that he had any to offer - and, indeed, was likely to just get in the way. Casting one last glance at the doorway, looking at the sinister mountain of a man coiling his muscle for another blow, he made his way for the back doorway, pulling it open and slipping into the empty hallway beyond.

Still, he couldn't just leave. In spite of the better half of his mind that agreed it was time to run, time to get out of the shop where he might at least call the cops, some strange sense of loyalty to his friend kept him from running. Pulling the door most of the way shut behind him, he let it remain open, just a bare crack, so that he could peek into the shop from behind. The view was unnerving - he was looking over Sam's shoulder, along the length of the shotgun barrel, which was now pointed unsteadily at the shadow of the man assailing the door.

With the next blow, the man punched a surprisingly neat hole right in the door, chunks of it falling away and letting his fist pass right on through, coming to a stop just inside the door. The man held it there for a long moment, as if brandishing his fist, little bits of glass caught in the coarse hair covering his forearm, letting it turn slightly before pulling it back and grabbing on to the raw edge of what Jonah presumed to have been bulletproof glass. With a grunt loud enough for him to hear, the man pulled on the glass hard, peeling it back with almost no resistance. When there was enough of a hole opened up, he simply barged his way right on in, breaking the door around his frame.

Sam, unsteady but unwavering, finally pumped the action on the shotgun, loading a shell with a threatening ka-chunk sound that even made Jonah shiver, keeping it pointed right at the intruder. "All right, mister, it's time for you to turn right back around and go back the way you came."

The intruder did not seem in the least fazed by the sight of a shotgun barrel staring him down, standing rather impassively in front of the wreckage of the doorway, gazing right back at the man with coal-black eyes. "Where is it?"

"Cops are on their way. I don't really care that you made a mess of my door, just turn around and leave and never come back, and that's the last you have to worry about this little mistake …"

"Where is it?" The man repeated his query, speaking in a deep, sonorous voice, the words a little unsteady and forced, and marred by a thick accent that Jonah could not place. With a grimace, he took a step forward.

Sam responded by tightening his grip on the shotgun. "I don't know what it is you're after, son, but it ain't worth a throat full of lead. I don't want to use this but I will if I have to. Don't make me do it."

Undeterred, the man took another step forward, and then Jonah's ears were suddenly assailed by a boom so loud that he could feel it in the chest like a fist. The shotgun jumped in Sam's unwieldy grip, the recoil forcing the old man to stumble backward while belching out a little plume of smoke. The big man, mountain that he was, stumbled backward several steps from the force of the blast, his shirt tearing open and his chest blossoming in an ugly spray of red before he tumbled backward into the wreckage of the front door.

Jonah had seen guns fired on television, had seen his fair share of explosions in movies, but this was nothing like it. His ears still rang from the blast, and the acrid odor of gunpowder on the air was already plucking at his senses. Then there was the man, crumpled on the floor, felled by a shotgun blast to the chest. He had heard that seeing death faked in the movies was nothing like seeing it in person. He was almost inclined to agree when he saw the man twitch.

He was still alive.

"Holy shit," he whispered under his breath, watching incredulously as the bulky man twitched again, rolled to his side, and began to slowly push himself back up to his feet. The wound on his chest looked far too shallow and inconsequential for the shotgun blast, the clothing sheared apart but the skin largely intact beneath, save for an oozing wound the size of a quarter.

Sam, too, must have been watching in disbelief, for the old man hardly budged as the wounded intruder pulled himself up straight, fixing that inky black gaze forward again and making his demand in that strange, foreign voice. "Where is it?"

"I don't … know what you mean," the old man responded, his voice now shaky and devoid of the conviction that it had only moments before.

The intruder took a few steps forward, now standing just in front of the counter, close enough that Jonah could now begin to smell the iron tang of his blood on the air. "The token. Where is it?"

The old shopkeep shuffled back a step, the shotgun forgotten in his hand as it drooped downward and then fell to the floor with a clatter. "Token? I'm sorry … look, the gold coins are right over there … this is just a coin shop …"

For a moment, the strange man seemed to consider the response, blinking dispassionately, hardly moving, and then worked his mouth slowly, as if trying to decide how to respond, himself. "Then you are of no use to me."

Suddenly the man moved with more speed than someone of his bulk seemed like he had any right to move, leaning forward over the counter and shooting a hand out in Sam's direction. The old man did not have a chance to respond before thick, meaty fingers closed around his throat, lifting him up off the ground, his thin, spindly limbs beginning to thrash in the air. Jonah could do nothing but watch while his old friend was lifted up into the air, wheezing and gasping for breath; he could do nothing but watch as those big, meaty fingers clamped down around his throat with a sickening crunch. The strange man relaxed his grip, and the shopkeeper collapsed into a pile on the floor, unmoving.

Jonah could do nothing but stare in horror as an innocent man was murdered less than five feet away. His hands and feet felt like they were made of stone, his jaw heavy as lead as it gaped open. "Oh my god …"

Inky black eyes snapped up and looked straight in his direction. Instantly the paralysis that he felt fled from his muscles, and Jonah wheeled around, fleeing down the hallway. He didn't have time to think, didn't have time to cry, to mourn for the fallen. He was probably pissing in his pants as he ran, but he didn't even have time to think about that. His legs urged him onward, his brain imagining that murderous bulk of a man pounding down the hallway after him. Making for the end of the hallway, Jonah kicked open the door and burst out into the fading light of the afternoon, shielding his eyes before glancing first in one direction, then the other, getting his bearings. Hardly pausing, he turned to the left and ran across the asphalt as fast as his feet would take him.

The man had to be behind him. He couldn't afford himself the luxury of turning to look back, sprinting for the end of the little strip mall, arms flailing as he turned to the left again and made his way for the parking lot out front. His motorcycle was there, tucked safely beneath the shade of a tree, and wordlessly he thanked himself for parking it facing out, away from the parking space. His feet pounded anxiously at the pavement. All he could do was hope and pray that he could make it before that man caught up to him. Fishing for the key in his pocket, he pulled it out and had it ready as he ran right up to the side of the bike.

He almost reached for his helmet strapped to the back, but the thought in the back of his mind of that man chasing him down made him forget all about it. Throwing his leg over the seat, his fingers fumbled with the key, trying to line it up with the ignition, taking what felt like far, far too long. Finally the key slid into the slot, turned to the side with a click, and his thumb was on the ignition. The bike roared to life beneath him, breathing out a high-pitched whine as he abandoned all sense of pacing, popping the clutch and twisting the throttle, clinging on to the machine in a sense of desperation as it lurched beneath him, the tire squealing for a brief second and then shooting out of the parking space. He thanked his stupid luck that the little parking lot was mostly empty as he careened through spaces that might otherwise have been blocked, hazarding a glance in his mirrors, catching a glimpse of the dark, foreboding man standing angrily where his bike had been parked only seconds before.

Hardly pausing to take a breath, Jonah guided his bike out of the parking lot, zipping right out into the roadway in spite of the traffic. The angry beep of a horn to his side made him almost jump out of his skin, but again he twisted the throttle, shooting away down the road, defying the speed limit as he sought to put as much distance between himself and the coin shop, as fast as he possibly could.

Half a minute and half a mile down the road, however, the rush of adrenaline wore off and the reality of the situation caught up with him. A little ball of tension in his stomach was beginning to writhe, and Jonah suddenly feared that he might throw up. Turning down a side road, glancing over his shoulder to make sure he wasn't followed, he finally pulled over at the side of the road, cutting the throttle, leaning forward and let out a long, painful scream.

Sam was dead. He had just witnessed the friendly old man murdered. He had just spent the last handful of minutes running for his life. These kinds of things weren't supposed to happen, not to quiet, normal guys like himself. He did not know how to react. His scream died off, and the sour knot in the pit of his stomach suddenly rose up in his throat - he had to lean over and empty the contents of his stomach onto the sidewalk next to him.

Empty, his stomach still churned and heaved. His legs began to quiver and feel weak, and Jonah feared he might black out. With barely enough sense to put down the kickstand of his bike, he stepped unsteadily off to the side, collapsing onto the sidewalk and rolling onto his back, clutching his stomach and moaning.

The sound of footfalls coming in his direction suddenly made him panic - had the man followed him, after all? Sitting up, he spied a man, much smaller, eyes wide with concern. "Hey! Hey are you all right?"

"No," he said miserably. He was not all right. Falling to his back again, he stared up at the fleeting clouds in the sky, and then closed his eyes as he felt another wave of nausea coming over him. "I'm not all right …"

The bystander spoke with a heavy Indian accent, but clear enough for Jonah to hear. "Is there anything I can do for you, mister?"

"Call the cops … please … I've just seen a murder …"

TWO

Jonah found himself in a room that was an embodiment of sterile serenity: plain, off-white walls, diffuse fluorescent lighting that cast only indistinct shadows, a quiet little oscillating fan sitting in the corner and pushing the air around at a leisurely pace. The little round table in the center of the room was plain and unadorned, as well, save for a conference phone installed in the middle. The plush executive chairs were comfortable, and helped to lend to the room a sense of calm and quiet, the perfect environment for introspection.

Introspection was the last thing that Jonah cared for. In the silence, he could still hear the deafening roar of a shotgun, the sickening crunch of a neck being broken, the dull thud of a lifeless body collapsing to the ground. When he closed his eyes, he could still see murderous black orbs gazing back at him through the darkness. It was enough to recall the sour feeling deep in the pit of his stomach. Cringing, he reached for the little bottle of water that had been left for him, hoping it might calm the churning sensation.

The quiet sound of the door creaking open, then, was something of a welcome distraction to Jonah. He looked up to see what was presumably another police officer walking in, this one wearing a simple white shirt, dark slacks and a blue tie. He seemed somehow stereotypical for the role, sporting a trimmed mustache and well groomed, salt and pepper hair cut close. Bright blue eyes locked on to him, seemed to observe him from the doorway, before the unnamed officer shut the door quietly behind him and pulled open a plain manila folder. "Hello, ah, Jonah. I'm Detective Franklin, I'll be here to ask you a few more questions, take a few more statements from you so we can get this whole thing wrapped up."

Jonah was already beginning to tire from the questioning. After the initial call to the police, he had been checked out by an EMT before being escorted to the nearby police station, where they had asked him to fill out a number of forms, making a number of sworn oaths about what he had witnessed. He understood that, for something as serious as a murder, the police would have to be thorough with their investigations, and they wanted to get as many details from him while the memory of the events were still fresh in his mind.

Still, Detective Franklin was the third such officer to come asking for some statements. Gritting his teeth, Jonah sat upright in his chair and set the bottle of water back down. "All right, fire away."

"All right, Jonah. First, I just need to inform you that your statements are being recorded," the detective said, gesturing to the conference phone in the center of the table. It was no different than what the first two had told him. "Also, just for the record, I need you to state your full name, age, and place of residence."

"Jonah Fischer, 27, Fort Lauderdale."

"Can you provide your full address, please?"

Jonah could not help but to sigh. "Look, I've already written it down on like a dozen forms already, you have all of the information there …"

The officer looked genuinely apologetic, but nodded as he sat down. "I'm sorry, but, there are important procedures to follow …"

With a nod of resignation, Jonah rattled off his full address for the machine to record. He also listened to the detective go through a short spiel about all of his rights, about the legalities and technicalities involved, how it was important that he be as thorough and truthful as possible. Again, nothing he had not already heard.

Satisfied, Franklin nodded and made a little note in his manila folder. "Thank you, Jonah. Now, if you wouldn't mind, can we just start with a quick statement, describing what you witnessed at the coin shop?"

He shot the officer an exasperated look, but the one he got in response made it clear that he would have to go through this again. "It was at Woolworth Coin Gallery, four in the afternoon or so. There were no other customers in the shop. This short but stocky man, black hair, black eyes, strange accent tried to buzz in but Sam wouldn't let him. Said he looked suspicious. The man punched his way through the door, demanded something. Sam shot him, he got back up, and the man …" Jonah had to force down a little swell of gall in his throat, snagging his bottle of water to guzzle down a swallow. "The man broke his neck. I had to escape out the back door, ran to my bike, and called the cops. Do you want all the gory details, again?"

"No, that'll be sufficient for now," the detective said, scribbling another note or two down in his folder. "Can you tell me what you were doing at the coin shop?"

"I was browsing," he replied, with a blink. This was new.

"Browsing?"

"Yeah, you know. Just checking out some new stuff that Sam had."

Another nod, and another scribble in the folder. "I see. You've said in a previous statement that you personally knew Sam Woolworth?"

Jonah breathed a sigh, slumping back in his chair some. "Yeah, for a few years, anyway."

"How did you know Mr. Woolworth?"

"From his store." Again he took a swig of the water, closing his eyes and trying to relax.

"You'd been shopping there for some time then? Without knowing Mr. Woolworth previously?"

Jonah peeked his eyes open again, looking back at the officer quizzically. Franklin did not betray any emotion, simply watching him expectantly. "Four, five years maybe. I'd heard it was a good shop, checked them out, and went back enough that Sam and I were on a first name basis, yes."

"So, you're a … coin collector, then?" The officer asked the question with a faintly dubious tone.

"Numismatist," Jonah corrected, feeling faintly irritated. "Why?"

The question was not answered, the detective choosing to move on with his own questioning. "So you've been purchasing items from Mr. Woolworth for some time?"

"Yes. I'd just bought a coin from him, just before the incident, in fact."

"That's not in your previous statements," Franklin noted, scribbling in his folder. "Care to show it to me?"

"Yeah, sure," Jonah said, still frowning in irritation as he reached into his pocket, fishing around for the little coin that he'd bought. His fingers brushed against his keys, a piece of gum, and a few random quarters that he plucked out and spread apart in his palm, but the strange coin seemed to be gone. "Dammit … shit, I must have lost it when I was trying to get on my bike …"

The detective nodded to that, grunting, making a little note. "I see. Well, no doubt the transaction will show up on your credit card statement …"

Jonah shook his head at that. "No, I paid cash for it. Fifty bucks."

"Cash?" Detective Franklin looked up from his little folder, pausing in his scribbling, gazing at him with those bright blue eyes again. "I don't suppose you always paid for cash, at Mr. Woolworth's shop?"

"Actually … yeah I did …"

The officer set the folder down on the table in front of him, folding it shut, and looking right across at Jonah. "So, basically, there's no real record of you having ever purchased something at the coin shop?"

"No, I guess not," Jonah began, and then stopped when a creeping suspicion began to rise up in his chest. "Wait … what are you getting at?"

"Nothing, Mr. Fischer. My job is to get at the facts."

The answer was clipped and rehearsed, and made Jonah all the more uncomfortable. "Oh, god … you think I had something to do with it?"

"I didn't say that," Franklin said, folding his arms on the table and leaning forward, leveling a piercing gaze at him. "Perhaps there is something else that you need to tell me?"

"Look, I told you exactly what happened. It's in two of your goddamned reports already, I've told you guys front and back the whole goddamned story," he sputtered, feeling the sickness starting to creep up in his stomach again.

"Your recounting of the tale is certainly consistent," Franklin said, an accusatory tone starting to creep up in his voice. "It's a little outlandish, though, don't you think?"

"It's what happened."

The detective shrugged, leaning back in his seat. "I'd like to believe you, really, I would. But I don't. Let me present a different take on the events. Based on the evidence that we've collected, so far."

Jonah's eyes began to go wide with disbelief as the officer cleared his throat, and began to speak again. "Sam Woolworth is sitting behind his desk, enjoying a quiet afternoon at his shop when a customer shows up. The fellow looks decent enough, friendly, young fellow who doesn't look like he's any trouble. He lets the man in, talks about some of his wares, shares just enough of his personal background with the man so that he could recount it at a later date.

"Then the man pulls out a weapon. A knife, a gun, who knows. Demands that Sam hand over everything in his register, all the gold in the display. But poor Sam, he can't just let it all go. It's his livelihood, his savings, his retirement, after all. He reaches under his display and pulls out a shotgun. Sam and the intruder have a little tussle; the shotgun goes off and misses. Hits the door, shooting a big gaping hole, and the rest of the glass falls out of place.

"Now our intruder is a little worked up at having been shot at. He reaches out and grabs the poor old man by his throat, strangles him out of retaliation, angry that he could have been killed. Poor Sam fights back, but he's old, weak, and frail, and suffocates. Our intruder never really meant to kill the old man, just meant to steal his things, so when the old guy falls dead to the floor, breaks his neck, and the robber freaks out. Turns, and leaves the store in a hurry, without stealing a dime. Gets on his bike, has a flash of guilty conscious, so he calls the cops to make up some kind of story about what happened …"

The anger that was rising up in Jonah's throat at hearing the story was making him quiver. "That's not what happened," he hissed, furious that someone might dare try and implicate him in the death of his friend.

The detective merely shrugged. "You tell me, Jonah. What's more likely? My story, or yours? You really want to stick with your story about some supervillain who has the strength to tear through a reinforced glass door, who can take a shotgun blast to the chest - point blank - and stand right back up? Who can reach across the counter and snap an old man's neck?"

Jonah wanted to argue. He was suddenly on the defensive; the cop's story did make sense, but it wasn't what happened. He wanted to defend himself, wanted to say something, but the little ball of sickness was growing more poignant in his stomach. Slumping back into his chair, he let out a deep sigh. "I think this is the part where I ask for a lawyer," he said, feeling deflated.

"Might not be a bad idea," the cop said, sitting back and smirking. "We don't wanna complicate things any further with lawyers, though, so if you're done talking, I'll tell you what. Much as I wish we could hold you on a hunch, we can't. You've got a clean record and no real reason to keep you here, so we're gonna have to let you go for the night. But if you're smart - if you're really innocent - then you better do the right thing. Keep your head down, keep out of trouble, answer the phone when we call, and by god, don't do anything stupid like try to skip town. Because our eyes are on you now, Mr. Fischer, and believe you me - the moment you try to take a step out of Broward County, we'll be on you like flies on dogshit, and you won't like what happens then."

"But I work in Miami …"

"I'm sure you have plenty of time off saved up. Perhaps it's best you take a little vacation from work for the time being. In case I wasn't clear before, let me just say it again. We're watching you. Not a foot out of the county, Jonah, and I mean it. Not a foot."

Detective Franklin accentuated his last point by jabbing his finger into the table in front of him before sitting back. The man looked frustratingly smug sitting there behind his mustache, behind his little file folder, and it made Jonah want to reach over and strangle him, at least. For all the anger that he felt in his chest he realized that an outburst would only make things worse at this point, so he swallowed it down. "Are we done, here?"

"We're done," Franklin said, pushing himself up from the table and walking over to the door. Holding it open and gesturing, he flashed Jonah an insincere smile. "Your bike is right up front where you left it. Be a good kid and wear your helmet this time around, eh? And remember, nothing stupid."

Jonah responded with a grunt of his own, hauling himself up out of the chair and pushing his way past the detective without so much as a word, when the officer spoke up behind him. "Remember. Nothing stupid. We're watching," he said, tapping his eyes with his first two fingers before pointing them back in Jonah's direction.

It was too much. Fuming, Jonah turned on his heel, stalking his way out toward the exit that was indicated to him. There was no way he could get out of there fast enough.

#

At last, Jonah made his way home for the evening. Pushing the door to his apartment open and flicking the light switch with a heavy sigh, he tossed his keys into a little bowl on the counter leading into the kitchen. The old fluorescent tubes took a second to warm up and flicker on, blinking their own sullen greeting before casting the small apartment in flat tones.

The half-finished soda can and the empty Chinese containers still sat on the counter, still lending the remnants of their odor to the air, but Jonah still did not bother picking up after himself. If he had lacked the energy and interest to do so before, he suffered from the same tenfold tonight.

Jonah crossed into the living room wearily, flopping onto the futon with another heavy sigh. His video game controller was conveniently close, as was the remote to the television, but none of it interested him this night. Lying back on the futon, his legs dangling over the wooden arm rest, he gazed up at a ceiling fan that spun in lazy circles overhead, its long, fleeting shadows dancing across the ceiling, stretching off into the corners of the room.

He longed for someone to talk to, but it was already well past ten, and for all the desire he had for human contact, he didn't know who he could bother with something like this. Sheer terror and disgust at witnessing the murder of his friend had permeated his mind for hours now, the incredulity and irritation at having been implicated by the police detective only adding an unpleasant layer on top of it all. He closed his eyes for a moment, then, fearing what he might see in the darkness if he let his mind wander too long, he opened them again to stare up at the lazy turn of the fan.

"What a day," he commented to the emptiness.

Before he had time to get too comfortable, he extricated himself from the futon and shuffled his way into the kitchen, pulling the door to the fridge open. He had almost forgotten how empty it was: a carton of orange juice, a pizza box that probably didn't have anything worth eating in it, a few sodas and beers as well as his hard boiled eggs. It was the beer that he was looking for, though, pulling it out and twisting the cap off. He threw his head back and guzzled down as much as he could before his throat began to burn, then pulled the bottle away. Breathing out a drawn-out "Ahhhh," he kicked the door to the fridge shut again, forcing the whole thing to rattle a little, before shuffling his way back to the living room and sinking back into the futon.

In an almost automated movement he reached for the remote, flicking the television on and letting the flickering dance of the image fill his eyes. His thumb found the channel up button, and he began to press it, again and again and again. News, late night talk shows, sports channels, classic movies and even weird, twisted cartoons that were obviously not meant for children. None of it really registered as more than blurred movement and white noise in his mind, though, and after a few minutes of robotic cycling through the channels he set the remote off to the side and left it where it was, an infomercial with a grandmotherly looking lady hawking some wonderful new kitchen gadget. Jonah didn't care what it was; the noise and dancing pixels in front of his eyes were a welcome break from his memory of the day. Lifting the beer bottle to his lips, he leaned it back and gulped down another swig of the beer without even tasting it.

It didn't take too long for him to kill of the bulk of his drink, only a few rounds of "But wait, there's more" echoing in his ears, the grandmotherly woman on the screen keeping track of time in measured little product pitches. The flashing 1-800 number in front of his eyes had just about burned its way into his short term memory when a sound like a knock on the door broke his little reverie, every bit as effective as an explosion in the otherwise quiet of the night, and leaving him feeling every bit as shaken. His heart suddenly felt like it was beating a hundred miles an hour right in the middle of his throat, and Jonah whipped his head around to stare at the door incredulously.

No one could be knocking on his door at this time of the night, he reasoned to himself, and continued to stare at the door as if it might divulge some kind of secret if he looked hard enough. Another moment passed, and there were no further knocks on the door, no sounds in his apartment other than the enthusiastic sales pitch on the television. Nearly convinced that he had merely imagined the sound, Jonah still felt a weird compulsion to make absolutely sure, querying the door with a meek "Hello?"

The words had barely left his lips when the door abruptly caved inward, literally flying off its hinges and crashing into the apartment, careening off the opposite wall in a shower of drywall and splinters. Instantly the same panic that he had felt earlier in the day shot through his veins, calling up the latter half of the "fight or flight" response, but sitting on the futon as he was he had nowhere to go. Arms flailing, he tipped backward over the arm of the futon and landed unceremoniously on his back, kicking his feet and pulling himself back up to standing, turning to stare at the gaping hole where the door to his apartment had once stood.

In its place stood the same black-eyed mountain of a man who had broken Sam's neck. With nothing between them, he got a better look at the man, a better feel for just how wrong he seemed. Eyes that were set too closely together, thick eyebrows that bled together over a wide, bony nose, ears that looked misshapen and folded in strange little points. It all looked like some kind of absurd disguise that was poorly fashioned and fit even worse.

"Oh shit," Jonah breathed, eyes widening in panic as he took a few unsteady steps backward. His mind instantly recalled the fact that, instead of being in a strip mall store with a back exit, he was in his third story apartment. The only exit was the doorway in front of him, and he certainly wasn't going to be making a break for it now. "Shit … shit shit shit …"

With the same lack of emotion and the same strange accent as before, the man spoke up. "Where is it?"

Jonah waved his arms in front of him, still clutching the beer bottle in one hand and sloshing what was left of it all over the ground in front of him. "Look, man, I don't know what you're talking about …"

Staring him down with that inky gaze, the intruder took a few purposeful strides forward, forcing Jonah to retreat instinctively. "The token. Give me the token."

"Token?" His mind racing, still trying to think of some escape, Jonah thought of the fire escape through his bedroom window. This man could move, though, and there probably was no way he was going to make it down the fire escape without being caught. He was also fresh out of any kind of weaponry to defend himself with, save the beer bottle, and he found himself brandishing it as if it were some kind of knife. "I don't know what the hell you mean! Just get the hell out of here, man!"

The man's fists tightened with an audible crack, a grimace full of crooked and twisted teeth the only hint of an emotional reaction that he betrayed as he took another step forward. "Give me the token and I will leave."

"Look, I don't have any freakin' token," Jonah began, feeling sweat begin to drip down his brows, getting into the corners of his eyes and making them sting, when he remembered the purchase he had made. "Wait … the coin? The coin with the dragon on it?"

"Give it to me," the intruder demanded, a meaty palm held open in Jonah's direction.

The last time he had tried to find the coin, he had come up empty. "Look, I don't have it. It fell out of my pocket, back at the store, when I was getting my keys … I don't have it but I bet it's still there, you just have to go back and get it, I could show you where I dropped it …"

The man paused, his inky black eyes blinking once. "Then you are of no use to me."

Jonah remembered with unwanted clarity what had happened the last time the sinister man had uttered that statement. In a weak effort to defend himself he lobbed the empty beer bottle, watching it bounce off the man's forehead without so much as leaving a mark. The man didn't even flinch, and Jonah could do little more than throw his arms up in front of him. So this is how it ends, he thought to himself, morosely.

Before he felt those meaty hands closing around his throat, however, another loud sound broke the quiet of the night, a sharp crack of shattering glass. Out of the corner of his eye he could see the main window of his apartment exploding inward, the blinds fraying and scattering in a shower of glass shards and an unidentifiable dark blur that streaked right across the room, smashing his television into pieces, before crashing head-on into the bulk of the intruder. The sinister man showed a brief flash of emotion - confusion - before he was bowled down to the ground, caught up in that blur, then crashing into the wall with an enormous thud that shook his framed posters right off the walls.

The insistent tinkling of little glass shards bouncing against each other, bouncing against the remnants of his television, filled his ears like a weird sort of rain shower, an otherworldly cloudburst that was just part and parcel to the continued shattering of his day. Whatever it was that had crashed through his window had been enough to send the hefty intruder crashing against the far wall with enough force to rend the drywall asunder and leave a yawning hole, where he could see his bedroom through the little white dust that had been kicked up. What emerged from that dusty hole, however, was the last thing he could have imagined.

It was a woman. A young woman, it seemed, about his age; fiery red hair, piercing green eyes, attractive in a strangely subdued manner. She was dressed simply, a loose flannel shirt and blue jeans that had been scraped and cut up by glass, covered in a fine layer of plaster dust that was still settling from the hole in the wall, little bits of drywall caught in her hair giving her a kind of wild look. Her gaze fixed directly on him, and she barked out a single, simple command: "Run!"

Jonah was in shock, and his feet felt like they were made of lead. Rather than run, rather than move at all, he simply stared, slack-jawed, at this strange woman who had materialized out of a blur that had come crashing in through his window with enough force to knock down a small mountain of a man.

"Is there something wrong with you? Run, goddammit, it's only stunned," she repeated, stepping forward and grasping him by the wrist with surprising strength, shoving him in the direction of the exit. This time he complied, if in something of a daze, his feet first shuffling beneath him, picking up speed as she pushed and shoved at him from behind, repeating the command to run with increasing urgency each time.

Jogging out the door and down two flights of steps, Jonah blinked into the cool night air, stopping when he got to the bottom of the steps and turning to look at the woman in a state of confusion. Shooting him an irritated look, she ran past him and grabbed him by the sleeve, tugging him along. "Did I tell you to stop running?"

He wanted to protest, wanted to cry out, wanted some kind of explanation, but the sound of heavy footfalls beginning to crash down the stairwell erased any sense of hesitation he might have. Picking up the pace, he followed the strange redheaded woman across the street. Her destination seemed to be a blue pickup truck that he did not recognize. Without any hesitation, she made her way to the driver's side and threw the door open, jumping into the cab in a fluid motion. Jonah could only stand and stare in confusion. "What ... what the hell is going on?"

"You're getting in my truck," she shouted, reaching over and kicking the passenger door open, turning around to glare at him with an angry urgency. "Now."

Blinking in confusion, he rounded the front of the truck and hopped in the opened door. The woman hardly waited for him to close the door before she fired the engine up and threw the vehicle in gear, mashing the gas and sending it screeching down the road. With a yelp of fear and surprise, Jonah swung his arms around wildly, grabbing hold of the safety belt and tugging it around his waist, fumbling to get it latched, when he heard her voice call out firmly once again. "Hold on tight!"

The truck lurched suddenly to the left, mashing him tightly against the door, with enough force that his head dangled out the window and he found himself screaming into the night. A flash of green suddenly caught his attention, as he realized a motorcycle - his motorcycle - was right there next to the truck. No one was riding it, however - the machine had simply fallen right out of the sky, crashing into the pavement in the exact spot where the truck had been only seconds before. With an angry crunch and squeal of metal, he watched as the bike's frame simply snapped in half, sending the front end careening off to the side, little bits of green plastic fairing and mechanical components shearing off, scattering across the road before the body of the bike came to a rest.

Whipping his head back, he saw the silhouette of the sinister intruder, standing right in the spot where his motorcycle had been parked, a menacing shadow that shrunk into the night as the truck sped on down the road. "My bike ... what the hell happened ..."

"Be glad it was just your motorcycle," the woman said, a little flippantly. "Would have been much worse if it was your ass he was lobbing around."

THREE

"Wait … lobbed … what are you talking about? You trying to tell me that guy picked my motorcycle up and threw it at us?"

Again her response was oddly flippant. "Sorry to be the one to break it to you. Hope you have good insurance."

Jonah could hardly believe that he had just witnessed his bike falling right out of the sky, but now she was trying to insist that a man had simply picked it up and thrown it at them, dozens of yards away. He wanted to comment on how incredibly insane that kind of statement was, when his mind suddenly reeled with the events that had unfolded in the last ten minutes. The strange murderer showing up at his door, ripping it off its hinges and demanding a coin from him. The strange blur that had come smashing through his window, which had, apparently, turned out to be a relatively petite woman his own age. All of this, on top of having been witness to the murder of his friend right in his own coin shop.

He turned to look at the woman again, his jaw slack, his mind already hurting with the unlikely string of events. In spite of the bits of drywall that still clung to her hair, in spite of the run, her face was strikingly serene - the look on her face almost slightly amused - as she guided the truck down the quiet nighttime streets. His jaw flexed, a hundred questions suddenly rushing to the fore, demanding to be asked, but instead he started out with the one that seemed to be the simplest. "Who are you?"

"Rebekah. You can call me Rebekah, though," she said, turning to look at him briefly with a playful twinkle in her eye.

The playful demeanor did not sit well with Jonah, particularly not in light of what had just happened. "No, not your name. I mean, who are you? What are you doing here?"

Though she did not turn to look at him this time, her gaze remaining fixed on the road in front of her, she flashed a rather jovial little grin.

"Saving your ass. You have a problem with that?"

"Have a problem with that?" Jonah felt himself starting to shake and sputter, the same angry reaction he had felt earlier in the police station, when he had been accused of being a murderer. "Look, I don't know what the hell you think is so funny, but do you have any idea what kind of a day I've had?"

"I know exactly what kind of a day you've had." The tone of her voice had taken on a sharp, surprisingly serious edge, a kind of unspoken rebuke that made Jonah retreat back into his seat some.

It was enough to douse some of the fire that had been building in his chest. "Then what the hell is so funny?"

"Never said anything was funny, Jonah. Just happy to be alive."

The absurdity of the statement caught him off guard, and for a moment he simply stared at her in silence. "Wait … you know my name?"

She paused before replying, stopping at an intersection and looking both ways, drumming her fingers on the steering wheel. "Of course I know your name. It's my job." She reached in to flip on the stereo, some contemporary rock station cutting through the silence. "Makes it a little hard to save your ass if I don't know anything about you."

Jonah huffed in irritation. "I want to know what's going on here."

"Long version, or short version?"

The hundred questions still bouncing around in his head were once again clamoring for their moment, but for now he held them in check. "Let's start with the short version."

"All right. Your friend back there, the big guy, he's after one thing, and one thing only. That token that you picked up at the coin shop. He'll do anything he has to in order to get his hands on the thing, right up to and including murder as you unfortunately know all too well." She paused briefly to take a breath, her head bobbing lightly in time to the music. "That means, as long as you've got the thing, you're in danger. My job is to get you safely out of that danger."

"Joke's on him then. I don't have the thing anymore," Jonah complained, rather bitterly.

Rebekah, as she had called herself, simply laughed out loud at that. "Oh, sure you do. It's gonna take a lot more than that bonehead back there to get it away from you, too."

"I do not," he insisted, stuffing his hand into his pocket. To his surprise, and his chagrin, his fingers immediately brushed against a coin that felt just about the right size. Pulling it out, he laid it flat in his palm, the shifting glare of the streetlights as they passed illuminating the stylized dragon on one side. "What … the hell?"

"It's yours, Jonah. That's what it was made for. Now that you've got it, it's yours to keep."

With a grunt, he leaned over to throw the coin right out the window. "Well if this is all he wants …"

"Stop," she interrupted, her voice suddenly firm and almost dangerous, enough to freeze him in his place. He turned to look at her again with a startled glance, but she did not look at him, her eyes still fixed on the road. "That would be a bad idea. Besides, as far as he's concerned, you still have the thing. He's going to be looking for you."

"Shit," he cursed, under his breath, feeling around in his pockets again. "I need to call the cops … they need to know about this … and I left my damned cell phone back in the apartment …"

"The cops?" She laughed, again, shaking her head. "You think the cops are gonna do something to protect you? They sure as hell weren't doing anything to keep him from finding you tonight. Look, my job is to keep you safe. Stick with me, you'll be safe enough."

The absurdity of the whole thing was beginning to creep up on him. Jonah grimaced as he shoved the coin back in his pocket, glancing up to see that Rebekah was turning the truck onto an on-ramp, getting on the Turnpike, the big green sign overhead proclaiming it was the way north, toward Orlando. "Where the hell are you taking me?"

"Somewhere safe. Try not to worry about it for now."

"Try not to worry?" He glanced out the window again, panic starting to creep up in his chest. Here he was, in a strange truck with a strange woman, who was making her way to the quickest route out of town. "Turn around … look, the cops already think I'm up to no good, I can't be leaving town like this … they said they're watching me."

Rebekah showed no indication of changing her mind, accelerating the truck quickly up to highway cruising speed. "Maybe they are."

Jonah's eyes widened a little as he realized that she wasn't taking him seriously. "Stop the truck."

"What?"

"I said stop the truck. Pull over, stop the truck, right now."

Finally she turned to look at him, that playful little grin back on her face. "What, right here, in the middle of the highway?"

Jonah bunched his fists and gritted his teeth. "I said stop the freakin' truck!" As soon as he had made the demand, Rebekah mashed her foot on the brake, and the truck responded by screeching angrily to a halt. Jonah was caught off guard, whipping forward with nearly enough force to smash his face right against the dash, stopped just in time by the tension in his seat belt snagging him about the chest. A vehicle that had been following not far behind them swung wildly about, the driver pounding on the horn, whining out a fading, angry song as it passed. When they finally came to a stop, he turned to look at the redhead with a wild, accusatory stare. "Jesus Christ, what the hell are you trying to do?"

"Stopping the truck," she responded, flatly.

"In the middle of the freakin' highway?"

All at once she turned to stare him down, those green eyes flashing with no small hint of anger. He found himself recoiling as he thought she was going to hit him, but instead she simply reached around him, pushing the passenger door open and gesturing out into the night. "Decision time, Jonah. You want to go crawling back to the cops, pray that they can keep you safe from that murderous madman? Well, the door's open, I'm not going to keep you here against your will. Get the hell out and out of my sight."

A part of his mind urged him to take that offer without hesitation, the urge to slip out of the truck and run as far away from this crazy woman as he could palpable enough that his legs twitched in anticipation. In spite of himself, he remained seated long enough to wait until she spoke up again. "Stay with me, and I'll keep you safe. Yeah, the cops might be on the lookout for you but I can keep you safe from them, too. I promise. But if you choose to come with me, you're going to sit back, shut the hell up, and do what I say. My job is to keep your ass safe, not suffer your whining and complaining. Got it?"

Another vehicle barreled past them on the freeway, again honking the horn, the sound about making him jump out of his skin. Against his better judgment, Jonah remained seated, reaching over and pulling the door to the truck shut, sitting back meekly in his seat. "Got it."

"Good," Rebekah said, her demeanor instantly brightening again as she threw the truck back into gear and quickly got it back up to speed. "You should sit back and try to get some sleep. We've got a long drive ahead of us."

Jonah didn't respond, at least not at first, but inwardly wondered where this woman was actually planning on taking him. After watching mileposts pass by for several minutes, he finally allowed himself to speak up again, to ask the question. "Can I ask where we're going?"

"North. Someone who needs to see you. A friend," she answered, cryptically.

With a heavy sigh, Jonah leaned back in the seat, closed his eyes and pinched the bridge of his nose. He found himself wishing that he were simply in a nightmare, that he would wake up in the morning to find the whole thing some figment of his imagination, that old Sammy would be alive and well in his shop, that he would find his bike in one piece. It had been just another day when he woke up that morning, and now his life had been turned completely upside down. "You gonna give me a straight answer to any questions?"

"What's that mean?"

Opening his eyes again, he turned to look at the driver, Rebekah, with a slightly disdainful grimace. "I mean, give me a real answer. One that doesn't include 'someone' or 'somewhere'."

She hadn't turned to look at him, her eyes fixed on the road ahead. "Depends on the question," she shrugged.

"Ugh. That's exactly what I mean," Jonah complained, leaning back again with another sigh. "You tell me I'm supposed to trust you, that I'm supposed to just sit back quietly while you cart me off to God knows where, and you can't even answer a few simple questions. This is unreal."

"Look. Jonah. I'm not trying to be difficult, I promise." Her voice was surprisingly gentle when she spoke again, furrowing her brows before continuing. "It's just that ... well, it's not easy to answer some of your questions. You aren't really ready for the answers, and I'm not really equipped to give them to you. Not here, not now. There are other people, better equipped to tell you what's going on, but in the meantime you're just going to have to take my word for it when I tell you that what's going on is ... important."

"Oh, hell," he spat, covering his face with his palm and just shaking his head.

Rebekah turned to look at him with a frown. "What?"

"I guess if you were some kind of psycho who wanted me dead you could have left me with Frankenstein back there," he mused a little sardonically, combing his fingers back through his hair. Briefly he paused, turning to look out the window and at the darkened landscape slipping on past, gazing off into the blackness in the distance. "But really? This nonsense about not being ready for the answers? That it's not the right place, the right time? Do you realize how ridiculous that sounds?"

"Look, I'm just trying to watch out for your best interests ..."

"So you've said," Jonah interrupted. "By keeping me in the dark. Right. What are you really on about? What are you really after?"

There was another brief pause, nothing but the sound of the truck as it made its way north along the highway. When the driver did speak again, she did so a little hesitantly, with more than a hint of frustration. "Fine. All right. Let's play it your way. What do you want to know?"

"Everything. Who are you, where are we going, what the hell is going on." When she turned to look at him with a withering glance, Jonah threw his hands up in the air and sighed. "Ok, well, what about Frankenstein? Just who was that guy? I mean, how the hell did he pick up a five hundred pound motorcycle and throw it at us?"

"He's a bull drake," she responded flatly, fixing her gaze on the roadway once again. "They're bred for brute strength and obedience, but they aren't exactly the most intelligent creatures you'll come across. I suppose it suits the role just fine, though. Not much room in that little head of theirs other than to carry out their assigned task."

Jonah blinked a little at the answer. "Uh, wait. Did you just say 'bred'?"
"Yes, I did."
He snorted a little at the response. "Like, as in, breeding animals?"
"Yes," she repeated, a little flatly.
"Okay," Jonah replied, a little dubiously, throwing her another sidelong glance. "So, like … genetic manipulation, or something like that?"
Rebekah shrugged but did not divert her attention from the road. "I suppose if that's what you wanna call it, but it's not like there's any test tubes or laboratories involved. No different than the way animals have been bred since the Stone Age."
"But, he's a human. That's different."
"No, he isn't. I told you, he's a bull drake."
Jonah blinked at the response, and wanted to sigh loudly, but merely shook his head. "What's that even supposed to mean?"
"Oh, sorry," she muttered by way of apology. "You really wouldn't know what that means. It's a kind of dragon. Less intelligent, more, shall we say, feral, but a breed of dragon all the same."
The unexpected patter of raindrops on the windshield announced the arrival of an unexpected downpour, steady but light, the kind of unpredictable weather that Florida was well known for. Rebekah flicked the wipers on, their steady and quiet thump, thump helping to fill the void of sound that now dominated as Jonah stared forward, into the night, not sure how to respond to that. It was only after a long moment that he spoke up again. "A dragon."
"Yes, a dragon."
He wanted to accuse her of being crazy, of being nuts, or at least of just playing some kind of stupid game, but he reminded himself of just how crazy the evening had been so far, of just how nuts it was that he was in a truck driven by some strange woman who had appeared in his apartment just as he was faced down by a murderer. Somehow it didn't seem right to call her out for being crazy. Instead, he answered with a rather flippant "Well, he sure didn't look like a dragon to me."
"Well, he was in human form," she responded flatly, shrugging again.
"Ah. Of course. Human form," he muttered, nodding, his voice still laden with sarcasm. "And you know this, because …"
She answered with another shrug, and once again in that flat voice. "Because I'm also a dragon."
He waited for her to turn and grin at him, or to laugh, or some other indication that she was enjoying a goofy joke at his expense. Instead there was nothing but the rhythmic sound of the wipers competing with the light rain, the rumble of the engine as it carried them along further northward. When it became apparent that she was not going to qualify her statement, Jonah shook his head with a derisive little snort. "Oh, God, what have I

gotten myself into … you really are crazy …"

"You asked for the truth."

Again he laughed. "The truth, yes. But dragons? You're crazy."

If she was offended she didn't show it. In fact, she continued to show no real emotion, keeping her gaze on the road, her hands relaxed while they clutched the wheel. "And how does that make me crazy?"

"Come on. Dragons? Really? That's ridiculous."

"I'm sure you have a better, less ridiculous explanation for how that man not only picked up your motorcycle but threw it a hundred feet, then. A better explanation for everything that's happened tonight, since this morning."

"Of course," he huffed, a bit indignantly.

Finally she turned to look at him, her lively green eyes looking him over with a little hint of doubt. "Well, out with it."

Jonah sputtered where he sat. He tried to tell himself that it was not really a question that should have been dignified with an answer, that he wasn't the one here who should be answering questions and explaining himself, yet at the same time he realized that he did not, in fact, have a satisfactory answer to the question. In truth he had no idea how any man could have the strength required for that kind of feat, but there had to be some kind of logical explanation, one that did not involve dragons. He, unfortunately, could not think of it.

Defeated for the moment, he folded his arms over his chest and shook his head again. "Christ. This is just … stupid. How the hell do I get caught up in this stuff? Wait, wait, don't tell me. That damned coin I bought is actually some magical coin, which sought me out on purpose, right? And, wait, let me guess, it's because I'm actually a dragon and never knew it, right?"

He thought he could see a little smirk forming on her features. "Well, actually …"

"Stop," he interrupted, shaking his head again and sighing. "Just … stop."

"Have it your way," Rebekah replied with another little shrug, the nascent smirk on her face fading away as she focused once again on the drive.

The silence was still uncomfortable, though, and while Jonah felt a bit agitated at the weird turn the conversation had taken, he realized that he wasn't quite finished with his questions. "So. Where is it that you are taking me?"

"Like I said, to see a friend. Someone who is a little better at answering these questions than I am," she said, her demeanor beginning to relax once again.

"Let me guess, he's a dragon, too."

The little smirk that had reappeared on her face bloomed into a full, if quirky, smile. "Of course."

In a way it was almost infuriating, for Jonah could no longer tell if she was indeed, crazy, or if she really was just out to make him look like some kind of fool. Leaning back in the seat once more, he closed his eyes and let out another low sigh. "Well. I suppose it's a good thing this road goes right through Orlando."

"Why is that?"

"You can drop me off at the Magic Kingdom. I could do with a dose of reality after tonight."

"Oh, very funny," she retorted, even if she did, in fact, let loose a quiet little chuckle. Once the chuckle died down, however, another bout of uncomfortable silence settled in. Jonah didn't know how to respond, didn't know if he even should respond. He wasn't sure which seemed like the crazier option - go along for the ride with some strange woman who claimed to be a dragon, or take his chances with some maniac who apparently had it out for him.

Again he found himself silently wishing that it would all turn out to be some kind of strange, twisted nightmare.

"Well." Rebekah's voice broke through the silence again, after a moment, a little hesitantly at first. "Like I said, we've got a long drive ahead of us, and you've had a long day. You should sit back and try to get some sleep. Everything will start to make a little more sense once we get where we are going."

Jonah didn't respond. He still was not sure how to respond. He wanted to know where she was taking him, wanted to know more about her, what her motives were. He did, in fact, have dozens of questions that he wanted to ask but did not know how to put into words. Wishing for nothing more than for the night to fade away into normalcy, he kept his eyes closed, and somehow drifted away into a deep, restful sleep.

FOUR

"They've found us. I don't know how, but they've found us."

The woman's voice, strained with fear, brought Jonah to attention, but what he saw in front of him was unexpected and confusing. He was sitting on a couch in a living room of sorts but the decor was terribly outdated. He had been watching television on an old console TV, encased in its own wooden frame and resting on a set of legs. The image on the screen itself was all in black and white and was nothing that he vaguely recognized.

At his feet was carpeting done up in a garish green color, and his surroundings were not much better. The lamps at either side of the couch, a fireplace in pastel colors, wallpaper that looked like it was better suited to an airport or a casino than a home; all of it screamed 'kitsch'.

He was viewing it all through a haze, too, unable to fully focus on anything that he saw. Standing nearby was a woman, black hair done up in a bouffant style, was dressed to match the surroundings. "Were you listening to me?"

Jonah tried to squint away the blur that was marring his vision but it simply would not retreat. To his surprise he found himself standing and he began to speak without even willing the words, as if he had been reduced to a mere spectator in his own body. "What? Are you certain?"

"I saw them at the grocery store. They had to have seen me, they had to have followed me back home," she said, her voice strained with panic.

Stepping over to a window and pulling back the curtains, Jonah took a look outside. Though his vision was still blurred, he could make out a scene that looked to have been stolen right out of some television show about nostalgic Americana. Big cars with gaudy fenders and whitewall tires lining the streets, well-manicured lawns, trees just beginning to shed their leaves - if the colors had been a little more faded it may as well have been a postcard he was looking at.

A pair of white, windowless vans coming around the corner caught his attention, and he frowned at the sight. Letting the blinds fall shut again, he turned to the woman who was standing nearby. "Get the children."

Jonah knew there would be precious little time. Watching the woman disappear down a hallway, he stepped over to the front door and latched the deadbolt shut. Turning down the hallway as well, glancing into one of the rooms in time to see the woman leaning over a small bed, he continued on toward the master bedroom. Without any hesitation he walked right into the closet, located a pump action shotgun that was hidden away on a top shelf, pulling a handful of shells from a box and hefting them in his hand.

Satisfied, he turned back toward the hallway, where the woman now stood with two small children. One, perhaps five years old, stood at her side and rubbed his eyes, while the other, hardly more than an infant, was fussing quietly in the woman's arms. Stepping past them, barely able to notice their bewildered looks through the haze of his vision, he moved with nervous intent. "Come on."

Once he was sure the little entourage was in tow, he made his way toward a sort of study that was located near the entrance to the hallway. Making his way straight for a bookshelf at the side of the room he pushed it to the side to reveal a darkened stairway leading down and out of sight. "We've talked this over before," he said, trying to remain calm, turning to look back at the woman with the children. "You know the plan."

He could see enough detail in her face to know that she was staring at him, wide-eyed. "You're not coming with us?"

"Stay down in the shelter for three days, not a second shorter, understand? Close the door behind you. It should be pretty soundproof down there but try your best to be quiet." Pausing to look down the stairway and catch sight of the heavy concrete door at the bottom, he turned once more to look at her. "When three days are up get on the first bus out of town. Don't pack anything, leave it all behind. Go at night if you can."

Shaking her head, the woman was trying her best to stay calm as the children were beginning to grow agitated. "Please. Come with us."

Jonah could feel the pit of his stomach sinking. He longed to be able to do what she asked; longed to be able to follow them down and to safety, but knew that he could not. "You know I can't do that. I've got to lead them away from here. Don't worry, I know what I'm doing; I'll be all right." As if to make his point, he started loading a couple of the shells into the shotgun.

"Please," she asked one more time, stepping forward and resting a hand on his shoulder.

"You know I can't," he repeated, shaking his head. Setting the weapon down on a desk at the side, he gently but firmly guided the woman toward the opening in the wall, briefly tousling the young boy's hair. "I'll meet up with you in Vegas. Just like we planned. Now go."

Doing her best to look stoic, the woman took a few steps into the stairway, turning around to look at him with wide eyes. "I love you …"

"I love you too. Three days," he repeated, then waited until the three of them had disappeared beyond the heavy door below, hearing it latch shut behind them. "Guess Khrushchev was good for something after all," he murmured. Pushing the bookcase back where it belonged, he took a second to make sure nothing looked out of order and then made his way to the front door.

A loud banging could be heard on the other side, and Jonah frowned grimly, knowing who was on the other side. "Time to play," he huffed, cocking the weapon before reaching out to unlatch the door and kick it open.

On the other side was a creature, scaly and terrifying, jaws agape and breathing hot, fetid air against him, the force of the dragon's roar pushing him back a bit as he fought to bring the shotgun up to level.

"Holy shit!" The very ground beneath his feet lurched back and forth, threatening to pitch him down, and when he tried to catch his balance he realized that he was no longer standing but was seated. His flailing hands latched not on to the hard surface of the mantle but grasped something smooth, curved and plasticky feeling. The scene out the window changed as his vision sharpened. Rolling green hills rose up in the distance, but in the foreground was a building of some sort, surrounded by asphalt; a parking lot.

"Decided to join the land of the living, at last?"

Turning around, Jonah had to shake a little confusion from his mind as his eyes settled on the redheaded woman sitting next to him, flashing something of a smirk in his direction. She was sitting in front of a steering wheel, he was sitting in the cab of a truck. The events of the night before came rushing back to his conscious thought, everything that he had wished were a nightmare making itself ugly reality once again.

Reaching up to hold a hand over his eyes and rub at his temples, Jonah groaned. "Christ. I was dreaming … a nightmare ..."

"I guess so," she said with a little shrug, pushing the door open and stepping out into the sunlight. "Was beginning to wonder if you'd ever wake up. Come on, let's get a bite to eat. I don't know about you but I'm starving."

A deep rumble in his stomach agreed with her assessment, and he merely nodded with a weary sigh. Pushing the door open and stepping out onto a somewhat gravelly parking lot, he squinted into the sky and noticed the sun was already high overhead. "How long was I out?"

"Ten, twelve hours?" She merely shrugged as she turned toward the building where they had stopped, a small roadside cafe of some sort.

"Twelve hours?" He blinked incredulously at the thought. He'd never been one to sleep very well in a moving car, and the idea that he could have been out for that long seemed ridiculous on its face, even in light of the events that had unfolded the night before. "Where the hell are we?"

Before she answered he looked around again, trying to get his bearings. The landscape was all wrong - far too hilly to have been anywhere near Southern Florida. It had the feel of a small town along the side of some highway, or perhaps the outskirts of some larger town, but he couldn't quite be sure. As he looked around, a small platoon of motorcycles rumbled their way down the highway, heading in the direction of the hills. "Ever hear of Deal's Gap?"

Turning to look at her with a frown, Jonah sputtered. "Deal's Gap? The Dragon's Tail?"

"Tail of the Dragon," she corrected with a smirk. "Thought you were mister sport bike enthusiast."

Deal's Gap - otherwise known as the Tail of the Dragon - was a stretch of highway that twisted and turned its way through the Great Smoky Mountains. It was also a world famous destination for motorcycling enthusiasts who regularly descended upon the location to test their skill and mettle against the numerous hairpin corners. A few of the guys in the riding group back home even sported little decals on their bikes proclaiming that they'd made the run a few times, themselves.

Still, it was supposed to have been up in the mountains, not in some small town. Jonah shook his head a little. "This doesn't look anything like the pictures I've seen ..."

"Haven't been there yourself? That's a shame. Technically you're right, though," she said, pointing up the highway with her thumb. "It was about half an hour back that way. You slept through the entire thing. Don't know how you managed that."

"So you mean to tell me that we're in Tennessee," he said, flatly.

She nodded with an overly perky smile, probably just to irritate him, as she held the door to the little diner open. "Yup. Come on, enough of the chitchat. I'm starving."

Begrudging and bewildered, Jonah followed in with a little shake of his head. The last time he'd so much as left the state of Florida was to visit his grandparents in New York, and that had been the first year of college. The thought that they could have driven to Tennessee, that he had slept the entire time, was a difficult one for him to process.

A waitress wearing too much makeup guided them over to an empty table that abutted the front windows where he could see outside and watch the stream of motorcycles continuing to come and go, seeming to corroborate her story that they were only just down the highway from Deal's Gap after all. They were provided with a couple of dingy menus that looked like they hadn't been changed for years, and a pair of tall glasses of water. Jonah realized that he was every bit as thirsty as he was hungry, and attacked his own glass with abandon.

It didn't take long for them to place their orders. Jonah had opted for a large omelet with sausage, his body hungering for breakfast in spite of the fact that it was apparently into the afternoon. His companion, Rebekah, had hardly looked at the menu and had decided to order a twenty ounce steak, rare. The waitress had asked her if she was sure about that and she'd only responded with a cheery nod of her head.

Neither bothered speaking while they waited for their order to arrive. Jonah spent the whole time looking back and forth from the scene outside the window to his companion. None of it made any sense, of course; he was still quite convinced that this was either some strange dream or someone's sick sense of humor.

Rebekah herself was a sort of contradiction in his mind. At once playful and serious, he didn't know how seriously he could take her. Even now as he turned to look in her direction she flashed him a strange sort of smile, one that he couldn't read. Was she being friendly? Was she mocking him? He didn't know if he could tell the difference. If she was part of a weird conspiracy to make him look stupid then of course it was all a front. If she was a figment of his imagination, it would be even more confusing - he had no idea why he would imagine her of all people.

He was equally conflicted about what he thought of her. She was not what he would describe as his type, between the unruly red hair, the outdated flannel shirt that she was wearing, and the carefree, unserious manner in which she presented herself. Yet he could not help but to find something oddly infectious about her, something that threatened to draw him in. Jonah was becoming aware that he was attracted to her on some curious level, a realization that was making him slightly uncomfortable.

Their meal arrived, mercifully in time to derail that train of thought. The food in front of him instead commanded his attention, his stomach instantly rumbling at the smell of it. An enormous cylinder of eggs drizzled in some kind of cheese sauce and topped with mushrooms, it spoke to his hunger and left him incapable of thinking of anything else while he dug in, assisted by a healthy use of the Tabasco bottle.

Unsurprisingly, not a word was spoke the entire time they ate, either. Halfway through the oversized omelet he began to realize just how much food had been plunked down in front of him. Pausing to sit back and let his stomach settle a little, he was shocked when he looked up at Rebekah's plate. She had been served a rather massive chunk of beef to begin with, and while he'd not been paying any attention to her she had managed to down almost the entire thing. Little more than a few bites of meat were left on her plate, a bloody mess from the rare steak left behind.

Part of him wanted to be disturbed or disgusted at the sight, but he found that instead he was simply amazed, staring. "Don't you think you're taking this whole 'dragon' thing a little far?"

She stopped to look up at him with a briefly confused stare, her jaw pausing in mid-bite, and then she simply furrowed her eyebrows at him. "Not sure what you are talking about," she murmured around the piece of meat, chasing it down with a swig of her water.

"Come on. Dragging me on up here through the Tail of the Dragon. Mowing down a slab of beef so rare that it's practically still mooing at you. Yeah, I get it. You're a dragon. So you've said. You think this little show is going to convince me of something?"

"No," she responded innocently enough, sitting up and dabbing at the corners of her mouth and continuing to look at him in a way that was either genuinely confused or mocking, he couldn't tell. "For one thing I happen to like my steak rare, and I haven't eaten since yesterday, so I'm a little hungry. Pardon me if it doesn't seem ladylike to you."

"Sorry, I didn't mean it that way," he muttered.

Shrugging it off, she continued. "Anyway, I didn't bring you through here to convince you of anything. I just happen to have been by this way a few times and just happen to like the food here, and it's only just a little detour from our route, anyway."

"Just where the hell are you taking me, anyway? You still haven't even bothered telling me that."

"I haven't?" She shrugged a little and took her time in responding, stabbing another bit of her steak with a fork and looking at it thoughtfully. "I thought I had. Well, anyway. We're heading to Detroit."

Jonah gaped at her openly at that, looking around him as if he expected someone to jump out at that very moment and announce that he was on camera. "Detroit? As in, Michigan?"

Chewing on the little bit of meat, she leveled a humorless look at him. "Do you know of any other Detroits?"

"Well, no ..."

"Then that's where we are headed," she deadpanned.

It was too much for him. He couldn't fathom why he had put up with the situation for as long as he had; but to be told that he was going to have to follow her all the way up to Detroit was beyond ridiculous. "All right, all right. I think I've had enough of this ... nonsense. Whatever you want to call it. There's no way I am going with you to Detroit."

With a vague sort of shrug, Rebekah continued to stab at her food a little absentmindedly. "No? Why not?"

"Because ... because it's insane. I don't even know what the hell I am doing here, right now. I should be back at home. Hell, I should be at work. Do you realize that the cops are probably out looking for me right now? God," he said with a pause, shaking his head. "The freakin' police are looking for me. I'm some kind of fugitive."

"You're probably right about that," she responded rather nonchalantly.

Once again he gaped at her openly, leaning forward in his seat some. "Are you serious? Like it's no big deal or something? Do you even realize what kind of trouble I could be in … what kind of trouble I will be in? I'm pretty sure that transporting a fugitive is a crime, too, you know. What do they call it? Aiding and abetting?"

"Something like that." Using a bit of bread that had been forgotten at the side of her plate, Rebekah swabbed up some of the ruddy juice that the steak had left behind, stuffing it in her mouth and swallowing it loudly. "But, hey, what are you gonna do about it?"

"What am I going to do about it? What am I going to do about it?" Jonah repeated himself with emphasis, glancing around the little diner again, growing flushed with frustration. "I'm going to do what I should have done a while ago. I'm going to get off this crazy train before things get any worse. I'm going to turn myself in to the cops, let them throw me in jail. Maybe they'll believe me when I say that I ran because I was scared. Doesn't matter, at least I don't have to worry about being chased down or getting in any deeper shit than I already am."

"Suit yourself. Payphone is over by the restrooms."

Her response caught him a bit flatfooted, and he sputtered angrily in his seat for a moment. Once again she was a contradiction to him; she had fought so hard to pull him from the clutches of the weird man who had attacked him, had done her damnedest to convince him to come along, yet now seemed rather unconcerned with his threat to call the cops, turn himself in and make it all for naught. Her blithe dismissal of his concerns seemed unfair.

"You don't even care, do you?"

Licking a bit of her food from her fingertips, she looked up and stared right back at him, her bright green eyes seeming to flare up for a second - but her voice remained calm and almost detached. "Look, Jonah, let me explain something to you. I have a pretty simple job to do here. Keep your ass safe and get you up to Detroit. No more, no less. I can keep you safe from the cops, I can try my best to keep you safe from bull drakes or whatever else gets thrown at us, but I'm sure not going to baby you."

She paused a moment before going on, her tone growing more firm as she went. "You're a grown man. You make your own decisions. Strange woman shows up demanding to take you to Detroit, and what do you do? Make your own decision. I'm not going to tie you up and drag you along kicking and screaming. If you are that intent on getting yourself in trouble with the cops, getting thrown in jail where there's nothing I can do to help you anymore, well, be my guest. I'm not going to stand in your way."

Jonah turned to look back at the payphone, just where she had said it was. She once again did not seem to be paying much attention to him, her own gaze turned back to a pile of mashed potatoes that accompanied her steak. Her indifference made him seethe. Clenching his fists, he pushed back from the table and began to march his way across the restaurant and toward the phones.

He didn't know what would happen, when he called them. They'd probably contact their local counterparts who would show up, detain him at a local police station until he could be extradited back down to Florida. Once there he'd probably rot in a cell until he could be put on trial. The evidence linking him to the murder was circumstantial at best, but his flight to Tennessee certainly wasn't helping make the case for his innocence. He'd probably be sentenced to at least some time in jail.

Still, he thought to himself. It had to be better than putting up with this nonsense. One last glance was cast over his shoulder, where he could see Rebekah seated by the window, plowing through her food as if he didn't even exist. Reaching into his pocket and pulling out his wallet, Jonah fished out the business card he had been given back at the police station, scowling at the numbers, before he picked up the handset.

He hadn't used a payphone in ages. It took him a moment to find where the rate for long distance was posted, digging around in his pocket once more to withdraw enough quarters to feed the machine. Settled in amongst them was the damned silver coin. The sight of it made his mood darken, and he contemplated stuffing it into the coin slot along with the quarters. Once more he looked at the digits printed on the little business card, and he sighed.

"Shit," he growled under his breath. "What the hell am I supposed to do?" Reaching up he let his fingers move across the buttons, punching them in one by one. He felt a knot form up in his throat as the phone began to rang, and finally it picked up.

"Hi! You've reached Donna and Mike," a pleasant feminine voice answered. "We're sorry we missed your call but we're not in at the moment. Please leave us a message and we'll get back to you soon. God bless!"

Jonah closed his eyes as he stuffed his wallet back in his pocket, letting the business card flutter to the floor. "Hi, mom. It's me, Jonah. Things have been kind of crazy over here, but I wanted to call and let you know I'm ok. I'll call you again soon. I love you." Setting the handset back on the receiver, he stumbled his way back to the table to sit down heavily.

Rebekah, who had been sitting there the whole time, her plate nearly clean, looked up at him with a slight smirk. "You know, you aren't half bad, Jonah."

"What do you mean?" He frowned a little at the statement, not quite sure what to make of it.

"Calling your mom like that. That was a nice thing of you to do."

Her voice was surprisingly gentle and sincere, a rather abrupt shift from the nonchalant and unserious behavior from only moments before. In a strange way it helped to defuse Jonah's growing anger, leaving him feeling deflated, defenseless, and unable to fight against her. He wanted nothing more than for the situation to end, to go home and pretend that none of this ever happened.

He didn't even stop to consider how she had known; there was no way that she could have overheard him across the restaurant. Running a hand over his face, he shook his head. "You know, this whole thing would be a lot easier if you could do something to convince me that you're not all crazy. That this story of yours is even remotely possible."

"Do something to convince you? You don't seem very open to what I have to say, Jonah."

He shrugged a little in annoyance, feeling slightly defeated. He didn't really want to be convinced; what he really wanted was for her to admit it was a hoax and let him be on his way. Yet he found himself unable to confront her directly, call her out on it like that. "Maybe you could prove your story some other way. You know, if you're this big mighty dragon, then why don't you turn into one?"

Rebekah laughed softly at that. The sound of her laughter was oddly lyrical, soothing to his nerves, and apparently genuine; she shook her head, smiling in spite of herself as she flagged down the wait staff to ask for the check before she bothered with any kind of response. "Somehow I don't think a dragon crashing around the place would be very appreciated by the locals."

"I don't mean right here and now," Jonah scowled, somehow irritated by the fact that her laughter was further defusing his bad mood. "Could find a quiet road that goes off into the mountains or something, somewhere private. Then you could show me. That'd go a long ways toward convincing me."

"Oh? Someplace nice and quiet in the mountains, no one around to see what we're doing? Just the two of us?" With a sly sort of grin she reached across the table and brushed a fingertip against his forearm. "Why, Jonah. If I didn't know better I'd say you were coming on to me."

All at once he forgot what point he was trying to make or where he was trying to go with his line of reasoning. He felt his cheeks flushing hot as he averted his gaze and sputtered. "What? No, no, that's not what I meant," he insisted, trying his best to ignore the little peals of laughter that his reaction had caused, the embarrassment transforming into irritation at being caught off guard like that.

Then, too, there was some part of his imagination that wanted to indulge in the thought of finding a quiet place where he could be alone with her. It was only a fleeting sort of afterthought, but it was enough to deepen his irritation.

"Of course it isn't what you meant. That's what I mean when I say if I didn't know better," she teased quietly, sitting back in her seat with another little laugh. "I'm sure you'd be rather ashamed of yourself, flirting with a girl you just met and hardly know."

Jonah was desperate to change the subject, and let the first words that would form in his mouth spill out. "Well, then, why don't you tell me more about yourself."

If her earlier tease had caught him off guard, his own question seemed to have much the same effect on her. Sitting back in her seat and blinking at him quizzically, she brushed an unruly lock of hair from her forehead. "What do you mean?"

"You expect me to follow you to Detroit. Fine. But that's what … another half a day's drive from here?" He didn't really know how long it was going to be, only that it was longer than any drive he had been on so far, with the possible exception of the travel earlier that day. "If I'm going to spend several hours in the car with you, I think I deserve to know a little more about you."

"I don't think that's necessary," she objected, the smile on her face wilting a little, her expression suddenly growing a little guarded.

Jonah, sensing that he had the upper hand in the conversation, even if for a moment, did not back down. "It's only fair. You've been stalking me long enough to know my name and God only knows what else. I don't want to be traveling across the country with a complete stranger. Come on, tell me something about yourself. Tell me what you do when you aren't dodging motorcycles."

For a moment it looked as if she were going to respond, or that she was at least considering it. Her mouth hung open uncertainly, her bright green eyes regarding him with a slightly wavering glance, but before she could get anything out the waitress reappeared with the check, setting it on the table with a pleasant thanks for their patronage. It had broken the moment, however, and Rebekah's expression hardened a little. "Look, we've got to get going. I don't want to get there too late."

Without giving Jonah a chance to protest, she reached into her pocket and withdrew a few bills, leaving them on the table and getting up to stalk toward the exit. Feeling once again trapped by the situation, unable to make any choice other than to simply follow along, Jonah pushed his own chair back and made his way after her.

FIVE

It was nighttime again when they had finally made their destination in Detroit. Nearly eight hours had passed since they'd left the little diner back in Tennessee, eight hours that had felt more like sixteen. Rebekah had been standoffish since they resumed the trip, and with the exception of a little idle banter about who would go inside to fetch drinks when they stopped for gas there had been little in the way of conversation.

Were it not for the radio stations that came and went as they made their way northward, the whole trip would have passed in near silence. It was enough to make him feel immensely uncomfortable long before the sun had set.

In the darkness Jonah had been unable to see much of the city, little more than a blur of nondescript buildings as they rushed along the interstate before pulling off an exit that dropped them right into the heart of the city. Though he had heard more than his fair share of horror stories about what a blighted town it was, the little part of the city that he'd had a chance to see that night seemed fairly normal enough.

Rebekah navigated the truck a few blocks away from the freeway, swinging around and coming to a stop in front of a skyscraper, rising some thirty floors up into the night, the concrete and stone facade fading into the darkness where the lights didn't illuminate it so well. It was hardly the tallest building Jonah had seen, but the rather staid colors and the stone seemed like such a contrast to the modern glass and steel buildings that dominated the skyline back in Miami. It seemed vaguely reminiscent of the Empire State Building in style; he could not help but to crane his neck a bit.

"Enough gawking. Time to get out."

He turned in time to see Rebekah swinging the door to the truck open and hopping out, casting him a glance that seemed more grave than was necessary. With a shrug of his own he opened his own door, stepping out and swinging it shut behind him, the sound artificially loud in the relative quiet of the night. "All right. What's this place?"

His unexpected companion seemed irritated at the questioning, as if she were still giving him the silent treatment. Squaring her shoulders, she began to stomp her way across the sidewalk and right up toward the entrance to the building. "Doesn't matter. Come on."

"What's got you all worked up, now? You're the one dragging me across the country with the insane story," he protested, but followed her up toward the entrance all the same. "You're damned lucky I haven't just walked away, or called the cops, or something."

After a bit of a sigh, she apologized in a slightly begrudging voice. "Sorry. Being behind the wheel for that long takes a bit out of me. The place doesn't matter. Just who."

"That's right. The guy who is going to answer all my questions. Make sense of it all, right?" He responded with a little more sarcasm than he intended to, and involuntarily flinched back as soon as the words had crossed his lips.

If she had noticed the sarcasm she gave no sign, and in fact did not react to his question in the least. Stopping at the door she reached out and rapped her knuckles against the glass twice, waited, and then repeated it once again. A light dimly visible in the distance responded by pointing in their direction and then bobbing, the silhouette of a man resolving itself after a moment. The guard briefly pointed his flashlight right in their direction, briefly blinding him, forcing Jonah to cover his eyes and flinch again while he heard the sound of a bolt being unlatched.

"Ah, Bekah! You finally made it. We were wondering when you'd finally get here … hurry on in. There's word that trouble might be on your tail."

Jonah found himself being ushered into the building a little hastily, the burly, uniformed guard giving him a not so gentle nudge inside as he passed the threshold, turning to lock the door behind them. If he had any protest to offer he wasn't given the chance; Rebekah spoke up first. "I think we're all right. He up in his office?"

The guard nodded. "He is."

Returning the nod, Rebekah then turned her head to glance at Jonah a little sharply. "All right, just follow me."

Their footfalls echoed in a disturbingly loud fashion against the polished stone floor, another product of the late hour. He imagined that during the day the lobby would be filled with people going about their business, but their slinking around in the night was beginning to feel increasingly inappropriate, illegal, or worse. "Wait just a second. Something doesn't feel right about this."

Stopping halfway toward the nearest elevator, Rebekah turned to shoot him a slightly irritated look. "What?"

"I'm not sure I'm comfortable sneaking around like this. It feels ... I don't know. Wrong."

"And letting a strange woman take you on a wild drive across the country feels right?"

Jonah bristled at that comeback. "Now you're going to give me a hard time for coming along with you?"

"Yes." She shrugged and turned back to the elevator. "Come on. After this, if you decide that you want to go back home and pretend like this never happened, handle it all in your own little way, then be my guest. Just see this out for me."

Feeling like he didn't really have much say in the matter, he simply shrugged in acquiescence and trudged along behind up to the elevator. The doors slid open immediately and they filed in; he watched quietly as she pushed the button marked 21, the elevator lurching slightly as it pulled them upward. With the exception of the quiet chime marking the passage of each floor, they passed the short ride in silence.

The doors slid open once again and admitted them to a quiet, darkened hallway. A directory on the wall in front of them pointed the way to various offices on the floor but Rebekah clearly knew exactly where she was going, not so much as pausing before she marched down the hall and to the left. Once again Jonah felt the urge to turn around and walk away, as he had for countless times in the past twenty four hours, but once again he felt oddly trapped by the circumstances. Rather unwillingly, he found himself following along. She led him straight to a door marked "Sawyer & Assoc", opening the door and stepping inside without so much as breaking her stride.

Beyond the door was something of a contrast to the rest of the night so far. He found himself in a small waiting room, well-appointed with plush leather seats and couches, the table in the center littered with highbrow magazines. The room was well lit, and some kind of contemporary jazz was being piped in through hidden speakers in the ceiling. A faint but cloyingly sweet and spicy scent lingered on the air, made him wrinkle his nose.

"Good to see you again, Bekah!" The voice belonged to a plump, middle-aged woman who was sitting on the other side of a sliding glass window, inside a comfortable little vestibule lined with innumerable pictures of small children and various pets. Festooned with rosy cheeks, curly auburn hair and horn rimmed glasses, the woman looked almost like a caricature of a secretary from a bygone era. "How are you doing? Oh, but, you aren't really here to chit-chat are you? He's been expecting you, go right on ahead."

For the first time in the night Rebekah managed a smile, albeit a weak one. "Good to see you too, Nanette. But, actually, I'm not the one who is here to see him." She turned on her heel, casting a glance back at Jonah and gesturing to a door next to the vestibule. "You're the one with the questions; he's the one with the answers. It'll be the second door on the left."

Jonah blinked in surprise. "What, you're not going along with?"

"Want me to hold your hand?"

Again Jonah felt himself bristling. He wanted to snap back that he'd been only too patient, too willing to go along with the insanity that was happening. He wanted to shout that he'd really done more than he rightfully should have, that any sane person would have gone straight to the police after the attack at his home, that any sane person would not have gotten into a truck with a strange woman and allowed themselves to be dragged more than a thousand miles across the country to a city they'd never been to before, to meet some mysterious person with all of the answers.

Before he could really let loose with his thoughts, however, he felt all of the ire inside of him suddenly deflate. He wasn't sure if it was the way she was looking at him, or perhaps some kind of morbid curiosity of his own to see where this was all leading, but once more he found himself incapable of saying no to her, incapable of fighting against what was happening. His shoulders drooping, he shuffled toward the door and pushed his way into another, shorter hallway.

The strange, sweet-spicy scent on the air seemed to grow thicker as he approached the second door on the left, as he was instructed. Pausing at the door, trying to decide whether or not he should knock, he was surprised to hear a voice calling out from inside. "Come on in, the door's open."

Jonah frowned, pushing the door open, and discovered the source of that odor as he was suddenly hit in the face with a thick cloud of smoke, pungent and faintly sweet. Caught off guard, he involuntarily breathed in a lungful of the stuff and promptly began to cough and wheeze, waving his hands in front of his face to try and push the smoke away. "Ugh!"

"You're not supposed to inhale the smoke like that. Just savor the flavor, the aroma." The voice, deep and sonorous, belonged to the man who was sitting on the other side of a sumptuous mahogany desk, the man who supposedly had all of the answers for him. A man who was apparently in the midst of enjoying a big fat cigar. "Come, sit, Jonah. I've been looking forward to meeting you."

Still coughing, Jonah frowned and squinted through the haze, flopping down on a plush leather chair on his side of the desk. "Everyone seems to know my name. Not very fair."

"Sorry about that. Name's Abraham Sawyer. You can call me Abe."

Getting a better look at the man behind the desk, Jonah had the strange thought that the man did not look like much of an Abe. Even seated behind the desk the man loomed large, his broad shoulders all but filling the big executive chair that he sat in. Abe, as he called himself, had a swarthy complexion and dark black eyes. Though he was completely bald, not a hair on his head, gray stubble adorned his jaw and chin in a sort of shadow of a beard. His scalp above his left eye was heavily pitted in what looked like an old burn scar. Something about his demeanor seemed to demand respect, but Jonah had had enough of granting strangers the benefit of the doubt. "You shouldn't smoke. It's bad for you," he blurted rather abruptly.

"So it is, so it is," the man conceded, speaking with a slight accent that Jonah could not readily place. After what seemed to be a moment of contemplation, he set the still smoldering cigar down, black eyes regarding it before he spoke up again. "Or, at least, that's what they tell me. But you aren't really going to try and deny an old dragon his favorite vice, are you?"

Folding his arms over his chest, Jonah frowned. "So. You're in on this dragon thing, too, are you?"

Abe grinned a toothy smile. "Well, of course I am. Were you expecting anything else?"

"Right." Much of the pent up frustration that he had been feeling the entire drive northward was beginning to bubble up inside of him. In spite of the fact that this man seemed to demand respect - the lavishly appointed office, the smart, double-breasted suit that he was wearing, the gold Rolex and fingers studded with rings, even the look of authority in his eyes - Jonah did not feel nearly as compelled to acquiesce to him, not in the way he felt helpless to demur to Rebekah. "And I suppose you're going to tell me that you're a thousand years old and you breathe fire or something like that."

The man faked an offended frown. "A thousand years old? Is my age really beginning to show? I'm actually only, oh, just turned seven hundred and forty five last week, actually."

Jonah just shook his head, suddenly no longer in the mood for these kinds of silly games. "Look. I promised that I would come here, listen to your little spiel, and I've held up my end of the bargain. God knows why. So, go on, say what you are going to say so that I can get my ass back down to Florida, before I get into any more trouble."

The faint hint of a grin on Abe's face retreated, leaving the man to regard him in a curious, cautious manner. "Spiel? Well, I suppose if you have to call it a spiel, go right ahead and do that. But it's more than that, Jonah, a bit more than that. You see, I'm supposed to be good at convincing people of things. Opening their eyes to the truth, as it were." The big executive chair creaked as Abe leaned back, folding his hands behind his head and relaxing. "I'm supposed to convince you of this whole ... how did you put it? Dragon thing?"

"The whole thing is just ridiculous. You're clearly not a dragon, even if there were such a thing," he grumbled a little angrily.

"Oh? And you know there is no such a thing how? Because you've never seen one? What if we just don't like to be seen?"

"Well I see you now," Jonah retorted, tapping his foot on the floor lightly, impatiently. "And you don't look a thing like a dragon."

Abe flashed another light, toothy smile. "Well, now, of course I don't. Wouldn't do to have a dragon sitting here running a law firm, now would it? I know Rebekah didn't tell you much but I thought she'd at least have the courtesy to let you know we don't usually wander around in our, ah, true form. Masquerading as a human has got certain advantages, as I am sure you can imagine."

Jonah sat up a little more upright, frowning pointedly at the man across the desk. "Bullshit. You can sit there and tell me about being in some kind of magical human form all you want, but it's just bullshit. I can sit here and tell you that I'm actually the freakin' Loch Ness Monster in human form. Anybody can say what they want. So prove it to me. If you're really a dragon, then prove it. Show me."

"It doesn't work like that, Jonah, you've got to …"

"Of course it doesn't," Jonah interjected a little angrily. "How freakin' convenient. Come on, if you can't come up with something better than that, then why don't we just stop wasting our time and let me be on my way. I don't care about dragons or any shit like that. Let me know what the hell you want from me."

"Ah, so impatient. So brash. Definitely a youngster," Abe said, coming across as vaguely amused as he, too, sat forward, resting a pair of big, meaty hands on the desk. Jonah suddenly remembered the sinister mountain of a man who had attacked him in his home, who had punched his way straight through a bulletproof door, and suddenly he felt a little more meek. Though Abe hardly had that same sinister mien, he was nearly the same build, and Jonah suddenly felt rather intimidated. "You a betting man, Jonah?"

Leaning back a little, eyes widening some, Jonah merely blinked. "A what?"

"A betting man. Would you like to make a little wager?"

The man looked dead serious in spite of the faint grin on his face, a certain amount of implied danger hidden behind that air of authority. It was the sort of thing that again seemed to demand cooperation from Jonah, in spite of his desire to be brash, as the man had put it. "Sure, I suppose."

Abe grinned a little more obviously. "Good, good. So am I. So here's a friendly little wager. A hundred dollars says that, before you leave here tonight, you're going to believe that not only am I a dragon, but you are, too. What do you say?"

It seemed like an easy bet, but just as he was about to open his mouth to accept his eyes lit upon the gold necklace that the man was wearing, or, rather, the pendant that it held. A round bit of gold, shaped not unlike a coin, and bearing a dragon symbol that was, for all intents and purposes, identical to the one that was on the coin he had in his pocket. Reminded of its existence, he could suddenly feel the shape of it digging in to the side of his leg. For some reason it took his confidence down a notch. "All … all right. It's a bet."

"Good, good," Abe repeated, leaning back slightly, shifting his hands on the desk slightly. "But that means you have to hear me out. Before we can get to the convincing part, there's a few things you're going to have to know. A few things about the situation at hand, a few things about yourself. A bit of a history lesson, as it were. Think you can manage that?"

He was still a little thrown off by the design on Abe's pendant, and let a moment of silence pass before he spoke up. "All right."

"Thousands of years ago, dragons freely roamed the earth. Mostly in what is now northwestern Europe. Germany, France, the British Isles, and so on. Life was good and simple for generation after generation. We had no real competition, plenty of land, plenty of game to hunt, open skies to soar. We had plenty of squabbles among our own kind, of course, but nothing serious. Life was good.

"Then, mankind showed up. At first we really couldn't tell them apart from any other lesser species. They hunted in packs like wolves, lived together in communities like bees, made all manner of strange sounds like the birds. But then we made the remarkable discovery that humans were intelligent, just like us. We could learn to speak with them, interact with them. Imagine the joy, discovering that we weren't the only sentient beings on the planet! That there was someone else to share our stories with, our lives with!"

Remembering his cigar, Abe picked it up and stuffed it between his teeth, chewing on it lightly as he continued his tale. "Back then, the humans did not fear dragons, and we were free to be ourselves among mankind. We made friends with them, and some went even beyond friendship. Some dragons learned to use their magic to take human form, settling in among the humans, even making families among them. There was a blending of cultures and peoples. For hundreds of years there was peace.

"But jealousy is a trait that has always bedeviled mankind. There were sorcerers among mankind who coveted the powers that the dragons had. They coveted our ability to take to the skies, the magic that we were born with that their own could not hope to match. Banding together, these jealous magicians sought to steal the power of the dragons for themselves. They discovered a power over us, a way to bring us down low, to wage war against the dragon clans. In the space of a few short years the long peace we had enjoyed had been forgotten, and all we knew was persecution at the hands of the Sorcerers' Syndicate."

Jonah coughed and shook his head. "Wait, wait. Sorcerers' Syndicate? Really?"

"Oh, they've gone by different names. A thousand years ago they were the Holy Order of the Magi. Before then it was probably something else. Now they call themselves the Sorcerers' Syndicate. More of a modern feel to it, I suppose."

It was really all too much. Jonah could hardly believe that he had been dragged over a thousand miles to sit in a smoke-filled room and listen to an imposing man named Abe spin a fanciful tales about medieval dragons. He couldn't help but to respond with a sarcastic tone. "Nice story. Have you thought of selling it to Hollywood?"

"Please." Abe sat up again, wearing a rather stern frown. "You promised to listen."

"All right, I suppose I did - but what does this have to do with me?"

"Just listen."

Jonah shook his head, folding his arms over his chest impatiently again but nodded. "All right, go on."

Abe cleared his throat, his gaze wandering upward as he once again delved into his tale. "Now where were we? Ahh, yes. The Syndicate had found a way to subdue, to subjugate the dragons to their own designs. With frightening speed, one clan after another was decimated, either brought under the sway of the Syndicate or wiped out in their entirety. The dragons were forced to go into hiding, taking on human form, trying to live out their lives in obscurity right in the midst of mankind.

"It worked, too, at least for a while. But the dragons have an ability, they can see through the disguise. When the Syndicate discovered this, they used the dragons in their control to sniff us out. One by one the dragons in hiding were captured, either to be enslaved or killed. One by one the clans began to go extinct, ancient familial lines being wiped out wholesale. We sought safety in lands beyond the Syndicate's control. South to Spain and Italy, east to Russia, and so on. And again, for a time, it worked."

Pausing for a moment, putting down his cigar, Abe looked in Jonah's direction to see if there was any response forthcoming, but the young man merely sat in his chair, arms folded over his chest, brooding a little. He had agreed to listen to the tale, not to chime in from time to time. Shrugging silently, Abe continued with a grin. "Now, that's where the story starts to get personal. For me, at least.

"My own branch of the clan had fled to Spain. Al-Andalus, as it was called, at the time. Led their lives in relative obscurity among the Moors, integrating into their society. I was born Ibrahim ibn Sawwar al-Maghribi, in the year 1267. Of course, one can't really go by the same name for seven hundred years. Abraham Sawyer, Ibrahim ibn Sawwar. Get it? Sixty years ago I was Ben Mackie. Before that I was …"

Abe looked to be rather pleased with his own cleverness in names, but Jonah was growing impatient. "Yeah, I get it. You were getting to the part that has to do with me?"

The big man looked slightly taken aback by the interruption, the grin on his face fading some, but he merely nodded and cleared his throat. "All right. 1267, right in the middle of the Catholic reconquest of the country, the Reconquista as they called it. Now, I don't mean to insinuate that the Syndicate was behind it all, but it certainly proved to be a worthy vehicle for their aims of rooting out pockets of dragons in the area. Hell, the Spanish Inquisition a couple centuries later was a perfect disguise for their witch hunt …"

Jonah blinked. "You're saying that the Spanish Inquisition was made to hunt down dragons?"

"No," Abe said, chuckling as he shook his head. "Not entirely, anyway, but the Syndicate was at least partially behind it. Dragons had been reduced to myth by this time; it's no coincidence that the Church had been describing Satan as a dragon, either. The Syndicate was not interested in the Church other than a means to an end. They couldn't openly hunt dragons anymore, but doing so under the guise of inquisitors was perfect for them. I … witnessed several members of my family burned at the stake under ridiculous charges. Blasphemy, heresy, you name it." By the time he paused again, the grin on his face had vanished.

For a fleeting moment, Jonah almost felt sorry for the man. On the verge of offering some kind of sympathy, he reminded himself of how ridiculous the situation was, frowning a little again before he spoke up. "And how does this bring us to where we are now?"

"Hmm? Oh, yes, of course. By the 1500s the Syndicate had managed to eradicate almost all of the dragon clans. All that were left were a disparate scattering of individuals who had managed to escape their net, individuals like myself. There were rumors of a few clans who had escaped into Russia and further east, but if they escaped the Syndicate or not, we never knew. Those few of us who remained made our way back north, regrouped in Britain, right under the noses of the Syndicate. Last place they'd think to look, right?

"I'm sure you can see where it's going from here. When word got out that the colonies in America were proving successful, most of us were on the first boat across the Atlantic we could get on. Migrated to the colonies, kept our heads down, kept out of the way. It worked, too, for quite a while. The Syndicate, they must have thought that they had us all done for. It wasn't until … oh … fifty years ago that they started hunting us down anew. Which just about brings us down to you."

"Down to me." Jonah frowned rather dubiously, briefly glancing around for a clock, or some way to know how much time had passed, but there were none. Sighing softly, he turned his gaze back on the man behind the desk. "This had better be good."

Abe drew in a deep breath, leaning back in his seat again and relaxing. "Right, so I'll just come down to it. The parents you know and love are not actually your own; you were adopted. You were born to two members of our clan who had gone into hiding to try and protect you from the Syndicate. When they realized they could not outrun their pursuers, they quickly and secretly put you up for adoption. They did good, as even we lost track of you until just a few years ago."

In a way, hearing someone tell him that he was adopted, that his parents were not really his own, was a harder pill to swallow than the insane concept that there were actually dragons. "That's ridiculous."

"You can ask them about it, if you like. You know you've wondered why you don't look anything like them," Abe intoned a little solemnly, folding his arms in his lap in front of him. "Look, being adopted doesn't mean they're less real, or less loving, it just means …"

"It means that you have no idea what you are talking about," Jonah protested, his voice taking on a slightly defensive tone to it.

Abe held his hands up in front of him, shaking his head. "Take it easy, kid. I'm just telling it to you the way it is."

"Ridiculous. Whatever. I didn't come all this way to listen to some fantasy, have some guy tell me that I'm secretly adopted, that I'm a dragon, blah blah blah. I just want to know how to get away from all this, to go back to my life. Get away from that guy … that … what did she call him, bull drake …"

"That's a bit more difficult than you know," the big man said, a bit apologetically. "Bull drakes are members of the clans who have been subjugated by the Syndicate. They've been bred, for hundreds, even thousands of years, to have a slavish need to fulfill the demands of their masters. Your particular bull drake has been tasked with finding the Silver Token, and he's not going to stop until either he finds it or he is dead."

Reminded of the coin in his pocket, Jonah dug it out and dropped it unceremoniously on the desk, listening to it ring as it settled against the hard wood. "Like I said before, I don't want it. Get rid of it, keep it, I don't care. I just don't want it anymore."

"I can't take it, and I can't get rid of it. It is a symbol of your place as the Silver Dragon. Leave it here and it'll just find you again, and so will the bull drake …"

"Bullshit," he retorted, slamming his fists on the desk and rising up to his feet. "I am sick of this bullshit. I don't know what you people hoped to accomplish by dragging me here and then feeding me this fantasy novel reject of a story, but the only thing it has accomplished is to convince me that you people are batshit crazy. I want out of here. Now."

Abe furrowed his brow but otherwise seemed rather unfazed by the outburst. "Now, Jonah …"

"No! Don't freakin' patronize me. I'm done."

Chewing on his lip for a moment, Abe let silence fall over the pair as he seemed to be considering, measuring his response. "All right. I thought you might appreciate a little background to help you understand what's going on. I hope that it'll prove useful to you at some point, but clearly it's not helping you right now. Come. I want to show you something," he said, rising up from his seat, briefly towering over Jonah before turning to the big, expansive windows behind his desk and pushing them open.

The window turned out to be a door, a fact that Jonah did not notice against the darkness of the night beyond. "What is it?"

"Just come here." Begrudgingly Jonah followed, stepping through the door and out onto a short, narrow balcony. Abe was already reclined against the handrail, gazing out into the sea of lights that spread out twenty stories beneath them. From here he could see the highway in the distance, the constant buzz of lights zipping along in one direction or another, the languid pace of the city as it slept in the deep of the night. "One of the things I love about this office, you get such a great view of the city. Detroit used to be quite the place, you know. Back in the day, back in the fifties …"

"What's this have to do with me?"

"Nothing," Abe said a little morosely, frowning. "But this does. For centuries our young have been born in human form. It's a way of protecting ourselves. Normally the whelps are taught their identities at a young age, an advantage you did not have. It's time for you to embrace who you really are, Jonah. To spread your wings."

Once more Jonah bristled. "Come on, this is ridiculous. Make this quick, I'm about to turn and leave."

With a sigh, the bulky man in the suit nodded. "Each dragon is different. Some of us breathe fire, some of us don't. We come in all colors and sizes. The one thing we all have in common is our ability to fly. I want you to fly, Jonah. Take a leap of faith."

SIX

"You're kidding me," Jonah croaked, peering out into the dark of the night that surrounded them. "You aren't really suggesting …"

"I am," Abe answered, gruffly, his expression dead serious. "Birds aren't taught how to fly, Jonah. There are no lessons, no practice sessions. One day they spread their wings and take a leap from the nest. It's long passed the time for you to take that step, too, Jonah."

Jonah took an involuntary step back from the edge, back away from the man as if he suddenly feared he might try to lob him over unwillingly. "You're insane …"

"Look. You said you wanted convincing. This is the easiest way to do it. Would it help if we did this thing together?" The big man proved rather spry for his frame, hauling himself up to the side of the little handrail and perching precariously right on the edge, turning back to extend a hand in Jonah's direction. "Here, come on."

"Jesus Christ!" He wasn't sure whether he was more afraid that he might be hauled over the edge or the man who suddenly seemed more the lunatic would simply topple off right in front of his eyes.

Abe smiled calmly, all things considered. "It's safe, I promise."

Still Jonah refused, shaking his head vigorously, taking a step back. "You people are goddamned insane. Even if I believed this shit do you honestly think I'd jump off a building?"

"Your body knows what to do." A slight breeze crossed the little balcony, hardly enough to set his disheveled bangs to flapping, but to Jonah it may as well have been a gale, and he responded by pressing himself firmly back up against the wall. Abe still seemed to be wholly unperturbed "You won't let yourself be hurt. You'll spread your wings and be soaring before you know it."

"No way." His voice was cracking again, and he was beginning to feel dizzy in spite of the distance that he had put between himself and the ledge. "No way I'm jumping off a building. Not with you, not for you, not for anyone. If you're out to kill me, there's better ways to get it done."

"Exactly."

The response caught him a little off guard. "What?"

"If we wanted to kill you, we'd have found a simpler way of doing it, don't you think?"

There was, in fact a certain logic to the statement; all the same, no amount of good logic was about to convince him to take up the offer. "I don't know what you people are getting at. Some kind of sick joke, some kind of twisted prank, I really don't know and I really don't care, but there's no way in hell I'm getting up there with you. Just forget about it."

"Jonah …"

Before he could try and make another point he was interrupted by the sound of a door opening inside the office. Both men turned to see Rebekah, her eyes widening at the sight. "Sorry if I'm interrupting something here … but we've got a problem."

With that same surprising grace, Abe hopped back down to the balcony, straightening out a little ruffle that his clothing had acquired. The calm, almost jovial expression on his face had suddenly grown more serious as he strode his way out of the chill night air and back into the relative safety of the office, Jonah right at his heels. "A problem?"

"We've got company."

The statement was enough to get Abe to pause in his steps, his brow wrinkling a little bit. "Company. So you were followed."

There was a brief twinge of something like regret in the young woman's face, but it passed quickly and she nodded in the affirmative. "So it would seem."

"Well. Looks like there is going to be a change in plans, then." The big man resumed his seat behind his desk, resting his hands on the edge and turning his gaze back up to Rebekah. "It's not safe for you to stay here. I want you to take my car, yours is probably being watched. Use the service elevator, down to the basement. It's parked down there." Pulling a drawer open, he fished out a set of keys and placed them on the edge of the table.

Gathering the keys up obediently, Rebekah nodded gravely. "The meeting, then?"

The course of the brief conversation was rapidly evading Jonah's understanding, and the fact was beginning to irritate him. He wanted to interrupt and ask who the company was, what this meeting was, and what was going on, but for the moment he held is tongue and watched as Abe nodded as well. "Yes. But I want you to make a stop on the way. Pick up Jeffress. We haven't been able to inform him, you know how he is."

"Of course. Anything else?"

"Keep him safe. Do what you can to convince him of the truth, but remember. He's got to discover it for himself, " the big man replied with a renewed grin, turning his attention back to Jonah. "Oh, and you. I believe this is yours."

Jonah looked down to see a crisp $100 bill being slid across the desk. "What … what's that for?"

The grin on Abe's face only seemed to widen. "I lost the bet. Now, the two of you get going. Stay close to Rebekah, she knows what she's doing. She'll keep you safe. You'll have another chance to figure yourself out, kid, soon enough, but we need you to be kept safe until then. I'm just sorry we didn't have the time tonight. We'll do our best here to keep our company occupied while you two slip out. Now get out of here!"

The man's statement ended more in the form of a command, one which Rebekah obeyed without hesitation. Before Jonah had a chance to object, she clutched him by the wrist and dragged him right on out of the office, down the hall, and back through the waiting area where the plump woman in the vestibule smiled and waved at them. "Don't worry about us, Bekah. We'll take care of things here, you just take care of yourselves!"

Rebekah acknowledged with a hasty wave, continuing to drag the rather befuddled Jonah right back out into the relative dark of the hallway. Finally he shook off the sense of surprise and confusion, yanking his arm away hard enough to extricate himself from her grip, frowning into the darkness. "What the hell is going on here?"

When she turned back to him her gaze was surprisingly sharp, enough that he flinched just at the sight of it. "Weren't you listening back there? Come on, we don't have time to wait around."

He followed behind as she took off down the hall again, but he continued to grumble quietly. "Something about company following us."

"Try your homicidal friend, and maybe some of his friends, too. I don't really know, but it doesn't really matter. Don't want them getting their hands on you, now, do you?"

"And just what do they want with me?" They had rounded a corner, passed the main elevators and stepped through a door marked "Restricted Access" that was nonetheless unlocked. It was, apparently, a service area, where there was access to a number of electrical, utility closets, and, their destination, the wide doors of the service elevator.

"Same thing they want with all of us," she finally responded, a little breathlessly, mashing the button to summon the elevator. A quiet, sluggish creaking sound filtered up through the elevator shaft, seeming to be in no hurry to reach them. "Use you for their own purposes. Kill you. Maybe both, just depends. Try not to think about that too much - at least I wouldn't, if I were you."

Jonah closed his eyes and shook his head. The entire situation seemed to go a little beyond simply surreal; people claiming to be dragons, asking him to leap from a balcony two hundred feet in the air, punching through bulletproof glass. If he had not seen it happen with his own eyes he would have thought it a fanciful tale. "Just … just tell me this isn't happening," he groaned, rubbing his temples.

"Wish I could, but it is. Now, come on," came the reply, coinciding with the sound of the elevator doors sliding open.

Opening his eyes just enough to follow her inside the oversized service elevator, watching her press the button for the basement, he backed himself into a corner and slumped back against the cool metal walls. "And what about you? What do you people want from me?"

Turning to look at him over her shoulder, Rebekah cast a quizzical frown in his direction. "What?"

"You. The bald guy upstairs. Whoever else you happen to be working with, the whole insane lot of you. What do you want with me?"

She blinked before answering. "To keep you safe. Protect you from…"

Jonah shook his head, cutting her off with a little wave of the hand. "Right. So you've been saying. But there's more to it than that, you aren't doing it out of the vast goodness of your hearts. There's something you want from me."

For a moment he was answered only with the slow creak and groan of the elevator descending down its shaft. Frowning, Rebekah turned away from him, facing the doorway and speaking a little more quietly. "I'll explain later."

"Explain now," he shot back, stepping forward and reaching for the button to stop the elevator in its tracks.

His attempt was cut short by a swift swing of her arm, batting his hand away, while she turned again to look back at him rather harshly. "I'll explain later. We have a long drive ahead of us, and I sure as hell don't want to spend it in silence like the last one. Besides," she said, punctuated by a little shudder as the elevator car reached its destination and bobbed to a stop. "The longer we stay here, the more danger we are in. Let's go."

The doors languidly opened to a largely darkened basement, lit only with exit lighting and whatever light made its way in through a large roll-up door that was open to the exterior. The elevator dumped them out onto a raised concrete platform, part of a dock that was built to handle large freight trucks. Beyond the dock were a few parking stalls for larger vehicles, and then a sort of small parking garage, presumably for the employees of the various offices in the building above.

It seemed to be their destination. Rebekah led him down a small flight of stairs and across the truck loading area, their footfalls echoing against the oil stained concrete, disturbingly loud in the quiet of the night. There were relatively few vehicles that were parked overnight, mostly cars that he guessed were to be used for business purposes only, and a few smaller delivery vans nestled up against concrete pillars. Something about the way they scowled at him from the darkness of their little parking stalls made them seem strangely sinister, a thought he tried to banish by shaking his head.

To his surprise, they stopped right in the middle of the garage, Rebekah coming to an abrupt halt and holding up a hand to indicate that he follow suit. In confusion he glanced around, watching as she seemed to listen before speaking up quietly. "Something isn't right."

"What do you mean?"

For another moment she seemed to be listening intently to the silence, the look on her face one of serious concentration. "I don't think we're alone."

The sinister feeling in the dark silence around him suddenly seemed so much more validated, and Jonah found himself glancing around a little wide-eyed, as if he might spot some kind of danger, as if he expected the dark-haired man to jump out from one of the shadows. "What? Where? Do you hear something?"

"Shh!" She brought her finger up to her lips, narrowing her eyes as she glanced around, her voice dropping to a mere whisper. "They've been here. Might still be here. More of them than we thought …"

The quiet of the night was shattered rather abruptly by the roar of an engine coming to life. The two of them jerked their heads in the direction of the sound just in time to see a pair of headlights flick on, pointed directly at them, blinding them both. A loud, angry squeal echoed against concrete, the vehicle's engine roaring all the more loudly. In confusion Jonah hunched himself downward, near the ground, arms thrown instinctively in front of his face when he was struck solidly on the shoulder, something bowling him to the ground and rolling him out of the way.

A rush of air reeking of burned rubber and exhaust wafted past him, and before he could get his bearings he felt a firm grip on his shoulder hauling him back up to his feet. Opening his eyes, looking about in a bewildered fashion, he could see an unmarked white van coming to a hard stop, tires squealing, shuddering as it was being turned back in his direction. The grip on his shoulder was Rebekah, her green eyes flashing at him wildly as she shouted a simple command : "Run!"

The command did not need to be repeated. He followed as she took off, his legs pumping as quickly as they would go, feet pounding against the oil-stained concrete beneath them. The angry sound of tires squealing and the engine revving behind them suddenly grew frightfully close. Just in time she ducked between a pair of parked vans in their stalls and he followed without question or thought, diving in the little space between the vans just as the one pursuing them caught up, screeching to a halt, boxing them in.

"Shit," Rebekah hissed breathlessly, fishing around in her pockets. "Black SUV. End of the row," she said, shoving something in his hand before pulling him further into the stall.

"What?" Bewildered, he glanced down to see a set of keys in his hand. He looked back to see her squeezing behind one of the parked vans, a tiny little space that was too narrow for him to follow. "Wait, where are you going … don't leave me here?"

The sound of a door sliding open and latching in to place caught his attention. Turning on his heels he stared as he saw a man climbing out of the van, blocking his only route of escape. The man was not tall but thickly built, his head topped with inky dark hair, and a pair of black eyes to match. It was the same man from the coin store, the same one who had torn down the door to his apartment. Jonah felt his blood go cold in his veins as he stepped backward and began to shake. "Oooh, no, no, no …"

The man's face did not betray any emotion, but Jonah could not help but to imagine that the loud crackle of his knuckles as his hands balled up into fists was something like grim satisfaction. He winced as the man took a menacing step forward, but the both of them were caught off guard by a loud and sudden shout from the right. "Now! Go!"

Before either of them could react there was a sudden blur of motion that crashed into the man hard enough to send him sprawling. It was the same sort of thing that he had seen back in his apartment just the day before, and instinctively he knew what it meant. Clutching the keys in one hand, Jonah darted out from between the parked vans, gaping at the sight of the sinister mountain of a man laid out flat on his back, briefly stunned, Rebekah's considerably smaller from holding him down. "I said go!"

With a nod, he ran right past them and glanced wildly along the row of parking spaces, trying to guess which car would be the right one. Fumbling with the key fob he mashed one of the buttons and was rewarded with a quiet beep, a black BMW at the end of the row of stalls flashing its lights on and off for him. Grunting, he sprinted off in the direction of the vehicle as fast as he could.

The sound of a struggle behind him caught his attention, though, and before he reached the car he stopped and turned around to look. The big man had gotten back up to his feet and was busy trying to peel Rebekah away from him, while she was busy grappling at him and writhing, trying to knock him back down by the looks of it. "Get in the damned car and start it up, we've got to get out of here," she cried out loud when she noticed him watching.

Just as he was about to turn back to the car, the small mountain of a man succeeded in peeling Rebekah off of him, holding her out at arm's length like one might hold an uncooperative cat. Jonah could only watch with a sense of creeping horror as the man sneered, growled, and then threw her against a nearby van with enough force to collapse the door inward, sending a shower of glass spraying in every direction while Rebekah's body simply disappeared into the gaping hole that had been left behind.

"Holy shit," he whispered breathlessly, eyes widening. Then he realized that the man was advancing on him anew, unwavering and determined. "Holy shit," he repeated, taking a few unsteady steps backward before turning and breaking into a sprint, crossing the distance to the car, tugging the door open and climbing into the driver's seat.

He fished around for the key, trying to find the right one, trying to find the ignition and coming up empty. A furtive glance upward showed the big man closing the gap much too quickly for comfort. "Shit, which one is it?" Jonah's hands shook as he fumbled through the keys, groping at the neck of the steering column, his heart racing as he tried to figure out how to start the damned car. All while watching his doom approach with unrelenting steps.

At last he found the key that fit in the slot, but to his dismay it would not turn. Before he pulled it out and tried again, his eyes finally lit on the big button marked "Start Engine." Jamming his thumb into the button the engine at last roared to life. Reaching for the gearshift he pulled it into gear and stepped on the gas, the vehicle jerking forward, tires squealing against the concrete.

It was not a moment too soon. The big man was standing where the car had been only seconds before, fists flexing at his sides, a menacing and impatient look on his face. Jonah watched the man with a panicked expression before remembering that he was driving. Turning his attention back in front of him, he yanked the steering wheel to the side just in time to avoid crashing into a thick concrete pillar, the tires again squealing beneath the car, his own voice crying out in a startled yelp before he finally pointed it in the direction that he thought the exit was.

Then, to his surprise, someone stepped out from behind another parked vehicle to stand right in the way of his escape path. It was Rebekah. Her clothes were a little torn, her hair disheveled and wild looking, filled with little shards of glass, a line of blood running down the side of her face, but otherwise whole. Jonah was so shocked by the sight that he almost forgot to stop, slamming his foot on the brake and coming to a stop only inches from where she stood, unwavering.

As soon as the car stopped, however, she was in motion. "Go," she shouted, rounding the front of the SUV and pulling the passenger door open, launching herself rather unceremoniously into the car and tugging the door shut behind her, shouting again before she even had a chance to sit up. "Go, go, go!"

In the rear view mirror Jonah could see the van whipping back around to point in their direction again, and he needed no other motivation than that. Mashing his foot on the accelerator, the car jerked forward once again, and he turned the wheel sharply to aim right for the exit door, whipping around again and finally exiting onto the road. "Where?"

"Back to the highway," she responded a little gruffly, finally getting properly seated and pulling the seat belt on. "Bastard Abe had better make sure my truck is taken care of," she grumbled, turning to look out the window as they passed where it was still parked.

It seemed an odd sort of thing to be concerned with, given the circumstances. Jonah could see the van rounding the corner and getting on the street behind them, following in close pursuit. The freeway was still a few blocks away, and, to his dismay, the light at the intersection ahead had just turned red. Somewhat hesitantly, he started to apply the brake.

Rebekah immediately hit him in the shoulder. "What the hell do you think you are doing?"

"The light is red," he objected, gesturing ahead of him.

"And do you think your friend back there cares? Go, dammit, go!'

Cringing, Jonah let off on the brake and punched the gas once again, urging the car forward and through the intersection. There was fortunately no traffic at this hour and they cruised through without incident, but he somehow could not help but to feel a little chagrined at the infraction.

Sure enough, the van behind them did not so much as hesitate. He realized it was moving faster than they were, closing the distance. Cringing once more he sped up, way too fast for these roads. "Which way," he asked, seeing that they were fast approaching the highway intersection.

"Not this one," she responded, after a moment of thought.

He turned to give her a confused and somewhat panicked look. "What?"

"Not this one," she repeated, pointing ahead of them. "Next highway. It's only right up there a few more blocks."

The van behind them was continuing to catch up, and Jonah was forced to continue increasing his speed. Luck was on their side and the next few intersections beyond the highway were all green and traffic was all but nonexistent, but at this rate all it would take was one person crossing the road at the wrong time to spell disaster.

It was only a moment before he realized that they were coming up to the next highway intersection. "Which way, then?"

She paused a moment. "West."

"West?"

"West. Right. To the right," she clarified

He nodded, peeking back in the mirror to see the van growing uncomfortably close. Looking forward again, his blood suddenly ran cold again when he realized that, just before the turnoff to the highway there was another intersection, a fairly broad and complicated intersection with more than one road crossing his path. This time the light was red, and this time there was some traffic. "Oh, shit," he cursed.

Rebekah only frowned. "Keep going."

"But it's red. There's traffic …"

"Don't stop."

Jonah felt himself tensing as they neared the intersection. "We're gonna crash. We're gonna get killed."

"And what do you think happens if he catches up to us?"

There was no time left to argue. Screaming involuntarily, Jonah simply mashed on the gas and tensed up. He wanted to close his eyes, didn't want to see what was about to happen but he could not. It all seemed to go in slow motion for a second, even the sound of his own voice becoming strangely detached in his ears as they sailed through the intersection, headlights glaring at them from either side. Tires squealed as vehicles in the cross traffic slammed on their brakes, beeped their horns furiously at him.

Yet somehow they passed through unscathed. Still screaming, he glanced up in his rear view mirror to see the van behind them barrel through the same intersection without so much as hesitating, weaving between the stopped and stopping cars, somehow managing to make it through as well. All he could think of was how insane it all was.

"The turn! Don't miss the turn!"

Rebekah's voice brought him back to his senses, somewhat, just in time for him to yank on the wheel and turn the car sharply to the right. The wheels skidded against the pavement, seeking traction as the back end threatened to slide away from him, but by some combination of luck and sound engineering the little SUV wound up pointed the correct direction, and again Jonah punched the gas and aimed for the freeway on ramp

The van behind them was not so agile. Older and heavier, it was forced to slow down considerably to make the sharp, sudden turn, buying them several seconds of precious lead. Jonah swallowed down a little gulp of relief as the car spat out onto the highway, easing in the light traffic and heading westward. "Where are we headed?"

"Nowhere, at least not until we lose our tail. Let's see how fast this thing can go."

They'd already sped up to 60 miles per hour, but he pushed it to 70, and then to 80. What little traffic there was on the highway at this hour was mostly going slower, so as he began to pass all of the cars, Jonah let his foot come up off the accelerator some, letting the needle come to a stop hovering around 85.

"What are you doing?" Rebekah turned to look at him harshly. "Speed up."

With a bit of a cry, he protested. "We're already going pretty damned fast ..."

"Not fast enough," she countered, jerking her head around to look behind them. "I told you, he's not going to stop till he gets us."

Peeking into the mirror, he confirmed her statement when he saw the headlights of the van weaving between a pair of slower vehicles, the lead that they had gained rapidly diminishing. "This isn't safe," he protested again, but complied by applying more gas, watching the needle creep on past 90, coming into the triple digits.

The van didn't slow down. The headlights that were in pursuit were no longer closing the gap so quickly, but at the same time they were not receding. Jonah could feel his heart thumping loudly in his chest, feeling himself growing tense and sweaty as the speedometer began to sneak up on 110. "Jesus, this is insane. This is too fast."

"Oh, come on, mister sportbike rider," she said, the tease seeming to be a little misplaced given the tension in the air.

Jonah frowned. "That's different."

"Maybe. But if he catches us ..."

She didn't have time to finish her statement. A sudden flash of blue and red at their sides along with a loud siren that quickly receded behind them cut her off. Jonah glanced in the mirror in time to see the police car swerve from the shoulder and onto the highway, behind the van now but rather quickly building up to speed. "Shit, now we got the cops to worry about?"

Rebekah was still looking behind them with a scowl on her face. "No, forget the cops. They're the least of our concerns right now."

"Forget the cops?" Jonah had seen his fair share of high speed chases on television. Even if that particular police car did not catch up to them, could not convince them to pull over, they'd call for backup. Use some kind of maneuver to push them off the road, use spike strips to disable them, something of the sort. There was no way he was going to escape this one. "I'm gonna wind up in prison over this!"

"No you aren't. Now, come on, give this thing a little more gas, we gotta get out of here."

Glancing down at the speedometer, he was surprised to see it had crawled up to nearly 130, the engine racing to keep up with the demands of the driver. In spite of his better judgment he stomped down on the gas but it refused to acknowledge him - it was stuck, hovering there at about the same speed. "It's not going any quicker," he protested, keenly aware of how quickly the other cars, the buildings they were passing were flying on by in a blur. He'd heard stories about the infamous car-swallowing potholes of Detroit. If they found one of those doing that kind of speed, he was sure they were doomed.

At the very least the headlights of the van behind him seemed to have trouble picking up speed, as well, creeping up on them only very slowly. The flashing lights of the police car were just behind the van now, undoubtedly calling out on the megaphone for the driver to pull over, but there was no way the van was going to budge.

"Jesus. Maybe you're right, we're probably gonna get killed before we go to jail," he muttered, doing his best to concentrate on the roadway. They came up on the cars too quickly, too fast for his comfort, each time he had to swerve around them he could feel his stomach churn, was certain that they'd lose control and go skidding across into the barrier in the median. It would all end quickly, at the very least.

"You're doing fine," she muttered, a little less than reassuringly, before her voice caught in her throat. "Oh, shit."

Jonah did not have to ask for clarification. A large piece of construction equipment, hidden behind a pylon beneath an overpass, had abruptly started moving right into the roadway. There was not enough time to react, not properly at least. Aware that he was once again screaming - this time accompanied by his passenger - he flicked the wheel to the right. It was just a fraction of a turn, but at the speed they were traveling it was more than enough. The car lurched heavily to the right, and then back to the left as he corrected. For one miserable moment it felt as if the wheels on one side were coming up, losing traction with the surface of the road, and the tail of the car began to skitter unsteadily behind them.

He was certain that they were going to crash. They were going to roll over, spin out of control, wind up in a fiery inferno along the side of the road. Yet again, more by luck than any skill, the car righted itself, having steered clear of the machinery in the road.

The cars behind did not fare so well. The driver of the van attempted the same correction but the larger, less nimble vehicle failed to make it, the rear corner clipping the edge of the equipment, throwing it around at a wild angle. Unable to skid sideways the van toppled over, bits of glass and debris flying skyward, glittering red and blue against the night sky, all while the van began to roll again and again, careening off to the side of the road. The police car tried to screech to a halt, a cloud of smoke rising from the back wheels before plowing headlong into the construction equipment, coming to an abrupt halt.

Then it was gone. All too quickly the SUV sped along down the highway, out of sight of the incident, leaving Jonah to shiver almost uncontrollably in the driver's seat. Rebekah, her voice quiet, tried to sound calm and commanding all the same. "Let's get off the freeway."

Too shaken to argue or question her decision, he maneuvered the car off the next exit and to a nearby parking lot. In silence they switched positions, Rebekah taking control of the car and plotting a new course, avoiding the highway, disappearing through the suburbs of the city. Neither of them would speak again until they had put the city far behind them.

SEVEN

"So. You had some questions for me."

It had been some time since they had left Detroit behind. Dawn had come and gone and the day was wearing on in to the afternoon by the time they had pulled in to a truck stop outside of Omaha to gas up and stretch their legs. Jonah had slept fairly well, all things considered; the luxury SUV had surprisingly comfortable seats, and after the adrenaline rush of the night before had worn off he had been left feeling physically drained. Once or twice he had woken up during the trip, when they stopped for gas, but otherwise most of it had been passed with his eyes closed.

Seated on a picnic bench outside of the truck stop, watching the traffic go by on the interstate, Jonah had been fairly caught up in his thoughts, munching quietly on a cheap hamburger, and was a little caught off guard when Rebekah spoke up. Shifting his gaze to where she was sitting, relaxing a bit, he blinked. "What?"

"You said you wanted me to explain some things to you, and I told you I would later. Well, now it's later. So, shoot," she said, drumming her fingers on the table.

His mind raced back to the previous night, the unbelievable events that had unfolded, and he could not help but to scowl a little bit. "That's right. I want to know what this is all about. Everything."

She had been eating a hamburger as well, finishing off the last of it before wadding the wrapper up into a ball and tossing it into a nearby wastebasket. "Everything? I don't think we have enough time for that, Jonah. You're going to have to be a little more specific. I'll answer what I can, but you're going to have to help me out a bit."

"Ok. What about these creeps that are after me, these … what did you call them … bully drakes?"

Rebekah laughed quietly. "Bull drakes. But that works, too."

Jonah did not really see the humor in his mistake, and frowned all the more. "What do they want with me? Why are they chasing me all around the country, killing people?"

"It's not you that they want, Jonah. At least not directly. You see, until you've had your first change you're indistinguishable from any random person on the street, they can't smell the dragon on you. As far as they know or care, you're just some unlucky sap who happened to get his hands on the Token. That is what they are after," she said, idly munching on a fry.

"Well, I guess that puts us in the clear, then. I left the damned thing on Abe's desk last night."

She smiled at him slightly. "You sure about that?"

"Positive," he said, reaching into his pocket. Much to his dismay his fingers brushed against something round and metallic, and when he pulled it out, he saw that it was, indeed, the silver coin with the dragon. "What the hell? I left this thing on the table. I didn't pick it up again, I'd have remembered that."

"Maybe, maybe not. Like I told you, the thing belongs to you. You're supposed to have it, and it's going to do its best to make sure it stays with you."

"You make it sound alive," he said, frowning down at the coin.

Again she laughed softly. "No, not exactly. It doesn't have any free will or power of its own, but it is imbued with a certain power. A way of influencing fate, random chance, little things like that to make sure it winds up in your hands and stays there."

Something right out of a fairy tale, he thought to himself a bit dismissively. As insane as it was, he had to admit that he could not explain why he still had the thing, how it wound up in his pocket again and again. "So what's so valuable about it, then? Why do these people want it?"

"I'm not entirely sure," she muttered, munching on another fry. "I suppose it's because they think that it has some kind of power over us. Like, if they get their hands on the Tokens, they might be able to use them to influence the dragons that they belong to. Control them. I'm not really sure."

"So what is it, really? Other than a nuisance," he murmured, prodding at the coin on the table.

A warm breeze fluttered across the table, ruffling the wrapper that his burger was resting on and causing Rebekah's bangs to cross in front of her eyes; she brushed them out of the way before continuing. "It's an insignia of your station, a sort of birth certificate, if you will. It's a way of proving that you are the Silver Dragon."

It was not the first time he had heard that. The night before, the bald man with the cigar had said much the same thing. "And what does that mean?

She chewed on her lower lip for a moment, as if considering her answer before speaking up. "Well, I'm sure you went over some of this with Abe last night so I'm just going to give you the Cliffs Notes version. A long time ago, thousands of years ago, there were a lot of dragon clans. Thirteen, as a matter of fact. The Syndicate went about wiping them out as efficiently as they could. When it started to get real bad, the two or three remaining clans, along with the scattered members of the others who were in hiding, banded together and created a single clan.

"The clan picked thirteen of its members to serve as surrogate representatives of the lost clans. Mostly symbolic, but still. These thirteen served as a sort of council to rule on important decisions that would affect the entire clan. The first thirteen imbued a small fragment of their souls into thirteen Tokens that were crafted for them. In the event of their deaths, that little fragment of their souls would seek out a spiritual successor to take on the mantle."

Jonah took a deep breath and then frowned. "You realize how ridiculous all of this sounds. Tell me, is there some novel you all have picked this stuff up from? Somewhere I can read it and memorize it, too?"

Rebekah frowned, as well, though her expression was considerably more annoyed than his own. "You asked for an explanation."

"Sorry, sorry. Go on."

"Right," she said, shaking her head. "Anyway. That's pretty much the point I was getting to, that being the Silver Dragon means you have inherited that position on the council. That the Token has sought you out and come to your possession is proof of this."

Suddenly he remembered that Abe wore a trinket around his neck that resembled his coin in more than a passing manner, albeit in gold. "So, was that Abe back there, the Gold Dragon? Looked like he had a token, too."

"You've got it," she said, the frown on her face fading and once more she was wearing a slight grin.

"So, does that make him some kind of leader? And does that make me …"

She laughed. "Second in command? Please. No, it does not work that way. We don't really have a leader in that sense, of someone who can command us or tell us what to do. Abe is one of the eldest of the clan, one of the eldest on the council, and as a result his word carries a lot of weight. We listen to his council not because of his title but because of his wisdom."

Jonah nodded a little blankly. "So you've got a seniority thing going on."

"Yes and no. Like I said, we don't really have anyone who rules, it's not a chain of command. We do have an elder, the oldest among us, who holds a special position of respect. He does have a few added duties and responsibilities as the eldest, and we all have a sort of special connection to him. He can feel us, and we can feel him, even from afar. You can too, even if you don't understand it yet," she said, with a slightly playful smirk.

"You don't have a chain of command but you've still got some kind of ruling council?"

"We don't rule, not in that sense. We convene from time to time in meetings called Convocations. No one forces the others to abide by what we say, but pretty much everyone respects the decisions that come from a Convocation," she replied.

Poking idly at the remains of his burger, Jonah did his best to mentally digest everything that he was being told. It took more than a little self-control not to deride the story as ridiculous once again, and he was certain that he'd heard of far more convincing sounding tales in various works of fiction. Still, there was a certain compulsion he felt about it all, a sort of curiosity to see where she was going with it all. "You say we. You a part of this, ah, council, too?"

She nodded. "I am."

"So, you the Bronze Dragon or something?"

"No," she replied, shaking her head, reaching beneath the collar of her shirt to pull out an ornately carved pendant made of some kind of polished wood. It was well worn and smoothed but he could still clearly make out the shape of a dragon. "Wood Dragon."

"Wood? What are the rest?"

She paused again, as if she had to think to remember them all. "Gold, Silver, Wood, Ivory, Stone, Bronze, Iron, Tin, Copper, Lead, Bone, Flint, and Obsidian. Three of the Tokens are missing, perhaps still seeking out the dragons to take their place, the Bronze, Iron and Flint dragons. The last ones have been gone for as long as I can remember," she said, her tone slightly downcast. "It's been almost fifty years since the Silver Dragon sat on the council, just so you know."

Jonah frowned a little, uncomfortable at the thought, as if it somehow was meant to make him feel a sense of reverence or purpose. "Why does it take so long?"

"I'm not sure. Things are not the same as they used to be, Jonah. Once upon a time there were thousands of dragons. Even when we were reduced to a single clan there were probably three hundred left in all. Now, I think we're down to maybe fifty. Maybe it just takes that long to find a successor, maybe it just takes that long for a replacement to be born."

Her tone continued to darken, the smile on her face having faded, and Jonah could not help but to feel a little guilty for it. "So how often are new dragons born, then?"

"Rarely," she replied with a slightly annoyed grunt. "There are only two that we know of younger than yourself, so, every five to ten years or so.

There's just not many of us left to keep things going. A single dragon can lay an egg only once every twelve years, so, you can do the math."

The mention of laying eggs and the implication that it carried - that he was hatched from one rather than being born in a hospital somewhere - was simply beyond absurd, preposterous. He was about to say so when Rebekah spoke up again. "Before you ask, no, I haven't done so yet. Eventually, but I'm in no hurry. I'm not that worried about the clan, yet," she added, with a smirk.

"I wasn't going to ask," he replied honestly enough, feeling embarrassed all the same and jamming some of his now cold hamburger into his mouth. "Besides. Abe back there told me something about all dragons being born in human form for centuries."

"True enough. I suppose it's a matter of speech to say that we still lay eggs," she offered with a shrug, her smile once more fading a bit, though at least this time it didn't transform into a frown. "You still think it's all made up, don't you? That this is some kind of elaborate fiction that I've put together for you."

Swallowing the food in his mouth, he frowned openly at her. "What do you think? I mean, honestly, this is an awful tall tale you're trying to sell me here. Dragons, sorcerers, ancient clans and magic tokens? Come on."

"Even now? After everything you've seen? The bull drakes? The coin mysteriously in your pocket again and again? You come on," she said, her voice still carrying a hint of playfulness. "Do you think we'd really go to this extreme? We're in freaking Omaha, Nebraska. Isn't that an awful lot to do for a prank?"

"Maybe. But maybe you, or whoever put you up to this, is just insane enough to go through with it all."

"All right," she said, pausing a moment, her green eyes still on him, studying him. "Well in that case I have a question for you."

Jonah squinted at her. "For me? What?"

"Why are you here? Why are you sitting at a picnic table in front of a truck stop a thousand miles away from home, Jonah?"

"Because you dragged me here," he shot back.

She shook her head. "No, that's not good enough. You're an adult, and no one is tying you up and dragging you along. You could have gotten out at any of the gas stations we stopped at. You could have run off in Detroit. You could run off right now, flag down a cab, call someone back home for help, but you're still here. Why?"

He had, indeed, thought of doing that on more than one occasion. It was a valid question, too, as to why he had not done so, and when she asked it he was forced to consider the answer, himself. There was still some strange compulsion to hear her story out, but more than that a weird curiosity driving him to follow along, to see what would happen, where they were going. Not that he believed a word of it, but in some way he felt compelled to see the story through. "I don't know. I guess I've never really gone on a road trip before, so why not?"

"Don't lie, Jonah," she accused.

"I'm not lying," he spat with a frown, flushing in his cheeks. "Hell, other than flying up to New York to visit my grandparents during the holidays I don't think I've ever been out of Florida at all."

Rebekah shrugged. "Maybe that's true, but it's not the reason you're sticking around."

"Fine. Maybe I'm a little curious as to where you are going with this, what it is all leading up to," he confessed.

"It's more than that, isn't it?"

He frowned and shook his head. "I don't know what you are talking about."

"Maybe. Maybe not. But you feel drawn to it Jonah, drawn to me, drawn to the story, don't you? Something about it is calling to you on a deeper level. A spiritual level. You can't deny that it's about more than just curiosity or the urge to go on a road trip," she said, smiling.

"Sure I can," he responded, a little impatiently. He didn't like where she was going with that, and did not like the fact that, at least in some small way, it felt like she was speaking the truth. It was a bunch of nonsense, and he didn't believe a word of it. He wondered if he should just cut it off there, not encourage her by continuing along, but he still felt that compulsion, despite what he said, despite whatever else he felt.

"Let me ask you something, then," she said, once more having to push her bangs from her face, the warm little breeze fluttering at a napkin on the table and threatening to carry it away before she plucked it out of the air.

Jonah shrugged his shoulders a little noncommittally, not sure he was interested in the conversation any longer. "Okay."

"Do you ever get the feeling that you're different from everyone else? That there was something more going on than you could see or explain?"

"No." He answered the question without any hesitation, his voice as flat as his expression as he looked back across the table at her, slightly confused with what she was trying to get at.

Rebekah kept her own gaze on him, her bright green eyes blinking slowly as she held her tongue for a moment, giving him the weird and slightly uncomfortable sensation that she was looking right through him. "You sure? I mean, haven't you ever wondered why you look so much younger than everyone else your age, for example?"

Again Jonah responded with a little shrug. "I suppose I get a little tired of being carded all the time, but I haven't given it a lot of thought, no."

"And your health? I've been watching you for a while now Jonah and I know you haven't ever taken a sick day from work. You never missed a class back in college, you've never so much as had to take a shot of cough syrup." Pausing a moment as if she expected a reaction, she leaned in a bit closer. "Come on, tell me when the last time you felt sick."

"Last night. Half a dozen times," he shot back with a smirk.

Leaning back again, she shook her head with a mock frown. "That's not what I meant."

"Yeah, yeah. I don't know," Jonah confessed, tilting his head back to try and remember the last time he had a fever, the last time he had suffered a cold. A weird sort of sensation came over him as he realized that he was having trouble even thinking of a single time. "I … well, it was probably when I was a kid, or something."

"Come on, Jonah, you're holding back on me. Holding back on yourself. You know you're different, even if you aren't going to admit it to me. You age more slowly. You don't get sick. Your weird obsession with silver," she said, putting emphasis on the last word. "There's probably more. You may not be a fan of running but I'd bet that you can go a long ways without getting tired. You're a lot stronger than a skinny guy like you should be …"

Each little fact that she repeated was true. Things that he had not stopped to think about before, bits and pieces of his life that seemed unremarkable to him before were suddenly being presented as something out of the norm, and he realized that, on the whole, she was right. The more right she was, however, the more uneasy it made him feel, and he finally had to cut her off. "All right, I get it. What's your point? Wait, let me guess. Somehow all proof that I'm actually a dragon and don't know it, right?"

Rebekah flashed him a slight little smirk. "You're catching on pretty quick. Being clever happens to be a common trait among dragons. Just like the rest of those traits."

Jonah rolled his eyes and shook his head. "Right. Look, that's all fine, but it's not that hard to pick a few random things out of my life and pretend they are 'common dragon traits'. You could just as easily have said that having brown hair and blue eyes are common dragon traits, too. Doesn't prove a thing."

"Maybe. But brown hair and blue eyes are pretty common. Those others? Not so much."

"They aren't all that rare, either," he protested. "Besides, if I were something other than a regular, everyday human then my doctor would have noticed. I've been to the doctor before, you know. Annual checkups, and I'm as healthy as can be. Nothing weird like being cold blooded."

Rebekah laughed softly at that, in that irritatingly attractive way. "None of us dragons are cold blooded, Jonah."

"Right," he responded, shrugging his shoulders.

She allowed another moment of silence to pass before she spoke up again, this time a little softer, almost reverently. "And the visions? You've started having them, too, haven't you?"

A little caught off guard, he glanced back up at her skeptically. "Visions?"

"Visions. Dreams. Ever since you came to have the token."

"I don't know what you are talking about," he answered, a little defensively.

The smile that she passed him was sincere and disarming, but he did not want to feel disarmed. It made him feel more open, more vulnerable than he cared for. "Surely you have. It's always strongest when you first are united with the token. Visions, fragments of memories left behind by those who held it before, those who were members of the clan you were chosen to represent. A legacy of those who have gone before you, Jonah. You know what I am speaking of."

Instantly he knew exactly what she was talking about, and the fact that she had zeroed in on that little fact made his blood suddenly run cold. For a fleeing moment he found himself wondering if there were a grain of truth to what she was saying, but he shook it off with a bit of a grunt. "You people are just ... playing with my head."

"And what about last night? How could you explain that? You saw me get tossed right through a car window and come out with hardly more than a scratch. That's gotta count for something," she said with a sort of smirk.

"Just means you're ... hard headed." Annoyed, he gathered up the remnants of his meal and stuffed it all back into the paper back, getting out of his seat to drop it in the wastebasket nearby. "We've probably been here long enough, right? Shouldn't we get going?"

"Changing the subject," she accused, but got up out of her seat as well. "But you're right. Long drive ahead of us."

"Big surprise," he muttered, stalking his way across the parking lot toward the SUV, pausing to look back to her before he got there. "Mind at least telling me where we are going?"

"Page. Small town in northern Arizona."

He shrugged as he reached the vehicle, stepping around and getting in the passenger's seat, buckling himself in. He waited until she was in and had the car started before speaking up. "And what's there?"

"A friend. We're picking him up."

"And then?"

She maneuvered the car out of the parking lot, turning onto the ramp that would take them back on the interstate, heading westward once again. "Then we're going to a Convocation."

"Of course," he said, shaking his head, settling into the seat with a sigh as they set out on yet another long drive. The scenery began to bleed away in a blur outside of the window, another long slog across the country to look forward to. Still, Jonah was not interested in passing it all in silence if he could help it, and in spite of his better judgment he still had a few lingering questions gnawing at him. He'd have to get them out. "Mind if I ask you a few more questions?"

She had just been about to reach for the controls to the car's stereo, turning to glance at him curiously with her bright green eyes before she shrugged. "All right."

"You're trying so hard to convince me of this whole dragon thing. I don't really know why. I'll grant you that some weird shit has been happening the past few days," he allowed himself to say, slowly, keeping his eyes trained out the window. "But I'm not going to buy the story about dragons. It's just too much."

"I thought you had questions."

"I'm getting there," he said, frowning, shaking his head a little. "I was just going to say, why don't you go for the obvious? If you're a dragon, just show me. Prove it to me."

She turned to look at him with a little frown. "Well, to be honest, if it were up to me I'd do it in a heartbeat. I'm kind of tired of you playing the part of Doubting Thomas over there in spite of all the evidence around you."

Her answer caught him off guard. He had expected her to spout some more nonsense about how it wasn't the right way, how he had to learn to fly on his own, something like Abe had spouted the night before. Something about her candor was both refreshing and disarming. "You say that like you don't have a choice in the matter."

"I don't. I was told to try and convince you in any way that I could short of just showing you. Something about you having to find out on your own." She shrugged, keeping her eyes on the road. "Pain in the ass, if you ask me."

"So ... this whole thing, everything you're doing. It's all about taking orders."

A brief moment of silence passed before she answered. "What're you getting at, Jonah?"

He sighed softly before he responded. He wasn't quite sure what he was getting at, himself, and wasn't really sure why he felt the need to broach the subject in the first place. "Look. You saved my ass last night, and it's not even the first time you've done that. I'm ... not really sure how I feel about that. Thankful," he added, a bit hastily. "But confused."

"Why confused?"

"I guess I just don't understand why," he muttered a little meekly, looking back out the window again, trying to gather his thoughts. "Why'd you do it. Stick your neck out like that for me. They order you to do that?

Put your life on the line?"

"No," Rebekah answered, a little hesitantly, as if she were carefully choosing her words. "They asked me to protect you but no one made me promise to do it at my own peril. What was I supposed to do, though, stand by and watch them murder you? Besides. You been watching over someone as long as I have been watching over you, and you can't help but to grow a little fond and protective of them."

Jonah felt a weird little lump in his throat and a heat in his neck that made him uncomfortable. Seeking to deflect the rise in emotion, he teased, "Makes you sound like a stalker. How long have you been … watching me?"

She laughed softly, that same laugh that was so easy on his ears. "Just a few years. And don't worry. It's not like I've been sitting in a dark room across the street, watching you through a pair of binoculars while you shower. At least not often," she said, turning to look at him with a sly grin and a wink, teasing him right back.

It worked, as the flush in his neck reached his cheeks. He closed his eyes, too embarrassed to look back at her, holding a hand over his face. "That's not what I meant …"

"You sure about that?"

"Please," he murmured, sounding exasperated.

With another soft laugh, she shook her head. "All right, all right. I'm sorry. Didn't mean to make you blush."

"I'm not blushing," he lied, keeping his gaze fixed out the window. She was merciful enough not to press the issue any further, and when he had mustered enough courage to turn around and look at her directly again she was once again focused on the highway in front of them. A smile still pulled at the corners of her mouth, but it was a genuine sort of smile. For a long moment he just watched her out of the corner of his eye, trying not to look like he was staring, realizing that once again he was finding himself admiring her in spite of the conflicting emotions he felt.

"Well," she finally offered, breaking the silence again. "I guess you could say that no one's holding a gun to my head and making me do what I do. Yeah, they ask me to do it, but I suppose I do it because I want to, too."

Jonah felt like he should leave it at that, but at the same time was not comfortable just leaving things hanging in silence. Without much forethought to where he was going with the conversation, he simply managed to blurt out the first thing. "So, ah, how old are you?"

Turning to level a sharp look at him with her green eyes, she blinked. "Why would you ask me that?"

"I guess … I mean, like I said, just thought it might be nice to get to know you a little better …"

"By asking me how old I am?"

Immediately uncomfortable, he found himself fidgeting in his seat again. "Well, you've been going on about how we're all older than we look ..."

"Look, Jonah. Even you are old enough to know that asking a woman's age is never a good thing to do," she said with a serious tone.

He couldn't tell if she was mocking him or not. He waited to see if she'd laugh it off and say she was kidding but when she did not, he felt himself growing increasingly discomfited, folding his arms over his chest. "I'm sorry."

Rebekah did, in the end, offer a good natured little chuckle but it was a bit on the muted side. "Well, fair bit of advice, then. There's better conversation starters than asking a lady her age. If you're up for a little tutoring I suppose I could offer you a few pointers," she added, her tone softening and a grin creeping up on her face once more.

In a way it irritated him even more to think that she might be willing to offer him advice on how he might approach other women. He realized he was developing more than a passing interest in Rebekah, for reasons that were simply beyond his understanding; with the exception of a few difficult to interpret teases, the interest seemed to be only one way. He wasn't comfortable with his feelings on the subject, and pushing them down, simply shook his head. "How far do we have to go?"

Shrugging, she looked back over the dashboard. "Going to take most of the day."

"May as well see what's on the radio, then."

EIGHT

A light rain had begun to fall over the last few hours of their trip, just as they had crossed into Arizona and passed through Monument Valley. It was beautiful in a strange, stark fashion, the way the low-hanging clouds hugged against the massive sandstone buttes, occasional breaks in the clouds forming fleeting rainbows against the gray sky. It was the sort of thing that Jonah had only seen in old western movies, in dazzling collections posted online by various accomplished photographers. The kind of scenery that he could only have imagined.

After a time, however, the novelty had worn off and the drive had become a monotonous trek through washed out reds and browns, punctuated only by the occasional small town or shack on the side of the road hawking "authentic Indian jewelry". When they passed by a power plant, its trio of smokestacks rising up from the ground like sore thumbs, even the familiar and drab industrial architecture seemed a welcome change to the scenery.

At last they rounded a small butte hugging the side of the highway and came across signs of civilization, turning at the first stoplight he had seen in hours, and they had arrived at their destination. Page was a fairly small town; it took them only a few minutes of driving along the main drag, passing by a row of churches and the brief commercial center of the city before they turned off along a quiet residential street.

Rebekah guided the car down a couple of turns before coming to a stop in front of an otherwise unremarkable home, situated on a row of likewise unremarkable homes. Except for the striking red color of the earth that surrounded them, the neighborhood looked like it could have been in any residential neighborhood. Stepping out of the car and glancing around, Jonah thought that the view might have been somewhat nicer in good weather; the homes were situated on a bluff that overlooked a lake in the distance.

"Come on, I don't want to stand here all day and get soaked," Rebekah said in a slightly annoyed fashion. The rain had picked up a little and had reached a moderate drizzle, so the pair made their way up the little walkway and huddled onto a cramped porch while she rang the doorbell.

Waiting for a response, Jonah stuffed his hands in his pockets, more chilled than he thought he should be in the desert. "Why here?"

"What do you mean?" Rebekah turned to look at him, ringing the doorbell again when there was no immediate answer.

"Why here? Why would someone pick a place like this to live?" He glanced around the neighborhood again, feeling slightly chagrined at the fact that one of the neighbors might have overheard him. "Kind of in the middle of nowhere."

With a shrug, she rang the doorbell once more. "How should I know? You're going to have to ask him. Some folks don't like living in the big city, you know. It can be pretty nice out here, what with the lake and all. Besides, I think he runs some kind of business here." Pausing to crane her neck, trying to peek in the window, she pulled the screen door open and rapped on the door. "Jeff? You home?"

Jonah shrugged his shoulders again. Perhaps she was right, but he could not imagine living in such a small town, so far away from everything else. It was just too quiet here for his tastes. "Maybe he's at work, then."

"Not unless he walked," she said, motioning to an old beat up truck sitting in the driveway, turning to knock on the door again. "Besides, it's getting a little late in the day to be out working, don't you think?"

"How should I know? Doesn't seem like he's home, either way."

"Maybe. Probably. Doubt he's gone far though," she murmured, giving the doorknob an experimental twist. When the door popped open, she managed a wry smile. "I'm sure he won't mind us waiting inside, not when it's all cold and wet ..."

Her voice trailed off when the door was pushed open to reveal that the interior of the home was completely trashed. Potted plants that had stood near the doorway had been overturned, the soil scattered in every direction. The face of a nearby grandfather clock had been shattered, and several of the chairs surrounding the table in the adjoining formal dining room were tossed about, while the china cabinet next to it had fallen onto the table, spilling now shattered dishes all over the place.

"Oh my god," Rebekah whispered softly, drawing her hand to her face, her eyes going wide. After a moment of standing in shock, she bolted across the entry way and through an arched passage into the living room, her voice rising to a shout. "Jeff! Jeffress?"

Jonah followed behind, not giving any thought to closing the door behind him. Rounding the corner into the living room he saw that it, too, showed signs of something violent having taken place. A large, flat screen television had been broken nearly in half as if something rather heavy had been thrown right into it, pushing it against the wall with enough force to cause the wall to cave in slightly. Parts of both of the couches had been shredded, slashed apart with the padding spilling out, cushions left haphazardly across the floor. A glass coffee table had been wrecked, and the curtains on the windows had been either torn or pulled down.

"Jesus Christ. It looks like someone let a wild animal go to town," he muttered under his breath, turning to look at Rebekah.

To his surprise, she was kneeling on one knee, near where the kitchen was. The wall near where she stood looked blackened and charred, as if a fire had been set and put out before taking the whole house down. The charred wall was not what had her attention, however; she was looking at the ground. When he moved over, glancing over her shoulder to see, he was at first confused by the strange brown colored stain on the ground. Until he realized what it was.

Without looking up, Rebekah began to speak. "Well. He put up a good fight," she said, reaching forward and gingerly touching her fingers to the spot on the ground, leaning over to inhale. "It's not his. Not very fresh, either. Two, three days at least."

"What … what happened?" Jonah felt a little stunned, looking around again, suddenly feeling as if the home might still be unsafe.

"I can't say for certain." After a moment, Rebekah pulled herself to her feet, looking around with a sober expression. "They must have found him. No idea how, but they found him. Gods. And there was a hell of a fight. There were at least two of them. Maybe three," she pondered aloud, brushing her fingers against the scorch mark on the wall and turning to glance into the kitchen.

Pots and pans were strewn about wildly, cupboards opened, some of them torn clean from their hinges. "They? Who are they?"

"The Syndicate. Or their goons, at least. Probably caught him at the door. Fought them off pretty good, drew blood back there in the living room. See, you can see where the wounded attacker bled his way into here," she said, pointing at a series of browns splotches that led into the kitchen, marring the tile floor. "Quite a bit, too. Jeff got him pretty good."

Jonah still felt uneasy about the home. It was too quiet inside, and too quiet outside, no sounds except for their own breathing and the steady patter of raindrops on the roof. He half expected to see the dark haired maniac that had been pursuing him jump out of the shadows at any moment. "And … your friend, Jeff? Is he …"

Rebekah turned to look at him a little skeptically. "Dead? Maybe. It's hard to say. One, maybe two of them and he'd have a chance. But these weren't just bull drakes. These were a different breed, more feral, quicker, nastier. It could have been a hit, but they might have been here to take him alive. Here, look," she said, pointing to a sliding glass door that had been shattered open, the hanging blinds swaying slightly in the breeze from outside.

There were obvious signs that the fight had made its way outside. There were several large divots in the lawn just outside of the door, a set of lawn chairs were overturned and tossed about. If there had been any blood stains on the ground here, however, the rain had surely washed them away. "Maybe he fought them off and got away?"

"Maybe." She wasn't immediately dismissive of the possibility, but as the rain was already beginning to wet her hair, she took a step back inside of the house, choosing instead to look outside from the dry safety within. "Anything is possible, but if he'd made it out he'd have contacted us. They took the elder alive, so maybe they took Jeff alive, too."

A part of Jonah still wanted to disbelieve what was going on. His life had been normal, dull even, only a few days before, but he had since witnessed the death of a friend, been accused of murder, dragged across the country only to be told he was a dragon. Now he found himself thousands of miles from home in a house that had been ransacked, signs of a bloody fight all around him.

What could have been signs of claw marks, of dragon fire blasting a wall, he could dismiss those in other ways. Knife fights, an attempt to burn evidence, things of the sort. Supernatural or not, however, he had been dragged into something big, something sinister. It was no dream, and he would have to deal with it somehow.

He just didn't know how. Sighing, he closed his eyes. "Now what?"

"Well, I've definitely got to tell the others," she said, stepping further into the kitchen and away from the chill that was seeping in through the broken doorway. "They've got to know what is happening. Somehow the Syndicate is finding us, tracking us down, and the others might be in danger."

"And your meeting? Convocation, or whatever you called it?"

Breathing in deeply, she seemed to square her shoulders and calm herself down a little. "Well that simply has to go on. Come on, let's get going."

"Right now?" Jonah almost gasped at the thought, and instinctively put himself in front of her to keep her from charging off. "Look. You've been driving all day. And all day before that. You've got to be exhausted. I'm sure there's a place in town here we can stay for the night …"

"Not necessary. I can go a long time without sleep."

He shook his head, defiantly. "No. You've said that before, and it might be true, but you look tired. I can see it in your eyes. Come on, at least a few hours rest."

She did look tired, and his pointing it out seemed to make it somehow more obvious. Her red hair was drooping around her face, her eyes dull and sporting a pair of dark, heavy circles. Nodding, sighing in resignation, she let her expression drop a little bit as well. "I suppose you're right. But no hotels. We may as well just stay here for now."

"What?" Suddenly he was regretting his insistence on delaying the trip, looking back over his shoulder into the relatively ominous darkness inside the house. "I mean, are you certain it's safe?"

Without answering right away, she stepped past him and into an unlit hallway. Flicking the switch on, the light revealed that the hall seemed to show no real sign of damage, the carpet unmarred and the doors all closed and intact. "They'd have no need to stay here, or come back here. Even if they've been tracking us, it'd take them a while to act. We can relax here for a few hours, anyway," she muttered, pushing one of the doors open and pointing inside.

It appeared to be a guest bedroom, made up neatly and not obviously used in a little while. With a wry grin, she turned on down the hallway. "You rest up, too, but since I'm driving I'm gonna use the comfy bed."

Again, he found himself wanting to protest. Something about the way she got over the shock of seeing the house in disarray, at the possibility of her friend being kidnapped - or worse - seemed too cavalier for him. The way that she felt comfortable inviting herself to the home seemed callous. There was a certain logic to it, but Jonah wasn't sure he felt comfortable with that logic.

Regardless, the room did look comfortable and he did suddenly feel tired. Luxury seating or not, sleeping in a car was only so restful and his bones ached to lie down in a proper bed. As he slipped beneath the blankets to warm himself up, the steady patter of rain on the roof lulled him rather quickly into a deep and needed rest.

#

The respite had been too short and not nearly sweet enough, and when Rebekah had come to rouse him Jonah felt a bit cheated. He had been lost in welcome dreams, back at home in the Florida sunshine, cruising along the highway on his motorcycle, the warm waters of the Atlantic swelling lazily to one side, tourists and local beach bums in scanty clothing sprawled out in the sand soaking up the rays.

Night had once more fallen, but the rain that had been falling when he dozed off had not abated. If anything it had graduated to a heavy and steady downpour, the constant dancing of raindrops on the roof transforming from a gentle and soothing rhythm to an almost annoying sort of buzz over his ears.

Standing at the doorway and peering unhappily into the night, the two of them seemed to be gauging the distance to the car parked along the side of the road, trying to decide on whether or not it would be worth the effort to run. "I thought this was the desert," Jonah muttered unhappily, sticking a hand out into the rain experimentally, pulling it back rather wet.

"Even the desert gets rain sometimes. Apparently sometimes a lot," she responded a with a crooked little smile, shrugging her shoulders. "Come on. It doesn't seem like it's going to let up anytime soon."

Jonah had decided to make a break for it, dashing across the yard and into the car as quickly as he could, but still wound up quite soaked for his efforts. When Rebekah fired the engine up she flicked the heater on to get it going, and, much to Jonah's delight, the seats themselves began to warm up. "I think I could get used to this kind of luxury," he said with a faint grin.

"Tell me about it," she replied, smiling as well, flicking the windshield wipers on.

"So. How much farther is it to … where were we going again?"

"Lake Tahoe," she responded, putting the car into gear and glancing behind to make sure there was no oncoming traffic before pulling out into the road. "Something like twelve hours."

Realizing that he did not know what time it was, Jonah peeked at the console and found the clock. Nearly a quarter after nine; it was going to be another one of those all nighters. "Any reason we couldn't have just stayed till morning?"

"Don't want to be late. Besides, I'm feeling pretty refreshed. Dunno about you," she said, still smiling, her voice taking on something of a perky quality to it. She was very obviously teasing him.

Briefly he was tempted to make some kind of snarky comment about it. She did seem to always be more positive than she should be. Even when they were being chased by someone, even when she had just seen the home of a friend torn apart, its owner gone missing. He had no idea how she could continue to smile in a situation like that, and part of him wanted to think that there was something wrong with that kind of attitude.

Even so, he realized, he wished that he could do the same. He had led a fairly easy, if uneventful life. He had little to be so sour about, and most every reason to be a more happy person. Hell, he could have considered the last few days the kind of adventure that he had always wanted but never worked up the gusto to actually undertake.

He also realized that she looked considerably nicer wearing a smile, quite attractive, really. It was not the first time the thought had crossed his mind, bringing with it a somewhat uncomfortable mix of emotion. As soon as it surfaced he dismissed it by shaking his head and glancing out the window into the night.

The wipers moved back and forth, thump-thumping in their steady rhythm, the sheets of rain falling fast enough to keep them busy. Small puddles had formed along the sides of the roads, forcing Rebekah and the rest of the light traffic to keep their speeds down. They passed a couple of shops, dark and closed up for the night, before finding their way back to the main road, passing a couple of small, older hotels before the road turned and wound its way down a short but steep bluff, hooking up with the highway once again.

From here Jonah could make out the sight of the dam nearby, holding back the significant weight of the lake behind it. It was too dark to see the lake, itself, but the dam was illuminated, the top of it easily visible, though the bulk of it was hidden away in a deep gorge. Craning his neck a little, he spoke up again. "That Hoover Dam?"

"Nah. That's closer to Vegas. This one is … uhm. I can't remember what this one is called," she confessed, shrugging her shoulders.

As the road dropped down the bluff his view of the dam diminished, until he could barely see the top of it lit. "I've never seen anything like it."

"You'll get a better view of it from the bridge. Heck, I could stop and let you walk out … well. If it weren't raining so hard."

Stopping for a moment to let some traffic pass by, Rebekah turned the car along down the highway and in the direction where the dam was at. He had not noticed it before, but there was a bridge just in front of the dam spanning the gorge. It was obviously their destination.

Signs just shy of the bridge warned of a slower speed, and Rebekah obliged, particularly in light of the heavy rain that was coming down. As they crossed from solid ground onto the bridge Jonah again craned his head, trying to get a better look of the dam, which seemed to glow a brilliant white, lit up as it was against the dark of the night. Even from this vantage point he could not see all the way down to the bottom, realizing that it must have been hundreds of feet from here to the river below. The thought of it suddenly made him feel a little dizzy. "Damn. That's a long ways down."

"Hey. No 'damn' jokes when we're by the dam, ok?"

The little attempt at humor made him smile, and he turned to look at her with a bit of a chuckle. As he turned his head, though, a flash of light ahead caught his attention, a vehicle pulling onto the bridge from the opposite side, a big tractor trailer. The bridge was fairly long, perhaps a quarter mile, but not so far that Jonah couldn't tell the truck seemed to be moving a lot quicker than the posted signs allowed. "Looks like someone is in a hurry."

"Yeah," she agreed, her voice lined with something like concern, her grip on the wheel tightening some. Her concern seemed to be warranted, however, as the truck crossed the gap disturbingly fast, halfway across the bridge already and, it seemed, picking up speed along the way. Abruptly the truck shifted lanes, swerving in front of them, tires beginning to squeal. "Shit!"

It all seemed to happen very quickly. Jonah watched with a strangely detached sense of horror as the big truck swerved wildly into their lane and then back into the other one, quick enough that the trailer behind it whipped around like a wagging tail, blocking their path. Rebekah slammed on the brakes and jerked the wheel of their car to the side, skidding, trying to stop, but Jonah knew that it was far, far too late.

In the fraction of a second before the trailer hit, Jonah thought he got a good look at the driver of the truck. Big, broad shouldered, with dark hair and a sinister expression. He'd seen that face before. Far too many times.

The impact jolted the car with enough force to nearly tear him from the seat in spite of the belt that he was wearing. Airbags suddenly appeared in front of him and to his side, keeping his head from slapping angrily against the window of the door, but they were not enough to keep him from being whipped around like a rag doll in his seat. The sound of crunching metal and shattering glass - along with a scream that came either from him or Rebekah, he could not be sure - assailed his ears. His view out the front window was briefly obscured by the airbag, leaving him bereft of any visual cues, but he knew that the car was tipping over, on its side, then to its back. Loose items in the car flew past him as it rolled, his arms flipping up over his head and then whipping back down again as inertia carried them, whipped him around, left him flailing.

Then, as soon as it started, it was over. There was one last grating screech of metal being sheared and then the car came to a rest, on its side. The airbags deflated, leaving his head resting on the window, and as he laid there, dazed, he could do nothing other than listen to the sound of rain dancing against the side of the car, the steady thump-thump of the wipers still going in spite of the crash.

After a moment of staring off into the blackness, he turned his head and looked to his side - up, now that the car had come to a rest - to see Rebekah, looking equally dazed but not obviously hurt. She was dangling a little awkwardly in her seat, held in tightly by the belt, her hair waving lightly above him while she breathed slowly, staring into the same blackness that he had been only a moment before. With something of a groan, he pushed himself up a bit and turned to look to his other side.

The black that he saw from that window confused him at first. There was a faint glimmer in the distance, and it took a moment for his vision to clear and try to resolve that glimmer, a sort of indistinct ribbon of reflected light. Twisting his head some to try and look behind him, he could see an odd sort of structure, straight, like the edge of a building resting right up against the rear door.

It took him a moment to register everything he was seeing. It was not the edge of a building, but the edge of the bridge. Sheared bits of fencing dangled from the edge. The glittering ribbon in the distance was the river below them. Far, far below them. The car had come to a rest on its side, its front protruding through the destroyed fence and hanging over the side of the bridge.

Dangling, precariously.

Panic seized up on him rather abruptly, a ragged sort of half-gasp rattling from his throat as the need to escape, get to safety welled up powerfully inside of him. Fumbling, he reached for the belt buckle so he could get out, when he heard a voice call out sharply. "Jonah! Shit, don't do that … hold still!"

Her words made sense, he could understand them individually, but somehow his mind failed to comprehend what she was saying. All he really knew is that the only thing separating him from hundreds of feet of free fall was a flimsy pane of glass, and the only thing keeping the car from toppling down to its doom was the way in which it had coincidentally come to a rest. He had to get out.

"Jonah, please, calm down! Look, I can get us out of this but I need you to stay calm, can't have the car tipping right over … Jonah, please, just try to stay calm and don't move, whatever you do, don't move …"

He had to move. He couldn't just sit there and wait for the car to fall, couldn't just sit and do nothing and wait for the end to come. His heart throbbed powerfully in his chest, his tongue felt like it was swelling up in his throat, and his vision was blurring. A full panic had set in and his mind was focused on getting out.

Rebekah's voice, for as calm as she was trying to speak, held an edge of panic to it, as well. "Just stop … don't move, please, don't …"

His hand found the latch, and he pushed the button in. It opened with a loud click and the belt let loose. He hadn't thought beyond undoing the belt and as soon as it no longer held him in place he fell against the door with a loud thud. Briefly the car seemed to shift, an agonizing creak of metal as it wobbled, just long enough for reason to clarify through the panic a little and make him realize that he might have doomed them all.

The car held. The swaying came to a stop, along with the creak of metal and the frightened scream that sounded from above him. Shifting a little, he looked up at Rebekah, her face filled with fear, as she stared back down at him. For another moment silence reigned, the sound of rain splashing against the window and the wipers dominating. "Gods," she breathed, shuddering. "Just … just stay put."

Panic still had him. For a moment he just watched, helplessly, as she unrolled the window next to her, opening them up to the chill of the air and the rain that immediately began to run over her hair and drip on him.

Unbuckling herself, she reached for the edge of the door and began to extricate herself, slowly, bit by bit. She was escaping, she was getting out.

He had to get out.

Twisting wildly, he looked toward the back of the vehicle, still resting on the bridge. That was it, all he had to do was climb back, squeeze himself between the seats. Flailing as he grasped at the back of the seat he pulled himself up a ways, tried to haul himself to his feet but he slipped, landing heavily upon the door again, setting the car to swaying and creaking on the side of the bridge. Frozen in panic, he watched, helpless again, while Rebekah's legs dangled inside.

Once again, the car came to a rest without tumbling, but this time there was a new sound, another creak of metal, something groaning under strain, snapping after the abuse of the crash. The door beneath him, no longer able to support his weight, swung open.

Reflexively he grasped for something, anything to grab on to as he felt gravity suddenly clutching at him, tugging him downward. For a brief moment his fingers clasped around the handle to the door, wrapping around it and clinging as hard as he could but he did not have the strength. The bulk of his body dropped out the door and yanked at him, pulled his grip free.

Suddenly he was weightless. Wind whipped past him but the raindrops no longer fell on his face; they fell with him. In a stark contrast to the panic he felt in the car he was strangely calm watching the sight of the bridge, the car dangling over its edge, retreating in his vision. He tumbled through the air and his vision shifted, and this time he saw the ribbon of the river below, rushing up to meet him.

His heart seemed to slow in his chest, a languid thud, thud that he could almost count. Inertia carried him, whipped him around, and again he was falling backward, watching the bridge slipping away, watching as the car's luck ran out, tipping over the edge and moving to follow him on his way down. There was no sign of Rebekah. He wondered if she had escaped.

Again he twisted and found himself facing the river rushing to greet him. He knew only seconds had passed - three, four, maybe five - but it seemed like an eternity. He knew from this height even landing in water would not save him. The river would break him, so fast that it probably wouldn't hurt, carry his body downstream. They might never find him. His parents back home, his friends in Florida would never know what became of him. As sad as it all seemed, he continued to feel strangely calm in his resigned state of mind.

But then there was a strange sensation. A weird kind of resistance to his fall, as if the air were suddenly growing thick, clutching at him more eagerly, tugging at him to slow him down. It was strangely insistent just behind his shoulders, clutching, tugging, pulling, as if he were being pulled back by cables.

He felt an urge, a powerful urge to flex muscles that he was only vaguely aware of, the rush of air resisting him for a moment. Something in the darkness caught his eye, something stretched out at his side, something moving just there at the corner of his vision. Something flapping on the left, and then there on the right, too.

A pair of wings?

As alien as the thought was to his mind, his fall had slowed rapidly. Again he flexed his muscles, gave in to the urge that was running through his body, and he felt himself pick up a little, soaring, gliding through the air. The rush of the river beneath him slowed, shifted directions, the surface beginning to spool out beneath him as he took on a more horizontal motion.

He was no longer falling; he was flying.

The sensation, as well as the immense confusion that it caused in his head, was short lived. Where once the river was rushing to meet him, now it was a solid and monolithic wall of sandstone in front of him as the river turned in its course. Panic gripped him again and he flailed, not sure what to do, not sure if there was anything he could do.

Abruptly the soaring came to an end and he found himself tumbling wildly through the air. He hardly had enough time to suck in a lungful of air before crashing into the surface of the river, slapping him hard and wet, enough to tear that precious gasp of air right out of him.

Jonah was only in the river just long enough for the water to seep through his clothing but it was enough. The water that issued from beneath the dam was icy cold and instantly gripped him in a bone-chilling vise. He found himself unable to move, his muscles stiff and unwilling as the water pulled him down and along.

Before he could resign himself to this new and unexpected fate, he was plucked out of the water and back into the air. His lungs seized upon the opportunity, drawing in a gasping breath. The wind whipped him angrily in the face, raindrops smacking with enough force to sting, but he didn't care. He could breathe, he was alive. By no effort of his own - he was limp and motionless, carried along by some unseen force - but he was alive.

For a moment he tried to turn, twist his head, get a look at his benefactor, who had plucked him from the river, but his body refused. The panic had left him bereft of energy, the cold of the river having sapped what was left. All he could do was let his consciousness collapse deep into his body and let the night take him.

NINE

In the daylight, the river winding its way through the hills far beneath him was not such a frightening sight. It was a distant ribbon of blue that cut its way through the verdant hills, meandering lazily through the little valleys. Unhurried, it cast little glints of silver and gold back up at him at times where it caught the sunlight just right, reflected it back up to him; in a way, it almost felt like the river was winking up at him, glad to have him overhead.

Jonah, too, was unhurried. He had no real destination, at least none that required his immediate attention. There was no timetable to be met, no deadlines, nothing to do other than enjoy the warmth of the summer sun at his back contrasting with the chill of the wind in his face. The sky was an inviting cerulean blue, marked only by the occasional puff of cloud drifting along the wind beneath him, white and pillowy, serene as could be.

Vaguely, he understood that he was dreaming. It was like the brief nightmare that he had endured before, minus the fear pounding in his chest. He was a spectator in his own body, unable to control his own actions, unable to choose his own destiny, but somehow it did not seem so jarring and confining in such a scene. It only seemed to put him more at ease, as if it freed him up to indulge in the vision without having to act; free to dream without worry.

More than a spectator in his own body, however, he was a dragon. Though there was no part of him that he could see he knew it instinctively. The way he moved through the air, the way he could feel his muscles as if he were rowing through the sky. Sensations that he had not felt before, not that he could remember, yet felt so natural to him.

Besides, he thought to himself - what better place for a dragon than to soar high in the sky?

A hint of movement below caught his eye, and he could make out a dark silhouette against the tops of a nearby cloud, the black outline of a dragon against the puffy white. A shadow, it wasn't his; craning his neck to look above and behind him he saw the owner of the shade. A graceful figure clad in scales of white, soaring high above him, approaching with a speed that he knew he could never match. The sight was awesome to behold, and his heart soared in his chest.

All at once the dragon in white dove out of the sky and beyond him, her tail flapping out behind her in an almost mocking fashion. Letting out a sort of yelp, Jonah forgot that he was dreaming and gave pursuit, trying his best to follow the graceful creature cutting through the air in front of him. He knew it was futile, knew that he had no hope of catching her, but he also knew that he could not help himself. He had to try.

She knew he would try, too, and seemed only to encourage it. With an ease of movement that all but drove him crazy she banked to the side and pulled up into a climb, an acrobatic maneuver that slowed her down and brought her ever so close, almost within grasp. But as he pushed through the air in her direction she kept just out of reach, the teasing flick of her tail cracking at the air behind her as she changed directions too quickly, leaving him abruptly far behind.

Letting loose another shout, half in complaint and half in a sort of laughter, Jonah did his best to stay in pursuit. The dragon in white flitted her way in front of a cloud and became lost as she blended into it. He was forced to circle high above the cloud, darting in and around it to try and find where she had gone before he heard her call echoing in the air.

Glancing to his side, he could see that she had already put even more distance between them, dipping downward toward the green earth below, toward the lazy meandering of the river. Tucking his wings in and diving down as fast as he could Jonah did his best to close the gap. The lyrical sound of her laughter filtered up through the air, teasing at him the whole way, reminding him that he would always be one step behind.

Not that he minded. She'd let him chase her around for a while, and eventually let him catch her. It was always the way it went and would always be how it happened, and he loved it every time.

She did not pick a direct path toward the ground, instead spiraling about in wide arcs, occasionally flitting her wings just right to change directions and zip away at an angle that he could not have predicted. It was all a part of the game, all a part of the tease, meant to give him the impression that he might catch up before he fell behind once again. He shouted out eagerly after her, and again heard the faint echoes of her laughter wafting up through the air behind her.

Then, a bit abruptly, she shifted course and arrowed straight downward, in the direction of the river. He followed behind as close as he could, but when she lit upon a rocky outcropping that crowned one of the larger hills the river nestled up against it caught him off guard; he had to circle overhead once before coming back around and landing next to her.

"Caught you," he said, stepping up and expecting a reaction, but once more to his surprise he got none. The dragon in white had her attention turned elsewhere, gazing down into the river valley. Leaning to crane his neck around her, he asked quietly, "What is it?"

"Look," she responded, gesturing downward. The hill itself was studded with a thick, pleasant stand of trees, a part of the forest that blanketed most of the landscape and was replete with game, a favored hunting ground of his. At the foot of the hills and nearer the river was a large break in the trees, open grassland that stretched along toward the horizon, and it was in this direction she was looking. He peered down at the river, squinting, momentarily confused before he finally saw it.

The movement caught his eye first. A dozen shapes arrayed near the banks of the river, some of them moving back and forth along the edge of the water. The creatures were strange by any standard - not overly large but they stood tall on two legs. Though they were mostly hairless they had the strange habit of covering themselves in the hides of other animals. He'd heard of them before but never seen them. "Humans?"

"Yes," she answered, her voice rather curious. "I've heard rumors that they had been moving further up the river but did not think it was this far."

He could not tell what the humans were doing from this distance, milling around at the edge of the river the way they were. They all looked the same to his eyes, dull and uninteresting, the only real difference in their size. "What do we do about them?"

"What do you mean?"

"I don't know," he said, mildly confused. "Do we eat them?"

"No!" The vehemence of her response took him aback, stepping away a little and turning to look at her with even more confusion. "I heard that one of the other clans has been taking a closer look at them. They speak, they have language, they have music … look, look at what they create!"

Some ways away from the river were a pair of odd blemishes on the hillside that he could not immediately identify. Unusual collections of bits of trees and stone and grass, built up into roughly rectangular shapes, each one with an opening in them. As he watched a pair of the humans broke away from the others gathered at the river. One was small, a child perhaps, and the larger one carried it up through a rough path that had been worn in the grass to one of the rectangular constructs, vanishing into the opening. "They've created homes?"

The white dragon nodded, her voice growing thick with curiosity and excitement. "Yes, yes, it's just as I've heard! They're intelligent, like us!"

"Bees build their own homes," he said a little dismissively. "That doesn't mean they are intelligent."

“That’s different,” his companion responded with a hint of irritation. “Besides, bees do not speak to one another, they don’t create music. These … humans. They are more like us. Don’t you see what it would mean?”

Jonah peered down at the humans again, scowling at the sight of their hide-clad bodies. “Yes, it means there’s going to be competition for game. I don’t like it.”

Turning to scowl at him in turn, the dragon shook her head. “There’s more than enough game in these woods to go around. Well, there would be, if it weren’t for that appetite of yours …”

“Hey!”

Laughing softly, she leaned in and butted her head affectionately against his shoulder before turning her attention back down to the valley. “Still. I think it should be wonderful if we could be friends. I … I think I want to go and try speaking with them …”

The idea seemed simply ludicrous to him. These humans, for as strange and helpless as they looked, still had some means of felling beasts larger than themselves, and whether they could pose a threat to a dragon or not was a question he did not know the answer to. “I don’t think that’s a good idea.”

“No. I’m going to try,” she said, and without any hesitation she took off into the air and started to glide down the hillside.

“Wait! No, please, wait!” He tried to chase after her, but he knew it was futile. Panic started to well up in his chest as he watched her, graceful white against the verdant hillside, winging down into an unknown and unpredictable encounter with those strange humans. Feeling helpless, all he could do is watch in horror while his vision slowly faded out to black.

#

When Jonah awoke the next time, he was lying in a bed; warm, comfortable, and relatively well rested. The myriad of dreams that he had experienced the night before still swam in the murk of his subconscious mind, competing with the memories of the startling events from the night before. The sensation of icy water lapping at his skin, pulling him down had become a distant memory tickling at the edge of his conscious, perhaps little more than a dream, itself.

Rebekah had mentioned that his previous dream had been a vision, a fragment of a memory left behind by those who had come before him. It had made little sense at the time to him; why, after all, would a memory like that be of any use to anyone, let alone himself? He had chalked it up to more of the nonsense that she and Abraham had been spouting. He had, after all, been the one to tell her that he had been dreaming. It was not much of a stretch for her to try and ascribe his dreams to some kind of mystical visions.

Dreaming about flying high in the sky, as a dragon, was not too hard to explain away with logic. For the past few days he had the thought pounded into his head that he was a dragon, had heard the tales about how dragons supposedly once roamed the skies freely over Europe, how they had first encountered human beings. It would not be the first time that some fanciful tale had worked its way into his dreams. Jonah could still vividly remember times when, as a child, an unsettling movie on late night television translated into poignant nightmares.

Even the events of the night before might have been a dream. The whole incident on the bridge, trying to grasp at the doorway as he fell presumably to his death. The sensation of growing wings and soaring over the river. The whole thing could have well been manufactured by his sleeping mind.

Perhaps the whole last week could be explained away as a weird and complicated dream. Perhaps he had never left Florida, never purchased that damned silver token, never witnessed a murder and never met Rebekah or Abraham or anyone who had silly ideas about dragons and Syndicates and the like. Even now he could be in his own warm bed, waking from that long and confusing delusion.

Sitting up, he realized that it must not have been the case. He was lying in an unfamiliar bed, in an unfamiliar room. The clothing that he had been wearing when he fell in the river was now draped over the back of a chair nearby, and still looked to be on the damp side. That, at least, seemed to tell him that what he remembered was real. Glancing around with a frown he looked for something, anything else that was familiar but found nothing.

The room was small, as was the bed he was in. The decor looked outdated and a bit kitschy, the sort of thing one might expect to find in a motel. The heavy curtains draped over the window and the heater tucked in beneath it served to reinforce that idea. There was a door with a peephole next to the window, and another door off to the side that led to what must have been a bathroom. Somehow he had, indeed, wound up in a hotel.

Sitting upright, letting the blankets fall away, he realized that he was clothed. A turquoise blue t-shirt with "Grand Canyon" emblazoned across a silk-screened representation of the landmark, and a slightly oversized pair of sweatpants. He'd never seen the clothing before, and certainly did not remember putting them on.

Swinging his legs out of the bed, Jonah shuffled a little unsteadily in the direction of the door. His wallet was laid out on a table next to the door, the contents next to it, presumably to allow them to dry out, too. Next to the door were a pair of cheap looking flip-flop sandals and no sign of his shoes.

On the table, next to a few wrinkled but dry dollar bills was the token. With a bit of a frown he scooped it up, held it up in the light and took a look at it once more. The stylized dragon, wings held aloft and head back, seemed to evoke a reaction in him but he could not be sure what it was. Confusion, irritation, perhaps even disgust. He wanted to rid himself of the damned thing.

Turning it over he looked at the vague impression of letters on the surface of the metal that had been mostly rubbed smooth over the ages. Briefly, he wondered what it had spelled out, what language it had been in, who had forged it to begin with.

Again he remembered what Rebekah had told him. The coin was supposed to be some kind of emblem of who he was, a token carried by the dragons who had gone before him, whose memories had somehow been rubbed off on the thing and were now invading his dreams. The vision of the white dragon sailing in the wind ahead of him was still fresh in his mind, as if he had been there only moments before. It was just a dream, he reminded himself, shoving the token angrily into the pocket of his sweatpants.

The dream had been real enough in his mind, though, real enough to confuse him. Real enough that the emotions still lingered in his heart. The white dragon had been someone to him. Someone he cared about. Now that the dream was over, he felt her absence, a poignant little hole somewhere in the middle of his being. It made no sense.

"The hell," he muttered to himself with no small measure of confusion and irritation. He realized that he was also quite hungry, his stomach growling quietly. Reaching out and pushing the door open, he saw that it was a bright, clear day outside, enough sunlight reflecting off a nearby building that he had to shade his eyes. More than that, though, he could smell food.

Scooping a handful of bills off the table and grabbing what he presumed was the key to the room, he slipped the sandals on, somewhat unsurprised to find them a perfect fit. Emerging into the sunlight, he shuffled his way along the row of doors in the direction that the smell of food seemed to be wafting from.

Emerging from the little row of motel rooms, he found himself in a little dirt parking lot nestled up against a relatively quiet stretch of pavement. In the distance more of the red sandstone bluffs rose toward the sky, empty desert stretching off toward the horizon. He seemed to have been in a small town, little more than a scattering of buildings strewn against the side of the highway. One of them seemed to be a restaurant, at least, and it was there that the smell of food was emanating from, and there he made his way with unusual haste.

The building seemed to have been constructed to evoke the image of an old western storefront, a rickety sort of wooden porch stretching across the front of it, big glass windows letting him see inside where all manner of trinkets and souvenirs were available - as well as a cafe. Stepping up to the door and pushing it open, greeted by the scent of coffee and pancakes. It was enough to make him smile.

"Welcome to Lee's Ferry Mercantile!" The voice belonged to an older woman who was stationed behind the counter, frumpy but friendly looking. "Here for the breakfast service?"

"Yes," he said, simply enough, nodding.

The woman laughed, a hearty, well meaning sound. "Well, of course you are. Breakfast service is $11.99, all you can eat. Includes your drinks. Go ahead and help yourself, you can pay on your way out. Oh, and if we're out of waffles just give me a holler and we'll have another batch whipped up."

He required no further encouragement than that. Nodding briefly to the woman at the counter, he made his way into the little cafe. It was a simple affair, a handful of booths and tables arranged at one side, a buffet line on the other. Breakfast staples like eggs, hash browns and bacon lay simmering in steel serving trays over cans of Sterno, pitchers of milk and orange juice resting on ice at the end. Simple but more than effective; Jonah found himself rushing to the stack of plates, going through the line and piling the food on as high as he could.

The little cafe did not seem to be a busy place. There were only two other patrons that he could see, an older gentleman who gave him a brief nod when he glanced that way, and a Native American who seemed too engrossed in his meal to notice. Jonah made his way to one of the unoccupied booths, sitting down and digging into the pile of food.

An older television was situated in one corner of the cafe, turned to some local news channel. For several moments he paid it no attention, but then a familiar sight on the screen caught his eye - the bridge crossing the gorge near the dam. The one he thought he remembered tumbling from. Chewing his food more slowly, he turned his attention to the television.

"And now we have a breaking update on the freak accident that took place at Glen Canyon Dam late last night," the anchor intoned. "For details we'll go to Derek Wachowski who is live on the scene in Page. Derek?"

The picture flashed to a reporter who was standing at the bridge, which had been roped off, numerous police vehicles parked on the surface. From that vantage point, he could make out the gaping hole in the safety fence where the car had been pushed through. "That's right, Tom. We've just gotten word from the Arizona Department of Safety that not one but both of the vehicles involved in the accident may have been stolen vehicles.

"Early this morning Don Madden, the driver of the semi-truck involved in the accident and presumed to be one of the victims, was found dead near a service station just outside of Kanab. Arizona authorities received the report from their counterparts on the Utah side of the border and are not releasing much information about Mr. Madden but it appears that he was murdered, the carjacker taking the truck south to Arizona and apparently causing the accident that took place on the bridge."

Jonah found himself feeling strangely guilty that someone uninvolved with them was also a victim of the same man who had killed Sam, the same man who had tracked him across the country. It seemed unfair, unjust, and he could not help but to feel in some strange way responsible. Frowning, he continued to watch the report.

The picture had switched to an aerial shot. The crumpled outline of the trailer could be seen jutting partially from the dark blue-green of the river, the rest of it fading into the darkness where the river was deeper. "Rescue divers were able to get a positive identification on the luxury SUV involved in the accident, and now reports are indicating that the same vehicle was reported stolen from a Detroit area business two days ago. Attempts to contact the owner have gone unsuccessful but it now appears that all the victims of the accident were involved in car theft."

"Well that's quite something," the anchor interrupted. "Do we know anything about the identities of the victims yet, Derek?"

"Not that we've heard yet, Tom. Rescue divers are continuing to scour the river from the foot of the dam downstream to Lee's Ferry, but due to recent snowmelt there's a lot of runoff coming down the river making the process a little difficult."

"I see. And any word yet from the authorities on the cause of the crash?"

The picture switched once again to the reporter, panning out to show more of the scene. "No, not yet. We still have the eyewitness accounts that indicate the driver of the semi trailer was traveling at a high rate of speed and jackknifed on the bridge, colliding with the SUV before falling off the bridge. Unverified reports also seem to indicate the SUV balanced on the edge a moment before falling in and that a woman was seen attempting to escape."

"Any word on whether she made it?"

The reporter shook his head. "Well as I said the reports are unverified but it would not seem that anyone made it out of this, Tom."

The scene then switched to the studio with the reporter in a little inset in the corner. "Thanks, Derek. What a terrible situation unfolding in Page this morning. We'd like to remind travelers that Glen Canyon Bridge is being closed until the investigation is complete and repairs can be made, no sooner than a week out, meaning that you will have to take an alternate route through Kanab and Fredonia. Now, for your Southern Utah weather, we turn to the weather desk …"

"Poor sons o' bitches."

The gravely voice broke him out of the brief little reverie, and Jonah turned his head to see the older gentleman standing nearby, gaze toward the television. "What?"

"The folks who went off that bridge. One helluva way to go." He paused, chewing on his lip a moment. "Can't imagine what it'd be like. Don't care if yer a car thief or what, no one deserves to go out that way."

Watching a news report on the accident that had nearly claimed his life was beyond weird, it was surreal. He could remember the incident, every tiny detail : the way the truck barreled down upon them, the squealing of tires and metal, the way that panic had taken control of him and caused him to tip the car over the edge to its doom. He wondered what had become of Rebekah, wondered how he was here, in this place, watching the story unfold on the television.

Hearing the old man comment on it only seemed to compound the strangeness of the situation. "Yeah. Can't imagine," was the only response he could muster.

"Mhmm. Too bad, really," the man commented with a little murmur, shuffling his way back to the exit. "Good day to you, enjoy the food."

Jonah glanced back down at his plate, having briefly forgotten about the mountain of food that he had served up for himself. Suddenly he did not feel much like eating, as if it seemed somehow inappropriate given the loss of life, the gravity of what had passed the night before. The hunger in the pit of his stomach, however, did not seem to care for such sentimental thoughts, and was not yet alleviated. Begrudgingly he picked up the fork and impaled a sausage, forcing it down to satisfy the hunger.

TEN

Jonah had finished his breakfast without much gusto, shoveling the food down more out of a sense of duty than anything else. The kindly woman at the desk had been paid, and he had pushed his way back out into the bright sunshine, spending several minutes just standing on the wooden porch, watching cars coming and going in either direction, buzzing along the highway to points unknown.

Even in this he felt an odd sense of detachment. These were normal, average people doing normal, average things. Going on a road trip, going to visit family, passing through for business purposes. Many of them would return to their homes at the end of the day, unperturbed by maniacs who sought to kill them or women who insisted they were dragons. No one would be asking them to take a leap of faith from a balcony. None of them would find themselves pushed off a bridge to their doom seven hundred feet below.

He found himself yearning to turn back the clock, just a few days, just long enough to go back to that moment before he'd set food in the coin store. Perhaps he could make sure none of this would happen. Sam would be safe, he would be at home, and life would be normal.

That, of course, would be impossible.

Feeling somewhat resigned, he shuffled his way back across the dirt parking lot, in the direction of the roadside motel where he had found himself that morning. He still had no idea how he had gotten there to begin with; part of him assumed that Rebekah had taken him here. He had seen no sign of her the entire morning, however, and was beginning to wonder if he'd ever see much of her again. The time to himself that he enjoyed that morning was something of a welcome respite after several days of being watched and "guarded", as she said, but in a strange way he was missing her presence.

So it was that when he opened the door to the room and found her inside, sitting on the edge of the bed, he felt a strange mix of surprise, resentment and relief.

Rebekah looked more composed than she had in days. Her hair was cleaned and combed straight, except for the little curls at the end that rested on her shoulders. She was wearing a fresh set of clothing, too, free of the scuffs and tears that her flannel shirt had acquired. She even smelled fresh, recently showered, as best he could tell. "Hi, Jonah. Get yourself some breakfast?"

"Yeah." He answered in a halfhearted fashion, pulling the door shut behind him and glancing down at his sandal-clad feet. "You … get all this stuff, for me?"

"Your other clothes were pretty wet. Couldn't leave you in them all night," she responded, rather matter-of-factly. "I'm sorry they didn't really have much in that store next door. It was either that or something with rattlesnakes. Oh, and, I'm sorry about the shoes. I couldn't find them."

Nodding, he shuffled his way over to the bed and sat down on the edge, as well, breathing a heavy sigh. There were a dozen questions that were suddenly floating around in his head, as well as a dozen doubts. Questions as to how he was still alive, what had really happened the night before. Doubts over whether or not he was remembering them correctly, whether or not he was starting to lose his grip on reality. "I've been out all night," he said, instead, rather lamely.

She smiled pleasantly at him. Again he thought the smile looked good on her, thought she should do more smiling, and found himself feeling strangely sheepish about the fact; he turned his gaze downward at his feet again before she spoke. "You had a rough night. I understand."

"What happens, now?"

"Well," she said, drawing in a deep breath. "I just got off the phone with Abe, told him about the car. He's pretty unhappy about it, of course, but that's what insurance is for, right? Anyway, he reported the car stolen, so we don't have to worry about it too much."

Still looking at his feet, he nodded. "Yeah, I saw the news report."

"News travels fast," she responded with a quiet chuckle.

Again he nodded, rather lamely. He didn't know what to say, didn't know how to respond - not without broaching a subject that he did not really care to approach at the moment. "Tahoe?"

"He's getting in touch with a contact in Vegas. They'll be on their way out here with a car to pick us up, but it's probably not going to be till later this afternoon. We'll just have to lay low here until then, and I'm afraid there's not a whole lot to do around here. He's going to notify the others. The Convocation is probably going to be delayed a day."

"Right," he responded, squeezing his hands together, resting them in his lap and closing his eyes. Again he felt at a loss for how to respond, and again he felt the powerful yearning for this all to go away, for life to return to normal.

A feather light touch on his shoulder caught his attention, and he lifted his head just enough to see her green eyes regarding him with concern. "Jonah? You all right?"

"Yes. No. I don't know," he murmured, casting his gaze back down, once again.

"Anything you want to talk about?"

He didn't want to talk about it, yet at the same time he did. He felt a need to get it off his chest, felt a need to air the confusion and doubt that was muddling his thoughts. More than that, though, he wanted someone to blame, someone to lash out against, someplace to direct the anger and frustration that he felt all wrapped up in one, but he knew Rebekah was not the one for that. He couldn't do that to her.

Instead he just sighed. "I just … I don't know. I mean, last night … I'm so confused …"

Again she touched him lightly on the shoulder. "Yes?"

Gritting his teeth, he forced himself to ask the question that he did not want to ask, the one that demanded to be asked, even if indirectly. "I mean … what really happened, last night, after we fell? Did I really … I mean …"

"You did," she said softly, her voice almost cooing at him. "Just for a few seconds, but you did."

He was not specific in his question and she was not specific in her response, but specifics weren't necessary. The implications were obvious, terrifying, and impossible. A little quiver ran down his spine as he shook his head. "I don't … I don't know if I can believe that …"

"Oh, Jonah." He felt her hand brushing along his shoulder, caressing softly. "I know it must be difficult for you but you know what happened, I don't have to convince you. You know how it feels, now. The wind at your wings. It's a part of you and you can't ignore that."

"I don't know. I don't know," he repeated, shaking his head, feeling suddenly dizzy as his mind tried to wrap itself around the enormity of what was going on, of what was being said. Once more he tried to convince himself that what happened was nothing more than a bad dream, a nightmare, something to be forgotten. Even the strange journey across the country could be chalked up to a weird psychotic episode, his mind's way of coping with perhaps a long unfulfilled desire to travel, that even now he might still be sleeping fitfully back in his apartment. But as he felt himself shuddering, on the verge of tears, he felt her arms wrap around him, pulling him against her shoulder, caressing and comforting. He could feel her, smell her. She was too real to be any figment of his imagination.

"I can't. I can't do this," he murmured, shuddering once again as he allowed himself to be held, leaned against her, let her support his weight.

"Sure you can." Her voice was positive, supportive, managed to ease some small part of his heart in spite of the confusion. "Just be yourself. It doesn't change who you are, at your core, Jonah. Just what you are. You're still the same person inside."

It sounded silly, cheesy, and made him laugh a little in spite of himself, even if he knew it was a genuine statement. "And what would you know about that? Who I am, at my core?"

"I know you're a good person." He couldn't help but to look up, see her smiling at him, doing her best to soothe his frayed nerves. It was working, at least a little. "Don't forget, I've known you longer than you realize. It's been my job to keep an eye on you, make sure nothing happens to you. When you watch someone for that long you get to know them fairly well."

"Do you realize how creepy that sounds?"

She laughed softly at the accusation, a sound that was as infectious as it was light. "You're right, that does sound pretty bad. It's not like that, at all. I'm not a stalker, I promise!" She smiled, laughing again, stroking her palm lightly against his chin, dragging against the stubble that had formed on his cheek. "But I mean it. You are a good person."

Jonah found himself smiling, if only just. "And you think this makes me a good … ah … dragon."

"Of course!" She smiled brightly, her green eyes shimmering a little as they regarded him, a faintly mischievous look playing at her features. "If only you could have seen yourself last night, Jonah. It'd make so much more sense to you. I suppose in time, it will, but if you could see yourself the way I saw you …"

"The way you saw me?"

She nodded. "The way I saw you. The way I still see you. You're a good man, Jonah, and you're a good dragon, too. Not to mention you look pretty good, as a drake."

He wasn't sure why but the statement suddenly made him feel uneasy, or at the very least uncertain of himself. He could feel his cheeks flushing, so he briefly cast his eyes back down toward his feet. "Thanks. I think," he responded, with a quiet laugh of his own.

A soft touch on his cheek caught him off guard, a surprisingly gentle sort of caress that seemed to be both soothing and somehow electrifying all at the same time. Looking back up away from his feet he found his eyes meeting hers, big green orbs staring right back at him in silence for a long moment. Jonah felt conflicted. On one hand, here was some woman he barely knew who had dragged him back and forth across the country, who had been trying to convince him of some impossible truth that he was just now learning might, in fact, be possible after all.

On the other hand, she had saved his life, more than one time. She had taken on the strange, murderous creature that had killed his friend, that had been after him ever since. She had, if her story was to be believed, plucked him out of a freezing river and brought him back to safety.

There had been the mixed signals that she had been giving him ever since they met. Warm, charming, even inviting at one moment, yet in the next she might come across as somewhat sarcastic and distant. Worse, still, was the fact that he had undoubtedly found himself attracted to her. Physically, to be sure; the longer he looked, the harder he found it to take his eyes off of her. But even now he found himself craving her company, the pleasant way in which she laughed, the smile that seemed to brighten her features in just the right way.

Yet he hardly knew her, he reminded himself. Jonah had never really been one to fall for someone head over heels, and the possibility that it was happening to him now was terrifying.

He wanted to pull back, wanted to leave, run out the door as fast as he could and leave her behind, leave behind all of the events of the last few days, run back to his existence where everything used to be normal and sane and boring. Yet, at the same time, he felt drawn in to those eyes, drawn into the surprisingly soft and gentle face. He might never have felt himself to be so torn before in his life.

So it was that he surprised himself by leaning in, abruptly pressing his lips against hers.

He half expected a swift and violent reaction, he half expected to be pushed away, feel a palm slapping across his face, or worse. There was a moment of hesitation in which she didn't move, her green eyes widening slightly at his advance and her hand moved - but not to strike him. It slid lightly over his shoulder, pulling him closer, pulling herself up against him, and leaned into the kiss.

Jonah felt something inside of himself shift, a barrier that he had been keeping up around himself collapsing down all at once. The fleeting desire that had been tickling at the fringes of his consciousness leaped up to the fore, and when she reciprocated by leaning into the kiss he knew that he wanted this, that he wanted her. Reaching out to slip his own fingers past her ear, feathering their way through her red hair and tilting his head he deepened the kiss. A soft sigh sounded from his throat as he tasted her lips against his own, closing his eyes to drink in the sensation.

She did not seem content to sit there and accept the kiss passively, either. She kissed him back every bit as firmly as he did, turning her whole body to face him more fully, shifting against the bed and holding herself against him. Pulling her lips briefly away from his own she leaned her head back, her voice suddenly coming up low and husky. "Jonah …"

With her head leaned back like that, her neck exposed to him, she seemed suddenly so open, so vulnerable. He would also had to have been a fool to have missed the desire that she was now openly signaling, and he did not fail to act on it. Ducking his head lightly he began to kiss softly at the side of her neck, her skin there so soft and smooth against his lips. Emboldened, Jonah let his hands slip down her back, all but pulling her into his lap, feeling her slender body quivering slightly against his own.

"This isn't part of my duties," she murmured with an obvious teasing tone to her voice, leaning back again and giving him a broad, mischievous smile - but there was now more than a hint of desire burning in her eyes as she playfully tried to push herself away from him.

Returning the impish smile, he tightened his grip, letting his fingers slip beneath the hem of her shirt and begin to brush against the bare skin on the small of her back. "You don't seem to be complaining."

Rather than complain, however, she simply took control of the situation Swinging her legs around she wrapped them around his middle, pushing on his chest suddenly and swiftly, knocking him on his back, gazing up at her from the bed. Shifting her hips again so that she was straddling his own, she began to grind on him lightly, leaning in with a sound that was almost like a growl, and caught him up in another rough, passionate kiss.

Jonah groaned quietly in response. He could already feel the rush of heat in the pit of his stomach, could already feel the familiar heat focusing in his loins in reaction to her advances. The barriers deep inside of him had already failed and were rapidly giving way to the swell of lust and desire that was building inside of him. He kissed her back roughly, firmly, lying on the bed, running his hands against her arms, down her sides and over her hips, pulling her back against him. God, did he ever want her.

Again she broke the kiss, tugging up on the bottom of the tacky souvenir t-shirt that he had been wearing. He didn't need any better encouragement than that to lift his hands up above his head, letting her tug the entire shirt up and off, leaving his chest and stomach bare. As she rested her hands on his tummy and grinned down at him, he suddenly realized that he did not remember putting either the shirt, nor the unfamiliar sweat pants, on. "Something tells me that this isn't the first time you've seen me shirtless," he teased, grinning.

In revenge, she slid her fingers up and tickled them against his armpits. Gasping, he squirmed and tried to bat her hands away. "No, it's not," she finally responded, relenting with the tickling so that she could sit up and follow suit, pulling her shirt off and shaking her hair loose as she did so. "But it's the first time you've seen me without."

Getting his first look at her without a shirt on, Jonah could not help but to grin. She was slender but not unnaturally thin, perhaps a little more musculature to her figure than he would have guessed before. Her skin was soft and smooth, every bit as much as her neck was, perfect and practically unblemished. She was not extraordinarily buxom, a gray sports bra concealing only a modest bosom, but it was just the kind of figure that he found unbearably attractive. "We … we're really going to do this," he whispered, almost in amazement, as he reached back to run his finger against her bra strap, intent on loosening it.

She only smiled at him demurely, licking her lips as she leaned in closer. "You have no idea how bad I want you, Jonah … can't wait to feel you, join with you …"

Just as his fingers caught the clasp, a strange thought suddenly popped up in the back of his mind. He could vividly remember the conversation they had back in Omaha, the discussion about how rare it was for there to be a new dragon born, about how she was one of the youngest of all of them besides him, about how she had been waiting for her turn to find a mate. Pulling his hand back with a startled gasp, he blinked. "Oh, god … you want me to … you want an egg, or something …"

The fiery passion in her eyes wavered, Rebekah leaning back a little to give him a confused sort of look. "What … what are you talking about?"

"You want me to knock you up," he sputtered, a little more abruptly and pointedly than he had meant to.

Any desire that had been in her eyes suddenly went cold, an angry and pained scowl forming on her face. "What … what the hell?" Reaching for her shirt she pushed herself away from him, jumping off the bed, taking a few steps back and holding the shirt up to her chest as if to hide it from his vision. "What the hell is your problem?"

The shocked and offended look on her face made him realize that he had just made a mistake. Shaking his head, he sat up, his voice continuing to sputter. "No, I mean … it's just, what you said before, and I was worried …"

"Oh, no. No, no, no," she said, shaking her head, her voice growing angry. "You thought that I wanted … gods, no! With a whelp like you? Shit, Jonah, there are better, stronger drakes for something like that."

Jonah blinked in surprise. "Whelp?"

"Gods, gods," she repeated, hastily pulling her shirt back on over her head and tugging it back around her midsection. "I can't believe you actually thought that. And now I can't believe I really was about to … and with you? What the hell was I thinking?" Turning on her heel, she stomped toward the door.

"Wait," he said, getting up to his hands and knees and waving urgently. "Rebekah, no, wait, I didn't mean it like that!"

If she heard him, she did not give any indication. The door swung open and she was briefly silhouetted by the bright sunlight beyond before the door slammed shut behind her with enough violence to make the window next to it shudder.

"Shit," he cursed, fumbling his way off the bed and looking around for his discarded shirt. "You really messed this one up," he accused himself. It had been a little while since he had enjoyed someone's company in that way, and to be sure his now frustrated libido was already castigating him, but it was more than that. Rebekah had looked genuinely offended, sincerely upset, and he felt like an asshole for doing it.

It was a confirmation in a way. He cared about the way she felt, cared about how she reacted - cared about her. Some part of him sunk at the realization, telling himself that he wasn't ready to care about someone like that. Not there, not then, and not with a woman who had dragged him well outside of his comfortable little world. He had himself to look out for; he couldn't afford the baggage of something like that.

Yet care he did. He knew he had to do something, he could not just sit there and let her go thinking he was that shallow. Managing to get his shirt back on, he patted the pockets of his sweatpants to make sure that he still had the key to the door and made his way outside.

The sun, high in the sky, illuminated everything with a brilliance that forced him to squint and shade his eyes. It had the effect of washing out the otherwise brilliant reds of the nearby buttes, lending the scene a sort of washed out and desaturated quality, seeming to match his recently deflated mood. Blinking away the brightness he glanced around for some sign of where Rebekah had gone, but there was none.

A few doors down there was a cleaning lady, standing outside a door and sweeping the dust off into the parking lot. Jogging over to where she stood, he cleared his throat. "Hey, excuse me, did you just see a woman with red hair go by?"

Peeking up at him with a hint of irritation for being interrupted, she shrugged her shoulders. "I saw a woman run past, yes."

"Did you see where she went?"

"That way," the housekeeper muttered, gesturing off in the direction opposite the nearby mercantile.

Jogging his way toward the pavement, he shouted back a halfhearted "Thank you!" When he got to the roadway, however, peering to his left where the woman had indicated, he was a little disappointed to find that he could not only see Rebekah or where she had gone, but did not see much of anything at all. There was a small unmarked building, and across the road another scattering of buildings but that was it. There was another small sandstone bluff that the highway curved around, but he could not see anything beyond.

"You sure she went this way?" he called back over his shoulder, looking back to the housekeeper.

The woman looked up again and frowned at him. "She went that way, yes."

"Is there anything down the road?"

"Navajo Bridge," she said, without any clarification as she had apparently decided the conversation was over, pushing her cleaning cart into the room and closing the door behind her.

Taking the woman's word for it, Jonah began to jog down along the side of the road in the direction indicated. The little bend around the corner proved to be longer than he realized, a good quarter of a mile at least, a handful of cars passing him along the way and leaving him to breathe in the dust and exhaust they left behind. By the time he had made it around the corner he was already wheezing and coughing in spite of himself.

Not too far in the distance, he could see a wide gorge opening up in the ground, not unlike the one he had encountered last night, and could not help but to feel a little twinge of discomfort deep in the pit of his stomach. Particularly when he watched the cars making their way across a bridge, there.

Before the bridge there was a little outcropping of buildings on the left side of the road. Again they proved to be a little farther away than he realized, and as he set off jogging in their direction, he found himself a little winded when he finally got close enough to read the sign that proudly proclaimed the buildings were the "Navajo Bridge Interpretive Center". Overhead a pair of flags, one for the country and the other for the state, flapped in the breeze, framed against the stark blue of the sky. A few travelers had stopped there, milling about outside the center, speaking a language that he could not quite place.

Stepping toward the buildings, he glanced back in the direction of the bridge, only to realize that there were actually a pair of them. One carried the traffic, the other, apparently older bridge, seemed to serve pedestrians only. There were a handful of people milling out upon the bridge itself. From there he could spot a shock of fiery red hair.

It was with no small amount of trepidation that he began to make his way over to the bridge, and it was not just his newly acquired skittishness about such bridges that was to blame.

Crossing onto the bridge, he looked briefly off to the side. The gorge seemed to be a bit shallower here but it was still hundreds of feet down sheer red and orange cliffs, all the way to the bottom where the green and blue river flowed more lazily along its course. It was beautiful, in its own way; most of the tourists on the bridge were busy lining up to take pictures of one another against the backdrop. Jonah even felt compelled to step closer to the edge to get a better look, in spite of his nervousness, but the scenery was not the reason he had come here.

Rebekah, too, was standing at the edge of the bridge, leaning against the guard rail and gazing off into the distance, the breeze causing her hair to flutter over her shoulders. He stepped up close to her, slowing as he neared, stuffing his hands in his pockets. He didn't know what to say, but she spoke up first, anyway, without turning to face him. "What do you want?"

"To apologize." She was silent for a moment, and Jonah stood there watching her. She really was beautiful, he realized, and somehow the backdrop of vermilion and blue made her look even more striking. "For back there. In the room."

"Forget it. I'm the one who should be apologizing for letting it happen."

He still wasn't really sure what to say. Part of him wanted to blurt out that it was not such a bad thing, that she had nothing to apologize for, that he only wished that he hadn't been such a heel. Stepping up to the edge of the bridge, himself, resting his hands on the guard rail, he peered over the edge, looking down at the river hundreds of feet below. "I don't think you have to apologize," he muttered, closing his eyes when he felt a hint of vertigo teasing at his senses.

She breathed a heavy sigh next to him. "No, Jonah, I do have to apologize. I'm supposed to be your protector; I swore to do the job ever since we found you. It's my duty, at least until we get to the Convocation, when you can be better … instructed. I should have known better than to do something like that. Our relationship needs to be more … professional. Detached."

"I see," he muttered, letting his eyes open again to take in the sight, the dizziness already passing.

"You sound disappointed."

He turned to look at her a little skeptically. It would have made things a lot less complicated if he could just leave it at that, but he was disappointed all the same. "Maybe I am, a little," he demurred.

"Don't be," she offered with a bit of a frown, finally turning to glance at him. "I'm not that good in bed, anyway."

"It's not … look, it's not just that. Yeah, you're sexy. Yeah, I was … I mean, when you kissed me like that, I was ready to go all the way," he sputtered, a little abrupt in his confession, fixing his eyes on the horizon so he did not have to measure her reaction. "But I don't want you to think I'm … you're an object to me. I think you're nice, and I … think I'd like to get to know you better …"

Again, she shook her head. "Please, Jonah. Don't."

"Look, I know you think I'm an ass, and that's fine, but …"

"No," she repeated, turning away from him. "We just can't afford to have this discussion. I don't really have time for … feelings. I just have a job to do. I'm sorry if I seem a little cold but I'm going to have to keep my distance."

Jonah breathed a sigh. "Rebekah …"

Once more, she cut him off. "No. Just stop. Look, our ride is going to be here in a couple of hours. We just have to keep things professional for a little while longer and then I won't have to deal with you anymore, I'll be done with my duty." Breathing a sigh of her own, she squared her shoulders and began to walk back in the direction of the motel. "Try not to get yourself into any trouble before then, hmm?"

"Wait," he blurted out, reaching out and grabbing her by the shoulder. "This isn't fair."

She turned to look at him with something of an irritated scowl. "Not fair?"

Jonah was sure that he could see more to her gaze than irritation. There was something else there, he told himself; a conflict within her own eyes, that all too familiar disconnect between a nascent and genuine attraction and the fear that it brought up. He could have been dreaming it all up, he realized, but could not help but to see that there was some glimmer of hope there. "You're not being fair to me, Rebekah. I can't figure you out. One minute you're flirting with me like crazy, the next you're as cold as ice. One minute you're a tease and the next just doing your job. One minute you're about to spread your legs for me and the next it's all business?"

Instantly he regretted the last few words that came out of his mouth, and the way that Rebekah furrowed her brows at him and gaped confirmed that he'd just made an even bigger ass of himself in the end. "Jesus, Jonah … just … just shut up. Leave me alone." Quivering with anger she turned once again and headed back the way she had come.

Jonah found himself at a loss for words. He wanted to call out, to apologize again, but even then he'd probably manage to find some way to bungle the situation worse. If she had any feelings for him before he had surely managed to douse those flames for good. Gritting his teeth a bit and balling his hands into fists, he watched as she stalked her way off the bridge, disappearing between the little buildings of the interpretive center.

Even then, he felt the odd urge to chase after her. Swallowing down the unsettling emotions, he turned his gaze back to the river flowing beneath him, scowling. He didn't have any time for this kind of confusion, either. He'd only known her a few days, it wasn't right to feel this way. He'd just have to find a way to get past it. Some way to get back to his own version of normal.

Shoving his hands in his pockets his fingers came across the little disc of silver that he had wedged in there earlier. Pulling the token out again, flipping it over in his fingers and watching the way the sun shone dully against the patina, he spoke out loud, as if to the coin itself. "This is why I don't do relationships. I don't … I don't want this."

Briefly he cocked his hand back, as if he meant to dispose of the cursed little coin right then and there, fling it out into the yawning chasm of the canyon where it would plummet down into the river, never again to be seen. Then he would be rid of it, and, perhaps, be rid of the rest of his problems.

Somehow he found himself unable to. Seething, he stuffed it in his pocket once more, turning to look back at the way Rebekah hand gone. Shaking his head, exasperated, he followed after in spite of it all.

ELEVEN

When their transportation had finally arrived, Jonah found himself relegated to the back seat in the otherwise spacious SUV, an entire row of seating separating himself from Rebekah and the driver, a fairly quiet man who went by the name of Davis. He felt as if he had been serving out some kind of sentence back there, particularly during the long, empty stretches of the roadway through the lonely heart of Nevada. Much of the trip was spent with him trying to find some way to get comfortable there in the back, sprawled out and doing his best to get a little rest.

After what seemed like forever they finally arrived at their destination. They had crested the mountains and dropped into the broad valley where the lake rested, hints of brilliant blue water bedecked by snow capped mountain peaks visible through the window in the back, but his view was limited. The sun was still low in the sky, the morning young, and he briefly remembered the lessons back in high school photography class about how it was one of the best times of day to view a landscape.

Yet he was forced to take in the view framed by the backs of two heads, people - dragons, by their own accounting - who had all but ignored him the whole way.

Their ultimate destination turned out to be a rather large, rather expensive looking home in an exclusive area along the shore of the lake, tucked away in a small valley and hidden away by trees; they had passed through more than one security gate along the way. When they had finally piled out of the vehicle, Jonah took the opportunity to stretch and take in the rarefied and crisp mountain air before giving the home another look.

Upon second inspection it looked more like a mansion, if not some kind of luxury resort. The main structure was enormous, done up in a style reminiscent of of an alpine cottage on a grand scale. The exterior was paneled in natural wood, a broad set of stairs carved out of logs cut lengthwise and set into the ground leading up to a large deck patio, over which hung a balcony that was equally large in size. The pointed roof seemed to tower over him where he stood, looking a bit out of place among the pines.

"Huh. Nice place," he muttered under his breath.

For the first time in what seemed like hours, Rebekah turned to look at him, her expression a little withdrawn. He thought it looked forced and unnatural on her face. "It's not my style," she sighed. "But Carolus had this place built years ago, and it's become something of an unofficial retreat for the clan."

"Carolus?"

She shook her head. "Just come along inside."

Watching as Rebekah led the way up the oversized steps, followed close behind by the ever quiet Davis, Jonah breathed out another quiet little sigh, and shook his own head. Conflicted on whether to press the issue at some point, he instead decided that he should keep a little distance for the time being, waiting for them to pass through a set of broad glass doors before following, blinking to let his eyes adjust to the dimmer light inside.

He found himself in a grand foyer, sumptuously appointed and practically oozing wealth and refinement from every corner. An ornate chandelier made of some kind of antlers hung high overhead, centered over a pair of winding staircases that led up to the second floor. A massive grandfather clock directly opposite the entrance ticked away the hour, while various works of art studded the walls in every direction.

"Glad to see you made it in one piece, kid!" A slightly accented voice broke his little reverie, tore his attention away from drinking in the sight of the wealth around him, and he was somehow less than surprised to see the big, balding Abe crossing from the other side of the foyer to clap him on the shoulder. "Though I hear it was a rough trip."

"Yeah. Sorry about your car," he offered a little lamely, turning to watch Rebekah making her way up the flight of stairs and to the second floor without looking back.

Though he had no cigar clamped between his teeth this time, Abe still smelled vaguely of tobacco, that sweet and pungent odor that made his nose wrinkle slightly. "Try not to worry about it, that's what insurance is for. Besides, I'll get a new one for my troubles," the man said with a slightly conspiratorial tone. "Anyway, I also hear that you had your first flight. Well worth the loss of a car to bring you to that, my friend. Congratulations."

Jonah found himself bristling at the congratulations, as if it were not the sort of thing he should be congratulated for, at all. He still was not quite sure he was convinced of it, himself; for as little sense as the whole night had made, he was sure that there was still some rational explanation that could be dreamed up, some sequence of events, unlikely as they might be, still more likely an explanation than dragons. "Yeah, thanks," he replied, unconvincingly, not in the mood to be confrontational about it.

"I'm sure the next time will be a little less traumatic for you. Come," he said, slapping a big meaty hand against Jonah's shoulder and guiding him up the stairs. "You two are the last to arrive. It's time that we began the Convocation."

At the top of the steps, he was led beyond a pair of heavy wooden doors into a large room whose description he could not immediately decide : dining room, conference hall, or something of the like. A long, wooden table was set in the center of the room, framed by a roaring fireplace on the wall opposite the entrance, the walls here decorated no less lavishly than the foyer below. There were enough seats for perhaps twenty, but at the moment there were only six seated, Rebekah among them.

"Jonah, I want you to come meet Carolus. He's the one who has so generously offered his private residence for our gatherings, and one of the only dragons older than myself. That'd explain his name, every bit as old and crusty as he is," Abe said in a jovial manner, gesturing to the man seated at the head of the table. "Jonah, Carolus. Carolus, Jonah."

The older looking gentleman nodded with a dour smile. "Fortunately I do not share your lack of respect and regard for tradition, Ibrahim. It is a name you were given at birth, you should be proud of it." His voice sounded harsh and authoritative, but Jonah thought he could detect a hint of playful prodding, as if between two old friends.

Abe merely shrugged with a smile. "Tradition only goes so far when it gets too old. Just like a fine wine, there's a point when more age doesn't make it any better."

Carolus sighed softly, before turning a pair of watery, light blue eyes in Jonah's direction. Wispy white hairs framed his face, somewhat tired but forceful, a smile cast in his direction that he could not quite read. "Ah, so, you are the new Silver Dragon. Allow me to welcome you to the clan; I only wish it were under brighter circumstances. Now that we are all here we mustn't delay the Convocation any further. Introductions with the others will come later, please have a seat."

Jonah nodded, withdrawing from Carolus with an odd sense of relief. Choosing to sit in an empty chair next to where Abe had seated himself, leaning back and watching with a skeptical eye as the meeting began.

Carolus stood, holding his arms out at either side and gesturing to both of his sides. "Esteemed brothers and sisters of the clan, welcome. As the eldest among us it falls to me to call to order this Convocation. All are present and accounted for save for our elder and Jeffress, who is currently missing. I need not remind you of the severity of the situation we are facing, therefore I fear we must bypass formal greetings and salutations, and get right down to the matter at hand.

"It is no secret among the clan that our elder was taken, kidnapped by agents of the Syndicate who left no demands. Now Jeffress has been attacked and is unaccounted for; we do not know whether he has been taken, as well, or killed. Further attacks have been perpetrated upon some of our youngest and newest family members. It is clear that the Syndicate is becoming more aggressive in the pursuit of our clan. We must now decide what actions to take."

Abe cleared his throat rather noisily, calling attention to himself before speaking up. "Carolus, we all know what sort of action you are going to propose. We don't need a Convocation to know that you are planning a rescue attempt to break him out of wherever they've got him locked up."

"Indeed, it is no secret what course of action I would propose, but that kind of decision can only be made in Convocation. Furthermore, there is information I would like to share. I believe we have tracked down the location where he is being held," the older man said, coolly

There was a brief moment of silence, and while no one spoke, Jonah could see the looks of shock and surprise that were passed between those gathered around the table. One of them, a middle aged woman with raven black hair and somewhat hawkish features to match, spoke up. "Then there can be no question, we must mount the rescue."

Several of the gathered nodded, but it was Abe who spoke up again, his jovial tone of voice dropping a little. "And are we certain this is the wisest course of action?"

"What other course of action could there be?" It was the same woman, turning to look at Abe a little incredulously.

"I urge patience, Jenna," the balding man said, calmly and pointedly. "We still do not understand this renewed aggression from the Syndicate. That we can still feel the elder, and know he is unhurt, is unprecedented. We do not know what they want from him, and we can safely assume he will be unhurt in the near future …"

One of the other men at the table, who looked to be close in age to the woman called Jenna, interrupted. "Nonsense! We know exactly what they want from him! We are connected to him and he to us. Surely they are looking for a way to subvert this connection, use him to track us down. How else is it they found Jeffress?"

"Jason. Jenna. Everyone, please, let us maintain our decorum and order," Carolus intoned, raising his hands as if to ask for silence. "Ibrahim has a valid point, one that we should all consider. We do not understand the motives of the Syndicate, and we do not know what their plans are. We will all have our opportunity to speak our minds, please, let us not interrupt one another."

"With all due respect," the man apparently named Jason said, folding his arms over his chest. "We do understand the motives of the Syndicate. They seek to destroy us at all costs, and I would daresay they have been succeeding of late."

Abe waited to respond, his voice measured. "With this, I do not disagree. Still, I must question the wisdom in letting our emotions rule our logic. Yes, we must mount a rescue attempt, but must we do so before we have exhausted all other avenues?"

"And what would you propose as an alternative, Ibrahim?"

"We know they have stepped up their attacks on us. It goes without saying that they are likely to do so again, in the near future. I say let them come. The next time, we will be prepared for them. We will defend one another in force, and capture the agents of the Syndicate, ourselves."

Jason spoke up again, skeptically. "To what end?"

Smiling slightly, as if he had just revealed some secret, Abe continued. "Interrogate them. The creatures in the employ of the Syndicate are simple-minded; if we can capture one uninjured, or with a minimum of injury, it could be … convinced … to divulge some of its secrets to us. We could learn of their methods. Perhaps then we could mount our rescue attempt, more well informed, and better prepared. Perhaps then, we could be on the offensive rather than constantly running and defending."

There was some logic to the man's words, enough that the others fell silent and did not offer any objection, not immediately, even if they looked displeased all the same. When no one spoke up, Carolus stood once again. "Then there is an alternate proposal to consider. Is there any other proposal? Any other comment? If not, then let us proceed with making a decision …"

The whole time up to that point, Jonah had listened to the proceedings, the little banter back and forth between the members of the "clan", trying his best not to dismiss it all out of hand. It all seemed rather silly and absurd to him, as if it were all made up for his benefit, to get him to go along with the whole dragon story.

Still there was that tiny nugget of doubt. Much as he wanted to believe it was all some fabrication, that everything on down to his imagined fall from the bridge was somehow made up, he knew that he could not just pretend the entire thing was a fantasy for his benefit. It was becoming easier to believe in dragons than a vast conspiracy to ends that he could not imagine.

Fact or fiction, it was time for him to get more involved in making decisions about what was going to happen to him. It was, after all, still his life to lead. "Wait. I have a question."

The entire gathering fell silent when he spoke up. All eyes were on him - Rebekah's included, her green eyes widening in surprise, as well as something that almost looked like admiration. Carolus, equally caught off guard, cocked his head. "You have something to say?"

"You asked for opinions, but before I can give one, there's a few things I have to know, a few things I have to understand. I'm supposedly a part of this thing, and … it's ok if I ask a few questions, right?"

Glancing to his side, he could see Abe practically beaming with pride, as if he'd taken some special interest in him. Oddly, he felt proud to see the reaction. "Very well," Carolus said, with a nod. "It is well within your right to speak at Convocation."

"Right. Well … first, I need someone to tell me about what's going on with this Syndicate. I mean, what's really going on. Abe told me about how they're hunting you down - hunting us down - but I want to know why. What do they really want with us?"

"To destroy us," the old man said a little severely. "Nothing more, nothing less. Those of us who they cannot subvert to their own means they will simply eliminate. They will not stop until the last of our clan is gone."

Jonah shook his head a little impatiently. "Yeah, I get that, but what's really going on? Surely you can't mean to tell me that it's nothing more than a thousand year old feud and they're just out to get us because they don't like us."

Carolus, on the other hand, seemed only too patient with the question. "That too is easily answered. The Syndicate seeks nothing more than power. Since the beginning they have viewed the dragons as the only thing standing in their way. They are both covetous of us and afraid of us."

"More than that," Abe interrupted. "They believe that mankind is destined to rule the Earth and that all the creatures are to be subservient to them. The existence of the dragons is an affront to that belief. The fact that we're still here, empowered on our own, and not fallen sway under their influence is the one great bane of their existence."

"All right. So let's say they get their way, let's say they hunt us down and win this little war," Jonah said, noticing that many of those seated around the table cringed at the very thought. "What happens, then? They going to enslave humanity or something like that?"

"No, I doubt that," the old man muttered, resting his hands on the table. "They have already worked their way deep into many of the power structures, governments, corporations, and so on. Without the dragons in their way they will have essentially achieved their goals of power and control."

Frowning a little at the answer, Jonah shrugged. "So, then, not much else is going to change, other than we're outta the picture."

"Yes, you could say that."

"So we're not like, fighting for the sake of mankind, the future of the world, anything like that?"

Jenna, the woman who had spoken up before, broke the silence in an almost animated fashion. "We're fighting for our lives. Isn't that enough?"

"Yeah, I get it," Jonah responded with a bit of a frown. "But, I mean, is it really worth all of this running and hiding and fighting? Don't you all get tired of it sometimes, wouldn't you just like to be done with all of that? Have a little peace and quiet?"

"Well, certainly," she spat back with a slightly irritated tone to her voice. "But that's not going to happen, not until the Syndicate is gone to the last man. I can accept that you are new here, that there's a lot you don't know, but you can't be so stupid as to believe we can accomplish that. There are hardly more than fifty of us anymore, and the Syndicate are numerous. They've wiped out every other clan and whittled us down to the few that remain."

"And are they ever going to stop? If they're just going to keep hunting us, just keep picking us off till there's only a few left then what is the point? It sounds as if you're saying we're damned if we do, damned if we don't."

The woman frowned again, but Carolus raised his hand to interrupt before she could respond. "It is the curse and the burden that we are all born with, Jonah. Would that it were different, that it could be different, and not a one of us here would not leap at the chance. Perhaps we are doomed to fail to the Syndicate in the end. Perhaps we are doomed to eke out a meager existence, hidden in the shadows and hanging on by a thread. Then again, perhaps fate will smile on us eventually and we may be allowed to flourish again. None here can see the future, Jonah, and so we must do what we can and fight for survival."

Shaking his head with a little sigh, Jonah considered letting it go there. He could not help but to wonder if the whole lot in front of him were simply resigned to their fates; perhaps they had been fighting so long they weren't even capable of finding a way out. "What if there was a way? I don't suppose anyone here has bothered calling this Syndicate up and seeing if you can't put together some kind of peace treaty, or something."

His suggestion seemed to have caused a shocked silence to fall over the assemblage, and it was a long moment of listening to the fire crackling before Abe spoke up, his voice rather muted. "A novel idea, kid, but I'm afraid it wouldn't work. The Syndicate does not want peace, they want control of us."

"And what if we gave it to them? Told them we were sick of fighting, that we'd agree to play by their rules, work for their team?"

"Utterly ridiculous," Jenna spat out again, this time not bothering to hold her tongue in the least. "To do so would be to abandon everything we've fought for, for generations. It would be no better than being yoked to work for them, to give up our own free will."

"So what?" Jonah shrugged from across the table, not feeling intimidated by the woman's ire. "Maybe working for them wouldn't be such a bad thing. It doesn't sound like they're out to destroy the world, so why not? Beats dying, if you ask me."

Several jaws around the table went slack, and the woman sputtered angrily before answering with nearly a shout. "Absolutely preposterous! Are we really going to sit here and listen to this whelp insult our very way of life by suggesting …"

"Enough, Jenna." It was Carolus, the old man, who cut her off once again and demanded silence - which he received. He regarded Jonah with an inquisitive expression, reserved but curious, as if he were trying to figure something out, as if he were trying to peer deeper into his soul. "He may be a whelp but Jonah holds the token of the Silver Dragon. It is his right to speak here, and he may have a point. Something none of us, set in our ways, would have ever suggested, never even considered. Let us not stifle his input."

Jonah found his confidence beginning to waver even as the old man made a point of defending him. Four of those assembled were regarding him with open contempt, the woman and the man who looked to perhaps be her brother, as well as two others who had been silent up to that point. Abe looked to be slightly impressed, and Rebekah wore an expression that was nothing short of incredulous. It all made him feel nervous, and he found that he could no longer speak. Even when Carolus asked him if he had anything further to say, he merely shook his head and sunk into his seat.

"Then," the old man went on, "I must ask if there are any other alternatives to the plans that have been suggested by the Convocation." Again there was a brief silence, a few heads shaking in the negative, before he continued once more. "Very well. The time to make a decision is upon us. First, the alternative proposed by our brother Ibrahim. That we take no immediate action with regards to the disappearance of our elder and Jeffress, and that we attempt to formulate a plan to capture an agent of the Syndicate for questioning. All in favor of this course of action, please indicate."

Abe raised his left hand slowly but resolutely; no one followed suit. Even as he surveyed those seated around him he still smiled pleasantly, nodding as his eyes met the others, each in turn. He did not seem to be either disappointed or surprised by the defeat.

Carolus looked around with a nod. "Now the second alternative, proposed by myself. That we assemble a group to assail the Syndicate compound where we now know that our elder is being held, and attempt his escape. We shall also attempt to locate our brother Jeffress, if he is held in the same location. All in favor of this course of action, please indicate."

Several hands went up this time. Jonah glanced around the table to see that Carolus, of course, supported his own proposal. He was not surprised to find that five other hands raised - in fact, everyone at the table except for Abe and himself had their hands in the air. And once again, all eyes were cast upon him, as if expecting him to do something.

He did nothing other than sink deeper into his seat.

"Very well. As there are enough in support of this course of action to proceed, there is no longer any need to consider further proposals," Carolus intoned, resting his hands on the table; he still seemed to be looking right at Jonah. "This Convocation is hereby concluded. All participants are expected to reconvene here in five days. Good day to you."

Just like that, the little meeting was over. There was some muted discussion, but for the most part the participants simply got up from their seats and made their way out of the room. Jonah was fairly certain that more than one of them paused as they passed his seat to scowl, but by now all of the defiance he felt earlier had washed away. When the woman Jenna stopped in front of him, he felt himself blanch.

"How you were ever chosen to be the Silver Dragon is beyond me. The drake whose place you take is likely rolling in his grave, as are those who came before him. You do a disservice to the name of the Silver Dragon and are a shame to the council." She scowled at him severely before she continued. "You would do well to keep your mouth shut and do as you are told, whelp. You don't deserve that token, and until you prove yourself worthy of it …"

Rather than meet her eyes, rather than try to justify himself, he simply kept his focus fixated on the table in front of him. "I didn't choose any of this. I'm sorry if you don't like me. I'm just telling it like I see it."

Instead of responding she merely shook her head and breathed a quiet groan before stalking away, leaving Jonah to feel strangely exhausted, disinterested in the rest of the gathered as they made their way past him. He was a little surprised, then, to hear himself being addressed once again.

"You know, that was pretty gutsy of you."

He didn't have to look up to realize the voice belonged to Rebekah. Looking up anyway, he almost cringed at the sight of her bright green eyes looking down at him; she somehow loomed large where she stood, looked bigger, somehow authoritative, even if her expression was one of muted admiration. He could only muster a little whispered "What?"

"Don't get me wrong. I don't agree with you, not in the least. I suppose it's like the old man says, though, you're just a whelp and only just got here, so it's not like you know any better. Still, it took a lot of guts to speak your mind in front of everyone like that. I admire that."

"Thanks, I guess," he managed weakly, shrugging his shoulders.

Mimicking the shrug, she turned to head toward the door, but not before adding, "There might be some hope for you yet."

Watching her go with no small amount of confusion and conflicting emotion, Jonah sighed a little before he caught sight of another figure approaching, Abe's thick frame and bald head unmistakable. "I gotta agree with her, kid. You showed a lot of spunk. I knew you had some real potential to you, and not just because you're the new Silver Dragon. But today you even surprised me. Not easy to do."

With a shrug, Jonah repeated himself. "Thanks."

"I should have warned you, before we started, that some of us are pretty old and set in our ways. These things can get a little political, but for all her huffing and puffing, not even Jenna is going to hold your opinion against you. It's all just old habit that dies hard," the big man responded, resting a meaty hand on his shoulder.

"If you insist. I swear she wanted to bite my head off."

Abe laughed heartily at that, leaning his head back and bellowing out a long, loud chuckle. "Try not to take her too seriously. She still has some strong feelings about the whole situation ... it's a little complicated to explain now, but just remember, she's a bit set in our ways. It's hard for her to change. Or any of us, for that matter. You've got a good head on your shoulders, and I for one am glad to get a bit of a fresh perspective going on here."

He was still not convinced that he hadn't made himself some enemies already, but did not think it worth belaboring the subject. Still shrugging he shifted the topic. "What now, anyway?"

"Well, you heard old Carolus. Tomorrow's going to be a busy day." Abe pulled his hand away, adjusting his suit a little as he stood. "Normally I'd say it was time for you to go and get some rest after your long drive, but, you don't really have that luxury just yet. We can't be dragging you off on one of these little excursions without a little proper training, first."

Jonah frowned dubiously at that. "Training?"

"My good friend here is correct," a voice from behind him sounded out. Turning, he saw that Carolus had approached, still wearing that cautiously inquisitive look on his face, making Jonah again feel as if he were being appraised. "But don't let that frighten you. You have a busy day ahead of yourself Jonah, but we are going to make certain that you are prepared."

In spite of the reassurance, Jonah could not help but to feel a sense of dread creeping upon him. Any hope of going back home and pretending that none of this had happened had already faded, but the thought that they had something like training in store for him did not sound in the least like something he was interested in. "What do you mean, training?"

The old man flashed a crooked smile. "Why, flying of course. Learning to take on your true form, and learning how to use it. You still have much to learn, regarding what it truly means to be a dragon, but we too have much to learn about your abilities, what you are capable of. That is what we mean, by training."

Jonah opened his mouth to protest, but the man continued, cutting him off before he could speak. "Now, I understand you still have doubts. Your first change was brief, and in dire straits; a part of you wishes that this were all still just a dream, no? A part of you wants to believe that we are all … how shall I say … insane. I can understand. I might well feel the same way, were I in your position."

The fact that Carolus seemed to be able to read him so readily made him feel moderately disturbed, and suddenly he found himself hesitant to trust the old man, in spite of his friendly demeanor. "Yeah, you could say that."

"Surely you can't be looking forward to this training, either. It's been a long day for you already, and it would be unwise for us to throw you to the wolves so quickly, so to speak. I will have my friend Ibrahim here escort you to your quarters shortly so that you may get some rest, and food will be provided. But there is one thing I must impress upon you," he said, stepping forward and resting a bony hand on Jonah's shoulder. "What you see and learn this evening will change your life, forever. For the better, I assure you, but you must be mentally prepared for it. I'm certain we can count on you."

Jonah wanted to retort with an insincere "gee thanks", wanted to brush the man's hand from his shoulder and back away. No small part of him still wanted to turn and flee from the compound, find the first bus headed east and make his way back to Florida, fend for himself, turn himself in to the police, perhaps.

Yet at the same time he realized that option no longer existed. Looking dubiously back at Carolus, he simply shrugged one more time. "I'll do my best."

"That's a good boy," the old man said, smiling crookedly again, patting him on the shoulder before turning back to Abe. "Be a gentleman now, and show our young friend here to his quarters, will you?"

He heard Abe say something in acknowledgment, turning to him to beckon for him to follow, but for a moment Jonah's gaze was fixed on the old man as he made his way to the door. He wasn't sure why, but he could not shake the feeling that there was something about him he simply could not trust.

TWELVE

"What if I don't even want to be involved in any of this?"

After having been given a few hours to rest in a rather sumptuously appointed guest room that rivaled his own bedroom back home in Florida - if not his apartment in its entirety - Jonah had been awoken by the old man Carolus and told that it was time to commence with his training, so that he would be "Prepared to participate in the effort to free the elder", he had been told.

The size of the home, the resort, or the compound, whichever it was most properly called, had not quite been apparent from the front of the building. Having descended more than one flight of steps as they moved through the section that was the guest wing, Jonah guessed that either the building was sunken into the ground or had been built on a slope; passing by a window that allowed some natural light inside, hints of greenery visible between the curtains, confirmed that it was the latter.

Abe had been wealthy. That much had been obvious from the man's choice in vehicles and attire, but it was the kind of wealthy that was not all that uncommon in modern society. This Carolus, on the other hand, seemed to be in a whole other class of affluence, if his property was any indicator. He did not know why, but that fact again made the old man seem somehow less than trustworthy in spite of his overt friendliness. If nothing else, it made Jonah feel a bit uncomfortable.

Passing through the hall into another large, open room whose function Jonah could not immediately guess, the old man turned to him in response to his question. "Pardon?"

Jonah shrugged, looking around at his surroundings. "I dunno. I mean, look. For whatever else you people might think of me, what I am, I'm not some kind of action hero. I don't know anything about this business of infiltrating compounds or rescuing kidnapped elders. Adventure for me involves two wheels and a helmet, that's about it."

"I see," Carolus said, regarding him with watery blue eyes. "While your continued reticence is somewhat baffling to the clan, it is clear to me that you still have more than a few doubts regarding your identity, Jonah. I do understand how difficult this can be. It will all be clear to you shortly, please believe me."

"To be honest, I'm not sure what to believe. You know, I still half expect someone to tell me this is all some kind of sick joke," he muttered, glancing around again with a frown. In a way he wouldn't be surprised to have cameras pop out from behind a hidden corner at any moment, some friend or acquaintance of his to laughingly tell him how he'd been punked.

The old man shook his head with an air of disappointment, stopping at a set of ornate French doors, resting his hand on the handle. "In a way it is largely our fault, Jonah. We should have been there to protect your parents from the Syndicate, and when we failed to do that we should have been quicker to track you down, find you and assure you were taken care of. To wait so long for your first flight, it is no wonder you are filled with doubt …"

"My parents took care of me just fine, thank you," Jonah bristled with a scowl.

"No, please, I didn't mean it that way," Carolus almost sputtered, apologetic. "Your adopted parents have raised you a fine young man, and doubtless took exceedingly good care of you. I was referring to your needs as a member of the clan, as a dragon."

"Yeah," he replied with a vague shrug. "Sure. Anyway, even if I was sold in this dragon stuff, what makes you think I'd still be up for tagging along on your little away mission? Like I said, I'm not into danger and action and adventure."

Carolus shrugged as well. "It is your duty as a member of this clan, just as it is the duty of each of us." With that he pushed the door open and made his way outside.

Jonah followed, shielding his eyes briefly from the change in light, but the sight that met them was astounding to say the least. An enormous wooden deck extended outward from the building, no less than forty or fifty feet wide, before falling away in either direction with no handrail that he could see. At the sides stately pine trees rose up to frame the view of the lake, placid blue waters extending out so far that the opposing shore almost faded into the horizon. The lake itself was all but surrounded with towering mountain peaks, still shrouded in snow, a sight that in and of itself still caught him off guard.

Breathless as the scene made him, he still felt internally uncomfortable at the last statement. "So you're saying that I don't have a choice, that I have to go along with it."

"Everyone has a choice, Jonah, but we are a rare breed, anymore. Our clan is dying, being killed off, and every time we lose another member of our family we feel the loss more keenly than the last. There are none among mankind who understand us, not fully. As such we are fiercely loyal to one another, loyal to the clan and its needs. I am certain that once your doubts about who you are have been eliminated that you, too, will understand why it is so important we do this."

Jonah had walked out to the edge of the deck while the old man was growing somewhat preachy, still paying attention even if halfheartedly. The deck was built so that it nearly overhung the shore of the lake itself, a short set of stairs leading down to a private dock that was currently empty. "Yeah, sure. I guess we'll see about that," he muttered, turning once more to frown at the old man.

Carolus merely offered a crooked smile. "I am quite certain that you will, as a matter of fact."

"You know, this would all be easier if you would just drop all of the mumbo jumbo and prove it to me by just turning into a dragon, or something," he responded with a slightly impatient shrug.

The smile on the old man's face widened fractionally as his eyes seemed to take on a bit of a twinkle. "Do be careful what you wish for, my boy."

It was the kind of expression that Jonah somehow did not expect to see on the man's face, and he found himself a bit caught off guard. He was about to ask what he was getting at when a sound echoed from across the lake behind him, a sound like a deep, sonorous horn that thrummed and grated through the air. A sound that made his skin suddenly prickle, the hairs rising at the back of his neck.

Whipping around, he faced the direction of the lake again. Just as before it was every bit as placid and undisturbed as it was, before. In the distance he could see a few boats skimming along the surface of the water, and he almost convinced himself that the sound must have been one of the boats. Another part of him, however, was convinced that the sound was more of a growl; that it was more organic in nature than a simple boat horn.

Aside from the boats floating in the distance, as well as a few feathery clouds that were beginning to take on vaguely ruddy hues from the sun as it was dipping low in the west, there was nothing that seemed amiss or otherwise unusual that he could see, and the sound did not repeat itself. Still, it had been so real, so visceral that he could still hear it echoing in his mind, the hairs on the back of his neck still stood and prickled at his skin. It was enough to make him shiver.

Just as he felt his mind beginning to calm a little at the serene view, an unexpected gust of wind buffeted him from the side, accompanied by a distinctive sound of something heavy flapping in the breeze. Wheeling around on his heel again, he caught sight of treetops swaying lightly at his side, but aside from the way the branches rustled as they moved there was no more sound that he could make out, no sign of what had caused the momentary gust.

Incredulously, he looked at where the old man Carolus stood, unmoving and apparently unmoved, hands resting lightly at his sides as he continued to smile. Working his jaw slowly, Jonah shook his head back and forth. "What was that?"

"I think you know, Jonah."

"No, there's no such … it's not possible," he stammered, half in response to that statement, half as a sort of reassurance to himself. Memories of the other night, falling off the bridge and soaring over the river, came rushing back to the forefront of his mind. None of that was possible, none of that could have happened but everything he had experienced seemed to insist on just the opposite.

The strange man who had killed Sam, who had punched through bulletproof glass, who had picked up a five hundred pound motorcycle and thrown it at them, he too came to mind. All things that should have been impossible. Rebekah should have been killed when she was thrown through a windshield but she escaped with hardly a scratch. That damned coin that should have been lost ages ago.

Experimentally he reached down and brushed his fingers against the pocket of the pants that he now wore, his fingertips tracing over the obvious circular shape. He didn't remember ever having put it there. "Not possible," he repeated, demanding somewhat weakly.

It was at that moment that reality would defy him in a bold, unequivocal manner.

A shape, silhouetted black against the darkening hues of the sky, rose abruptly from beyond the massive resort home and shot high up into the air. Lack of a good perspective made it hard for him to gauge the size of the creature, and the contrast between light and shadow made the details vague and indistinct. Still, the shape of it was fairly obvious; a long, slender body, a pair of massive wings cutting through the air on either side. A fairly sinuous neck and an equally long tail ending in what looked like a spade were all obvious from this distance.

He could not have imagined something that looked more stereotypically like a dragon if he tried.

Jonah faltered a little as the beast bellowed out another sonorous, trumpeting roar, the sound reverberating in his ears and setting his nerves on edge. With an incredulous expression, his jaw agape, he watched as it wheeled overhead, cutting gracefully through the air in a series of progressively more acrobatic maneuvers. In other circumstances, he might be impressed; it was not unlike watching an air show.

The fear rising in the pit of his stomach, however, kept him from doing much more than staring in open disbelief. It did not help when the creature pushed its way through the air to circle briefly over the lake, dipping down low and practically skimming the surface of the water before turning and heading straight in his direction. For a brief moment he was afraid that it was going to come right at him, and then the fear transformed into certainty as the dragon lifted away from the lake just enough to come level to him, bearing down on the deck with frightening speed.

Almost too late, Jonah turned to flee from the beast with a frightened, strangled sounding yelp. Just when he was sure that the creature was going to be upon him, images of razor sharp talons clutching for him to pull him away from the deck he dived to the wood, crashing against it rather heavily. A heartbeat later there was a powerful gust of wind and the rush of the dragon passing mere feet overhead, cutting through the air with an audible whisper.

There was a sound of laughter lost in the rush of wind, and as he rolled himself around and scooted up to a sitting position, he realized it was the old man, Carolus, standing unperturbed and apparently amused. Before he could protest he caught sight of the dragon again, arcing through a graceful loop before landing on the edge of the deck with a rush of wings, flapping hard, buffeting him once more with a surprisingly powerful gust of air.

Jonah could feel the deck shudder beneath the weight of the creature, the wood groaning lightly before settling in. It only took a second for the dragon to come to a rest, massive wings folding neatly at its back as it craned its graceful, serpentine neck in his direction, a pair of brilliant green eyes regarding him with an expression that seemed frightfully disdainful.

The dark color that he had seen before wasn't just an illusion of light, for the dragon was, indeed, dark as night, covered in glossy black scales of varying sizes. Up close he realized it was not as large as it had seemed in the air, not much bigger than a horse, perhaps, but still seemed every bit as deadly. A pair of ivory white horns grew out from the back of its skull, a stark contrast to the black of its body, matching the color of its talons that splintered the wood where it had landed.

He realized that he could hear its breathing, a heavy rushing sound timed to the swell of its flanks. He also realized that he was beginning to shake where he was, pushing back against the deck, away from the dragon unsteadily. "Holy shit," he whispered, eyes wide, as it continued to stare him down.

"Don't worry, Jonah." He remembered Carolus again as the old man spoke up, calmly. "Regardless of what she might think of you, she will not harm you. Come, stand."

As much as his mind was reeling at the impossible sight that was now staring him right in the face, there was some small part that retained enough clarity to deduce that the dragon must have been Jenna, the woman who scowled at him at the table earlier. Though he still shook with fear he managed to pull himself to his feet, staring wide eyed at the dragon, repeating his breathless curse. "Holy shit."

The dragon's disdainful look, if that was indeed what it was, seemed to soften a little as she settled down on the deck, snorting and shaking her tail out behind her. Carolus took a few steps forward to stand at her side, resting a hand lightly on her flank before turning his attention back to where Jonah practically cowered. "Well, come along. Come closer, Jonah. I understand this cannot be easy for you, but please, you must confront your doubts and your fears before you can continue."

He had not heard such a severe understatement in quite some time. A large part of his mind continued to rebel against what he was seeing, tried to find some way to rationalize what he was seeing. A hallucination, perhaps, a product of the stress and fatigue that he had been made to endure over the last several days. But this was no mean hallucination, no simple figment of his imagination. A dragon was there, ten feet in front of him, living and breathing and watching him all the while.

The strain that the reality caused on his brain was so intense that it almost hurt.

Jonah forced himself to take an unsteady step forward, followed by another. The dragon made no move other than to watch him, and Carolus continued to look on expectantly. An intense curiosity began to rise up, compete with the fear and the uncertainty and incredulity. He reached a hand out, flinched when the dragon's gaze shifted to look at it, and then reached out once again.

His breath caught in his throat as his hand neared, reaching out to the dragon's snout, only a few feet away, then inches away, then close enough he could feel a slight heat radiating from those scales. As his fingers finally made contact there his mind reminded him of how they were mere inches away from what must have been massive, sharp teeth lining her now closed mouth. He almost pulled his hand away.

"Holy shit." Jonah felt a bit like a broken record but no other words would come. The scales beneath his palm were surprisingly smooth and supple, and the heat that he felt radiating from them was more poignant against his skin. He felt himself shuddering in spite of the fact that the dragon was relaxed, breathing slowly, showing no outward hostility. It wasn't all that different from the first time he'd touched a horse, when he was a child, if the emotions were magnified a hundredfold.

He felt a hand on his shoulder. He had been so focused on the dragon so intently that he did not notice when Carolus had walked over, the old man smiling at him crookedly once again. "Now you see," the old man said, quietly, almost reverently. "I am sorry that it had to be this abrupt, this difficult for you. If there were some way to turn back the clock and make this easier on you I would, but it is now time for you to accept the truth as you see it."

Again it came across as a massive understatement. Jonah merely shook his head, letting his palm gently run against the dragon's snout, his fingers gingerly touching against her scales, his eyes going wider all the while. "It's … it's really real," he finally muttered, his voice croaking a little as he gawked. "This … this Syndicate. Your clan. This whole business of running off to rescue some elder … bull drakes … this goddamned coin in my pocket."

"It is," came the quiet, calm response.

Then the real truth of the matter hit him. His hand falling away from the dragon's snout, hanging limply at his head, he whispered quietly with his lip quivering. "Then that means … that me, I'm …"

Carolus responded in that quiet, almost reverent voice, barely enough to compete with the smooth and even sound of the dragon's breathing. "Yes, Jonah. You are a dragon, too."

Jonah did not need to hear the words for the enormity of the statement to come crashing down on his head. Psychological though it might be it did, indeed, feel entirely physical to him, his knees beginning to buckle slightly under the weight, sending him down to a kneeling position with his hands on either side of his head. He felt dizzy, short on breath, an angry buzzing sound starting to ring in his ears as he felt dangerously close to fainting.

Once again he felt the rather gentle touch of a hand on his head, barely made out Carolus' voice through the ringing in his ears. "Calm yourself, Jonah. It may be difficult but you are not alone in this."

It was not the thought that he was alone that was sending his mind reeling, of course. It wasn't the first time that Jonah had encountered a radical shift in his life, learned to see it through and come out on the other side relatively unscathed. There had been the moves all throughout childhood, getting his own apartment after college, changes in his job duties and the like. Events that forced some kind of major adjustment, sometimes right on down to the way he thought.

This, however, was entirely different. Everything he thought he understood about life, the world, everything he thought he knew about himself was turning out to be a fraud - or, at least, an illusion. Grasping feebly at the reality slipping around him, he managed to mutter "Everything … everything I thought I knew …"

"Is still true. Mostly," Carolus spoke through the ringing once again, his voice distant and thin. "The sun still rises in the east. You still enjoy the occasional meal of a burger and fries. You're still Jonah, the person that you have known since childhood. Who you are is unchanged. What you are is still unchanged. You have just discovered something about yourself that was previously hidden."

"It's not that simple," he managed to protest, shaking his head as some semblance of calm was slowly beginning to settle back upon him. "This isn't … this isn't just like learning that you're actually German when you thought all along you were English."

"As I told you, your life has changed forever. You will always have the burden of this knowledge to carry until the day that you die. How you handle this knowledge is up to you," the old man intoned.

Jonah still felt weak, but the dizziness that was clouding his head was beginning to pass, the shock of the moment slowly losing its potency. Still, he leaned himself back so he was sprawled out on the ground, opening his eyes to the sight of a dark blue sky, the clouds streaked with orange as sunset approached. Carolus' face was hovering over him at one side, and at the periphery of his vision he could see the dragon regarding him from the other. "And how am I supposed to handle it? Yay, I'm a dragon. Now what?"

The old man smiled down at him. "As I have said, you are still yourself, Jonah. This does not mean you must change who you are. Your outlook on life, your goals, your dreams, wishes and desires need not change."

"But I'm still supposed to help you out. Help the clan out."

"Yes," he said, a little more hesitantly. "But again, it is my hope that you will choose to do so of your own will, as we cannot and will not force you to do so."

Jonah pushed himself back up to a seated position, fixing his eyes on the black dragon resting nearby. Looking at it was, in a way, a defiance of the way the shift in his reality had unsettled him, as if doing so were somehow confronting his problems. "Well, like I asked. What happens now?"

"Unless you are feeling ill, and unless you object, your training should begin …"

He did not know in the least what that meant, but the raw absurdity behind the notion of being trained as a dragon somehow made him smirk. In his mind, he saw it as yet another opportunity to confront his situation head on. "All right," he said, pulling himself up to his feet once again. "How do we do that? And I don't want to hear any 'wax on, wax off' shit. Get down to business."

Carolus regarded him with a bit of surprise and skepticism, but he supposed that he could not blame the old man. A little hesitantly, the older man nodded and cleared his throat. "Very well. First you must learn how to summon the ability to assume your true form, as well as how to control yourself in flight. Now, just as the young bird learns to fly through trial and error …"

"Remember. No lecturing," Jonah interrupted, a little impatiently, scowling perhaps unintentionally as he regarded the black dragon.

"Jonah, it's important to understand why things happen before simply doing them …"

Once more he interrupted, finding that he was losing patience - or losing the ability to force himself along. If he had time to think about it he might falter, might allow the doubt to come seeping back and unsteady him. He had to have answers and had to have them fast. "Yeah, well, you've said yourself that this situation isn't normal. Please, humor me."

The old man almost scowled, as well, taking a step back and folding his hands in front of him, striking a pose as if he were making some kind of assessment. "Indeed it is no normal situation. If you prefer, we will do it your way. The ability to call on your true form is something you will learn to control in time, but for now it is summoned instinctively by need. Falling, as you have seen, will trigger the reflex."

"Tell me about it," he responded a little darkly, recalling the night on the bridge, a memory he would just as soon discard.

"When in flight, it is much the same. I cannot tell you how to flap your wings, how to soar, how to bank, or any of these things. You must simply learn. Your body will do its best to keep you from falling to the ground or from crashing in to objects. Trust your body, trust the signals it sends you. It should not be hard for you to pick up on the basics fairly quickly if you simply follow your instincts and get a feel for it."

All of it still sounded so absurd. Were it not for the fact that a dragon was standing feet away, watching patiently, he would have assumed it was, indeed, absurd. Part of him still wanted to believe it was absurd, too, but there was no better way than this to find out for sure. "All right. Easy enough. So how are we going to actually train?"

Carolus still looked a little skeptical and reserved, but he was starting to open up at least, adopting a less stiff posture. "Once you take off and manage to fly more than a few feet without crash landing, you'll be pursued by your training partner," he said, indicating the black dragon with a tilt of his head. "Her task is to try and catch you, run you down, force you to the ground by any means necessary. Your task is equally simple : evade her."

Casting a dubious glance at the dragon, Jonah scoffed. "Any means necessary?"

"She won't hurt you. Not seriously, at least. That much I promise you."

The answer he got was hardly reassuring, but again, he supposed it was no more or less absurd than everything else going on. "And do I have a goal? Something I am supposed to do, beat her to it, win?"

"There is no goal. This exercise is not intended to be won, Jonah," the old man said, with something approaching a faint smile. "She will catch you. That, too, I can promise you. Your only goal is to evade her for as long as you can. If you feel up to the task you can try fighting back, try to buy yourself a little more time. There are no points for how long you last, and no punishment for quick failure other than to try again and again until I feel you have mastered the basics of flight. Do you understand?"

"Almost," he said, with something of a dismissive shrug. "How do you propose I go about, ah, changing in the first place?"

Carolus pointed in the direction of the lake. "How does my friend Ibrahim put it? A leap of faith?"

Jonah remembered that quite well, standing on a balcony with the eccentric, bald man urging him to jump off twenty stories high. The deck might not have been so tall, but he had seen enough to know that a fall from that height would do some serious damage if not kill. Worst case scenario, he might get a running jump and make it to the edge of the water, where it was just deep enough for him to drown when he knocked himself unconscious.

All the same, this was a moment of truth, it was his moment of truth. Even the day before he would not have imagined himself in this position. He was still certain that Rebekah was nuts, that Abe was nuts, that they were all either nuts or just plain sick. He still half believed that when he jumped from the deck the only thing he would accomplish would be to break his neck, but even then he would have an answer. Something he would not get just standing there.

He had spent long enough sitting around, letting himself be dragged from point A to point B, waiting for someone to do something - waiting for something to happen. Sucking down a deep breath, he let out a bellow that surprised even himself and ran for the edge of the deck as fast as he could. Fifteen, maybe twenty feet away, it came up on him quick, and then he was at the edge. Too far to stop, too far to turn back, he was committed to his course. Resisting the urge to close his eyes, he leaped.

Throwing his arms out in front of him in something of a ridiculous Superman pose, he felt himself starting to soar, flinging himself from the edge of the deck as hard as he could, the ground below spooling out beneath him, bringing him closer to the edge of the lake. For a brief moment he thought that he had, indeed, jumped far enough to make it to the water.

Gravity, however, had other designs. In another blink of an eye he was falling rapidly toward the ground. Suddenly his arms and legs were flailing, and Jonah found himself screaming as he had quickly gone from a graceful sort of soaring motion to a veritable death plunge toward the lake.

It wasn't going to happen. Nothing was happening, he could feel no difference in himself, could feel no urge to flap wings or do anything other than scream in terror as the earth rose quickly to meet him.

Somewhat miserably, he at least realized that he would have his answer.

THIRTEEN

Then there was a strange but slightly familiar tugging against his back, behind his shoulders. He remembered where had felt it, tumbling through the air toward his doom at the bottom of a canyon. This fall was nowhere near as far, nowhere near as long but scared him every bit as much, and when he felt that strange sensation something else suddenly leaped to the forefront of his conscious mind. Carolus' admonition to follow his instincts.

Without time to think about it, he pulled his arms and legs in tight against his body, pulling at muscles in his back that he wasn't even sure were really there. The little tug behind his shoulders suddenly became a powerful pull, trying to yank him upward, the air around him seeming to thicken, his descent slowing in an agonizingly long moment.

Just when he expected to become one with the ground, it began to pull away from him once again. The urge to pull on muscles at his back renewed, and he gave in to the urge, flexing his body, feeling himself push against the air. From the corners of his eyes he caught a glimpse of movement at either side, thin and indistinct as they moved up and down in time to the flexing.

Wings. They couldn't be anything other than wings.

Jonah was aware that something felt distinctly different. It seemed to evade comprehension, the way that he seemed to wear the world around him in a different way. Everything looked slightly different, felt different. Somehow he still could not wrap his mind around the thought that he was, indeed, a dragon; glancing down to try and get a look at his reflection in the water now beneath him he could see only an indistinct shape. The wings at `1his sides moved too quickly to get a look at. Though there was no explanation, his mind still had a hard time with the thought.

What was much simpler for him to comprehend was the simple fact that he was flying. Soon he no longer had to consciously think about the way he had to flex the muscles of his back - flap his wings - and it came almost as naturally as walking. Watching the blue waters of the lake spool out beneath him, catching a red glimmer from the waning sun, a sense of euphoria began to come over him, and he could not help but to let out an exultant cry.

It sounded surprisingly like the sound he had heard before, a deep, resonant trumpeting that rumbled and grated through the air. Again he tried it, bellowing out a deeply excited roar.

He discovered that turning was surprisingly similar to riding his motorcycle. Leaning his body to the side, putting his shoulder into it he began to wheel about, the horizon shifting around him as he slowly turned his way back in the direction he had come from. He was surprised to see that the villa he had come from had receded to little more than a point on a distant shore.

The part of his mind that continued to resist the idea was becoming more and more quiet, quickly overtaken by the raw and unmatched joy of cutting through the air, the way the wind whipped him in the face and flowed over his body.

As he approached the shore, however, something else caught his eye, a black shape moving gracefully through the air, approaching him with an almost frightening speed. At the last second he realized it was the other dragon, the one who had been tasked with taking him down. The creature had is claws out, pulling its wings back to reach out in a grasping fashion, roaring loudly at him.

It was going to collide with him; it was going to get him.

He tried to turn hard, but the thickness of the wind forbade him. His body suddenly twisted through the air as it yanked at his wings, pulled him around, sending him tumbling about end over end. The sky wheeled overhead, the horizon twisting and turning at crazy angles as he completely lost control of himself. He was vaguely aware of the other dragon passing by at a dizzying speed, the air itself seeming to quiver and reverberate as his passing, but she missed him, this time at least.

Still, he was tumbling through the air. Jonah could feel his heart thumping angrily in his chest as he flailed about in the air, his limbs trying to grasp at something that wasn't there. Once more he had to let his instincts kick in, obeying the urges to tense and relax his muscles independently. He could feel his wings cutting through the air, catching against it here and there, slowly allowing him to level out, the crazy tumbling of the world about him slowing and coming to an end.

At last he righted himself mere feet above the surface of the lake, skimming the water with his limbs before pulling skyward, letting out a triumphant shout of relief.

His relief was short lived, however. The black dragon had already come about, effortlessly arcing through the air over the lake and coming right back at him. While Jonah found himself in awe at how easily she seemed to move, he still felt a little more confident now that he had made it this far. Building up his speed he aimed right for the dragon, pushing himself harder, harder, counting off the seconds in his head before he knew he'd have to pull up and out of the way to keep from crashing into her. There was no way she would expect him to do something so bold.

There was also no way for him to have expected just what she would do. Just prior to that moment when he was about to pull up she pulled her wings high and came to an abrupt, rapid halt in the air, facing him down with her jaws agape, as if she were about to roar at him, but instead it was a brilliant gout of fire issuing from her maw. Jonah almost flinched, the plume of fire spreading out rapidly into an intense ball, but then he realized that dragons must be flameproof. Undeterred by her attempt to throw him off, he pushed on ahead.

Immediately his assumption was proved wrong. A searing heat enveloped him, intense enough that he could not help but to react instinctively, shutting his eyes and pulling his wings in tight around him, forming a protective embrace. His hide stung, the heat screaming at him as momentum carried him through the fireball and out to the other side. Pulled into a ball as he was, it was only seconds before he plummeted straight into the lake with an enormous splash.

Water surrounded him in a cool blanket, briefly a welcome respite to the burning sensation that he had felt. His lungs, already starved for air, urged him to come up to the surface, his limbs flailing till he broke he surface once again, drawing in a deep gasp, opening his eyes again while he paddled in the lake that was becoming rapidly very cold.

He was strangely dismayed to see that it was with normal, human hands that he was splashing in the water. Glancing upward, he could see the black dragon wheeling up and away, starting to circle him like some kind of vulture. "Hey! Hey, what's going on?"

"Natural talent cannot overcome the failures of overconfidence," a voice called out behind him. He recognized it as Carolus' voice, if somehow a bit deeper and more sonorous. Whipping around to get a look at the old man, he was startled to see instead a dragon hovering nearby, over the surface of the water.

A stark contrast to the graceful black female he had been trying to evade, Carolus in dragon form was somehow more stereotypical and frightening. Covered in ash gray scales, numerous horns and spikes seemed to issue forth from his hide in multiple locations : over his eyes, along his spine, the sides of his tail. He was larger, too, if not quite twice the size, and instead of being slender and graceful he was a massive, bulky beast.

Gray eyes that almost matched the color of his scales loomed down at him, jagged fangs overhanging the dragon's bite.

Jonah realized he was gawking, shaking a bit of the water out of his hair as he looked up at the dragon. "Carolus? You can talk?"

"Of course I can, we are not mute creatures! I have been near the whole time, watching you. You embrace your agility well, but you must learn to better respect your foe," he rumbled, loudly.

"She cheated! She spat fire at me," he protested, realizing that his skin was still a little singed, feeling almost like a light sunburn.

"Cheated?" The big dragon's voice seemed almost amused as he flapped, his wings pushing the air down and creating a series of ripples in the water. "She has done no such thing. Those who would do you harm will not hesitate to use such powers against you, and powers more damaging and deadly still."

Jonah sputtered a little, the little waves splashing him int he face and forcing him to squint. "Why didn't you tell me how to breathe fire?"

The big dragon huffed a sort of grumbly sigh. "I do not know if you can breathe fire, and even if you did I could not help you. It is not a talent I have, myself. Many dragons are endowed with many powerful gifts, but these cannot be taught to you. You must learn them on your own."

"Great." He sighed a little as he paddled in the water again, and then frowned. "What do I do now? I'm not a dragon anymore … what happened?"

"Sometimes a great shock can force you back out of your dragon state. Falling in the cold water, for example. That, too, is something you must learn to overcome, Jonah. To lose your concentration in a difficult situation could have dire consequences."

Jonah just shook his head. Once more the situation seemed beyond ridiculous, floating in a freezing cold lake and talking to a dragon about techniques. A few hours ago, it was something he would not really have imagined, and even now something about it seemed practically offensive to his sensibilities. Still, he could not sit and float in this lake forever. "Well, now what? How do I get back to this, ah, training?"

The big dragon dipped down without so much as a word, and before Jonah could so much as flinch a massive set of talons clutched him and hauled him right out of the lake. Carolus was as gentle as he supposed he could be, those massive talons holding on tightly enough to grip him but not enough to tear his sopping wet clothes, but something about being gripped like that was intensely frightening, enough to nearly make him cry out.

If the sensation of being grasped like that wasn't unsettling enough, the dizzying speed with which he was hauled upward did not help. The big dragon flew almost straight up, each beat of his massive wings pulling them higher and higher into the air. The waves on the lake quickly faded into what looked like a smooth blue, and then he could spy the massive building on the lake shore like a small toy model, shrinking away. Still they climbed, higher and higher, surpassing even the mountain tops, into the clouds and beyond, where the sun still shined brightly.

Just when Jonah wondered how much higher the big dragon might take him, the talons released. For a moment there was hardly any sensation of movement, the brief sensation of floating there persisting until the wind rushing past him whipped into a frenzy. He fell through the clouds again, the distant lake shore beneath him slowly growing once again.

Once again, too, he was aware that he was screaming. Once again, nothing was happening. He was just a helpless human being tumbling through the air high enough for skydiving, but without the benefit of a parachute.

The last two times he had not changed until he was about to hit the water below, until just at the last minute when he could pull himself back from the brink of disaster. He didn't have to know how fast he was falling to know that if he waited that long now there would simply not be enough time; he'd hit the water with enough force to shatter every bone in his body.

The others had told him that it was a natural reaction, that his body would simply know that he must change and die, that it would protect him instinctively. Instinct would not be enough here, and his conscious mind knew it well enough to send him into a panic. Flailing, grasping, he tried to convince himself that he had to do it now, before it was too late.

Still nothing happened. He whipped by the wispy clouds in a second, tumbling end over end. Third time is the charm, he thought to himself morosely. He supposed he could only escape death by falling so many times.

Then Jonah remembered the way it felt when he was in control, the way the wind slipped past his body, the way his wings cut right through the air when they needed. He pulled his arms in against his sides, straightened his legs out behind him and allowed himself to dive headfirst through the air, no longer tumbling but becoming a sort of missile driving ever more quickly toward the ground. The wind buffeted his face harder, whistled past his ears all the more angrily, letting him know he was picking up speed, hastening the arrival of impact.

Somehow, in the middle of all the fury of wind whipping around him, he found a kernel of calm in the center of his being. He closed his eyes tightly, giving himself over to the embrace of gravity, imagining the sight of him plummeting through the atmosphere, how he must have looked from the distance.

He could see his body lengthening, stretching, a tail whipping out behind him to stabilize his descent. He could see a pair of wings folded tightly to his back, reaching out slightly to cut into the air. He could feel the now familiar plucking sensation behind his shoulders, the little drag that the leathery membranes of his wings created.

He remembered the way it felt to be in control. He knew the way it felt to be in control. He was in control. Opening his eyes again, confronting the sight of the lake rushing ever nearer, he could feel himself smiling. He was in control.

Instinctively he knew that to open his wings and try to brake against his fall would be disastrous; they would snap like twigs at this speed, breaking his bones long before he hit the water. Instead he let them stretch out, following the contour of his body and letting the air simply slip over them, and tilted them ever so slightly so that he would start to pull up.

Though it worked, his descent beginning to shallow, gravity was not so eager to give up its prize. The shift of his direction subjected him to its pull in an odd way, something he vaguely remembered in the form of g-forces, making his limbs feel immensely heavy beneath him. His wings shuddered a bit from the pressure but they held, stretching wider to catch more and more of the air as he plummeted.

Painfully, slowly, but successfully he leveled his descent. The effort paid off when, several seconds before he would have plunged into the water he was no longer falling but was soaring forward at a terrifying rate, much of his downward motion translated into forward speed. The lake rushed out beneath him much faster than he could have ever dreamed on his motorcycle.

It was raw speed, pure freedom, absolute exhilaration. He didn't have to move his wings, only hold them out aloft so he could glide, shooting across the lake with the wind sliding effortlessly over his hide. He felt his heart swell with pride and excitement, the adrenaline rushing through his veins strong enough to make him almost feel dizzy. So he did the only thing that felt appropriate in the situation : he bellowed out an exuberant "Ya-hoo!"

His cry was answered by a distinctly irritated grumbling in the distance. He could see the black dragon now, flying level with him and some ways ahead but closing fast. Momentum was still on his side, however, and when he saw the dragon belch out another gout of flame all he had to do was lean into a turn and bank sharply to the right. He had too much speed for her to match, and he left her far behind long before the flames could hope to lick at him.

Jonah felt almost invincible. Taking a cue from the many dogfights that he had seen in movies, he suddenly banked upward, sharply, rising into a tight loop that had him flying upside down for a moment, his senses complaining when the world was all turned upside down. Instinct and inertia guided him through the loop, and as he leveled out he was more than satisfied to see the black dragon gliding in front of him, away from him. He had succeeded in getting behind her.

The maneuver had cost him some speed, and wind resistance was beginning to take its toll. He found that he had to start flapping his wings again in long, slow beats to keep aloft, but he was still gaining on her. Not knowing how to breathe fire - or if he even could - he opted for the simpler choice of going in to physically grapple at her, turn the tables and send her plummeting into the cold water.

Seconds before he caught her, however, she banked hard to the left and whipped almost instantly out of view. Startled, he tried to follow, but realized that he was not, after all, as agile or as experienced as he thought. Lumbering through the turn, he realized he'd lost sight of her.

Thrown off guard, Jonah glanced wildly to his left and then to his right, but could find no sign of the black dragon. Her bellow echoed in his ears again, nearby, but the wind whipping around him left him unable to track the sound. Craning his neck to look behind him he still saw nothing, save for the shape of Carolus hovering some ways in the distance. She bellowed again, and he suddenly remembered to look up.

The attack, however, came from below. Coming up at a sharp angle she barreled right into his chest with enough force to knock the wind right out of him and send him tumbling once more. Caught off guard as he was he could not retaliate at all, and could only watch as her sleek shape slipped through the air and away from him, probably circling back around to deliver another blow.

It was hard enough for him to stay aloft, let alone try and counter what he thought would be her next move. After wheeling through the air with his limbs thrashing Jonah managed to stabilize himself, pumping his wings mightily in spite of the shortness of breath that he now felt, trying to gain some altitude and speed. The sun had already slipped behind the mountains in the distance and the sky was darkening, giving her some advantage as her black form started blending in. Still he could see her behind him, and still he had a chance.

Ahead, he could see the shore of the lake coming up fast, the pine trees rising up abruptly just beyond. Deciding to try a slightly different tactic, he dropped himself to a level that he hoped was just above the treetops, urging his wings on a little quicker, wanting to reach the shore before she caught up to him. He could hear the surge of her own wings growing ever closer; he had to stay out of range of that fire.

Jonah was not quite sure he was high enough above the trees, and felt himself cringing as the lake below gave way to the earth. A second later he was at the treeline, close enough that the treetops were forced to bend and sway mightily beneath the force of the wind coming off his wings, but he had calculated right. He had just missed them.

Making a hard turn to the left, he struggled to keep the altitude he needed. Flying so close to the treetops put a significant limit to how much he could maneuver, but he knew that she would be suffering from the same handicap. He might not be able to pull away from her, but at least he could maintain his distance.

An angry bellow behind him seemed to confirm his thinking, and he couldn't help but to grin. The trees would also serve as a deterrent to more balls of fire; surely she would not want to start the forest alight.

It worked, for a time. Jonah could make out the shape of Carolus off in the distance, observing, but the big dragon was too far away for him to read an expression. He could hear the black dragon close, as well, too close for comfort but he still kept the lead. It would only work for so long, however, as there was only so much room for flying around above the trees.

Abruptly his path took him right over the mansion where they had been staying, but he only caught the quickest little glimpse of it. Without intending to, he had come full circle. To his dismay, just beyond was a rather large meadow, one that would take him several seconds to cross. One that would give his pursuer several seconds to maneuver, or worse.

To make matters worse yet, his lungs were beginning to burn for lack of air. He knew they were already at a high altitude, the air here much thinner than what he was used to, and he was already exerting himself to the limit and beyond. His heart was thumping angrily in his chest, and he knew he was growing exhausted. He'd have to think of something soon.

Jonah passed over the meadow before he had a chance to come up with a plan. Almost instantly the black dragon behind him made her move, a sudden and rapid surge of energy pushing her wings faster than he thought possible, and she started to arc right around, coming fast at his side.

He tried to turn out of her way and failed. Already exhausted, his wings simply would not comply in time. He faltered in the air, and a second later she crashed right into him in a flurry of wings and talons and claws. Jonah was flipped on to his back a second before crashing into the ground with enough force to knock the breath from him anew.

The black dragon pinned him to the ground, flashing her teeth at him in a snarl, but the effort was not really necessary. He lacked the energy to fight back, and merely collapsed onto the ground, gasping for air.

"You have done admirably, child," Carolus intoned a moment later, settling himself down at the edge of the clearing with a surprising amount of grace for a creature so large. "Better than I would have thought you capable of in such a short amount of time. Please, stand."

The dragon atop him had released him already, stepping back and away so that Jonah was left to clamber to his feet on his own. His joints ached mightily at the crash, his muscles burned and complained with the effort, but he managed to get himself standing mostly upright. "Then that's it?"

"For now," the big dragon said with a low rumble, turning to look back in the direction of the mansion just beyond the treeline. "It has already grown late, and I can't afford to have you flying about in the dark just yet. There will be time for that later, when you are ready; I'd rather not have you killed in a mock battle."

"Then you could tell her not to try and fry me next time," he spat out a little more upset than he meant to.

A familiar voice behind him startled him, and when he whipped his head around he was surprised to see Rebekah standing where the black dragon had been moments before. "I can go easy on you next time, if you like."

Jonah felt his jaw go slack at the sight. "It was you, all along?"

She shrugged her shoulders nonchalantly. "Carolus asked me to take care of you for this training. I guess my job isn't quite done, after all."

He didn't know why he was so caught off guard by the fact. He had expected that his opponent was the woman Jenna who had shown some hostility to him before, from what Carolus had mentioned just before the training began. Inwardly he wondered what the old man had meant when he used the words in spite of what she thinks of you. "You could have killed me."

"But I didn't," she answered with another shrug. "Like I said, next time I can go easier on you if it makes you feel better."

"No," he fumed, feeling his wings flutter a bit behind him in irritation. "I just ... didn't expect that you'd ... and how do you do that? You're a human, again."

"I'll tell you in a minute, but there's something I want you to see, first."

Scowling, frowning, he craned his head back to get a look at Carolus, who only nodded patiently. "What is it?"

Rebekah just smiled slightly. "Actually, meet me back on the deck," she called out over her shoulder as she darted off between the trees and disappeared.

"Come, child," the old man growled before lifting himself up off the ground, the wind kicking up dirt and debris around Jonah's head before he followed suit. It was not far to the mansion and the deck behind it, fortunately lit, but even that short flight left him feeling achy and exhausted.

He tumbled to the wood a little unsteadily, falling flat on his underbelly instead of landing gracefully the way Carolus did. "Perhaps tomorrow, you will practice landing," the big dragon said with something of a smirk.

Before he could respond, Rebekah stepped out onto the deck, carrying a fairly large rectangular object. "Jonah. Over here. Take a look."

Scowling, he turned to look at the object she had as she held it out for him to see. It was a portrait of a dragon, an off white color and decked with irregular, rust colored stripes. The painting seemed incredibly lifelike and detailed, the way the bright blue eyes in the picture seemed to sparkle at him, almost staring right back at him. The dragon did not look otherwise remarkable, a set of wings folded neatly on its back, a pair of ebony colored horns sprouting out from the back of its head, with a set of smaller ones jutting out from behind its jaw. Slender, unlike the older dragon, but somewhat bulkier than Rebekah.

He was about to ask her what the point was when he saw the image of Carolus moving in the background of the portrait. Except that it was no portrait - it was a mirror.

He was looking at himself.

Jonah reacted by drawing in a sharp, startled breath, backing away from the mirror with some haste, as if it had just bitten him. Rebekah seemed to have some pity on him, lowering the mirror so it no longer held his reflection, but she smiled all the same. "See. Told you that you were a pretty good looking dragon," she said, before she turned on her heel and headed back toward the doors.

"Wait," he croaked hoarsely, his throat feeling dry. "How'd you do it … become human again …"

"Think about it, Jonah. How'd you become a dragon? Works the same way," she called out without turning to look at him, disappearing into the house.

It really hadn't been hard when he figured it out at last, and wondered if it could be so easy. Closing his eyes, he imagined the way he looked … was supposed to look. No wings, no talons, no claws. Just skin and hair.

When he opened his eyes again he was surprised to find himself on all fours but quite human once again. Feeling absurd, he quickly pushed himself up to his feet and turned around.

Carolus was standing there, the old man looking human once again, nodding in his direction. "Very good, Jonah. You may take the rest of the night to relax. Have a good dinner, get to bed early. Tomorrow will be more training."

"Of course," he responded with a mutter, reaching back to rub his neck. His muscles were still sore and achy.

"There are still several things I wish to speak to you about," the old man paused, reaching out to rest a hand on his shoulder. "Tomorrow, or the next day, perhaps. When there is more time. But since you seemed eager to learn how to reassume your human form, there is one thing I must tell you now before I forget."

Jonah found himself frowning slightly. "What's that?"

"When you take on human form, you are human for all intents and purposes. With all of the same frailties and weaknesses that it comes with. A fire that merely singes you as a dragon might incinerate you as a man."

"Wait," he protested. "I remember Rebekah getting thrown into a car. That bull drake got shot in the chest, and they both seemed ok."

Carolus breathed a little sigh at that and nodded. "All right, let me rephrase. Some of the strengths and protections that you enjoy as a dragon you will still enjoy. Long life, excellent health, strength and resistance to being wounded. But it is not the same. You are still much more fragile, much more ... mortal, in human form. Take care that you do not forget this."

The warning seemed a little oddly timed, and he could not help but to continue frowning. "Why do you mention it, now?"

Carolus smiled crookedly. "Just seemed like something you ought to know. Now, go along and rest. Tomorrow will be another big day."

As he watched the old man make his way to the door and disappear inside, Jonah grumbled again. It was the kind of statement that he was getting used to hearing, and one that he would rather not keep hearing. One big day after another; one life altering event right on the heels of the last. What he would not give for a day that did nothing other than leave him bored to death.

The rumbling in his stomach reminded him that he hadn't eaten in hours. Tomorrow, for whatever it might hold, would have to wait. The faint smell of food wafting out the doors brought him back to the moment, and Jonah just shook his head as he followed the old man back inside.

FOURTEEN

Dinner had largely been uneventful. Jonah had been led to a large dinng room where food had been laid out on a large table, a veritable banquet that had set his mouth to slavering. He'd almost have thought it an early Thanksgiving based on the spread, but he had to remind himself that there were several other adults there who were likely just as hungry as he was.

He had hardly spoken to the others for the entire meal. The others came and went at their own leisure and seemed content to let him occupy a quiet seat at one end of the table, removed from the quiet conversation that he mostly ignored. He hadn't seen Abe the entire time, and Carolus had excused himself not long afterward. He recognized Jenna, the woman with the dark hair and the hawkish gaze that he tried to avoid. Though she did not openly confront him and seemed to mostly ignore him, as well, he could not help but to imagine she was sneering at him. It made him uncomfortable.

Briefly, he had been introduced to the two others who had been at the Convocation, the ones who had not spoken during the meeting. First Ryan, every bit as bald as Abe but lacking the man's imposing stature, who had friendly if somewhat tired looking features, and then Flor, a veritable waif of a woman with flowing black hair and almond shaped eyes that gave her a subtly exotic look. Both had been warm and friendly with him, but Jonah had not been much in the mood for conversation, and they had both excused themselves before long.

Rebekah, too, had been there at the table. Her reaction to his presence had been frustratingly difficult to read. At times he could have sworn that she was smiling at him, perhaps even subtly flirting with him again, while at other times she seemed to flash him a vaguely disdainful look, if she even bothered acknowledging his existence at all. After what had happened the past few days he was not sure he could entirely blame her, his own feelings regarding her almost as infuriatingly difficult to sort out. Still, he felt uncomfortable on the receiving end of her uncertain gaze.

As the evening wore into night the quiet sounds of conversation died off around him, the regular clatter of silverware and dishes becoming irregular and then hushing altogether as the others excused themselves, one by one. In the end, Jonah was all but alone at the dining table, shifting the remnants of his peas around on the plate with a fork while he tried not to contemplate the day's events too much, when an unexpected voice spoke up nearby. "I have to apologize for my sister."

Glancing upward, Jonah found himself face to face with Jason, one of those who had spoken at the meeting. He was fairly short in comparison to most of the others, his black hair flecked with bits of white, the skin around his gray eyes slightly stretched into suggestions of crow's feet, as if he were coming up on middle age. Frowning unintentionally, Jonah blinked at him. "What?"

"Jenna, my sister. I … she was a little hard on you back there. I just want you to know it's not because she hates you or anything ..."

The familial resemblance was obvious now that Jonah thought about it, though at the time he didn't realize the two were siblings. With a little sigh, he shrugged his shoulders. "If you insist. Abe tried to tell me the same thing before. What's she got against me, anyway?"

"It's complicated," the man began.

Jonah just shook his head with a sigh. "And that's exactly what Abe told me, too. I'm kind of tired of hearing that, to be honest. Things are too complicated to explain to me. It's not the right time. I just have to be patient and take it all on faith," he said, his voice taking on a sour edge to it as he closed his eyes. "I mean, hell. Here you people are asking me to fight but … why all the secrecy? I'm tired of feeling like I'm being kept in the dark, like I'm not really being told what's going on. I thought I was supposed to be, like, an equal member in your little club here ..."

"She was married to the last silver dragon," Jason interrupted.

Jonah blinked as he was cut off, and then paused a moment to let himself process that little bit of information. "Christ," he muttered, slumping into his seat a little bit as he put two and two together. "Which means he … and she blames me?"

"No," came the rather swift response, Jason shaking his head vigorously. "No, she doesn't blame you for his death. No one would. It's just that she took it hard, and even though it's been years she's still not really over it. Seeing you had dredged up some of those feelings in her, it's probably made her relive it a little bit. It's not personal."

The mention of reliving the loss made a chill run down Jonah's spine, although he couldn't quite figure out why. Hugging his arms around his chest as if to ward off the chill, a frown cemented itself on his face. "Well.

I guess I get that stuff about me not being worthy, then. Big shoes to fill, from her perspective."

A smile was offered and a hand rested lightly on his shoulder. "You got it. But like I said, it's not personal. In time she'll get over it, she'll remember that you're just you. In the meantime, she still knows you're a member of the clan, and even if she's not your biggest fan she'll at least respect you as such."

Jonah nodded a little at that. He realized that the man was trying to be sensitive to his needs, was trying to extend a hand of welcome, as it were, but he was still not in much of a mood to accept the offer. He wasn't certain what kind of mood he was in, at all, except that he found it all too easy to latch on to just the wrong part of what was being said. "She'll put up with me because I'm a part of the clan, huh?"

"Well, yes, but ..."

He interrupted with a little shake of his head. "See, that's another thing about what's going on. Clan this, clan that, you're expected to put up with some newcomer just because he's a part of the clan. I'm being asked to stick my neck out for some elder I've never met because I'm a part of a clan, like it's my duty or something. The only duty I know is taking care of my own ass. I don't know if I can do this."

He realized that he was unfairly unloading on the man, who he had only just met, but the opportunity was there and he'd been itching to get it out. For as unfair as it might have been, Jason was trying his best to respond. "Most of us were raised as a part of the clan, Jonah, so it's more than just that. We're family. It's not really a sense of duty as much as it is a sense of … well … taking care of one's family. None of us had to discover we were dragons, or discover the clan. We knew about it from as early as we can remember. You didn't have that luxury."

"Tell me about it," Jonah responded in a mutter.

"Still. Even if you don't see us as family yet, Jonah, we all see you as such. Even those of us who aren't comfortable with you yet. Any one of us would stick our necks out for you, without so much as a second thought."

"And you expect the same of me."

"We don't expect it," he answered in a friendly demeanor, once again reaching over to clasp Jonah by the shoulder. "We hope for it, yes. We hope someday you'll feel just as comfortable with your identity as the rest of us, but we're not stupid. We know it'll take time. Just try to stick with us till then?"

Jonah closed his eyes and pinched at the bridge of his nose before pulling his palm down over his face. "I just … why now? I mean, Rebekah told me you'd been watching me for years. If this shit is so hard to handle when you get old, why not break it to me sooner? What kind of sense does it make to throw me into this when things get tough?"

There was a long pause before the answer came, as if Jason was measuring his response. "The council had actually considered letting you live out your life without knowing, without intervening. Some speculated that if you never had a chance to change into a dragon you might live a normal human existence, grow old like other humans, blend in without ever knowing the difference. It wasn't until the Silver Token came to you, that we knew you were the silver dragon that we decided to intervene, and even then ..."

"I wish you'd never have told me."

"Jonah?"

Jonah sighed heavily again. The thought that he might have been able to go on with his life, without ever having been thrust into this madness, that maybe he could have been left alone made him feel sick to his stomach. "I didn't ask for this. I don't ... I don't want this. I want to go back to my life ... why did you have to drag me into this, if you had a choice?"

"It's not like that. We didn't have a choice, not once the token came to you, not once the bull drake tracked you down ..."

"No!" Jonah interjected, nearly shouting as he pounded his fist into the table. "No! I'd have let him have the damned thing and he'd have gone on his way. I don't care what he'd have done with it. I'd have been found innocent of the murder and then gone on with my life like none of this happened, and I wouldn't be here now."

Jason held his ground in spite of the outburst. "It's not that simple, Jonah. I mean that, when I say we literally didn't have a choice. Do you really think the bull would have let you live after giving him the token? And even if he did, the token would have found its way to you again. These kinds of things are out of our hands."

"Out of your hands. Out of my hands." Jonah wanted to be angry, wanted to shout and pound on the table again, but the powerlessness of the moment quickly eroded any real anger he might have felt. Instead, he folded his arms on the table in front of him and let his face droop against them. "Doesn't anyone have any say in what goes on around here? I don't ... I don't believe in fate ..."

"Maybe it's fate. Maybe it's destiny. Or maybe it's just what happens." Again he could feel that hand on his shoulder, as if it were supposed to be reassuring. "Maybe we don't have any power to control what goes on around us, Jonah, but then again maybe that's not what matters. But there is one thing that we can control. We're always in control of how we respond to what happens. That choice is always ours."

He didn't know how to respond, not to Jason's words, not to the situation, not to what was happening to him. "A week ago I was Jonah Fischer," he mutterd quietly, his voice muffled a bit against his arms. "I was one of a dozen people working in a department. I was one of a hundred people living in my apartment building. One of a million people in my city, just … just a person. Someone who went to work, who came home at night, who rode his motorcycle on the weekends and life was good. It was boring, it was sane, it was good."

"Jonah ..."

With a heavy sigh, he shook his head and went on. "But now? Now I'm a dragon. Something that's not even supposed to exist, something that's just a legend. I'm fighting for my life, running from people who want me dead. And now I'm supposed to be fighting for the survival of my whole goddamned species? Against some shady Syndicate filled with monsters and magicians? How the hell am I supposed to do this?"

Again Jason responded by squeezing his shoulder. "Jonah, I know it's hard ..."

"No you don't!" Again the anger was coming back, and he pushed himself back upright, clenching his fists and pressing them in against the table. "None of you know jack shit about what's going on! Were you dragged away from your comfortable little life and thrust into something like this? Were any of you?"

"No," the older man replied with a slightly stern expression. "None of us were thrust into this, but we're no strangers to the reality of the situation. We've been fighting the Syndicate for years ..."

"Exactly!" Again Jonah thumped his fist against the table. "Exactly! I've been dragged out of my comfortable little life only to be told I'm going to spend the next thousand years constantly watching my back, fighting for my life. Hell, Abe says he's been dodging these people for centuries. I don't want to be looking over my shoulder for centuries, dammit! I want to go back. I want to work in the rat race. I want to worry about whether I need to buy new tires for my bike, not how I'm going to rescue an elder. I want to go back."

In spite of the continued outburst, Jason was able to remain calm. "I understand this is difficult for you Jonah, but you must understand that you can't go back."

Jonah wouldn't accept that. "No, it's not true! I don't care what you think. I don't care what any of you think. I'm a human, goddammit. I'm not a dragon. I can go back ..."

"You've always been a dragon, Jonah, even if you didn't know it."

"Bullshit," he spat back, shaking his head. "I … I don't have to be a part of this. I want to go back. I've always been a human ..."

This time it was Jason who cut him off. "I was there when you were born."

That revelation cut his outburst short, leaving Jonah unable to do anything but turn back with his eyes wide and his jaw slack. "What?"

"Well. Not exactly there at your birth, but shortly thereafter," he responded, a faint and vague smile on his features. "I knew your parents well. When you were born, the council dispatched me to Dallas to visit with them, to visit you and to offer the congratulations and the blessings of the elder."

"You knew my parents?"

Again Jason nodded. "They were good people. Good dragons. No one was as devastated as I was when we heard what had happened to them. At first we feared the worst, that you had been lost as well along with them, until we discovered that they had given you up for adoption shortly before. They knew they were being hunted, and they knew you were in danger as long as you were with them. I know your parents. I know how enormously difficult it must have been for them to let you go, the sacrifice that it was for them. They had to do it to keep you safe."

It was more than he could take. The anger that had managed to build up in him anew had completely wilted away, leaving in its wake a void that was rapidly being filled by a confused and poignant sense of loss. He opened his mouth as if to say something but no words came out, his voice catching in his throat in a quiet little croak of a sound.

"You've always been a dragon," Jason repeated, expression somehow stern and soft at the same time. "You've always been family to us, Jonah, from the start. I hope you come to see us as family, too."

The wild mix of emotions was just too much. Part of him still wanted to be angry, wanted to lash out again. He did still want to go back to his previous existence, comfortable, dull and predictable. He did still want everything to go back to normal, to not have to worry about bull drakes and tokens and training.

He thought of his family back in Florida, his mother and father, who he had known and loved since as far back as he could remember. There had been jokes in his youth about whether he had been adopted, as he really looked nothing like either of them; the possibility that those old jokes were rooted in fact left him feeling uncertain.

And then there were the dragons. Strange characters, all of them in their own ways, come barging into his life and now wanting to be made a part of his family, as well. He looked up at Jason, who smiled to him faintly.

It was all just too much. Suddenly, tears began to well up in the corners of his eyes, making his vision swim and blur, and he found himself fighting the urge to blink, to keep them from spilling out. "I … I just don't know what to do ..."

"Just hang in there with us, Jonah. Do your best. We'll take care of the rest."

It all seemed somehow too easy an answer, yet Jonah didn't know how to refute it, how to come up with any alternative scenario. He felt like he was caving in to some sort of inexorable force working against him, pushing him onto a path he was neither ready nor willing to embark upon.

At last the tears got the best of him, spilling out over his cheeks. As his vision blurred into incoherence, he felt a strong grip on his arm, pulling him up to his feet, and then hands embracing him firmly around the chest. Without thinking about it, Jonah accepted the embrace, burying his face into the offered shoulder and let himself go, sobbing like had never done before.

FIFTEEN

For the next four days, Jonah had been put through the most demanding series of tests and trials that he had ever encountered. He had been instructed in all manner of aerial maneuvers, how to float aloft for long periods of time, how to catch thermal currents and use them to his advantage. He had been taught how to land without bruising himself, and how to take off from a standstill without toppling over.

Carolus supervised most of it, while Rebekah served as his training partner. He had learned how to better evade her attacks, her fireballs. She had shown him how to balance the need to control his flying while at the same time tracking, evading, and sometimes attacking an opponent.

It had all been a strange mix of exhilarating, exhausting, and patently unbelievable. Though Jonah had actually spent most of his time over the last few days as a dragon, flying through the air, some stubborn part of his mind insisted that it was impossible, and that he must have been hallucinating, perhaps stuck in some protracted dreamstate. Even when he was soaring high above the lake that tiny bit of doubt remained lodged there in the back of his subconscious.

At the end of the fourth day, though, there wasn't much room for anything other than exhaustion in his thoughts. The sun was setting over the lake again, and Carolus had gone inside to consult with Abe and a few of the others about the following morning when they would make their assault on the Syndicate compound. Jonah didn't know if he felt ready, but at the moment he didn't care.

Sprawled out on the deck with his head drooping slightly over the edge, he was trying his best to recover when he heard Rebekah's voice next to him. "Didn't wear you out too much, did I?"

Turning to look at her, he realized that she had already gone back into human form, and was wearing that strangely unconcerned smile that she always seemed to wear. By now he had come to realize that it was a sort of mask, something that made her real emotions hard to read, something that made her generally inscrutable. It was frustrating. "You did, but, I suppose that's the point."

"I suppose you're right," she agreed, sitting on the edge of the deck with her legs dangling, peering out over the lake. "I wanted to tell you that you've been doing great. Carolus thinks so too, he's awfully proud of you."

"If you insist. Don't know how much it's going to matter, tomorrow."

A slight breeze ruffled her ruddy locks of hair, something that he had seen many a time. She was still beautiful to him, and while she had not come across as anything less than friendly since the day after the incident at the hotel, she still felt unapproachable to Jonah. It was immensely frustrating. "Well, try not to worry about that. Just do your best and we'll take care of the rest. It's not like they're going to throw you to the wolves, and besides. I'll watch your back."

He almost scowled at the thought. She had grown abruptly so friendly since they had arrived at the mansion that he simply could not help but to imagine she was doing it out of a sense of duty, and for some reason that infuriated him. "There's a few things I've been meaning to ask you," he muttered, almost experimentally.

She twisted her head around to regard him a little coolly with her bright green eyes, narrowing ever so slightly. "What do you mean?"

It was something of a confirmation for him, and he could not help but to sigh. "Just a couple of questions. About the training."

"Okay," she nodded, seeming to relax slightly. "Shoot."

He felt a little deflated, suddenly a little disinterested in asking anything at all, but there were one or two things he had been wondering about since they began. "Well, first of all, what are we doing here? I'd have thought that we'd be off somewhere a little more secluded and hidden. Middle of nowhere in Alaska, or something."

"Why's that?"

"I realize that we've got some privacy here and the lake is big, but it's also busy. I see boats out there all the time, there's a lot of people around." He paused to squint out at the lake, certain he could make out boats at that very moment. "Isn't it a little risky to be flying out over the lake all the time?"

For some reason she chuckled a little at the question. "Maybe a little, but … well that's actually kind of tricky. Something about the way the human mind works. If someone does happen to see us from a distance, their brains will pick the first thing that makes sense. Birds, kites, maybe even airplanes. People don't believe in dragons so they're not likely to see us for what we are. Probably for the best."

"What if someone wandered too close? It'd be pretty obvious then."

"You'll probably have to ask Carolus about that," she shrugged. "Some kind of magic ward or something he's placed over the area. Does something to their perception, or their memories. I'll be honest, it really kind of goes over my head, some of the things that the older dragons are capable of."

His next question was something of a natural segue to her response, but he regretted asking it as soon as it left his mouth. "How old are you, anyway?"

He had been rebuked the last time he had asked the question, and he expected much of the same. She had already shifted her gaze back over the lake. While she visibly stiffened at his question she did not turn to look at him, not betraying her true reaction, though when she spoke up again her voice was noticeably darker. "Isn't that a kind of personal question?"

"I'm sorry," he muttered.

Again she shrugged. "I'm sixty four, if you must know."

He tried to mollify her with a friendly suggestion. "Well, that's pretty young for a dragon then, isn't it?"

"Not nearly as young as you, whelp," Rebekah responded, but there was at least a little hint of a playful jab in her response.

It did ease him, if only slightly. "Well, anyway, that wasn't one of the questions I wanted to ask. There's another thing I've been wondering, something that's been bothering me quite a bit."

"What's that?"

"Where do our clothes go when we, well, turn into dragons? And how come I still have them on when I change back?"

That question, at least, seemed to lighten her own mood quite a bit as she let loose a soft laugh. "You know, that's a good question."

Jonah peered curiously in her direction. "You don't know, then?"

"Not really. Well, sort of." She laughed again, shaking her head, though she kept her gaze fixed at some point over the lake. "Problem is no one really knows how we take on different forms. We just do it. It's kind of like how we don't really understand the inner workings of the brain, we just know it works, you know? I guess no one has ever thought to question the clothes thing, or if they did, they haven't told me. Maybe you can ask Abe or Carolus."

If nothing else, she seemed to be feeling a little more at ease. Something about her laugh was disarming, and certainly put him at ease, enough for him to broach the more sensitive question that he had in mind. "Why are you here?"

She turned to look at him again, her brow furrowing a little. "What do you mean?"

"Here, out here, training with me. Why?"

The little way her brow furrowed deepened into something of a more outright scowl before she turned to look away once more. "Carolus asked me to do it. Closer to your age, closer to your size, and I suppose he figured that spending a few days with you on the road meant that I'd gotten to know you, or something."

"That doesn't answer my question," Jonah said, a little more directly. "I mean, why did you go along with it? You told me yourself that you could say no. That no one gives orders, right? So tell me why."

"Jonah." Her voice was quiet and soft but held a certain edge to it. "Don't."

He was undeterred. "I just want to know …"

Again Rebekah spoke up, quietly but with a bit more of an edge to her voice. "I mean it, Jonah. Please don't do this. Not again."

For a moment he hesitated. She had warmed up to him a little in the last few days, had started smiling and laughing again as if she had forgotten what had happened - or at least forgiven him for it. It might be better if he'd just leave it alone, but he couldn't help himself. "Please, I just want to know why, I mean, I have to know …"

"Really?" Her bright green eyes seemed to burn little holes right through him as she stared, her voice snapping, the look on her face trending dangerously close to rage. "Fine. If you really have to know, it's because I just can't tell Carolus no. Don't you understand anything about loyalty and commitment? I would do anything, anything for the good of the clan. Anything, you get it? Even put up with your sorry ass," she spat, stomping away in an angry huff.

Jonah felt his heart sink, and he really didn't know why. Why he was so attracted to her, why he had such a need to try and get back on her good graces - and why he was so terrible at it. A part of him longed to call after her, or even chase her down before she vanished from sight, but for the moment he felt too miserable to do anything other than watch her head back inside the house.

"What the hell am I even thinking," he muttered to himself, sprawling out on the deck, closing his eyes and simply letting himself go limp. It had been a week now since he had been dragged out of his comfortable, boring life, and for what? To learn he was a dragon, to somehow fall for a woman he barely knew, and to screw it up not once but twice. Now, he was on the verge of being sent off on some insane mission that, even after the four days of training, he knew nothing substantial about.

None of it made any sense at all. A part of him longed to wake up suddenly, finding it had all been a long and twisted dream. "Hell," he thought out loud, rolling to his back so that he could regard the stars winking into existence overhead as the day gave way to night. "I'd be better off if it were all some kind of mental episode. If I'm lucky I'll wake up in the loony bin."

He knew it wasn't the case, he knew that was not going to happen. He would wake up in the morning and have Carolus or Abe or someone else drag him out of his comfortable rest and into some new flavor of insanity, as if all that had preceded it were not enough.

There was no one to hear his complaints, no one to console him now. He wondered if anyone back home in Florida, his coworkers or one of his few friends, had bothered to notice he was missing. He wondered if the police were looking for him, now convinced that he was guilty of the murder of Sam. He wondered if any of it made any difference, at all.

The stars overhead went on twinkling, of course, oblivious to his plight. As the night deepened and the air took on a sharp chill, more and more of them winked into existence out of the darkness. Before long he could make out the wispy swath of the Milky Way cutting across the black curtain of the sky, the rapid flit of satellites as they zipped their way around the planet, and more stars than he could count in a lifetime.

It all went on, spinning and moving and unchanging. No matter how bad his life got, the world still turned as it always had and always would. Billions of other people with their billions of problems knew nothing of his own, and they, too, went along their way. The thought had a way of chilling him to the core as he stared out into the vastness of space; Jonah could not be sure whether it was comforting or damning.

"They're beautiful, aren't they?"

He hadn't heard anyone approach, so when he heard Carolus' scratchy voice at his side he nearly jumped. At some point he had slipped back into his more comfortable form, without even realizing it, and he pushed himself up to his feet rather abruptly. "Yes, they are," he muttered a little weakly. "Never seen anything like it."

"We're a ways away from the city here, so less light to drown them out. I do enjoy coming out here and just gazing at them as they float overhead, move on by, gazing into the vastness of space. Has a way of making one feel small, yet somehow important," the old man mused, his hands stuffed into the pockets of a coat that he was wearing. "The air is thinner here, too, so there's less of it to get in the way of the light."

Jonah didn't really know what Carolus wanted, or if the old man wanted anything at all, but something about his presence made him feel slightly uncomfortable. "I'm not in the way, am I?"

The old man turned to look at him, his watery blue eyes indistinct in the darkness, though a crooked smile could be made out on his face. "In the way? No, not at all. So long as you don't mind an old dragon reminiscing on the days when the skies were this dark just about anywhere you went on the planet. When we didn't understand things like the thickness of the atmosphere, when there were no satellites infringing on the stars."

"Mind if I ask you how old you are?"

"Not at all," Carolus said, still smiling crookedly. "912 years old. Born in the great city of Constantinople. The Crusaders had just captured Jerusalem and were crawling all over the empire at the time, the Syndicate along with them. It was a dangerous time and a dangerous place for a dragon."

Inwardly Jonah wondered why the old man had apparently decided it would be good to come and divulge all of this information to him, and again it made him feel slightly uncomfortable. He didn't know how to respond; he half wanted to retreated back to his quarters for the night, but felt compelled to remain. "Sounds like the Syndicate has been after you your whole life."

The old man laughed softly at that, hugging his arms around himself. "More true than you know, boy. To be sure, many of the clan can make the same claim, but after nearly a thousand years of moving, staying one step ahead of the Crusaders or the Inquisition or some other handy guise for the Syndicate to root us out … it's easy to get a little worn down."

"I don't think you came out here to talk about ancient history," Jonah muttered, shrugging his shoulders.

"Ah, you've a point there my boy. No, it is not the reason I came out here to speak to you, but there is something I've been meaning to talk to you about," he said, stepping a little closer, a bit too close for comfort. "Regarding your comments at the Convocation."

Jonah flinched backward involuntarily, shuffling. "Look, I'm sorry if I ruffled a few feathers … I guess I just don't really know the situation, don't really know what I am talking about."

Carolus waved a hand and shook his head. "Nonsense. You are new to the clan, new to the council, and you bring a fresh viewpoint that many of us would not have considered. You may have ruffled a few feathers, as you put it, but you also brought up a valid point. I must confess that your suggestion does speak to a certain part of my soul, Jonah."

"But it was like the complete opposite of your own suggestion," he said, still muttering a little.

"And so it is. I stand by my belief that our first and foremost priority should be the rescue of our elder. Whatever else happens, we cannot leave him at the mercy of the Syndicate, and we cannot sit and wait for them to make the first move.

"That said," the old man continued, shifting on his feet a bit, "some of us are indeed growing weary of the long and endless battle. As you pointed out the Syndicate has been nipping at my heels for the better part of a millennium. It has a way of wearing down one's resolve. Your suggestion speaks to that part of my soul, the part that desires rest, the part that desires peace."

Once again Jonah shrugged. "Yeah. I can see why it would."

Carolus seemed to be moving in a way to make sure Jonah did not get too far away, making him feel a little trapped in spite of the friendly look on the old man's face. "As I am sure you could guess, I am not the only one with such feelings. Ibrahim does not desire a confrontation. There are others too, no doubt, and whether or not they are a part of the council does not mean their voices should not be heard. In a way, your voice at Convocation is their voice, Jonah."

Cringing, Jonah shied away from the old man, turning his gaze outward toward the lake, a dark expanse beneath the night sky. "Yeah, sure. I'm not sure what you mean, though. I'm not sure what you're getting at."

"Well, then, allow me to get straight to my point. A time may come in the future when we are faced with a decision that may not appeal to the others, a time when we may have to choose between peace as you have suggested and continuing to fight in vain." The old man stepped closer, close enough that he could almost feel him looming behind him, setting his nerves on edge. "I need to know where you stand, should the issue come up again."

"I'm sorry," Jonah sputtered. "I'm not really sure I follow you … I'm not really into all of this political stuff."

"Please forgive me if I'm giving you the wrong impression," Carolus offered, taking a step back to give him a bit more breathing space. "I am not seeking to sway you in one way or another, Jonah. I simply desire to know, that when the time comes to make a decision, will your voice still be one seeking to make peace with the Syndicate?"

The space that he had been offered helped, but he was beginning to feel genuinely uncomfortable around the old man. He could not help but feel that he was still being manipulated, in a way, especially weird since he was essentially being asked if he would support his own suggestion again in the future. "Yeah, I suppose I would."

The old man nodded, seeming to shrink back further. "You must understand that to do so would mean to accept the rule of the Syndicate over us. It is the only way we could sue for peace, the only way they would accept our offer. You truly see this as a better way? That to accept their rule and 'work for them', as you put it, is better than our fight?"

"Look. I'm not really qualified to answer. I don't know much about you or them or your fight," he responded, a little sharply. He felt as if the question were some kind of trap, as if he were being tricked into providing an answer, as if the wrong answer might make things somehow … difficult for him. "To be totally honest, I'm not sure I really care. Maybe someday I will, but for now it's still all kind of strange and confusing to me. But I'll just put it the way I put it before. It sounds better than dying, to me."

Carolus only responded with a slow nod, not making a sound for several long seconds. Wrapping his arms around himself, he offered another crooked smile. "I believe I agree with that sentiment, Jonah. Perhaps in time we shall indeed be able to find a way to make peace with the Syndicate. To work with them, as you have suggested."

The old man seemed quite sincere in that sentiment, and Jonah could sense no guile in his reaction, but somehow he was still a bit put off by the whole encounter, and eager for it to end. "Yeah. Sounds good."

"I fear that time is not now, however. The decision to rescue our elder has been made, and it is one that I hope I can count on you to support, as well. Please, Jonah, I urge you to get some rest. We will be meeting tomorrow, at daybreak." With that, the old man turned to head back into the house, calling out behind him. "Goodnight."

He watched as the old man crossed the deck and made his way back into the house, the sound of the door latching shut behind him sharp in the clear night air. Jonah breathed a soft sigh of relief when he was alone. He couldn't decide why Carolus made him feel on edge like that; for the past few days the old man had been watching over him, albeit in dragon form, and had never seemed anything other than benign.

No, Jonah could not decide why the encounter made him feel so awkward and unsettled. His skin prickled as a chill ran down his spine, but it was not from the cold. Hugging his arms around himself, he waited for several minutes to pass before following suit, making his way into the mansion and toward his quarters for the night.

#

The meeting the next morning had been called with little fanfare and conducted in a straightforward manner. Jonah had been roused just before sunrise by Abe, allowed a few moments to get dressed and freshen himself up before he was escorted back into the same room they had met in previously. In addition to those who had been present at the Convocation there were four others seated around the table, dragons not on the council who had presumably been drafted into the effort.

Carolus briefly explained that, according to the intelligence that he had gathered, their elder was being held in a small Syndicate compound a few hundred miles to the south, tucked away among the mountains that straddled the California-Nevada border. The security there would be relatively light, the Syndicate relying more on the facility's remoteness and obscurity to guard their prisoner.

Still, as there was only a single road leading to it, they would have to make an aerial assault to avoid detection and ensure the elder's safety; it would have to be a night raid. The dragons would be transported by van to a secure site fifteen miles away and cover the rest of the trip on wing and under the cover of darkness.

The actual plan when they arrived was relatively simple. The guards outside of the compound would have to be dealt with swiftly, in a coordinated manner to ensure that the alarm was not sounded. This task was to fall to a team composed of the older, larger dragons while the rest held back. When signaled, the others would come in and enter the compound in three teams at three known access points.

Somehow Carolus or his operatives had delivered a sketch of the interior of the compound, indicating a few potential locations where the elder was being held. The three teams would sweep through each spot and regroup at a predetermined location, whichever group having encountered the elder would take him there. One group was to be led by Carolus himself, another by Abe, and the last by the Jenna, the woman who continued to scowl at him.

They would wrap it up by flying back to the vans, assisting the elder if he was in need of it. With any luck they would be back on their way to Tahoe before the Syndicate even knew something was wrong.

There was no discussion afterward. Carolus adjourned the meeting and the group filed out the door where a trio of plain white vans waited to whisk them away. Whether by intent or some circumstance, Jonah wound up in a van with no one he knew and only Jenna to continue scowling at him. Though she did not speak a word to him the entire trip, her disdain for him was palpable; he could not help but to wonder if he had violated some deeper taboo than simply disagreeing with her.

The route they traveled took them along the foot of the Sierra Nevada range, and for the next few hours Jonah got to watch out the window at the passing mountain peaks, giant granite sentinels to the west that loomed over them along the entire trip. Grand and majestic, he thought that he should be somehow more stricken with awe at the sight. Perhaps another time he would, in other circumstances.

For now, however, he could not afford to do more than glance at them a little morosely through the window of the van. Once more he was being dragged along, no longer actively in control of his destiny. Once more, he was being pulled toward something unknown, and he hated it.

The vans stopped briefly in a small town called Bishop to refuel before heading south along the highway, then turning east. It soon became clear to Jonah why they had left so early in the morning in spite of the night raid ahead of them : the vans soon turned off the highway and onto a dirt road, forced to slow down considerably. Though the mountains that the little road wound between were nowhere near as tall as the granite peaks to the west, their progress was nevertheless sluggish, passing through narrow valleys and over rather precarious looking switchbacks.

After what seemed like forever, the vans reached their apparent destination. The road straddled a high pass between mountain peaks, empty and deserted valleys stretching out in every direction. As Jonah made his way out of the van, following the others, he shaded his eyes against the light of the setting sun, looking for some sign of the compound they were to raid, some sign of civilization. He saw none.

Carolus led a sort of informal procession up a stubby little outcropping of rock, his hair whipping slightly in the breeze as he looked out into the valley ahead of him. Jonah followed, hanging toward the back, coming just close enough to hear the old man speak. "We all know our duties in this, my brothers and sisters. Do not forget that we do this for the sake of our clan and its future. While I expect our plan to unfold smoothly it is not without risk. Please, everyone, be on your guard and to not underestimate the foe. I would like to see every one of us here return safely to the mansion tonight."

Again the wind whipped at his hair, Jonah imagining that it was somehow snatching the old man's words away and spilling them down the side of the mountains, where they would be lost in the valley below; the whole landscape made him feel strangely alone, even among the crowd, as if he might be swallowed up by it, never to be seen again.

The old man paused a moment to look over the assembled group, nodding. "There is no need to hesitate. We fly." With that he turned, leaping from the edge of the outcropping, his body stretching and shifting into the shape of the massive gray dragon that had been hovering over him for so many days. Carolus' wings caught the wind easily, sailing off to the south, silhouetted against the dying light.

One by one the others followed suit, some jogging, some running along the length of the rock outcropping before leaping out, arms spread, each quietly assuming his or her true form, and before long there were almost a dozen dragons, wings outstretched, gliding and flapping their way over the mountains. The sight was absolutely surreal.

"Let's not stand around waiting here all night, I'd rather not get lost and have to find my way back on my own."

Jonah assumed he had been the last to hold back, and was startled to see Rebekah standing behind him, her hands on her hips. Blinking at her, he stammered, "Rebekah … you're still here?"

"Yeah. Guess who has been tasked with watching your ass to make sure you don't get into trouble."

He cringed again at the ire that was lining her voice. "Sorry," he muttered weakly.

She responded only by thrusting her finger outward in the direction of the departing dragons. "Look, you can apologize and grovel all you want later. I'm dead serious when I say that I don't want to get lost out here. Get your tail in motion before we lose sight of them or else."

Jonah would have to wait until later to feel sorry for himself, he supposed. She was right, after all; the other dragons were already beginning to fade into the distance, hard to see in the failing light, and he had no idea where they were supposed to be heading. Sucking down a deep breath, he threw himself at the edge of the outcropping, arms spread wide, and let the wind take him.

SIXTEEN

Fifteen miles passed with surprising speed, flying over the hills and mountains. It was a short, uneventful flight, no more than half an hour, with nothing other than the occasional fit of turbulence spilling over some of the taller peaks to shake him up a bit. Even in the waning dusk light, the sight of the landscape rising and falling beneath him, the rush of mountains covered in rock and brush was something of a breathtaking sight. Flying over a lake was fun, he supposed, but it lacked the impact that flitting around a towering mountain peak could make.

As quick as their flight was, night was even quicker in hastening itself along. Were it not for the half moon hanging overhead he might have lost sight of the other dragons altogether; as it was, he saw them more as inky shadows against the faintly lit night ahead of him, dancing over the hills and mountains, following along in a sort of grim procession.

The mountains abruptly gave way to a broad, open valley a few miles across. Tucked away at one end of the valley was a small lake positioned just right to catch the rays of the moon, briefly transforming into a gleaming argent mirror on the ground, the rest of the valley cast in the strange bluish light of the moon. Opposite the lake was the compound, their destination. Jonah leaned a bit to the left to head that way, aware of the other dragons now flapping in slow circles high above it.

Jonah could count four shadows dropping out of the air to swoop downward before they became too indistinct to see. The compound itself looked rather out of place in the remote valley, a large, sprawling structure that was a dark, blocky shape against the otherwise featureless earth. Though he could not see it in the dark, he knew that a fence surrounded the perimeter of the compound, a hint of something rectangular off to the side suggesting where the guard shack might be.

The outline of the building itself was given away by the series of lights on the exterior, but Jonah was too high to see what else might have been down there. Settling into a nice circular pattern, keeping a comfortable distance from the nearest dragons, he let his wings scoop up the air and keep him aloft, gliding lazily while he kept his eyes downward, peeled open in anticipation of the sign.

It didn't take long. No more than five minutes after they arrived, a brief plume of dragon fire rose up from one side of the building. Somehow seeing that signal made the whole thing suddenly seem a lot more real, and Jonah felt strangely energized. He had not been looking forward to this, but now that it was under way, now that his role in the mission was to be played, he could not help but to feel some small hint of excitement.

He was, after all, a part of something now. Something real, something important. Something dangerous.

One by one the dragons landed in the dirt next to the building, almost immediately shifting into human form. It was a technique he had not quite mastered, the art of landing, rearing up on his hind legs and shifting all at once. Done properly it was a fluid, flawless transition that could enable a dragon to land on his feet, running. Jonah, in spite of his best efforts, could not keep himself from tumbling forward, nearly falling on his face before hopping back up to his feet.

The others noticed, of course, but no one said anything, and the embarrassment he felt heating his cheeks quickly fled, replaced by the rush of adrenaline as he watched a series of silent hand signals being made. The group was being split into three, just as planned.

Carolus quickly singled out three dragons who came to his side, with Abe doing much the same. The rest, himself and Rebekah included, were called over to Jenna with a brief flick of her wrist. Any irritation she felt at him before would have no place here, as she did not so much as let one stray scowl fire off in his direction. Once the groups had been formed the three split apart, Jenna leading the way in a quick jog around the corner.

From here, the compound did not look so imposing but was still out of place in the otherwise empty valley floor. It was as tall as a three story building but lacked distinctive windows, giving it an appearance more akin to a warehouse than anything else. Lights placed every several feet kept the sides of the building illuminated, but there was no sign of any guards.

For a moment, Jonah found himself curious as to how they had been handled.

He wouldn't have much time to think about it, however. After another moment, Jenna came to an abrupt stop in front of a large door that looked to have been pried open forcibly, claw marks evident in the metal siding. Signaling everyone to gather around, she spoke up quietly, her voice harsh all the same. "Listen up, we've only got one shot at this. If anyone sounds the alarm, it might mean disaster for the elder. Let's make sure no alarms are sounded.

"Stay close to me. We're not sure what kind of resistance to expect here, but security should be light. We don't think they have any dragons working for them here, but there might be mages among the human guards."

Jonah felt a sudden sinking sensation in his stomach. No one had mentioned to him before that the Syndicate might be employing some kind of magic against them, and nothing in his training had brought that up, either. He had no idea what he should do in a situation like that. He wanted to protest, but a soft touch on his shoulder pulled him back a bit; it was Rebekah.

"Don't panic, Jonah. Just stay close. I've got your back."

He wanted to argue that panic was exactly what he was about to do. All of his his training had been focused on fighting in dragon form - aerial combat, flying maneuvers, how to land correctly. They were about to go into a building, on foot, where such training would be absolutely useless to him, and he hadn't been given any kind of weapon at all. He knew nothing at all about hand to hand combat.

Suddenly the entire thing seemed absolutely absurd, again. He had no place here, he had nothing to bring to the group, he added nothing to their effort. He wanted to protest, wanted to say that he should stay behind, but he could not. With a grim nod, Jenna darted her way into the building, and he followed behind as if he had no other choice.

If the compound resembled a warehouse on the outside it was for good reason. Once inside they found themselves very much inside of a warehouse, or at least a portion of the building that was one. With only the emergency exit lights on Jonah could not see very far or in much detail, but it was enough to make out several rows of boxed items on pallets, some larger items covered in sheets or tarps. He wondered what this place was normally used for, what on earth they could have been storing out here in the middle of nowhere.

Jenna kept the group of them close to one wall of the warehouse, skirting around the corner rather than crossing the wide open space in the middle. They moved in near silence but there was nothing to compete with them, nothing else moving. In fact, Jonah thought that the warehouse had a slightly musty, disused odor.

It didn't make much sense to him.

On the far side of the large open space they came across a stairway angling up to a door above, and this was where they were headed. Their footfalls seemed to echo more harshly on the steel grating of the steps, but there was no sign at all that they had been heard. One by one they filed their way up the stairs and through the door into a cramped hallway beyond.

The hall was even darker than the cavernous warehouse they had just left. Dim emergency lighting was just enough for Jonah to make out a few doors on the left before the hall opened up into a larger room beyond. As they made their way into that room, passing by a small bank of cubicles, he realized that the compound seemed to resemble some kind of office and warehouse building he might expect to see in an industrial complex.

Again he thought it seemed to be wholly out of place here, in the middle of the mountains, tucked away in a forgotten corner of the country miles from any city. It was making less and less sense as they went on.

"Something isn't right."

Though the sentiment mirrored his own the words did not come from Jonah's mouth. A man with whom he had not been acquainted, a muscular, balding man who looked to be in his mid forties, had been the one to whisper into the deathly silence around them.

They all paused, Jenna turning around to shoot the man a fairly harsh look, but remained where she was for the moment. "What do you mean?"

"I mean, something is not right about this. Where are the guards? If this is truly a Syndicate compound, where have they all gone? This place seems abandoned."

"Carolus told us it would be lightly defended," she offered, sounding less than confident in her own answer.

"Lightly defended?" The man spoke in an incredulous fashion, shaking his head. "Undefended seems more like it."

She seemed to consider his response for a moment, eyeballing the others one by one before glancing around again. "I must admit this is not what I had been made to expect. Something feels wrong but I don't know what it is. Still, I don't see that we have any choice but to continue onward."

It was Rebekah who voiced her concern, then. "And if they have been alerted, already? They could be expecting us. They could be lying in wait, it could be an ambush."

"Perhaps," Jenna said, wearing that perpetual scowl as she looked on ahead. "In that case we'll just have to stay on our guard. Keep an eye out behind us for anyone who might be following. Let's move."

The thought that they might be walking into some kind of ambush made Jonah's skin crawl, made the fear rise up in his throat anew. Once again he was keenly aware that the was without weapons and without any ability to fight in this state. Though he would never have admitted it, he was suddenly rather glad that Rebekah was the one pulling up the lead and not himself.

Their route through the compound took them through a few turns in the otherwise unremarkable halls of the building, each one as dark and abandoned feeling as the last. Twice they stopped to check the side rooms, each time finding the doors unlocked, the rooms either completely empty or filled with items that had not been disturbed in some time. Each time there was a growing sense of frustration in the group, and each time Jonah felt that things were going more and more awry, ever more certain that something was, indeed, very wrong.

Finally, as they rounded another corner, there was some change. Jenna brought them all to a halt with a silent gesture of her fist, then pointed at a door down the hall whose frame was illuminated from light within, more light than could be explained by simple emergency lighting. There was no sound from the room, and no sound in the hallway, but Jonah could feel his heart beginning to thump in his chest as they moved forward again, slowly and carefully, nearing the door.

Surrounding the door, two on each side, they waited and listened. Though there was no sound he could swear that his heart was beating loud enough to be heard, rattling in his chest, thumping as Jenna counted down from five silently, waving her hand in the air : five fingers, four, three, two, one …

Kicking the door open without otherwise making a sound, the woman twisted around and all but jumped in beyond the door, the balding man just behind her. Jonah gasped when he felt himself being shoved from behind, right through the doorway, waving his arms in front of him as he flailed in the sudden brightness of the light.

The room was empty, just as the others had been, with one important exception. In the center of the room, positioned exactly beneath a bare light bulb hanging from the ceiling, was a simple wooden chair. Tied to that chair was a man.

He was old, well past middle age and into the golden years of his life. Wispy strands of white hair fell at either side of his face, unkempt and a bit wild. The face that his hair framed was gaunt and sallow, tired looking skin stretched over his cheekbones in a way that made his eyes look sunken in, dark eyes glazed and unfocused as they flitted back and forth. Several days of stubble had grown over the creases and wrinkles of the man's cheeks, his nascent beard holding the dried remnants of drool running down one corner of his mouth, his cracked lips quivering around words that would not form themselves.

Jonah didn't have to be told to know that this man was the one they were looking for; he was the clan elder. Whatever clothing he might have normally worn had been stripped away and he had been dressed in a plain gray shift that hung loosely around his shoulders. The man looked positively emaciated, his arms little more than bony spindles held behind the chair with rope. He looked to have been starved, neglected, or worse.

After only a momentary hesitation, Jenna moved right up to the man's side, kneeling on the floor and reaching back to start untying his bonds.

"Elder! It's me, Jenna. We're here to rescue you," she whispered, freeing his hands before gripping him gently by the chin and twisting his head lightly to the side. "Can you hear me? Are you all right?"

He didn't respond. Jonah watched as the bald man turned back to the door, poking his head outside and keeping guard while Rebekah joined Jenna at the elder's side; Jonah could do little more than stand off to the side, out of the way, feeling rather useless.

Jenna looked the man over a little more critically, peering into his wandering eyes, leaning in to sniff at him. "He's been drugged."

"Will he be all right?" Rebekah assisted by pulling the cords away from the incapacitated elder, throwing them off to the side and then helping to hold him up, keep him from tumbling out of the chair.

"Eventually. Even now he fights the effects of the drug. He is trying to see, trying to become aware of what's going on around him, and he is trying to say something," Jenna said, not hesitating to give her own little interpretation of what was happening. "Either way we have to get him out of here, and fast. Ryan, come here and help me get him up and carry him. Jonah, get to the doorway and make sure that we don't have any surprise company. Move!"

Jonah jumped a little when he was spoken to, watching mutely while the bald man quickly moved toward the chair and began to help the elder out. Shaking away his confusion he stepped back out of the door and into the dark passage beyond, peering into the shadows, half expecting to see someone lurking there, waiting. He still had no real way of defending himself or the others, and didn't really know what was expected of him if company did show up.

He couldn't help but to imagine that small mountain of a man bounding his way down the hallway with murderous intent in his eyes, that same bull drake who had caused him so much grief. He shuddered with the thought.

The others came out of the room, the bald guy named Ryan helping to hold up the elder along with Jenna, followed by Rebekah who turned to shoot him a cautious glance. No one spoke, no one had to give the order to start making their escape with haste. A few more turns through the corridors brought them to a pair of double doors that had been thrown open wide, and to their surprise the rest of the dragons were gathered there, waiting for them. It was the rendezvous spot.

More than one gasp went up among those gathered there at the sight of the elder being carried in, a few stepping forward to help along. For a moment, no one seemed to be in a hurry to speak, only to offer a helping hand.

"We've got him," Jenna gasped a little breathlessly, her shoulders slumping as someone else relieved her of the burden. "Let's get going."

Abe, who was one of those who had rushed in to help, shook his head.

"Hold on. He looks pretty rough; we will have to make sure he is in any shape to fly before we can go any further."

She responded with a look of urgency and incredulity. "He is in no shape to stand, let alone fly. He will have to be carried. The sooner we get out of here the better, too, I don't want to get caught here now that we've finally got him!"

"I believe all of the Syndicate agents here have been taken care of already. Did you encounter any resistance?"

"Well, no," she began, frowning, before she was cut off again.

"Then we don't need to rush. Let's make sure that he is in any shape to be moved around, at all. He does look pretty rough, as I said."

Relenting, Jenna nodded as the elder was gently laid down on his back, surrounded by the others who stared down at him wide-eyed. The elderly man was still for a long moment, his lips chewing over unspoken words, his eyes unfocused and glancing around wildly. If Jonah did not know that he had been drugged, he would have thought the elder some insane old invalid who was on his way out.

Abe leaned in, resting a hand on the elder's chest while he listened to his breathing, looked into his eyes and then nodded slowly. "Yes. Yes, I have seen this before, I have seen this drug used. Distilled from dragonsbane. Causes the mind to close in on itself, shutting it out from the world around. Potent stuff but not long lasting; I think he's beginning to come to, already."

Almost everyone seemed to lean in a little closer at that revelation. At first there was no obvious change, unfocused eyes continuing to wander around aimlessly, but then Jonah realized they were beginning to move in a pattern, back and forth, pausing to look at the assembled, one by one. Trying to focus, leaving him looking a little panicked as he lie there, his mouth moving over and over.

"He's trying to say something," someone whispered. "Hush, everyone be quiet. He's trying to say something."

The old man did, indeed, look as if he were trying to speak. His tongue flicked out and wetted his lips, moving a little faster with each passing moment, closing his eyes as he drew in a breath and exhaled, repeating it again and finally managing to form a single word. "Fools."

Jonah hoped he was not the only one confused by the elder's response. Jenna, again kneeling at his side and stroking her fingers lightly through those wild, unkempt locks, whispered softly back down to him. "Elder, we can hear you, we hear you … what are you trying to tell us?"

"Fools," the man managed to whisper hoarsely once again, opening his eyes to look at them with increasing clarity. "What … you doing … here?"

"We've come to rescue you," she answered, offering him an encouraging smile.

He reacted by coughing violently, a spasm running over his frail looking body before he clutched at Jenna with a bony hand, pulling himself up into an unsteady seated position. "No," he muttered, shaking his head, glancing at them all one by one again, blinking away the confusion. "No, no ... it is not. Don't you know ... smell ... a trap ... when you see one?"

The mention of a trap made Jonah's blood run cold. Several of those gathered around looked up and around warily, a sense of nervousness about them at all, yet there was no immediate danger to be found. As far as any of them could tell, they were all there alone. "There are no more Syndicate here," Jenna said, quietly but firmly. "There's no trap. We're going to get you out of here."

"No," the old man repeated, shaking his head and waving his hand in front of his face, then pinching at the bridge of his nose in frustration, as if he were struggling to put together the words. "The Syndicate ... no. One of you, one of you ... a traitor."

If the mention of a trap had set some of them on edge, the accusation that there was a traitor in their midst made them all instantly uncomfortable. Jonah watched as everyone paused, taking a moment to look at one another, well aware of several pairs of eyes that glanced in his direction in a searching, scrutinizing manner. It all served to make him feel ever more uncomfortable, the urge to find the nearest exit and head off running rising in his chest.

"That's not possible," she retorted, a little uncertainly, but insisted on getting to her feet and pulling the trembling elder up with her, throwing an arm around his shoulders. "Come on, we've come this far. We've got to get out of here. Everyone. Let's get moving," she said, beginning to shuffle toward the other exit of the room, the one that led outside into the cool night air.

A shadow passed in front of the door, and then the shape of a man filled the doorway. "I'm sorry, but you won't be going anywhere," Carolus intoned, stepping out of the shadows and blocking the way.

The tension that suddenly gripped the group was palpable. For a long moment no one spoke, no one moved, but old Carolus and Jenna, standing in front of him, locked eyes in something of a battle of wills. It was the elder, however, who spoke up, his voice still trembling and feeble but gaining in coherence. "Carolus? You were the one behind this all along, then?"

"It's nothing personal, Nathan," he answered, watery blue eyes turning on the elder as he flashed a crooked smile. "I just couldn't think of any other way of getting the entire council together in one place to deliver to the Syndicate. I do hope they didn't mistreat you too badly."

"You old snake," Jenna hissed angrily. "I'll tear you from limb to limb for this."

Carolus frowned dismissively, raising one hand in the air. "Now now, I am hoping violence won't be necessary here," he said, as two bulky figures appeared at either side of him. Bull drakes, by the looks of them. Two more appeared as well at the door they had entered by, blocking both exits.

Several in the room assumed defensive postures, preparing for the worst, while Jenna continued to face off with old Carolus, all the while supporting the elder around the shoulders. "Four … five of you against twelve of us. You aren't that stupid, Carolus. Reconsider what you are doing. Get out of my way before I have to hurt you."

"I'm afraid that won't be happening, either." This time it was Abe who spoke up, a rueful smile on his face. "A ward has been placed on this room to prevent you from accessing your true forms, and there are more bull drakes and Syndicate mages standing at the ready. You are quite surrounded, outmatched, and outnumbered."

Jonah had felt strangely vindicated when Carolus outed himself as a traitor. While he had never imagined the man capable of something like this, he had instinctively distrusted him, and at least now he knew why. But when he watched Abe step over to stand at Carolus' side, he was dumbfounded.

Nor was he the only one to be caught off guard. With a disappointed sigh, the elder leaned heavily on Jenna and closed his eyes. "Et tu, Ibrahim?"

Abe continued to smile apologetically, shrugging. "I'm afraid I'm with Carl on this one. This war has gone on long enough and I see no other way of ending it. I had hoped to find another way, something less dramatic. I tried to offer you a solution but none of you would take it. I'm sorry, but it's out of my hands, now."

"Bastards," Jenna spat, the rage plainly visible on her face, echoing the sentiment that the rest of the assembled were feeling. Angry, betrayed, and suddenly helpless. "Don't go hiding behind these Syndicate lapdogs. Come in here and lets handle this like dragons, and I'll show you another way of ending this."

"This is precisely why I had to do this," Carolus said with a dour frown. "With attitudes like yours, peace with the Syndicate is something that can never come about. You have forced my hand in this, Jenna, you and those like you."

"Liar. What have they promised you, Carolus? More money? Agree to put you in some position of power?"

"Please." This time it was the elder who spoke, his face suddenly tired, his voice exhausted. "Please. I can not bear to see brothers and sisters at each others' throats this way. It pains me to witness the downfall of the clan, come at the hand of our own," the old man said, shaking his head. "Carolus. You have known me since you were a whelp. Your lust for power is no secret to me, but this? You are capable of selling your family for this?

"And you, Ibrahim. For centuries you have been my most trusted friend and most reliable confidant. You were more than a brother to me, you were more than a clanmate. You were my best friend. How could you do this to me, do this to the rest of us?"

Abe looked genuinely remorseful but merely shrugged. "I'm sorry, Nate. I just don't see any other way."

"Nevertheless," the old man continued, shaking his head sadly. "It is by your hand that we are delivered to our destruction. Please, whatever fate you have in mind for us, make it swift. I have suffered much at the hands of the Syndicate; honor me at least in promising that the rest of my clan will be spared such injustice.

"The rest of you," the elder said, turning his eyes over the others. "I beg of you to surrender peacefully. I do not wish to see any bloodshed tonight."

Jenna seethed, and spoke for the rest of the crowd. "I'm sorry, elder, but how can we do that ... we must fight as we always have ..."

"Please. Honor a dying old dragon's wish. Let us meet our fates with our heads held high and our dignity intact. Let it not be said that bloodlust brought about the end of our kind."

A sickening hush fell over the group, their spirits seeming to be crushed by the quiet one by one, the fires in their eyes going out. The gravity of the situation had caught up with them, the futility of their escape becoming evident; Jonah, who had begun to feel some fire of his own felt it die out just as quickly. They would surrender.

Carolus gestured with his hand again, and the bull drakes began to step their way into the room, looming over each of them in impassive yet threatening poses. "Take them to the holding areas. We will begin dealing with them tomorrow," the old man muttered rather impassively, watching as the big men began to escort the defeated dragons away.

Just as one of them was reaching for Jonah, the old man called out again. "Not that one. Jonah, you come along with me."

Instantly he felt eyes burning on him, accusatory, hateful stares coming from the dragons who were being led out. Jenna, the woman who always seemed to scowl at him, now regarded him with something more akin to open hatred. The elder, who he had never before met, regarded him with sad, watery eyes. Rebekah stared at him with unmitigated contempt, her green eyes boring holes right through him.

"I'm not a part of this," he croaked in a lame protest.

"Nonsense." Carolus smiled at him and beckoned, a gesture that made him feel sick to his stomach. "You aren't like them, Jonah. Come along with me."

He wanted to protest again, wanted to run away, just wanted to go home. The hatred and animosity that the others were showing for him burned him deep to the core, and he wanted to yell after them that he had had nothing to do with it; he'd just been dragged along unwilling the whole time.

None of them turned to look at him anymore. They all marched out of the room, heads hung low, leaving him alone with the sinking feeling in the pit of his stomach as Carolus reached out and rested a hand on his shoulder.

Jonah had never felt more alone, more wretched, or more abandoned in his life than he did at that moment.

SEVENTEEN

"I suppose you're expecting some kind of explanation, aren't you."

Jonah had watched as the members of the clan had been marched away one by one to parts unknown. The whole time he had just stood by with a lame sort of expression, unable to do anything to help, unable to so much as meet their gazes. There didn't seem to be any way to convince them that he had no part in the deception; standing there next to Carolus had been enough of an indictment for them.

The old man had led him away from that room and back into the building, accompanied by two of the bull drakes. Neither of them had been the one who had been hunting him but the similarities were enough to set him on edge. He'd half expected some further deception, half expected that one of them would pluck him up off the ground at any moment, snap his neck as well, finish the job that their compatriot had failed.

Carolus had led him down a flight of stairs and into a section of the compound that bore more resemblance to a modern office than anything else. Well lit, well appointed, clean and in obvious use. Stepping into a side room with leather couches on either side, the old man had settled in comfortably, offering him a drink.

He had declined, and had remained silent while Carolus poured himself a glass of whiskey Even when the old man mentioned expecting an explanation - which, he in fact, found that he did not care to hear - he offered no response other than to scowl quietly. While he was not especially fond of most of those in the clan who had been dragged away, he did not have any interest in playing part in their betrayal.

After waiting for a moment the old man shrugged, sipping at his drink. "It's for the good of the clan, after all. Of course none of them will see it that way, not at first. But you understand where I am coming from, don't you Jonah? How did you put it? Better to work for them than run and hide all of the time? I came to that same conclusion myself. Years ago.

"The others? Too damned idealistic to see past their own pride. Give them a few more centuries of it - a millennium of running and hiding will change the way one sees the world. But by then it would be too late. The Syndicate would have wiped them out. This was the only way. I'm certain you understand."

Until that night, Jonah had not felt any real connection, any real loyalty to the clan. He supposed that hadn't really changed yet, as most of those who had been captured were still effectively strangers to him, many of whom he did not even know by name. Still, he had finally come to recognize the fact that they were like him, and he like them. They did, at least, share a common bond.

Bonds notwithstanding, he could not help but to feel that they had been wronged when they were betrayed by Abe and Carolus. "You're just trying to justify your actions."

"Am I, Jonah?" The old man shifted in his seat, smiling crookedly in that way that made his skin crawl. "Come now, you haven't been among them so long as to be blinded by their fanatical dedication to the cause. Truer words were not spoken when you dared loose your tongue and suggest we work with the Syndicate. And now they will. Peace will be had."

"What do you want with me?" Jonah folded his arms over his chest, impatient.

Carolus chuckled a little. "Straight to the point. Very well. I need your help, Jonah."

Scowling at the old man, he shook his head. "I don't see any reason to help you. Besides, it looks like you've won this battle, what could you possibly need me for?"

"Winning a battle does not mean the war is over," he prattled. "There are still others to be convinced. Members of the clan who are not a part of the council, who were not here tonight. Without the council they will be leaderless and directionless, and will probably lash out in irrational strikes against the Syndicate. They will be their own undoing.

"They need leadership. Ibrahim and myself are ... well, tainted. They will believe we have done this for our own selfish reasons, and rebel against us. But you? The newest member of the council, young and headstrong. You would be better suited to convince them of their follies, convince them that they must lay down their anger and come into a peaceful accord with the Syndicate."

Jonah frowned. "You're trying to tell me that there's nothing in this for you, that you're doing it all out of the goodness of your heart?"

Carolus laughed again, sipping from his glass. "Please. I don't wish to be known as a liar. No, I will be rewarded for my service to the Syndicate.

When the dust clears from this, when we have convinced the others of the need for peace, the mantle of leadership will fall to me. I will be the elder of a new clan, a stronger clan, a clan working in tandem with the Syndicate to advance our common goals."

"So it's all about the power, then."

"Don't mistake my motives, Jonah." Carolus leaned back, smoothing the hair back over his brow. "For many years I have been forced to watch as that fool Nathan continued to lead the clan down the same decaying path that his predecessors trod. A path of constant war and loss. Have I yearned for the day when I would become elder and lead the clan in a new direction? Yes. Do I have a selfish desire for power? Yes. But you must see that it is for the good of the clan."

There was an odd, insidious logic to the statement. Jonah could not argue against the fact that the fighting seemed to be taking its toll on the clan, from all he had heard, yet at the same time he could not find himself agreeing with the old man's methods. "And Abe?"

"Ibrahim? My friend has no interest in power or ruling the clan. His day will come, to be sure. He is many decades my junior and will inherit my position when my time is over." Carolus paused to put his drink off to the side. "But Ibrahim is interested only in pursuing his love for wealth and women. The end of this conflict will mean he can devote more time indulging in his vices."

"And the others? Who support the elder?"

Carolus sighed a little heavily at the question. "They will be made to cooperate in one way or another. I pray that they will come around before it is too late, but the situation is fairly grim. That fool Nathan will not change his mind, and he likely will not survive the Syndicate's methods of convincing. As for the others? I am not sure how they will turn out."

Jonah scowled darkly. "Methods?"

"You've seen the bull drakes. Years ago they were members of an independent clan. The Syndicate applied some kind of magic to sway them, force them to fight for their cause, abandon their identity as a clan. It has been centuries and I do not know that the current Syndicate mages are well practiced in the art. The results may be ... less than satisfactory."

"And you are okay with this?" He glowered down at the old man, incredulously. "You are willing to sit by while they experiment on your friends? Look, I know you might disagree with them but ... you're ok with putting them through this?"

Carolus responded with a scowl of his own, his voice taking on a slightly darker edge to it. "Do not think me some kind of monster, Jonah. As I have said there is no other choice. It is either this or allow them to die fighting, one by one, until they are all gone, until the clan is wholly destroyed. That is why I am asking for your assistance in this. I thought I could count on you, I thought you would understand. Do you, Jonah? Can I count you among my allies?"

There was an inherent danger in the question, and Jonah could feel his skin beginning to crawl once more. Suddenly he felt like was being observed once again, the old man's watery blue eyes fixing on him with a calculating stare. It was as if he were suddenly on the edge of a precipice; one false move and he might find himself in deep trouble. One false move and it might be his last.

He was not ready to commit to Carolus and his cause, but could, at the very least, understand what the old man was saying. He didn't see the sense in wasting time and energy on a pointless fight, dying over an old and rotting principle. Yet, as the thought crossed his mind, he also realized that he did not see the value in forcing peace upon those who did not want it.

"I'm still not sure how I can help. I don't think they trust me, anymore," he finally answered, in a slow, measured voice.

For a long moment, Carolus seemed to hesitate, as if trying to make a decision. For that long moment, Jonah worried that the old man might not believe him, might not give him a chance, after all. Finally, however, he nodded, reaching over for his drink again. "No, I suppose they will not. Not at first, no. We'll just have to try and be more convincing, won't we?"

"I don't follow," he responded, confused.

"There's no need to. The others are being held here in the compound overnight and it will not be until tomorrow that they are transported to a more secure facility. We don't anticipate any other interruptions, so tonight, at least, we can all relax. Our friends here will show you to a room where you can get some rest. Tomorrow I believe Ibrahim will have a good discussion with you on how to be more persuasive," the old man said, smiling crookedly, waving a hand and summoning one of the big bull drakes to escort him away for the night.

#

It was morning still when he arrived at the city, the heat of the desert having not yet reached its full fury. The sun at his back was still pleasant, warming rather than burning, and it cast the city in sharp contrasting shadows, making it stand out from the otherwise dull scenery around it, a vibrant oasis of sorts that should have looked welcoming and vibrant after his long trek across the countryside.

But something was different, he realized, something going on within the city itself. From his vantage point on a small hillock approaching the city he could see more movement among the streets than might normally be expected, in spite of the approaching holiday. Something about it felt ominous, and it was with some anxiety that he picked up his pace and made his way toward the vibrantly colored buildings.

The streets were, indeed, rather teeming with people. As he tried to make his way toward his home on the opposite side of the city he found himself increasingly forced to push his way through the crowd, ever thickening as he went, until he found that he was no longer able to make his way. The crowd itself had been pushed to the side, forcing him up against the facade of a shop while he heard distant shouts demanding the gathered to move to the side. There was some kind of procession making its way down the street, he realized, and as a result he was being forced to wait.

It was difficult to see what was going on from where he was, pinned to the back of the crowd, but the clamor around him began to die off as a more solemn atmosphere fell over the assembled. The sound of a bell tolling began to approach, rising up above the din and was finally the only sound he heard as those around him fell silent. Trying to peer in the direction of the sound, he finally was able to see something moving through the mass of people, bobbing up and down as it moved between them : a cross, shrouded in black cloth, held aloft.

The sense of trepidation he was feeling in his gut intensified, and he craned his neck to try and get a better look. When he realized he had no hope of seeing the procession from where he was, he forcibly pushed his way through the people, eliciting some minor but irritated protests as he went, until finally he was close enough to see the procession go by.

He caught sight of a number of clergy and other officials making their way through the streets but it was those who followed that commanded his attention. Clad in yellow sanbenitos decorated with various symbols of evil and malice, bearing the names of their crimes written on the cloth, labeled unmistakably "herege condenado" : convicted heretic.

They passed toward the city's plaza, one by one, eyes downcast and defeated. It was the auto de fe, the elaborate trial orchestrated by the Inquisition. The very sight of it made his stomach turn.

At the last were those convicted of the most serious crimes, accompanied by a pair of friars each, heads hung low. These were the ones condemned to be taken to the quemadero outside the city and be burned at the stake. This he could not watch, and with a heavy heart he shook his head and turned away.

Just as he glanced away, however, his eyes caught hold of one particular sanbenito decorated rather ostentatiously in demonic looking dragon figures. As the condemned passed he hazarded a glance upward, his eyes happened upon the name, Estefania de Ribadeneira. A glance up at the flowing black hair that was tied behind her head was enough to make his heart sink.

His beloved wife, being dragged away to die.

Without so much as a second thought he leaped over the barricade that had been erected to hold back the crowd and bolted in her direction. "Estefania! Estefania!" The friars at her side turned to look at him with a startled expression and the crowd around him gasped in surprise but he paid them no heed.

She turned around to look at him with those midnight black, almond shape eyes that he knew only too well, reddened with tears and wide with surprised. "Alvaro, no!"

The sound of hooves clopping against the ground filled his ears but he paid them no heed. Long before he could reach his wife something hard and heavy smashed into the side of his skull and sent him crashing to the ground, the world spinning around him wildly. More screams sounded around him before an angry looking official loomed over him, sneering. "What are you thinking, interrupting the procession?"

Groggy, dizzy from being hit like that, he merely shook his head and groaned. "Estefania … Estefania, you can't take her … she is innocent!"

"That is not for you to decide. It is between her and God, now."

"No," he moaned, pulling himself up to a seated position before he was cuffed soundly against the head again, sending him sprawling. "No … you can't take her …" As he rolled on the ground he could see her being led away down the road toward the plaza, her back turned to him again, her body heaving as if she were sobbing.

The official who had smacked him down gave him a kick in the ribs, as well. "Unless you have something to confess as well, I would urge you to stay out of the way." With that the official got back on his horse, rejoining the procession and blocking his view of Estefania.

Sobbing, he pulled himself back up to sitting, some of the crowd having dragged him back to the side so the procession could pass. "No," he sobbed, reaching in the direction he had last seen her. "No …"

"Hey, Jonah. You awake in here?"

Abe's voice tore him rather roughly from the dream. For a brief moment he found himself lying on his back in an uncomfortable cot, staring up at the ceiling and wondering what had just happened until the realization that he'd been experiencing another one of the strange dreams - visions - once again. A sick feeling at what he had witnessed still stuck in the pit of his stomach, and he was in no mood to deal with the man. Turning his head, he frowned openly at his visitor, turning his eyes back upward toward the ceiling. "No."

Abe chuckled heartily in spite of the response that he got. "Well, come on then. Sleepwalk with me."

He didn't really see much point in arguing or fighting, so he pulled himself up out of the cot with a quiet grunt and followed as Abe led him out of the compound, passing by several of those big, silent guards, the ones that gave him chills in spite of the fact that they no longer seemed interested in him. His guide seemed to respect the fact that he was not feeling chatty in that morning, speaking only to let him know they were heading outside, pushing the doors open at the end of a hall and stepping out into the brilliant morning light.

The valley hidden away between the mountains was just as quiet as it was during the day as it had been the night before. Stretching out before him for the better part of a mile, the valley floor was flat and featureless, dotted with scrub and some kind of grass, surrounded by rocky hills that surrounded them. In a way it was like a whole other line of defense for the compound, keeping the rest of the world out.

It was also eerily reminiscent of some of the desert landscape he had seen in the vision, summoning some of the images anew. Closing his eyes and shaking his head, he tried to will them away.

Abe spoke up again, stuffing his hands in his pockets as he strode away from the building and apparently toward no specific destination. "So. You decided to work with Carl after all, then? Smart man."

"Like I had a choice," he protested, all but growling under his breath.

"Of course you had a choice," the bigger man said with a soft chuckle, pulling a pair of sunglasses out of his pocket and pushing them onto his face. Even here he wore a sharp double breasted suit, his black leather shoes kicking up little plumes of dust that made him look very out of place. "You always have a choice."

Jonah grunted quietly again and shrugged. "Well, it was that or get thrown down into the dungeon with the others."

"It was still your choice."

Staring at the bald man as he strode a few steps away before stopping, he shook his head. "What are you getting at?"

"Just a little friendly chit-chat," Abe said, beckoning him to continue, following a slightly worn path in the dirt that cut between some of the knee-high scrub brushes. "You could have picked that option. Gone to your doom with them, retained a little sense of pride, or something like that. But you didn't."

"Sorry. I'm not in the mood to die," Jonah answered a little dryly, confused and somewhat suspicious at the strange course of the discussion. It almost felt like Abe, a traitor himself, was admonishing him for choosing to save his own hide.

Not that the larger man seemed to be passing any judgment "Neither am I," he replied, flashing a big, toothy smile back over his shoulder. "So it's not like you picked to go along with our little plot out of principle. Just out of self preservation. I can respect that."

Once again, Jonah felt like he was being judged, put on some kind of impromptu trial. Once again he felt like he was standing on the edge of two fates, and whatever he said here would determine which path he would go down. Much to his irritation, Abe had stopped at a spot where the path split into two, illustrating his predicament. "I still don't know what you're getting at. You make it sound like there was no right choice to make."

"You could have embraced Carl's plan wholeheartedly. None of this cowardly halfway stuff."

It was more than he could take. "You know what," he spat out, balling his hands up in fists and shaking one of them at his somewhat surprised companion. "I'm sick and tired of getting pushed into these kinds of things. You want to trick me into saying something that gets me thrown into the basement? Fine, call your thugs and have them take me away now. Let's just skip the trick questions and the traps."

Abe pulled his sunglasses down some to look at him over the frames, his expression growing dead serious. "You mean that, Jonah?"

"I don't care. I just don't really care anymore," he said, nearly exploding. "What does it really matter, anyway? You all have it out for me, anyway, so let's just get it over with. I'm tired of the games."

Pushing the shades back up his nose to cover his eyes, the big guy grinned once more. "Well. You've got it half right, kid."

In his agitated state he was only confused by Abe's reaction. Jonah was half tempted to simply let loose with the anger that was building up and assail the man standing in front of him, in spite of knowing that he wouldn't stand a chance. Not this way, not as a dragon, not at all. He would be outmatched, taken down in a heartbeat.

But at least it would feel good.

Still, the cooler half of him prevailed, keeping his anger at bay for the moment. "What do you mean by that?"

"Someone's got it out for you, Jonah, that much is for sure. But it ain't me. It's not even ol' Carl, really. It's the Syndicate. They've got it out for all of us. You, Carl, me, the rest of the clan. They don't really care a lick for a single one of us. Yesterday was only the first stage of the trap."

"I don't get it," he practically hissed, furrowing his brow. Abe was not making any sense.

Stuffing his hands in his pockets and resuming his slow walk, Abe cleared his throat. "Carl is so eager for this all to go off right that he can't really see it for what it is, but it's pretty obvious when you think about it. Step one, corrupt someone influential in the clan. Step two, kidnap the elder and set a trap for the whole council, all in one fell swoop. Step three," he said, pausing, shaking his head with a sardonic chuckle. "Set a trap for the rest of the clan. Bam, finish them all off."

"Wait," Jonah interjected as he tried to wrap his mind around what the big man was saying, new layers of intrigue and confusion wrapping themselves around the whole situation and serving only to muddle his thinking. "What are you saying? Carl wants to use me to lure in the rest of the clan, so they can be … whatever is being done to the others?"

"Not Carl. The Syndicate. Carl sees you as a pawn in his scheme, but in their scheme he is every bit as much the pawn. As soon as they get their hands on what they want, they'll take him down, too."

"Why are you telling me this? Hell, if you have this all figured out … why are you working for them?"

Once again Abe laughed softly. "Working for them? Well, I suppose I am, aren't I? You could call me something of a double agent, then."

Jonah squinted at him dubiously. "You're not making this all up to make me look foolish? To find some reason to get rid of me, get me out of the way?"

"If I wanted you outta the way, kid, I'd have you locked up by now. No, I don't want you out of the way. I need your help."

He leaned his head back at that and breathed out a low sigh. "You need my help."

"That seem so strange?"

"No." He shook his head a little bit and closed his eyes. "It's just, if I hear that again … I don't know. Today has been such a strange day. A strange weekend. Look, this whole last week has been … I don't know. To be honest I'm just not really sure what's real anymore, if I'm imagining the whole damned thing or what."

Abe nodded a little more soberly at that. "I know a lot has happened to you, kid. If it were up to me I wouldn't be so quick to try and turn your life upside down, but I don't really have a choice. There isn't much time."

"Time?"

"Yeah. In just a few hours from now the Syndicate will have transport here to start taking the others to a more secure facility. I guarantee you that once they're loaded up and taken away we'll never see them again - at least not in the way that we remember them." The big man shifted his posture a little bit, glancing back in the direction of the compound. "If we're going to act it has to be right away."

Jonah shook his head a little. "Ok, let me see if I can get this all straight. Carolus has this big plot to lure us all here so that the Syndicate can scoop us up and carry us away. Somehow you've gotten in on this but you're actually playing the part of a double agent, and now you want me to do something about it?"

Abe flashed another one of his big, toothy grins. "That's about the long and short of it, yes."

"God." He held his hands behind his head, locking his fingers together and started to pace back and forth between a couple of the scrub bushes, kicking up little clouds of dust as he went. "I'm still trapped, aren't I? I mean, if I go along with you I'm risking my neck. I get dragged along with the others and I'm done for. I decide not to, go and rat you out and all is well until the Syndicate finishes what they're doing and hauls us all away. That's all assuming you're telling me the truth …"

"God's honest truth," he said, raising his right arm to the square as he chuckled. "Look, kid. I realize there's not a whole lot I can do to convince you that I'm not making it up, so I'm just going to play the part of a bad guy and manipulate you into doing what I want."

Jonah blinked in confusion. "Manipulate me?"

Abe stepped over to loom large in front of Jonah, resting a meaty hand on his shoulder. "Don't make this about you and me, kid. Selfish motives can only take you so far. What really counts is when you do something for someone that you care about. Me, I'm doing it for the clan. I'll stick my neck out all day long. But you? There's a young lady locked up in that building that I happen to know you care about. Do nothing and she's going to be dragged off in a few hours to have her brain scrambled, or worse."

Jonah blushed hotly, his gaze heading downward to his feet and looking away. "That's ridiculous. I don't know what you are talking about …"

"Nonsense." The grip on his shoulder tightened a little, just shy of painful. "I don't blame you, kid. A lot of fire in that one, a lot of spunk. If I were a little younger … a few hundred years, maybe … but she's more in your league, kid. Don't let her go. Don't let them take her. Do something about it."

"She can't stand me," he muttered beneath his breath, still looking down at the ground. He could remember the way she smiled from time to time, the sound of her laugh and how infectious it was to him. Something about her drew him in; in only a week's time he had fallen completely head over heels for her, it was true.

It was obvious that she did not return the sentiment. He could also remember the way she scowled at him, the angry look she had given him, and the unmitigated fury that last time he had seen her eyes. He shook his head and grunted.

"Doesn't matter." Abe clapped him lightly on the shoulder and pulled his hand back away, pausing a moment before speaking again. "That's not what it's all about, Jonah. You do things for people because you care about them, not for any other reason. I'll say it again. Don't let her go. Help."

Jonah clenched his hands into tight fists, tight enough for his knuckles to start going white. He wanted to argue but found that he could not. He had no response other than to breathe a long, low sigh. "What does it matter? There's nothing I can do."

The sound of Abe's deep laughter was enough to get him to look up, the bald man beaming a broad smile. "I've got that all taken care of, kid. All I need to know is that I can count on you. Will you help me? Help her? Help all of us?"

"Just tell me what to do," he muttered a little hesitantly, still refusing to meet the man's gaze.

"Your job will be easy enough, Jonah. All you've got to do is get locked up with the others."

That was enough to get Jonah to look up and meet him in the eyes - or, at least, the impenetrable black lenses of his sunglasses. "Wait, what?"

One again Abe laughed. "Ok, let me explain. Right now they are being held together in a single large room. Just like the room where you were captured, the room has a ward that has been placed on it to keep them from taking on their dragon forms. If that ward were to come down and they were able to change then they would have a real, fighting chance to escape."

Jonah frowned skeptically. "So you want me to somehow take down this ward? I don't know anything about it."

"I got that one kid. The problem is that even if I take down the ward, there's no way for the others to know it's happened. It's going to take a coordinated effort; I'm going to have to take care of that at the same time that you bring word to the others, and let them know that it's time to make a break for it."

"Right. And just how do you propose I'm supposed to get down there?"

Once again the bald man flashed a toothy grin and a soft chuckle. "That's also easy. I'm going to escort you down there myself. Pretty easy when you've decided to rebel against Carl and I. We don't want you running around up here causing trouble."

Shaking his head, Jonah sighed. "Do you realize how cliché that is? Smuggling someone in as a fake prisoner?"

"Cliché, but it doesn't matter. Will you do it?"

"I don't know. I don't see how it's supposed to work." Jonah turned his gaze to look back at the building behind him, wondering exactly where it was that the others were being held, wondering what they were doing at that very moment. "It's not like they're going to believe me, anyway. Not now. Not after seeing the two of you get all buddy buddy with me. As far as they know we're both traitors, too."

Abe shrugged slightly, and started to make his way back toward the compound. "That part will be up to you, kid. Beg, cajole, do whatever it takes to get them to cooperate. It'll be their only way out, and once you're committed to this thing, the only way for you to make your escape, too."

The thought briefly occurred to him that he might try to escape while Abe was turned away, walking toward the building. If he got a running start, perhaps he could transform and fly away to safety. They'd give chase, of that he was sure, but he might be able to get far enough away, enough of a lead that he could hunker down and hide until the whole thing blew over.

As quickly as it came to his mind it fled. Sighing again, he started to follow behind. "Anything else I should know about this?"

"Like I said, your job will be pretty simple," Abe called out behind him. "Once you are in, give me ten minutes. I'll hold the ward down as long as I can, but it won't take long for them to catch on to what I'm doing. At that point I've got to make a run for it, myself, so you've got maybe fifteen minutes, tops."

"What happens after we make our break for it?"

The big man faltered in his step a moment and then chuckled. "Afraid I don't know the answer to that one. We'll have to play that one by ear, but, there is one thing I can say for certain. Once you guys break out of that room all hell is going to break loose. The Syndicate will unleash everything that they have at their disposal. You will have one goal, and one goal alone at that point : make it out alive."

A powerful chill ran down Jonah's spine as he nodded. "That it?"

"That's it. Just do me a favor and make it out of there safe and sound. I'll do my best, too. Let the others know that anyone else who makes it out alive, we will regroup to the north and decide what to do from there."

Before Jonah had a chance to respond, the big man turned around and snatched him by the shoulder with surprising speed and strength, pulling him out in front in a rough motion. "You won't be escaping now, whelp. I thought we could trust you, but you've proven me wrong," he said, rather loudly.

The ruse had begun, and so suddenly that it was only too easy for Jonah to feign surprise and fright. The nearest door to the compound swung open, a thick necked guard peering out severely.

Abe shoved him against the bull drake roughly, hard enough to knock the breath from him as a meaty, powerful arm wrapped around him and held tight. "Take him. Lock him up with the others. I don't want to see this rat's face again," he said, twisting his face into a scowl before turning on his heel and disappearing into the doorway.

The point of no return had already come and gone. Without hesitation the bull drake dragged him into the building, forcing him along one of the corridors. Jonah struggled in vain to escape the man's grasp, his hands like vises clamping down on his arms, twisting them back at a painful angle that made him cringe and gasp.

No words were spoken when they arrived in front of another doorway, guarded by two of the massive men. One of them unlocked the door, pulling it open, and he was shoved in and to the floor while the door slammed shut behind him.

Still gasping and reeling from being thrown around, Jonah rolled onto his back coughing and shuddering, shaking the dizziness from his eyes. When he was finally able to focus on his surroundings he felt his blood suddenly run cold. Never before had he seen so many glances of raw hatred cast at him all at once.

"This isn't going to be easy," he whispered to himself, working up the strength to push himself back to his feet.

EIGHTEEN

"What the hell are you doing here?"

He wasn't sure who had spoken, but Jonah realized it didn't matter who it was. All of the eyes upon him were livid, steps away from something like murderous, he thought to himself. Shivering, he hugged his arms around his chest and peered around, going from one angry face to the other. "I'm here to help."

"You've helped enough for one lifetime, don't you think?" It was Rebekah who spoke up this time, her green eyes burning with rage.

"No. Yes. I mean," he cringed, fumbling over his words. "Look, it's not like what you think. Abe sent me."

This time it was Jenna, who had always openly despised him, who shot him the fiery, hateful glance before speaking up with a voice every bit as vitriolic as her stare. "One traitor sends another? To what end, to taunt us? You've truly done enough around here, whelp. Go back to your murderous conspiracies. We will have nothing to do with you."

The force of her words and her gaze were enough to make him stammer, and he had to look away to get a hold of himself. There was no safe direction to look, however; no matter where he turned, there was hatred and anger. "No, you don't understand. He's on your side, we're on your side! We're trying to save you!"

"By turning us over to the Syndicate? Please. We already know what your idea of peace and prosperity is. Go, leave us alone," she hissed dangerously.

Jonah felt like he was on some kind of timeline. He didn't have a watch on and there was no need for a clock inside the room, and he felt a sense of panic beginning to rise up in his chest. "Listen! There isn't much time. Ten minutes, he said ten minutes and then the ward would be down, we'd have a chance to escape …"

He was only just able to speak in something approaching coherence, but the others were quickly losing interest. Frustrated, irritated if not disgusted, they began to turn their backs on him one by one, and each time he felt a little more panicked. "Please! You don't understand … the Syndicate is coming for you! They'll be here in a few hours. He told me! They're going to take you away, do something to you … brainwash you … I don't know. But you can't stay here."

"You should be happy," Jenna answered him, looking back over her shoulder at him. "That's just what you wanted for us from the beginning."

"No, it isn't. It isn't at all. Look, I didn't understand what was going on. To be honest I still am not really sure what is going on, I'm not sure I get all this Syndicate stuff anyway. But I'm sorry. It's not what I want. Please." No one answered him again, their backs turned to him once more, arms folded over their chests, doing their best to ignore him. Infuriated, he felt like running up to the nearest one and pulling them around, beating on them until they would listen.

"Please," he begged, a little more lamely than before as he feared the time was slipping away too quickly. "Please. I don't really care what you think of me. I don't care what you think of me later, either. I'm not asking for forgiveness. Just hear me out. Ignore me for the rest of your lives after, turn your backs on me all you want, but not right now. Hear me out. Please!"

A few of them turned back around to face him, hesitantly, dubious expressions on their faces - but they were not ignoring him. Gasping at his small victory, Jonah found himself beginning to pant a little as fear was creeping up on him. Once more, Jenna turned to face him, rolling her eyes a little as she chose to indulge him one more time. "Make it quick. I don't even know why I am listening to you."

"Abe … he's not working with Carolus. He only pretended to, so he could … so he could …" Realizing that he did not truly know what Abe's motives were or what drove him to play along, he stumbled a little over his words before continuing on. "So he could figure out how to stop him. He sent me here so we could get you out of here. He's going to do something, shut down the ward protecting this room. He's putting himself at risk so we have a chance, so we can escape."

Jenna glared at him for a long moment, her eyes narrowing as her gaze became briefly distant. When they snapped back into focus, she sneered at him angrily. "Liar."

"No! I'm not lying, he said that after we should meet to the north …"

"Liar," she interrupted him once more, shaking her head. "This room is still warded. I don't know what you hoped to accomplish coming here with that story. Get our hopes up so you could laugh at us when we failed? Well, forget it. Insult us all you want; we won't play your games any longer.

Now, just go."

Jonah felt his jaw going slack, gaping at her incredulously while she turned around one last time, the others following suit. "Wait … no, wait, he said ten minutes. He said to wait ten minutes. God, I don't know how long it's been but he said ten minutes …"

None of them budged. Any hope that he had begun to feel was withering inside of him, and in desperation he began to ponder what options he might have, how he might convince them. Beg, plea, get down on his knees. Continue raving like a madman. Scream at the top of his lungs until they got the point. Something. Anything.

He ran up to Jenna and grasped her by the shoulders, trying to pull her around, but the woman was too strong, too solidly placed. "Please," he begged to no avail as she would not move. He turned his attention to Ryan standing next to her and tried as well, tried shoving him forward, but the bigger man would simply not budge, solid as stone. "Please, someone, anyone," he tried, his voice cracking as he turned around.

"Rebekah," he croaked when he saw her turned away, the red locks cascading over her shoulders making it obvious where she was. "Please, you know me. You know I'm not a traitor, that I don't work for the Syndicate … please, you've got to listen to me, make the others listen to me," he started, crossing over to where she was and touching his hand to her shoulder.

With frightening speed she whipped around, backhanding him across the face with enough force to send him reeling backward, falling flat on his ass. Reaching up to clasp a hand over his jaw and stare up at her incredulously, he found himself drawing back as she spoke up. "Stay away from me. Don't touch me, don't get near me. I never want to so much as see you again, you bastard."

Jonah was so stunned by the outburst that he could do little more than gape up at her, pulling his hand away from the corner of his mouth without even noticing the little spot of blood that it left behind. There was something inescapably terminal about the way she finally turned her back to him, leaving him alone in the center of a semicircle of backs.

They would come soon enough. Abe could only hold out for so long and then he, too, would be captured. They would be dragged away to some place far away and meet some fate that he really didn't understand. Brainwashed, given a lobotomy, he didn't know and wasn't sure he really cared. His heart sank in his stomach as he realized he was going to fail.

The one time when others really depended upon him. The one time in his life when he put himself in harm's way to help. The one and only time when he was acting for the good of someone else rather than simply to satisfy his own needs and desires. Abe was right; there was something different about it when you were fighting for someone else.

Yet he was going to fail. When it counted most, he was going to fail.

He felt the world beginning to collapse in on him. The wall of turned backs around him began to spin, his vision began to slip as he let himself fall to his side, starting to curl up in a fetal position. His life would end on this, on what could have been his greatest moment, left curled up on a floor, already dead to those around him.

Darkness crept into the corners of his vision, blurring as his eyes began to well up in fat, stinging tears. He felt like if he exhaled long enough, deep enough that his spark might give up, that he might let himself pass into the yawning abyss that was threatening to engulf his mind. Get it over with, and not prolong the suffering. Concede to failure.

"No."

The voice was his own, and he surprised himself by whispering it. The spark inside of him did not give up, and suddenly he realized that he had not yet failed. He still had hope, he still had a choice, and he was still in control of his destiny. He could choose to lie down on the ground and give up, cry like a child, and accept his failure.

Or he could choose to fight.

"No," he repeated, a little more firmly, dragging himself up to his feet slowly, staggering a little, but finally getting there. He wasn't sure if any of the others had heard him, if they were paying any attention to him at all, but it didn't matter. He would not let their ire control his destiny. He was still in control.

"No," he repeated one last time before turning his eyes on the door that held them in. While it was no proper prison cell it was still a solid, metal door with no window or opening to the hallway beyond. Bolted and locked behind him as he was cast inside, it was their only way out. Squeezing his hands into tight fists, shaking at his sides, he focused on that door, crouched slightly, and then threw himself in its direction.

The door seemed to rush him all too quickly, and before he knew what was happening he had crashed into it headlong. It would not give, and the impact sent him reeling, all but bouncing right off the wall, a sudden loud ringing buzzing in his ears. He rolled once, gaping up at the ceiling, and then came to a stop splayed out on his stomach, struggling to focus, struggling to banish the dizziness that was bouncing between his ears.

When he finally managed to shake it off, he immediately became aware of two things. First, all of the occupants in the room - Jenna, Rebekah, every last one - had turned and was now staring at him in disbelief. But he also spied the sight of a leathery wing draped on the ground at his side, heaving lightly with his own breathing.

He had changed.

In an instant Jenna's expression transformed from one of bewilderment to one of stark determination and focus. Her eyes fixated on him in a commanding stare, and she pointed in his direction, shouting. "Move. Now!"

At the same time, she leaped forward. Her body twisted slightly in the air, stretching and expanding, wings suddenly extending outward where there was none before, and within the blink of an eye Jenna was standing there in all her glory, an emerald green dragon whose size rivaled that of Carolus, and was in fact too bulky to fit comfortably in the room, her back pressed against a ceiling that was now straining to keep itself intact. Her jaws opened wide and she inhaled deeply, and Jonah found the strength to pull himself out of the way.

Hardly a second afterward she exhaled sharply. There was no gout of flame, however; instead, a sharp crack filled the air, and the door simply burst outward, not only tearing it free from its hinges but separating the door frame completely from the wall and blowing an enormous gash in the side of the room. The sound in his ears was like an enormous booming, as if a shotgun had been fired off next to his head.

She did not hesitate in repeating the gesture, breathing in deeply before exhaling all at once, the entire wall in front of her tearing to shreds and exploding outward with enough force to penetrate the outer wall beyond, blowing open into the brilliant daylight outside. Jonah thought he saw a pair of bulky, crumpled bodies flying outward like so much detritus. The sight made him go wide eyed.

"Go," Jenna shouted again, clawing her way forward through the wreckage of the wall and toward freedom, tearing away whole chunks of the ceiling as she went. Others sprinted past her, leaping to freedom beyond and shifting as they did, immediately taking flight and soaring upward, out of sight. It was mesmerizing to watch them flocking outward like that, so much so that he nearly forgot to escape, himself.

His head still rung from the impact against the door but it wasn't enough to keep him from scrabbling his way to his feet and darting for the newly created exit, spreading his wings as soon as they tasted the air outside of the compound. "North," he shouted as loud as he could, hoping the others would understand what he meant. "North!"

Jenna seemed to lead the charge. She was obviously the largest of all the dragons now in flight, joined at her side by another green dragon, slightly smaller. Her brother, perhaps. She wheeled around overhead once, turning back to fire off another bone rattling shout at the building behind her, the force of her voice punching an enormous hole into the roof with all the efficacy of a wrecking ball. The roof began to collapse in on itself around the gash, and the big green dragon wheeled around once more and pushed her way northward.

She had understood. They had all understood. The flight of dragons was rapidly beginning to make its way across the valley, speeding toward the ridge line ahead, speeding toward freedom. In that moment he felt his heart beginning to soar on the wind.

His moment of elation was cut short by the sight of a massive dragon rising up from behind the ridge, covered in ash gray scales and a series of menacing spikes along the ridge of his back. Carolus.

"Turn back," the big dragon growled threateningly in front of them, spreading his wings wide to make himself look even larger. "Turn back, and there may yet be a chance for you to beg for forgiveness."

Jenna did not bother with any kind of comeback. Instead, the big green dragon reared her head back, her chest puffing out as she inhaled deeply and prepared to fire off one of those shock waves at Carolus. Jonah did not know what effect a force like that would have on a dragon of Carolus' size, but he still could not help but to imagine broken bones being the least of the dragon's worries.

Carolus, however, was faster. He did not have to breathe in so deeply, did not have to exhale in a gust of force. The big dragon simply spoke a few words in a harsh, unfamiliar language, and instantly Jenna shuddered. Her eyes rolled back in her head and her wings ceased their steady beating, and all at once the green dragon began to fall out of the sky. Two others dived after her, trying to get under her and keep her from crashing into the valley floor below.

The other dragons paused in their exuberance, falling back as if they had hit some kind of physical wall in the air. Jonah watched with a sense of foreboding as the big gray dragon just kind of hovered in place, menacing the others with his mere presence. "As I have commanded you. Return and you may find some mercy yet."

"Carl!" The voice from behind him caught them all off guard, again, as a large crimson colored dragon came zipping in from the direction of the compound, passing overhead with enough of a rush of air that his wake nearly knocked Jonah off course.

Carolus growled angrily at the approaching drake. "Ibrahim. You fool."

Abe wasted no breath on any further speaking, any further taunts. He was zeroing in on Carolus with that same frightening speed, not slowing down in the least until he was mere seconds away. At the last he threw his wings open to clutch at the air, rearing up and grasping with the talons on all of his legs, not giving the gray dragon enough time to evade or fight back. The two big dragons began to tumble downward, grappling as they went in a flurry of wings. "Fly! Fly!"

The remaining dragons were somewhat scattered and disorganized. "North," he urged again, pushing his way through the middle of them all and taking the lead. It was something he didn't even have to think about, and he didn't even care what anyone might think about it, but at least he knew to pick a direction.

A low, resonant rumbling from behind him shook him deeply, and he whipped about to try and see what it was. Several shapes were rising rapidly from the partially collapsed compound, four, five, and then six of them. All dragons, and all very large - larger than Jenna, larger than Abe or even Carolus.

Someone shouted. "Bull drakes!"

The approaching bulls left the dragons in disarray once again as they started to scatter in multiple directions. Far below he could see Jenna's green form splayed out on the ground, attended by two other dragons who had landed at her sides, but from here he could not tell if they had succeeded in slowing her fall. There was no sign of what had become of either Carolus or Abe, the pair having somehow vanished completely out of his awareness.

It was a dismal, disheartening sight, but he did not have much time to think about it, for the bull drakes were closing fast.

Now he understood what was meant when they were said to be a different breed. They all looked fairly similar in color, a sort of dark olive, and their shape was similar to one another but different from all the rest. Their bodies were thicker, more massive, their skulls boxier and more menacing. They each wore numerous spikes, and the ends of their tails were studded with yet more of the sharp appendages, already swinging them around like wicked clubs.

One of them was headed straight for him. The sight of it practically made him freeze in his tracks.

"Jonah!" Before he could look for the source of the voice, a brilliant fireball erupted right between him and the bull, enough to force the big male to veer off course. A flash of glossy black darted across his field of vision, another heavy gout of fire lighting up the air. It was Rebekah.

She had succeeded in diverting the bull drake away, the big male changing course and now wheeling around in hot pursuit of her, instead. Out of the corners of his eyes he could see similar chases going on in the air around him, the big bull drakes plowing through the air in pursuit of the smaller dragons. Some of them spat fireballs at their enemies, others tried to evade them with all manner of aerial acrobatics to keep out of their clutches.

It looked like a rout.

Rebekah's voice tore him out of his brief reverie. "Jonah! Don't just sit there, damn you … help!'

While she was certainly more nimble than the big bull dragon Rebekah simply could not outpace him, and he was starting to close fast. Jonah silently cursed the fact that he had not discovered any kind of powers that he might have, no gouts of fire, no ability to crush things with a sonic boom. He wasn't helpless, though; tucking his wings in, he darted straight for the big dragon, intending to use nothing more than his weight to try and return the favor, knock the drake out of course.

It must have seen him. Seconds before he was able to reach out and grasp, the bull flicked his spike studded tail, whipping it in Jonah's direction. He barely had enough time to react and jerk his body out of the way, those dangerous spikes whistling in the air right in front of his face. It had caught him off guard enough to make him miss his mark.

Rebekah and the bull drake pulled away from him as he readjusted himself, pulling hard on his wings to gain a little altitude and go for a different angle. Whether Rebekah had seen him or not, whether she knew what he was doing she seemed to be reacting in just the right way, coming about and back in his direction, keeping just out of the drake's reach.

Jonah could not hope to match the bull's speed, but here he had the benefit of altitude. He waited until they were close enough, until the angle was just right before he tucked his wings in and dove, coming at them from above and ahead. Out of reach of that deadly looking tail club. He mimicked what he had seen Abe do only moments before, waiting until the last second before spreading his wings wide like sails, splaying his talons to grasp on.

The bull drake was quicker once again. When it seemed like there was no time left to react it whipped around and came face to face with him, snarling, its own talons stretched out wide. Jonah crashed into the dragon's bulk as quickly as he had meant to, but now it was the bull who was clutching and grasping at him, pulling him in. Trying to fight back, he scrabbled his claws against the bull's thick scales, his talons lodging between them but failing to penetrate, failing to do any real damage.

Once more the bull whipped his head around and before Jonah knew what was happening he felt razor sharp teeth latching on to the base of his neck, biting down and piercing right through his softer scales. A sharp pain ran right up through his spine, leaving him to cry out a painful roar into the air, desperately trying to pull himself away from the bull but failing. The male was simply too big, too strong, too fast.

A powerful jolt rocked the both of them with enough force that the bull lost his grip. Seizing upon the opportunity, Jonah pushed himself free and away from the creature's clutches. He ached where he had been bitten, was vaguely aware of blood seeping from the wound but it didn't seem to be serious. He was still airborne.

Rebekah must have crashed right into the bull, tumbling several feet away before regaining her attitude and pulling up into a tight loop. The bull roared in anger at having been robbed of his prey, turning his ire on the black dragon once more, powerful wings scooping at the air to close the distance.

Trying to keep up, Jonah willed his wings to move faster, cutting through the air quick enough to make him hurt. "Rebekah! Behind you!"

She must have heard him. Whipping her head back she belched out a pair of fireballs at the pursuing bull, but he seemed to have grown more determined in his anger. Instead of evading the gouts of fire the creature simply flew right through them, and the effort had quite the opposite from the intended effect. It had slowed her down so that the bull was just beyond reach.

With one terrific gasp, Jonah pushed himself hard to try and intervene, try to push the drake out of the way, tried to do something to help.

He was too slow. Unable to do anything to help, he could only watch with a creeping sense of horror as the bull drake pushed himself forward, closed the gap, driving himself forward and snapping a pair of heavy jaws at Rebekah. She evaded the first, the second, and even the third snap of the jaws before her luck ran out. The edge of her wing got caught in those jaws, her body shuddering while she let out a cry of pain, but the drake was undeterred. Another powerful lurch forward and he was atop her, clutching her smaller frame to his body, wrapping his limbs around her, and then the pair fell out of the sky.

Jonah tucked his wings and tried to follow but he simply could not keep up. It didn't take long for him to realize there was nothing he could do save watch them plummet toward the earth. A mighty roar in the direction of the compound was only just enough to tear him away from the sight, the sick, hopeless feeling lingering in his craw.

Winging in their direction was yet another dragon, the largest he had seen. Twice his size and then some, larger than the bull drakes, this new dragon was a dark midnight color, little flashes of deep blue iridescence to its scales as it flapped its wings. A thick pair of spiral horns jutted from the sides of its skull, chipped and weathered, matching a generally worn down look; its wing membranes were tattered at the edges, its scales pockmarked and uneven. The great dragon seemed to tire as it flew toward them, the wind heaving around it.

Instinctively he knew that it was their clan elder. The old dragon seemed to survey the sight, dire indeed; the bull drakes had succeeded in grounding two more of them, only a handful left to dart in and around and try to evade the four remaining pursuers. Jenna was still splayed out far below on the ground, having not moved from the spot where he had seen her before. Rebekah and the bull drake had tumbled away, out of sight.

The elder bellowed out another mighty roar that shook Jonah's bones, and this time his call was answered. The four remaining bull drakes immediately forsook their targets, turning on the oversized newcomer and were on him in an instant, swarming about him. The elder rumbled deeply at their approach, the air around him seeming to swell and twist, a weird kind of distortion that made it hard for Jonah to see what was going on.

The elder was the largest, and probably most powerful of them all, but it was still one against four.

Abruptly a flash of crimson erupted from beneath him, Abe flying into view from wherever he had fallen with Carolus. The dragon looked to have been fairly badly injured, several gashes visible on his side and his motions were unsteady, choppy, as he bellowed out to the others. "Quickly! To the north!"

The other dragons who were still airborne flapped around, one of them crying out, "But the others! The elder! He is being attacked!"

"He purchases our escape with his own capture. Quickly. Let us fly!"

Jonah looked down at the floor of the valley for some sign of Rebekah but still could not find one. The dragons around him chattered in a brief argument, and he could see movement around Jenna's fallen form, one dragon he did not recognize trying to drag along a recalcitrant Jason.

Again he glanced back at the elder, confused by what he saw. The big dragon, as well as the bull drakes, had grown somehow indistinct, their forms blurring together in a sort of writhing mass of motion in the air, taking on a form of its own. Sharp cries and bellows emanated from the unnatural looking fight, reverberations that struck out and caused his bones to rattle in his body, the earth to groan beneath them.

"Enough arguing! We remain at our own peril. Don't let his sacrifice go in vain, we must escape," Abe shouted through the air.

"We cannot abandon him! We cannot abandon any of them!"

The red dragon growled, looking quite miserable with his wounds. "Nor can we assist them now. We fly, so that we may come to their aid again in the future. We are doomed if we remain any longer." At that he began to flap his way to the north, limping away from the scene of the battle.

It was, indeed, a rout. Slowly, reluctantly, the other dragons fell in behind Abe, hunching away from the sight of the elder fighting behind them. Far below, the other dragon had succeeded in getting Jason airborne, the green dragon flying with his head low, his wings limp, looking utterly defeated. Half of those remaining, Jonah included among them, were wounded.

None of them wanted to leave, but none of them could stay.

The sick feeling in the pit of his stomach had returned. Jonah cast one forlorn look back at the wreckage in the valley behind him before turning back to an unknown and somewhat unwelcome future.

NINETEEN

Hours after they had escaped the Syndicate compound, the small company that remained looked anything but victorious.

There had been no way that they were to return to the vans they had parked in the mountains and use them for an escape. Abe had told them that while he had successfully battled Carolus to a standstill the older dragon was still alive and well; as Abe had put it, somewhat grimly, "We're still going to have to deal with Carl again down the road." The dragons had winged their way westward to the edge of the mountains, as far as they dared and risk being sighted. They had hiked the rest of their way to a highway before hitching a ride in the back of a rancher's truck into Bishop.

Exhausted, they had rented a few rooms in an old but clean motel in town, gathering in one of the rooms to sit together and lick their wounds, decide what course of action to take, but no one really had the energy for talk. Abe was in particular exhausted from his struggle with Carolus and the walk down the mountain, his crisp suit somewhat frayed at the edges and dusty, lending him a somewhat absurd appearance. Jason was despondent; though it turned out that Jenna had survived the fall thanks to his and Ryan's efforts, they had been unable to rouse her and were forced to abandon her on the valley floor.

Jonah was not much better, himself. His own wounds on his neck had translated into a nasty bite mark in human form, obvious enough that the proprietor of the hotel had asked him if he'd had a run-in with an angry dog. Still, the wounds were superficial, requiring little more than a bandage and some washing up.

The wounds in his mind were deeper. Since before they had arrived on the hotel, for the entire ride in the back of the friendly rancher's truck, he had replayed the sight of Rebekah being snatched away and pulled earthward by the attacking bull drake. Again and again he saw it happen in his mind, close enough to see the look of terror in her big green eyes, but too far to reach, too far to catch up, too far to help. He'd even begun imagining alternate scenarios, tried to think of what he might have done differently. How he could have helped.

Worse, still, was when his mind wandered a little and began to speculate on what became of her afterward. Perhaps she had plummeted to the ground with the drake so quickly that the both of them had been smashed to pieces on the valley floor, beyond all hope and all recognition. Morbidly he wondered if a slain dragon would stay that way or turn back into a human at the moment of death.

Still other scenarios ran through his head. Perhaps she had been snatched up and taken back to the compound, tossed in one of those rooms, beaten and helpless to await her fate. They might have already come for her and taken her to whatever secure location they had in mind. They might even already be experimenting on her. Jonah could almost hear her screams in his head, and shuddered.

All in all, only nine of them had escaped capture or death. He just wasn't sure which was worse.

Some time had passed while the group gathered silently in that room, little more said than a few hushed conversations, whispers that Jonah could not really make out, before anyone had really paid him much attention. It was Abe, who had pulled himself up off the bed a little stiffly and made his way over, resting a meaty hand on his shoulder. "Don't be so hard on yourself, kid."

Glancing up at the bald man, Jonah tried to frown but it came across as more of a lame grimace. "Don't know what you're talking about."

"Don't be silly," he responded with a weak but sincere smile, nothing like the toothy grins that he was accustomed to flashing around. "I saw it all happen, actually. I saw that you tried to get her back. But take it from me, it wasn't your fault. You tried your best but there was no way you were going to get to her. Hell, not a one of us in this room could have made it turn out any differently."

"If that's supposed to be comforting, I'm afraid you're wasting your time," he muttered a little darkly, folding his arms around his chest and looking down to his feet.

Abe shook his head, sitting on the edge of the bed next to him slowly, with a bit of a sigh. "It's not meant to be comforting, kid. It's just the truth. There isn't a one of us in this room who isn't hurting, who isn't regretting what happened, who isn't mourning the loss of a friend or a loved one, and that's fine. It's part of what makes us human; it's part of what makes us dragons.

"But I don't want you beating yourself up over it. What happened, happened. It's not your fault, it's not my fault, it's just the way the chips fell. If you want to hurt over what happened then I encourage it. No one here should be bottling up that kind of pain. Just don't add more pain to your misery by making yourself to blame."

"Easy for you to say," Jonah retorted, shaking his own head and tucking his arms more tightly against himself. "You didn't see the whole thing happen, did you? She rescued me from that monster. If it hadn't been for her he'd have gotten me instead. It should have been me … should have been me."

There was a somewhat drawn out pause while Jonah was allowed to consider his own thoughts, once again reviewing the scene in his head, watching it unfold before Abe spoke up again with a little puff. "No, I didn't see that happen, but it doesn't change the truth of what I said. Maybe she pushed you out of harms way, but then you tried to do the same for her. Would that have made it her fault that you got caught, if you'd succeeded?"

"No, but …"

Abe did not give him a chance to finish with his objection, cutting him off smoothly. "No, of course not. You could go back and forth like that till you're blue in the face but it doesn't matter. One of you got caught. Call it fate, call it chance, call it bad luck, but whatever it is, it's not your fault that she's the one."

Jonah just shrugged miserably. "Still. I wish she hadn't done it. It should have been me to go down."

"Nothing could have stopped her from doing it, just like nothing could have stopped you from trying to return the favor. Just comes natural; anyone would stick their own neck out for someone they cared enough about."

Feeling his cheeks beginning to flush a little, Jonah kept his eyes fixed firmly on the ground. "That obvious how I feel about her, isn't it."

At last Abe managed a little chuckle. It was nowhere near as hearty as the ones he had been prone to dispensing since Jonah had gotten to know of him, and was lined with a sort of weary pain, but it was nevertheless a sincere sound and it was still good to hear. "It is, kid, it is. But that's not what I meant."

It took Jonah a moment to realize that he was talking about Rebekah and her feelings, and the thought made the flush in his cheeks run downward to his neck, making him feel uncomfortably hot there as he snorted. "What? You've got to be kidding me. I don't suppose you've actually seen her around me?"

"I saw her around you earlier today," he countered with a knowing look.

Jonah simply shook his head and forced a bit of a laugh. "Look, what she did for me today is something that anyone would have done, right? I mean, isn't that how it works with you and your clan?"

Abe shrugged a little at that. "Well. I suppose you've got me there," he said, briefly feeling around his pockets before shrugging again. "But I also saw her around you before that. Back at Tahoe. Back in Detroit."

"And?" Jonah waited expectantly, with a bit of a sneer on his face. "If you were paying any attention you'd have noticed that she isn't exactly fond of me. Not that I really blame her, I guess, not after what happened … but … hell, she could hardly stand to be around me. If it weren't for Carolus making her work with me, I'm sure she wouldn't have gone near me for the whole time. He probably did it to punish her, for some reason."

The bald man simply nodded at that, not answering immediately as if he were digesting the information he were being given. "I see," he said finally, slowly, pushing himself back up to his feet with a light sigh. "Ah, what I wouldn't give for a cigar right about now. But, let me ask you a question, kid. So she was a bit harsh around you. Probably called you a few names, right? Made you feel like an idiot? Made it pretty clear she was disgusted by you, yes?"

"Yeah. Thanks for reminding me of it, too …"

Abe cut him off with a little wave of the hand. "And that means that she couldn't stand you, right?"

It seemed like an obvious enough conclusion that to hear it repeated came across as mildly insulting. "Of course," he responded a little crossly, growing tired of the line of questioning and the line of reasoning.

"Of course," came the rather unconcerned sounding reply. "Let me tell you one thing about women then, kid."

"What's that?"

The bald man leaned in and clapped him lightly on the shoulder. "You've got a lot to learn about them."

Jonah glanced up sharply at that, furrowing his eyebrows and scowling. "What's that supposed to mean?"

"Exactly what it sounds like," Abe responded, once again wearing one of his signature grins. Before Jonah had any chance to respond to that, though, the big guy continued speaking. "But, here, something a little more important than that. Something a little more immediate to the moment. Regardless of what she thinks of you - of what you think she thinks of you - she's worth fighting for, isn't she?"

He was still a little put off by the whole thing, still feeling sore at having been made to think back on what had happened between them, as if losing her only hours ago were not bad enough. But he was right about that, at least. It was the sort of thing that Jonah would not have understood, himself, only a few weeks earlier, the concept of caring about someone enough to fight for, to put his life on the line for, in spite of whatever feelings might have been returned.

Even that, though, was hopeless. "Yeah," he said, looking back down to his feet with a soft sigh. "At least, she was worth fighting for." Though the thought crossed his mind, he did not care to add that he no longer felt like much of anything else was worth the effort, anymore.

"Tell me something, kid."

"What?" He didn't look up as he croaked a somewhat pitiful reply. "Something else to remind me how much shit sucks right now?"

Abe laughed in spite of the pained tone in his voice. "You still got that hundred bucks I gave you back in Detroit?"

The question seemed a little out of place and caught Jonah off guard a little, enough to make him look up with a confused frown. "The … what?" He found himself fishing around in his pockets, pulling his wallet out and opening it almost by reflex before he realized what he was doing. "Well … as a matter of fact, yes I do. What's it got to do with anything? Don't tell me you want it back."

"Of course I do," he answered with another chuckle. "But I'm not just going to ask for it back. I'll actually give you a chance to double it. I'll be willing to bet you a hundred dollars that Rebekah is still very much alive and well, and still very much worth fighting for."

It was not what he expected to hear, and it was enough to catch him off guard and leave him dumbfounded for a moment. "What?"

Abe mocked a little frown. "Not good enough for you? Five hundred more your style?"

Jonah shook his head a little bit and sputtered. "Wait. You're trying to tell me that she's still alive? How could you possibly know that?"

"I don't know that, kid. That's why it's a wager and not a sure thing. But I'll tell you what I do know. The elder is still alive; each and every one of us knows that. We can feel him. I also know that the Syndicate prefers us alive to dead. We're more useful to them that way, in the end. They aren't shy about eliminating us when we get in the way but if things go the way they want, they capture us, not kill us. I also happen to know that Rebekah is one tough cookie. Take a little more than a wrestle with a bull to finish her off."

"You really think she's alive, then?" He realized that he was coming across as far too credulous and eager than he ought to, somewhat like a young child who was being told that Santa Clause might actually exist, but the possibility was the only good news he had heard all day. Some part of his soul had caught on to that little glimmer of a hope and held on to it tight.

"No guarantees," Abe said with a friendly, almost fatherly sort of smile this time. "But I'd put a hundred bucks on it. I'd put a thousand on it. What do you say, you a betting man?"

Jonah coughed a little where he sat. "I don't think I can take that bet. You don't really expect me to bet on her being … gone … do you?"

The bald man smiled with a wink. "Good man," he muttered, clapping him lightly on the shoulder before glancing at his watch and nodding. "Like I said, still worth fighting for and I sure as hell hope you've still got some fight in you, kid. But that reminds me. Something that we've all got to discuss," he said, raising his voice at the end to catch the attention of the others who had been gathered around.

All of them save Jason turned their heads in his direction and looked to him with tired, worn expressions; he alone remained despondent, unresponsive, gazing blankly down toward his feet. Satisfied he had the attention of the majority, Abe nodded again. "We've all had a very long day already, and we're all worn out. I realize we have a lot on our minds, and while I'm not going to ask anyone to try and just forget about it, I am going to ask that we all try to gather our wits about us enough to get some rest."

"Rest?" One of the gathered men who Jonah did not recognize spoke up, his voice ragged and thin. "How can we be expected to rest when our clan is in shambles? We abandoned them, for God's sake."

For the first time Abe's expression darkened to one edging up against raw anger, his jaw clenching a bit. "No one abandoned anyone, Samuel. That idea I want you to get out of your head, right now. Forget about it. Any of us who had dared stay there would be captured now with no hope of making any further rescue attempts. We did not abandon anyone today, we retreated to regroup and regather."

"Regroup? You said it yourself, Abraham. They're already on their way to a secure facility. There's only six of us, and we're in no condition to fight." Samuel, as he had been called, just shook his head sadly. "What hope do we have?"

"Plenty. You're right about one thing, we're all beat up and worn down. That's why we've got to get some rest. None of us are going to be of much help until we do that," he said, balling up his hand into a fist. "I happen to know that the clan are all being shipped away to Washington State. Nothing is going to happen to them until then, and that's not going to be until later tonight. We'll take that time to rest up and recover."

Ryan, who had been sitting near Jason the whole time, spoke up. "Washington? And how the hell are we supposed to get up there? The Syndicate has got to be watching our every move."

Abe finally seemed to relax a little, the fire in his eyes cooling slightly. "I've already got that taken care of, and it's going to rely on a little misdirection on my part. Working for the Syndicate means I know of some of their methods, some of their bases, but it also means they are keeping strict tabs on my business and my funds. That doesn't mean that I don't have a few friends who managed to keep under their radar, however.

"I've already gotten in touch with a friend of mine who is arranging for us to fly to Reno on a local charter flight; there's a little airstrip just outside of town here, if you hadn't noticed. He'll pick us up there and fly us to Seattle on his executive jet. At the same time I have another contact in Los Angeles who has access to one of my personal accounts. I'm going to have them withdraw some funds later this afternoon from an ATM in the area. Give them the impression that we're headed south, the wrong direction."

To Jonah it sounded reasonable, if a little light on details. The others did not seem entirely convinced, skepticism still lining Ryan's voice. "So you can get us to Seattle. What then? The Syndicate isn't going to just sit back and follow through with their same plans as before. They have to know that you are still alive and going to be running the show here. Surely they are going to change their plans."

Abe nodded to that. "I don't doubt it in the least, and in fact I am counting on it. The Syndicate won't abandon their plans to take the clan to the area; it's where they have their base of operations in this half of the country. To try and transport them back East would be a logistical nightmare and a risk that they won't take, but they will have to pick another facility in the area. That change of plan will cost them time, time to give us a chance to make our move."

"But what good is time if we don't know where they are going?"

"We don't have to," he responded with a grin. "Not at first, anyway. It's a simple matter of infiltrating their regional headquarters in Seattle and extracting that information. The Syndicate is nothing if not organized and bureaucratic. They'll have the information readily available there."

Ryan scoffed and shook his head. "A simple matter of infiltrating their headquarters?"

"You don't think I spent my entire time inside the Syndicate spying on ol' Carl, do you? I've made a few valuable contacts inside the organization, know my way around the system. I'm not saying that it will be a walk in the park but I know what I am doing and I know how to get at what we need. Just leave that part to me."

The others still did not seem convinced, although for a moment they were unable to voice any specific concerns. "Look, we'd all love for nothing more than to rescue the others. And I'm sure you've given this a lot of thought and you're sure that you've worked out all the details but … I don't know. It's a lot for us all to just take at face value."

Jonah expected Abe to react with some indignation at the doubt, but the bald man simply shrugged with a genial smile. "Well, Ryan, if anyone else has a better plan or a better idea, then please. Let them speak it. This may not be the full council and we may not have the luxury of our usual order of doing things, but let's be open to suggestion. We are still all brothers and sisters and still all have a voice. Speak."

An uncomfortable sort of silence settled over the room, and for a long moment nothing other than the slow hum of the ceiling fan churning overhead could be heard. Jonah could see the conflicted emotions running through the heads of some of those gathered, and he too could feel the same conflict inside of himself. On one hand, the possibility that there was something he could do to fight back, some glimmer of hope that Rebekah might be rescued after all, burned bright in his chest and urged him to follow along, to do whatever it took to accomplish.

Yet at the same time, he realized how hopeless the situation seemed. He was sore and hurting, and he knew that he would be in bad shape for any kind of fight that they might encounter. More than that, he knew that in spite of all of Abe's planning it was still a wild plan cobbled together at the last moment, that any one variable would throw it all off. If he were wrong, and the Syndicate took them in a different direction … if they anticipated his actions, if they already knew where they were hidden … any one misstep would unravel the entire thing.

No one seemed to have the temerity to speak up against Abe's plan, to point out how fragile it all was, yet at the same time they all seemed to lack the courage to throw their lot in behind him, to voice support for the effort, no matter how ill conceived it might be.

When someone did finally speak up, they were all surprised to see that it was Jason who spoke the silence. His eyes, blue rimmed in pained red, wavered a little as he finally looked up and fixated on Abe where he stood, his voice coming out thin and dry. "Ibrahim. You can save her? Save Jenna?"

"I can't promise you that," Abe answered with stark sincerity, his smile fading ever so slightly and taking on a sort of grim resolve. "But I can promise you we will do everything in our power to do so."

Jason's eyes seemed to wander back and forth, considering the statement as he nodded slowly, licking his lips before he spoke up. "Then … if I die trying, at least I die trying. I cannot sit here and wait without doing at least that."

The statement did not fail to rouse an emotional response in the others, ranging from quiet little gasps to an even quieter, reverent nodding. Abe, on the other hand, merely nodded firmly. "Then we will fly, my brother. Be it into the arms of victory or the jaws of defeat, we fly together. We fly as brothers. We die as brothers."

One by one the others in the room began to echo the sentiment in their own ways, grim promises of going to battle as family, side by side, facing death together if need be. The sentiment had caught on, proven infectious, and not a single one could fail to fall in to line with the plan, to make their stand. Even when it came around to Jonah, he could not simply stand by idly and not feel swayed by the grim determination around him.

All the same, he was in no hurry to die and was not afraid to say so. "I'm with you guys on this one, if it means we might get them back. But if it's all the same to you, I'd rather go in expecting to come back alive."

A few stray chuckles echoed in the little room, and Abe leaned over to clap him firmly on the shoulder once more. "Ah, once again the wisdom of the young ones is apparent. Perhaps we've been around too long, come face to face with death so many times that we come to expect that familiar risk at every turn. I like your attitude though, kid. Let's all go into this one with a little more hope, a little more optimism, why don't we?"

There were a few nods of assent, the big man raising his fist upward in the air. "For Jenna! For Rebekah!" The others repeated in somewhat muted shouts, slowly picking up in enthusiasm as they went. "For our elder! For our clan! For dragons wherever they may be on the face of this Earth! For each other!"

#

Hours later the brief fit of enthusiasm they had felt together in that hotel room had become a distant memory. A long, bumpy flight on a turboprop into Reno, followed by a much smoother and more comfortable trip northward to Seattle on the posh corporate jet had put more than simply miles between them and the hurts of their loss in the valley. Even the sensation of hope that the little cheers had instilled them with felt like they had fallen away into the past, tempered by long hours in the relative quiet of the flight.

Finally the jet had set down in Seattle, when the night had worn long and the wee hours of the morning had come along. A hired limousine had taken them from the airport to a small hotel south of downtown, where they had briefly set up in accommodations much more luxurious than the little motel in Bishop had offered.

The luxury meant little to them, however, and did even less to ease the aches and pains that they had felt. When Abe had assembled them once again in the suite they had rented for the night he had not been able to rouse them to the same level of energy, the same enthusiasm as before. The determination was still there; not a one of them wished to shirk from the moment, not a one of them would have suggested turning back and trying to find some other way.

Some of them looked even more tired and despondent than they had back in California. The glimmer of fire that had burned in Jason's eyes at the talk of rescuing Jenna had become little more than a smoldering flicker hidden behind a visage that looked gaunt and worn like he had not slept in weeks. Two of the others looked little better than walking zombies, apparently having not slept at all either at the hotel or on the flight north. Jonah didn't feel much better himself; though he had managed to fall to sleep in the motel, his sleep had been unsettled, riddled with replays of

Rebekah's fall, of the death of his friend Sam back in Florida, of the sinister look of that bull drake behind the wheel of a semi seconds before pushing them of a bridge.

When Abe had announced that only he and Jonah would be going to the Syndicate headquarters in search of information, the protest had been earnest but muted. Even when he had attempted to allay their concerns by telling them that once the location of the clan had been determined they would return to regroup once again and assault the compound as a whole, the others had protested, or at least tried to.

Abe had finally prevailed, however, and while the others agreed to remain behind for the time being, Jonah was dragged up to the the roof of the hotel, where he could see the glimmering lights of the city splayed out around them. It was still dark, still very early in the morning, and a chilly wind spilled over the rooftop, making him shiver. "Tell me again. Why do we have to do this now, at this hour?"

"This is a little different than flying over Lake Tahoe, kid. There's a few million people living in this city, and we could cause a real stir flying overhead during the daytime. We're headed right into the heart of downtown, too, so there's no real way around it."

"Right," Jonah responded with a little mutter, stuffing his hands into the pockets of the hooded sweater that he had picked up down in the hotel lobby. "Remind me again why the two people to go on this little trip are the oldest and the youngest among us."

Abe smiled in spite of himself, dressed once again in a clean, well pressed double breasted suit. A fresh, unlit cigar was clamped between his teeth, but it seemed enough to satisfy him for the time being. "You're going because you're young enough to recover from earlier. I'm going because I happen to know the way."

"I wish that explanation didn't make so much sense."

"I can get someone else up here to take your place, if you really want," the bald man offered, peering out over the city.

Jonah shook his head. "Nah. I just wish that I was more sure about this," he said, turning to look at Abe again and level a sort of accusation in his direction. "You don't intend on coming back here for the others, do you."

"That obvious, is it?" It was Abe's turn to shrug his shoulders again, sighing as he stuffed the unlit cigar into his pocket. "Look, kid. I won't lie to you. What we're flying into is dangerous. Real dangerous. A good chance we could be caught, but if we were dragging along half a dozen half dead dragons we'd be as good as captured already. Two of us, we just might be able to sneak in and get the job done without getting caught."

A faint breeze snuck up and ruffled at his hair, the chill making him shiver slightly as he looked out over the city. "I know this isn't the best timing, but there's something I've been meaning to ask you."

The bald man turned to look at him curiously in the dark. "I suppose it's as good at time as any, as long as you can make it quick."

"I've been having these strange dreams lately," he said, not wasting any time. "Rebekah called them visions."

Abe nodded. "Right. You would be starting to have them about now, yes. We all get them, all of us on the council, anyway. You want to know something about them?"

"Yeah," he said, with a bit of a shrug. "She said they were some kind of ... I don't know how she put it. Fragments of memories, or something, from those who have gone before."

"That's fairly accurate. None of us are exactly sure how they work, or how they were originally made. They've been around since the beginning, really. Your token has been carried by every Silver Dragon to sit on the council, and then by every leader of the Clan Silver before that." Abe peered off into the distance before turning to look at him with a faint smile. "A lot of memories locked up in that little bit of silver."

Jonah shot him a quizzical look. "You mean to tell me that this thing is thousands of years old?" Without thinking about it, he reached down and felt the hard little disc through the fabric of his pocket.

The bigger man chuckled. "No. It's just a piece of silver. Eventually these things get worn down, broken, ruined or the like. When it does we fashion a new one." As he had been speaking he pulled his own out from beneath the jacket that he wore, dangling on a gold chain, letting it glint in the faint light cast by the city. Even in the faint light Jonah could see that it was, indeed, much newer looking than his own.

"But how? If you don't know how they were made in the first place, how can you make a new one? Transfer all of the ... well ... whatever it is that's in it?"

"I can't say for sure, but I'll tell you my theory. See, I think that when you hold the coin, the memories, the bits and pieces of the others that it has inside of it, actually go inside of you. They become a part of you. Their memories become yours. When you fashion a new one, they just go into it when the time comes. We don't know how but we don't have to. Just happens all on its own."

The explanation was a bit on the weak side and left Jonah feeling dissatisfied. Once again it seemed all too convenient and simple, but he felt like he had no choice other than to accept it. "Gotcha."

Abe nodded and once more looked out over the city. "That answer your question?"

"Actually," he started, drawing in a deep breath. "That wasn't really my question. What do the visions mean? Why am I having them? Is the token ... or whatever, are they trying to tell me something?"

"Well," the big man paused, stuffing the gold token back beneath his jacket, pulling the cigar out of his mouth and stuffing it in his breast pocket. "Again, no one knows for sure. But if you follow my theory - that the memories become a part of you, a part of your own being - that it's no different than any other dream. That it's your own mind pulling them up, drawing them out of your memories, turning them into dreams. If there's a reason for them, the reason is your own. Not so much that the memories are trying to tell you something, but it's something else. Your subconscious, perhaps, is trying to tell you something."

The possibility that the strange and unsettling visions that he had been experiencing were supposed to be some message from the deeper recesses of his mind - that he was the one dredging them up all by himself - was perhaps more unsettling than the dreams. Before he could ask any further questions, however, Abe spoke up, clearing his throat. "I hate to rush things, Jonah, but we've really got to be going."

Frowning a bit, shrugging it off, Jonah merely nodded and tried to put his mind back to the task at hand. "All right. You really think we can do this? You really think we have a shot?"

The bald man smiled at that, turning away and glancing one more time over the lights of the city, fixing his gaze on the silhouettes of the skyscrapers rising in the distance. "Only one way to find out," he replied with a chuckle, abruptly hopping off the edge of the roof and into the night. Realizing there was nothing more he could do, Jonah sighed softly into the night and followed.

TWENTY

"Stay close," Jonah heard Abe call out in the darkness ahead of him, his voice taking on the deeper timbre and slight growl to it that was the hallmark of being in dragon form. He didn't really need to be reminded, however; it was painfully dark over the city at that hour, and even close by he could only barely make out the larger dragon's silhouette. If he lost track of him now, he wouldn't have any clue where they were going or how to get there.

Fortunately Jonah's scales proved to be somewhat resilient against the cold, for as soon as he'd jumped off the roof of the hotel and taken flight he had stopped shivering in spite of the wind now rushing past him. In a way there was an odd kind of serenity to the night flight, no sound except for the air flowing over his scales and the quiet beat of his wings, nothing other than the sea of lights spooling out beneath him to detract him from the sensation.

The air, thick with moisture had a unique smell to it, vaguely reminiscent of the way the ocean smelled back home in Florida but at the same time quite different. The cool humidity had a way of making him feel disarmed, strangely at comfort aloft over the city. Were it not for the grim errand that they were on, it might feel almost relaxing.

Having to keep up with Abe's silhouette flitting through the night sky in front of him was the only thing that kept him grounded enough in the moment not to let him lose himself to the sensations.

They had to cross several miles of hilly terrain, trying to fly fairly low to the ground to reduce the risk of being spotted by air traffic while at the same time keeping high enough that they didn't catch the attention of any of the night owls below. In spite of the distance, however, it seemed to pass fairly quickly, and soon Abe was picking up altitude, circling his way around as the huddled mass of skyscrapers closed in like a looming, blocky mountain of its own.

Jonah had no clue which one they were actually heading toward. Trying to keep close, he only let his vision stray once, to catch a glimpse of the iconic Space Needle off in the distance, but it was just long enough that he nearly lost track. Abe's shadow was all but lost against the looming shape of a dark colored building ahead, dipping in toward the roof. Jonah felt his heart skip a beat as he angled in afterward, reaching his talons out to grasp at something, trying to make out a safe landing spot in the dark. He didn't want to think of what would happen if he missed his mark here.

Somehow, through some combination of dumb luck and chance, he landed almost perfectly on the roof of the building, only a brief little stumble before he came to a rest. Abe had already shifted back into human form, and he followed suit with a little gasp, coming up to his feet and looking around, slightly dizzy from the sight.

Abe reached out a meaty hand to steady him, leaning in to whisper quietly. "Steady yourself, kid. This is where it gets serious." The man's voice had enough of a deadly sober tone to it to make him suddenly feel a little uneasy to his stomach, and was about to ask exactly what he meant before Abe went on.

"Now, listen. We're going to try and make this as quick as we can. In and out. The Syndicate headquarters only make up the top four floors of this building so we won't have far to go. We're not looking for anything specific, just any computer terminal connected to their network should do the trick. Got it?"

"Got it," Jonah nodded.

"All right. I'm hoping we don't run in to much trouble, not here, not at this time of night. They shouldn't be expecting us and shouldn't be expecting any trouble to come from up top. With any luck all of their security is focused down below and we'll have pretty much free run of the place," he continued, making his way over to a rooftop door nearby. "If we do run into trouble, it's not likely to be bulls. Not here. Could be some trouble if they've got mages running security."

Jonah blinked in confusion at that. "Mages?"

Abe paused at the door, turning to look at him a bit critically. "What? Damn, that's right … we never really taught you how to handle mages. Look. Good news is mages can't sniff out a dragon. So if they do run into us, they're likely to take us for common criminals and just try to shoot us or something like that."

"That's good news?"

"It sure beats having them try and unleash their magic on you. Trust me on that one, a gun is a bit less frightening than that. Just, whatever you do, try not to let anyone here realize who you are or what you are, got it? And, god forbid we do have to deal with magic, try and let me deal with it," he muttered, trying the door and looking a little surprised to find it was unlocked and opened right up for them.

Once again Jonah shook his head, and breathed out a little puff. "Right. Whatever you say."

With a curt nod the big man took the lead and began to descend quietly into the stairway, ill-lit save for a few emergency lights and exit signs. Three flight of stairs down they arrived at the first doorway, rather conveniently fitted with a small window that Abe could look into. Shaking his head, they bypassed the floor and continued down a few more flights of stairs to the second. Again, he shook his head and continued down until the next door, where, finally, he nodded and pushed the door open.

The hinges creaked quietly, but the sound still set their nerves on edge. Abe held the door partially open for a moment, glancing inward for a moment as if he were waiting for some response to the quiet creak. None came, and he pushed the door open the rest of the way, beckoning for Jonah to follow along in near silence.

It was unremarkable, as office buildings went, Jonah supposed. A quiet hallway, also lit only by emergency lighting and exit signs, with little more than generic looking art prints hung at irregular intervals to break up the monotony. He could make out a little alcove in the distance where it looked like a copy machine was tucked away, the fronds of a silk plant jutting slightly out into the hallway from where it turned the corner.

Altogether it seemed rather unprepossessing for the regional headquarters of some powerful organization like the Syndicate, but then Jonah realized that he didn't really know much about them at all.

Abe betrayed no real emotion at all as he moved down the hall. There was something slightly absurd about the sight of the big man slinking down a hallway as quiet as a cat, but it was effective; their footfalls made nary a sound against the carpeted floor of the hall, and as he made his way to the first, nearest door, testing the handle, he managed to do that even in silence.

It was locked. The next two were locked, as well, and it was not until the fourth door, just opposite the little alcove with the copy machine that they found an office door that would open for them. After peeking inside, Abe turned back to look at him with a faint smile, mouthing the word "Bingo" before stepping inside and making room for him to follow.

Just as the hallway beyond was unremarkable, the office itself seemed to be indistinguishable from the countless other offices Jonah had seen. A bookshelf to one side lined with various texts and stacks of folders, one or two pieces of generic art on the walls, and a desk sporting a small handful of personal affects and a half finished coffee mug. None of that interested Abe, of course, who was motioning to Jonah to close the door to the office as he pulled up a seat behind the desk and smiled.

As luck would have it, the computer was already on, the sound of its fans humming softly in its case breaking the silence in the room. They would not have to wait for it to boot up. Once the door was closed Abe clicked the power button to the monitor, his face lighting up in a slightly eerie glow as he cracked his knuckles. "Here we go," he whispered, almost imperceptibly.

Jonah stepped around behind him to get a look at the login screen, frowning. "So, you're going to just log in to the thing like it's no big deal?"

Abe just smiled, resting his hands on the keyboard a little awkwardly. "I did work for the Syndicate, don't forget that."

"What, you don't think the first thing they did when you betrayed them was to revoke your access to their system?"

"Oh, of course they did," he whispered, starting to peck out the keys with his pointer fingers, none too quickly.

Jonah frowned at that, shaking his head. "Wait, don't tell me. You know the system well enough to hack in, or something like that."

Abe had to stifle a laugh, covering his face with a big hand and shaking his head. "Goodness, no. I can barely operate these damned things, to be honest," he said, resuming his slow typing, punching a few keystrokes into the password field before reaching over for the mouse, giving it a click.

To Jonah's surprise, the login screen vanished and the desktop began to load up, populating with various icons. "Well then how the hell did you do that?"

"Don't forget, Carl works for the Syndicate, too. You suppose a guy who hasn't bothered changing his name in nine hundred years is going to take the time to change his login password?"

In other circumstances it might have come across as a funny joke. Even now it still was a little humorous, listening to Abe sneak in a little dig at Carolus like that, but there was no time for laughter and lighthearted banter now. Indulging himself with nothing more than a smirk, Jonah nodded. "All right, but do you know what you are looking for? Where are you going to find information about where the others are at?"

"Old Carl is in pretty deep with these guys and their operation. He was basically their lead man back at the compound in the valley, he's probably the one who had to give them the bad news of how it all went down," Abe answered, slowly but methodically bringing up Carolus' email, clicking through some of the more recent messages with a little nod. "It's probably right in here somewhere. Even if it isn't we just have to access … ah, no, here it is. 'Relocate to Olympus'. Well there we go."

"Olympus?"

"Very remote. Very secure. About a hundred miles west of here," he responded, frowning a little as he clicked through some of the other messages, skimming through them. "Just like we thought, they predicted that we'd come after them, and they aren't taking any chances. Olympus is a hell of a location to try and break into."

Jonah frowned as well. "So now what? Do you even know where it is."

"I do. And we're going to do exactly what we set out to do, kid. I said Olympus is a hell of a location to try and break in to, but not impossible. Might make them complacent, too, thinking that we don't know where they are. Give us the element of surprise." Abe was still perusing through some of Carolus' emails, breathing a quiet little chuckle. "Looks like they took the bait. Caught on the transaction out of LA this evening and dispatched a team to find us there."

"You aren't worried about them catching your friend?"

Abe shook his head. "Nah. They'll chalk it up to a stolen card or something once they realize it wasn't us," he began, before his voice trailed off and a frown began to creep up on his features again. "Still. Old Carl knows me fairly well, all the same. They're expecting us here, in Seattle, expecting us to do exactly what we're doing now."

Jonah felt his skin starting to crawl, his heart thumping a little quicker in his chest at the thought. "They know we're here?"

"No. Not yet, at least. They think we're still in California, that we're traveling by car. Probably not expecting us up here by later this morning, at the earliest," he said, abruptly sitting up from the desk and stepping to the back of the office, throwing the curtains open and examining the window behind it.

"Wait - what are you doing?" Jonah stepped over to the window as well, looking on in confusion.

"Looking for a way out," Abe muttered, running his finger against the seam and pushing on the pane here and there, the frown on his face deepening. "Damn. Got to love these decorative windows. Don't even open to let in a little breeze."

The sense of panic starting to creep up into the corners of his mind again, Jonah found himself glancing nervously back and forth between the computer, the door, and the window. "But you said they aren't expecting us yet. They don't know we are here. Why not just go back out the way we came?"

After another futile shove against the pane, the bald man took a step back away from the window and puffed his cheeks a bit. "I said they don't know we are here yet. The Syndicate doesn't think we'll be here tonight but they're also not willing to take chances. Carl's account activity is being monitored, and if someone on their end is on the ball - and they usually are - it won't take them long to put two and two together, realize it's not him up here tonight logging in to his email."

"So you're saying they could be tracking us?"

Abe nodded curtly, flicking the computer back of before moving in the direction of the door. "No, I am saying that they are tracking us. It's just a matter of how quickly one of them realizes what's going on. The sooner we get out of here the better," he grunted, reaching for the door and pulling it open.

Almost without hesitation he shut it again, turned to push Jonah into a darkened corner of the room, and held up a finger to his mouth to demand silence.

For a long, tense moment, nothing happened. Jonah huddled back into the corner, wide-eyed and confused, his heart thumping angrily in his chest and nervousness gnawing at the edges of his awareness, watching as Abe crouched next to the door, unmoving and silent. He wanted to ask the big man what he had seen on the other side of the door, why he had pushed him into the corner, what the hell was going on - but dared not break the silence, especially after getting that look.

Then the door was pushed open from the hallway, someone stepping inside. Jonah hunkered further into the corner of the office as he watched a flashlight being shoved into the office, pointed directly at the desk, the little cone of light disrupting his night vision for a moment, enough that the shape of the man wielding the flashlight was indistinct and blurry at first. He really could not make out any detail, but thought that the man seemed to be wearing some kind of uniform.

Cautiously, the man took another step into the room, sweeping the light back and forth over the desk, over in the direction of the bookshelf. "Hello? I'm with building security … is there anyone there?"

Abruptly Jonah found himself blinded when the flashlight flicked over in his direction, bearing down right on top of him and leaving him helpless. The panic he felt redoubled when he realized that he'd been caught, but at the same time could not see a thing, could not do a thing to defend himself. "What the," he heard the guard start to shout before there was a dull thud and a crunch.

The light fell away from his eyes with a metallic clatter against the ground, followed by a much louder thump, but for a moment Jonah could still not see, his eyes still trying to adjust to the changing in the light. He heard an indistinct ruffling sound as he tried to blink away the darkness, and then Abe spoke up. "You ok there, kid?"

"I can barely see," he hissed, assuming that the silhouette now moving in his direction was Abe. "What's going on?"

"Guard," the big man said simply enough. His vision slowly began to return to normal, enough that he could make out Abe moving to kneel at the side of the guard's fallen form, patting down his sides and looking for something, perhaps. "Probably not the only one, either, so we'd better get moving."

"I thought you said that they weren't on to us yet!"

Abe shrugged. "If they aren't yet they will be very soon," he said, pausing as he plucked something away from the guard's side and hefted it up in the air; Jonah was a little disturbed to see that it was a handgun. "I don't get the impression that the guards here are authorized to carry these things. You know how to use one?"

Jonah blinked, nodding as he stammered a bit. "Well, yes, I do …"

"Good," the big man cut him off, shoving the weapon in his hands before turning to look out the door once again, up and down the hallway.

While he was hardly squeamish about guns Jonah had not ever used one outside of the context of a shooting range that he occasionally went to for the purpose of letting off a little steam. He did not have to be told that if one guard was packing heat the others would, as well. Nor did he have to be told what he was being given the weapon for, but the thought of actually shooting a gun at someone - even in defense - made his blood run cold.

He was still fumbling uncomfortably with the weapon when Abe spoke up again. "Come on. Coast is clear, let's get moving. Back to the roof." Abandoning the need for stealth and quiet, the pair made their way out into the hall and hastily back in the direction of the stairwell.

"Chuck? That you?" The voice came from behind them, in the opposite direction of the hallway, suddenly lighting up with another flashlight. Jonah looked back behind him instinctively at the sound of the voice, and when the light flashed in his direction he tried to shy away from it, bringing his hands up in a futile attempt to ward it off. In the process he mistakenly pulled on the trigger of the gun, firing it off loudly if harmlessly into the ceiling overhead, causing little bits of plaster and other materials to cascade down onto them.

The guard who had just called out to them dove for the ground, the flashlight dropping and rolling off to the side. Abe shot him an incredulous look before pulling him along toward the stairwell. "I thought you said you knew how to use it," he complained.

"I do. Sorry. I got startled."

Noisily they began to pound their way up the stairs, passing a doorway on their way up, coming around the landing when the door to the last floor before the roof opened up and three more of the security guards spilled out. "Freeze," one of them shouted down, the others pulling out their weapons and immediately firing off a volley of shots. Their aim was poor, the bullets ricocheting off the walls and sparking against one of the guardrails, but it was enough to send both Abe and Jonah tumbling to the landing and scurrying for cover around the corner.

Jonah found himself screaming in confusion as he was hauled back up to his feet, Abe starting to drag him bodily down the next flight of stairs while the guards above gave pursuit, firing off another volley of bullets that rained down around them. "Jonah! How about you use that thing now?"

Startled but nodding, he finally pulled the weapon up and aimed it in the general direction of the pursuing guards, firing off a couple of shots. He was certain neither of them would hit anyone but the report of the gun, the sound of the bullets bouncing against the stairwell above had the intended effect. The pursuing guards dove for cover, as well, giving them enough time to push their way into the door on the next landing. By some stroke of luck there seemed to be none of the guards on this particular floor.

"Well, I'd say they're on to us now," Abe muttered, very briefly looking for some way to secure the door behind them, and, finding none, he abandoned the attempt and turned to look for some other escape route.

This floor was completely different than the other. Rather than quiet hallways full of small offices, they were in some kind of broad foyer with a reception desk, an elevator sitting quiescent off to the side, plush looking couches and end tables covered with magazines. There was also a set of oversized double doors, and it was toward those doors that Abe was making his way.

Following close behind, Jonah shouted out, "Why don't you just take them on as a dragon? We could fight our way out a lot easier that way!"

"These guys aren't dragons, themselves. Might be mages, but I don't know. Either way they might not know who or what we are, either, and I'd like to keep it that way as long as possible," Abe said, pushing the double doors open and stepping into the room beyond.

It was a large sort of conference room, several tables arranged running the width of the room in rows six deep before stepping up to a sort of elevated podium. Behind the podium was a series of broad windows that presumably gave a panoramic view of something beyond, but it was still too dark to see outside.

Jonah protested. "Does it matter at this point?"

"The longer till they catch on to what we are doing, the more time we have. Look, if they think we're just some random thieves breaking in to try and steal some equipment, they might still think we're down in California, on our way. Soon as they know we are here they'll alert Olympus. Then our cover is blown."

"You honestly believe they think we're just random thieves?"

Abe paused for a moment, his chest heaving as he was breathing, looking around with a fairly dismal expression. "You never know. We could get lucky. Here, give me the gun."

Jonah blinked. "What?"

"The gun. Give it to me."

Nodding but confused, Jonah turned the gun over to Abe, who made his way up to the elevated podium in front of the window. "Get your ass over here, and when I tell you to duck, you'd better do it if you're fond of having your head attached to your shoulders."

Once again Jonah nodded and complied, making his way past the tables and up on to the podium, wondering what the big bald guy had in mind. There was no other way out of the room other than the way they had come, and somehow he doubted they would be lucky enough to go long without being noticed in that room.

Their luck did not hold out long. Only a moment later, fully half a dozen armed guards came pouring into the conference room, taking up positions at the far end of the room that looked frighteningly reminiscent of a firing squad, each one of them with his weapon drawn and trained directly at them. Abe stood with his own gun drawn, pointed right back at them, unmoving as the lead guard shouted at the top of his lungs, "Freeze, we've got you trapped!"

"I'm as frozen as I'm gonna get," Abe called back, quite unmoving, true to his word.

"Put the gun down on the ground slowly, put your hands over your heads, and get down on your knees," the guard yelled back, his voice firm and commanding.

Abe still did not waver, the look on his face taking on that broad, toothy smile that he was accustomed to wearing. "Now why would I do that? Soon as I put my gun down you boys are going to start shooting."

"No one is going to start shooting as long as you comply with our orders. We don't want anyone to get hurt tonight, so please, just put the gun down, get on the ground, and let's handle this like civilized men."

"I don't like that idea one bit," he responded, almost teasing in his tone. "But I don't want to see anyone get hurt, either, so how about I make you a deal. You boys put your guns down, step out of the way, and my friend and I here will be on our merry way. No one gets hurt, everyone gets to go home to their families, and we call it a night. Mmm?"

The lead guard seemed a little irritated by Abe's less than serious tone, shifting nervously on his feet before he spoke up again. "I'm afraid that's not possible, sir. We cannot allow you to leave this building on your own."

Abe simply shrugged. "Well, then I guess we're not leaving."

Jonah watched the interaction with a sense of detached bewilderment. None of the guns were currently trained on him but he had instinctively put his hands up in the air when the guards had assembled, leaving them there, growing heavy over his head. He looked to the guards and then back to Abe, his heart throbbing in his throat as he wondered what would happen. He knew that it would take only a few seconds for them to cut him down with their bullets, and then he was certain those guns would be turned on him to finish the job.

What the hell was Abe trying to accomplish?

"I will ask you one more time, to put the gun down, sir," the lead guard shouted, irritably. "We do not want to shoot you but if you do not comply we will be forced to do so."

"That'd be a hell of a shame. You boys start shooting and I'll have to do the same," he said with a smile.

The lead guard did not look in the least amused. "Do the math, sir. There are six of us and one of you. If things get ugly then you will not be walking out of here alive. Please. Put your weapon down and cooperate with us, I will not ask you again."

"I'm fairly good at math, boys, and I'm sure you can do it too. I get one, maybe two shots before I'm down? I might only take one of you out with me. Let me ask you, which one of you is ready to be the one to take that chance? Which one of you is the betting man?"

The tension in the room, already palpable, became thick enough to cut with a knife. For a long moment no one moved, no one spoke, though Jonah could see a few furtive glances cast among the guards who had been assembled. He wondered if any of them had ever really been in this kind of situation, if they had been prepared to face this kind of risk, if it was what they even signed up for. None of them, at least, seemed very eager for the prospect.

He also wondered what Abe hoped to accomplish. The big man stood there, cool as a cucumber with the gun in his hand, while the whole time Jonah was shaking. He had already put his hands back at his sides, continually glancing back and forth, waiting for the other shoe to drop. He expected the gunfire to begin at any time, he expected to be cut down before he knew what was happening, and the anticipation was starting to become downright painful.

"Well?" Abe spoke up once again, flashing that winning grin. "Which one of you is the betting man? Any of you? Who is going to take the first shot?"

No one answered at first, and when the lead guard finally spoke up again his voice was somewhat subdued. "Sir, I will give you one more chance …"

Abe cut him off before he could finish. "No, I didn't ask for more chances, and it looks to me like none of you are willing to be the one to take a chance, either. This is what we call an old fashioned standoff, boys. Unfortunately I don't do standoffs. I play to win. Hey, kid, remember what I told you to do? Well now's the time."

Jonah blinked at him in confusion. "What?"

"Duck," the bald man said, simply enough, before he squeezed the trigger of his gun. Almost too late Jonah remembered and threw himself to the ground, vaguely aware of Abe's shot going high, over the heads of the guards and shattering a light fixture near the back of the room. The guards reacted almost immediately, firing off one volley of shots after another, a veritable hail of bullets crisscrossing the room, the constant boom of gunfire echoing in the small space again and again with enough ferocity to mimic the rumble of thunder.

Jonah didn't realize he was screaming as he watched Abe fall limply to the ground, fearing the man had been shot, riddled with bullets and cut down without taking out a one of the guards. He cowered behind the heavy podium, aware of the sound of the wood being shredded and torn by the projectiles screaming around him, joining the sound of glass being shattered again and again.

The mad cacophony lasted only seconds, the guards emptying their collective magazines in the direction of the podium over the space of only a few heartbeats, but it felt like forever to Jonah as he cowered, constantly expecting that one shot that would find its mark and end his life. Somehow it never came, and when the hail of bullets ended he was amazed to find himself still breathing.

Still cowering, still cringing at the sound of glass falling and shattering against the ground for a moment longer before that, too, came to an end, leaving the conference room in an eerie and uncomfortable sort of silence. His ears rang almost painfully against the sudden lack of gunfire, but even that was a strange reminder that he'd survived.

He was even more shocked to hear Abe's voice cutting through the ringing in his ears. "Come on, kid, let's go!"

Turning around to find the source of the voice, he was slightly stunned to see the man standing in front of the window, now shattered to bits by the hail of gunfire and left open, gaping to the darkness beyond, a few random papers fluttering on the chill breeze that floated into the conference room. As Abe stepped out and leaped into the darkness, it suddenly all made sense.

"I'll be damned. He had it figured out all along," he muttered to himself, getting to his feet and sprinting for the open window. Just as he was about to jump out, himself, he turned around to get one last look at the guards, watching as they stood with gaping expressions while he dove out into the darkness.

TWENTY ONE

They had flown for nearly three hours straight after their flight from downtown Seattle, much farther than any single flight Jonah had attempted thus far. He had tried to follow Abe's lead and soar when the currents allowed for it, giving him some kind of rest, but when they had finally arrived at the point the bigger drake had chosen to set down Jonah was more than ready for a break, his muscles eager to relax.

Hints of dawn had been visible on the horizon when they escaped from the Syndicate headquarters, the eastern horizon tinged with pale color, but they had been well enough away from the city before it had grown light enough for them to worry about being sighted. They had been forced to take a long detour around a naval base of some kind, Abe warning that they would need to keep a good distance away to avoid running in to trouble, adding more time to their flight.

The scenery had been beautiful, at least. When enough light had filtered into the sky and the pair had lifted high into the air he could make out the numerous arms and bays of the Puget Sound far below, glistening gray that hugged up against the verdant islands and strips of land below. From so high in the air it had a sort of peaceful look to it, and he could not help to imagine that it was serene down there, below.

Before too long, however, the seascape had given way to a range of rugged mountains that rose up before them. Not as tall or striking as the granite sentinels of the mountains he had seen in California, this mountain range was nevertheless impressive to his eyes used to the flat landscape of Florida. Many of the peaks were lined with snow, and unlike their travel in California this flight took them directly over the range. To his eyes the mountains seemed to go on forever, one wrinkled valley after another cutting across the fast expanse of terrain.

It was also as remote as it was rugged. The signs of civilization had quickly ended at the foot of the mountains, and as they settled into one of the valleys he constantly looked for any hint of mankind, only to see none. Jonah knew places like this existed, all over the country, and in many places in the world, but somehow it still struck him as wild to see it with his own eyes.

At last Abe had picked a ridge line, coasting toward it and settling down on the bare rock, near where the snow covered the ground. There seemed to be nothing extraordinary about this spot, nothing to give Jonah a hint as to why they had settled in there, but for the moment he did not bother asking why. His lungs relished the opportunity to refresh themselves.

Abe broke the silence first, peering away into the distance. "I'm afraid that we're going to run into some difficulty here, kid. I really wanted to get out of that place unnoticed, but … well. Things didn't go exactly as planned. We made a bit more of a ruckus than I had hoped."

"A bit of a ruckus?" Jonah shook his head, sighing as he looked out into the distance as well, perhaps hoping to spy what the bigger dragon was gazing at. "That's something of an understatement."

With a bit of a nod Abe chuckled at that, a sound that was more hoarse and somewhat gravelly when he was in dragon form - but somehow still managed to convey all the mirth that his voice usually held. "So it is. Look, I'm going to be honest with you here. The past several days have all gone by rather quickly for you, but it hasn't been out of choice. None of us really wanted to throw you in this kind of a grinder, expect you to learn everything we've tossed at your way. There just really hasn't been much of a choice."

It had been something Jonah had wanted to bring up more than once. To say that the last week had been overwhelming was an understatement in and of itself; trying to accept and digest the fact that dragons were real was hard enough on its own without having to add in the fact that he was one, himself. "I still have so many questions. There is so much I don't know, don't understand … it feels like I'm going into all of this blind, Abe. It's scary."

"I know. It's just, it's been bad timing. We didn't expect to bring you into this, we expected to go on this little adventure and leave you alone, but the Rebekah called and told me you'd gotten the token, that the bull drake had attacked. We didn't have a choice at that point." The big dragon heaved a bit of a sigh of his own. "And here again I'm about to throw you into a difficult situation unprepared."

"What do you mean, by that?"

"They're going to be expecting us, up there," he responded, gesturing toward the distant ridge with a little flick of his head. "They've probably got more than just a few guards with guns, too. Ol' Carl is probably there. Bull drakes, mages too."

Jonah turned to look at him with a bit of a frown. "This supposed to be some kind of pep talk? Because all you're accomplishing is making me wonder if this is a suicide mission after all. How the hell are we supposed to stand up to all of that?"

Abe tried to sound positive, but even his voice carried a strain of doubt with it. "There are some advantages to coming in only a pair, like we are. We're quicker and more nimble than a whole flight of dragons. They probably aren't expecting just the two of us. We might even be able to slip in under their radar and still get a bit of jump on them, after all. But more than that, kid, we're fighting for the right thing. That always helps."

"If you insist." Jonah sighed once more, tucking his wings against him as the chill of the mountain air nipped at his sides a bit. "Still, I don't know what good I'm supposed to be. I don't know anything about these mages you keep talking about, and I'm fairly useless against those bull drakes. I don't even spit fire or do any tricks. I don't have any special, ah, dragon powers or whatever you call them."

"Sure you do. We all do," he answered.

"Care to let me in on the secret? I sure as hell don't know anything about it."

Abe huffed quietly again, turning to look at him critically. "Afraid that's not something I can do for you, kid. We're all a little different, and as a result it's not something that can be taught. You just have to discover it for yourself, and I'm afraid I can't tell you how to do that, either. If it makes you feel any better, I was in a similar boat. Was sure for ages I had no abilities myself, or that I'd never discover them. Took me over a hundred years before I did."

"That's not much consolation given the situation," he replied a little morosely. "What do you do, anyway? I don't think I've seen you use any power or anything."

"That's because I don't really use it, it's more of a defensive capability. Turns out that I'm completely immune to the effects of other dragons' abilities. Dragon fire, acid, you name it. Even ol' Carl's Power of Persuasion."

Jonah frowned lightly at that. "Power of Persuasion?"

Abe nodded a little slowly to that. "It's one of the rarer and more dangerous powers a dragon can have. It's not really an attack, but it allows him to put an immense amount of persuasion behind a single command, so much so that his target is unable to resist, man or dragon. You saw him use it against Jenna back in the valley; all he did was tell her to sleep, and she was helpless to do anything other than pass out."

"I guess I can see how that's dangerous," he agreed. "But then why didn't he just use it on all of us? Seems a little like an unfair advantage."

"Maybe it is an unfair advantage, and maybe the universe does have some sense of fairness to it. Our abilities take a lot out of us, physically, and the greater the exertion the more it takes out of us. The amount of effort Carl has to put into commanding one of us depends on how difficult it would normally be to convince us to do that very same thing. To persuade a hungry dragon to eat would be easy, but to persuade an angry attacking dragon to go to sleep is difficult. It took a lot out of him, and left him unable to try again until he gathered his strength anew."

Jonah found it difficult to listen, difficult to concentrate on what he was saying. It was once more going over his head, once again seemed all too bizarre and convenient. If it weren't for the fact that he were perched atop a mountain in the form of a dragon, he would again be tempted to think that the whole thing was some kind of strange, elaborate setup designed to take advantage of him in one way or another.

He was even still tempted to believe that he was trapped in some sort of vivid, extended dream, unable to wake up, unable to get back to the real world. He knew that wasn't the case, he knew that what he was seeing, hearing and feeling were very much real, but the desire to dismiss them all as some kind of fantasy was more than simply tempting, more than just alluring.

All he could do was sigh and shake his head. "Can I ask you a question, Abe?"

"Shoot, kid. Whatever you want to know."

"Do you think we can do this? I mean, do you really think we have a chance?"

The big dragon seemed to pause for a moment, thinking about the question - or perhaps his response - before answering. "Sure I do, kid. Don't forget, I'm a betting man. The way I see things, there's always a chance, no matter how slim. The longer the odds, the bigger the payout, and really that's what being a betting man is always about. I wouldn't be where I am today if I didn't think there was always a chance, and let me tell you, this is one chance definitely worth taking."

Jonah breathed in heavily. "Then what do you think our odds are?"

Abe breathed a deep, gravelly chuckle at that. "Do you really want to know the answer to that question?"

"No." He shook his head and closed his eyes, sighing once more. "No."

"Then it's time to roll the dice, kid. Every minute we sit here gabbing is one minute longer that the Syndicate has to do whatever it is that they're doing to our friends. Let's go make a difference."

"Wait," Jonah interjected, opening his eyes again and staring back at the larger dragon. "What's our plan?"

"Our plan? Follow my lead. Or don't. I can't tell you what to do this time, Jonah, so just do what feels right. This is the real thing, we're fighting for our lives, for the lives of our loved ones, that big desperate fight where the stakes are too high to plan on doing anything except succeeding. Got it?"

Abe did not give him a chance to respond, the big dragon simply turning his attention back to the distant ridge before pushing himself up and forward, heaving his wings and taking flight. Feeling as if he had no other choice than to follow, Jonah let his own wings unfurl to catch the air and go in pursuit.

Their destination was not immediately clear to him, other than the fact that they were headed toward the far end of the valley, where the bare stone of the mountain ridge rose higher than where they had rested only moments before, the peaks well covered with snow that did not look like it melted even in the middle of summer. It was not until they had crossed the valley and drew closer to the opposing mountains that he could finally see it, an unnatural sort of blemish against the natural rock, a few sharp, regular lines that did not look like they belonged.

It was little more than a bunker tucked against the mountainside, as far as he could see. Built from a concrete whose color closely mimicked that of the natural stone it was well hidden, but even when he realized it was there, there was little to see. A small, low-lying structure with no more than a pair of windows open to the cold mountain air, flat and completely unadorned, with no identifying marks.

There was also no sign that it was occupied, nor any sign that it had been in recent times. He thought he could make out the vestiges of an old roadway that had been carved up the mountainside, hints of switchbacks rising up from the floor of the valley below, but if a road had existed there it had not been used for some time. As he passed overhead and got a good look, he could see the rocky scree that had built up along either side of the bunker looked undisturbed.

He was about to ask Abe if there had been some mistake, if they had come to the wrong place, when he heard a low, trumpeting call sounding from just to his side. Whipping his head around to find the source of the sound, his eyes went wide when he saw the great emerald dragon rising up from behind a smaller ridge line, previously hidden behind an outcropping of rock, her wings now spread wide as she sailed to meet them.

"Jenna," he said out loud to himself, realizing who it was.

While she was still some ways away from him she stopped, pulling her wings back so that she briefly hovered in place, inhaling deeply, her chest swelling before she let it all out in one single burst. Jonah watched with a curious sense of detachment as the air in front of her suddenly convulsed, distorting her image into a weird, twisting image like trying to watch her through a swirling glass of water. The distortion grew as it neared him, and he was practically mesmerized by the sight of it, incapable of moving until it was too late.

Just before the shock wave caught him, Abe came about and threw his large frame between Jonah and the attack. Much of it dissipated as it crashed against him but he was unable to absorb it all, and the air around Jonah suddenly came alive with the sound of a sharp crack, the shock wave smashing into him with enough force to knock the breath from his chest, enough force to slap his wings back and fold them against his sides.

Limp and useless, he fell from the sky as quickly as a stone. The shock had dazed all of his senses, leaving him unable to react, but he was coherent enough to be aware of Abe flapping nearby, beside him, above him perhaps, and he could feel talons scrabbling against his scales, clutching, finally snagging him before he landed on something hard and unforgiving.

At some point after beginning his fall to the ground, he had unwillingly reverted back to his normal, human form. Perhaps it was after the impact, either way he could not tell, but when he came back to his senses he was lying prone on a flat concrete surface, his head throbbing, blue sky and the hint of a mountain peak visible in the corner of his vision. For a brief moment he was unable to move, his muscles refusing to cooperate.

A familiar voice reached his ears, however, one that made his skin crawl. "Ah, brother Ibrahim. We've been expecting you, I just wish you hadn't kept us waiting so long." The voice undoubtedly belonged to Carolus.

"Sorry to disappoint you, Carl. We've been a little busy."

"Making a mess of the offices back in Seattle, so I heard. Really that was quite uncalled for, you could have given me a call and I would have only been too happy to let you know where to come."

"I'm sure," Abe responded, rather sarcastically.

Jonah tried to move his head to get a look at what was going on, and while his muscles protested he was able to twist himself just enough to get a look at Abe standing next to him, also once more in human form, his double breasted suit a little dusty but no worse for the wear. Nearby was Carolus, also neatly dressed and looking well groomed, his watery blue eyes fixated on the bald man with a curious lack of anger.

Nearby, Jenna was perched on an outcropping of rock, the big emerald dragon looking down at all of them with a rather dispassionate gaze. As he tried to look further his muscles complained, and he groaned softly in response.

Carolus turned to regard him with those watery blue eyes, mocking a smile. "And you brought your young protege with you, too. Is that all? I had kind of hoped we might have a bit of a reunion, Ibrahim."

"We can still have a reunion, Carl. Lot of folk are pissed off at you and rightly so, but you can still turn your back on this foolishness. Come back with us."

"Please." The old man turned his attention back to Abe, wearing a rather disappointed looking frown. "What reason could I possibly have for doing that? Things are proceeding quite well here, perhaps it is you who should reconsider. The Syndicate can be rather accommodating of those who seek forgiveness, as can I."

Abe turned to look up at Jenna with more than a hint of pain on his face. "Is this your version of success, Carolus? Look at her. Look at what you've made of her."

The old man fumed a little bit at the accusation, shaking his head. "Come now, Ibrahim, you misjudge what is happening here. You know as well as I do that she would never have given up the fight. The Syndicate only want peace, just as you and I only wish for peace. They grant it to those who wish it. More drastic measures are required for those who reject their offer."

"This is not peace, Carolus," Abe responded, once again using the old man's proper name, as if to underline the sobriety of his statement. "This is slavery. I know how power hungry you are, but is this really the kind of clan you dreamed of ruling over? Mindless zombies?"

"She is no mindless zombie. She has only been made to see the error of her ways, and now she serves those who seek true peace."

The bald man shook his head and frowned. "You are fooling yourself if you believe that, and you are fooling yourself if you believe the Syndicate is going to let you stay in your position of power."

Carolus frowned as well. "And what is that supposed to mean?"

"Look at her," Abe repeated, gesturing toward the impassive Jenna perched nearby. "Look at what power they have. When you have subdued the rest of the clan, what possible use could the Syndicate have for you? Why would they bother leaving you in charge? You're a middle man, Carolus, and disposable to them. Look at what they have done to her, and know what they have in store for you when you have outlived your usefulness as a pawn."

"Ridiculous," the old man spat, growing angry. "Absolutely ridiculous."

"Think about it, Carl. Please. I'm telling you this as a brother, not as …"

The sound of footfalls approaching caught their attention, both Carolus and Abe turning to look and see who it was. The former responded with little more than a curt nod, but Abe's eyes widened a little and his jaw went slightly slack while an unfamiliar voice spoke up. "Carolus, what is this nonsensical argument out here about?"

"I am merely hoping to convince my brother Ibrahim of the error of his ways," he responded dourly.

"The man is a traitor twice over. There is only one purpose left for him, and we've only a few of the others left. The latest conversion was another easy success, I do not believe we are going to lose any others to the process."

Abe's expression went from one of shock to terror to raw anger, clenching his jaw and shaking his fist. "Lost? Carolus, what has happened here?"

The unseen man was the one to answer. "Not that it is any concern to you, but we lost two of your miserable compatriots who fought against our methods. However you can rest easy knowing that we have perfected our methods, and when we are ready for you there will be no risk of any permanent damage."

Jonah managed to shift himself a little more, rolling partially to his side to get a look at the man. He did not look particularly intimidating, a rather thin and unassuming man with plain brown hair and gray eyes set behind a pair of glasses, dressed in a business suit less gaudy than Abe's. Yet, for some reason, Abe did not attack the man in spite of the anger apparent in his eyes as he turned to look back to Carolus with a shock. "Lost … Carolus … is it true?"

The old man looked away for a moment, frowning visibly. "There were unfortunate results in the first experiments, yes."

"Carolus …"

"Enough," the unidentified man interjected, cutting him off with a frown and summoning over a pair of bulky men - bull drakes, by the look of them - to stand at either of Abe's sides and grasp him roughly by the arms. "We'll get to him later, but he is no longer any concern of ours. What of the young one?"

Jonah realized that he was referring to himself when the man cast a rather disinterested gaze down in his direction. Carolus cleared his throat a little, sounding somewhat resigned. "He is young and idealistic, but I fear that he has spent too long under Ibrahim's tutelage. It will take me some time to properly convince him of our cause …"

"Useless," the bespectacled man said, shaking his head and stalking away. "There's no time for that, Carolus. He can follow his tutor right into our own methods of persuasion."

Carolus continued to look at him with those watery blue eyes, a curious mixture of anger and disappointment as he shook his head and gestured to someone out of Jonah's vision. Another bull drake appeared, leaned over to grasp him by the shoulders and haul him to his feet. It was too fast, too sudden, and all of the blood seemed to rush from his head, letting the darkness wrap around him and knock him unconscious.

#

"Jonah? Hey, kid, you all right?"

Light came back to his vision with an uncomfortable jolt, accompanied by a sharp stabbing pain in the back of his skull. With a pained groan, he reached back and pressed his palm against his head. He was lying on his side on a hard, uncomfortable surface, and after a moment he pushed himself up to a sitting position, slowly. "Ugh. What happened?"

"You took a pretty good spill back there. Knocked yourself on the head." It was Abe, though Jonah could still not yet bear to open his eyes, the light causing the stabbing pain to increase. "Was afraid we might have lost you for a moment."

The memories of what happened came rushing back to him fairly quickly, the confusion bleeding away where the pain would not. He remembered plummeting from the sky, remembered lying flat on his back while Abe and Carolus had their brief argument. Forcing his eyes open, he squinted to try and get a look around.

He was in a small room that amounted to little more than a concrete box, lit by a bare incandescent bulb hanging overhead, unadorned with any furniture. A heavy iron door, partially rusted, closed off the only exit to the room that he could see. "Where are we?"

"Carl had us thrown in here after … well, after what happened. It hasn't been that long actually, maybe an hour. Haven't heard a word from them since they left us here," he replied a little morosely.

Pushing himself back against a wall to support himself, Jonah pulled his knees in against his chest and breathed a quiet sigh. "So then we're trapped. No way out of here, is there."

Abe shook his head a little, trying his best to retain his grin in spite of the circumstances. "Afraid not, kid. The whole places is probably warded and there's not a thing we can do to help ourselves get outta this room, and even if we did there's nothing but traitors, bulls and mages on the other side."

"Then that's it." His head throbbed lightly again and he let his eyes rest shut. "We're done. And it's all my fault."

"No need for that kind of mood, it's depressing enough that we're locked away like this."

Jonah shrugged it off. "Does it really matter? Besides, it's true. If I'd just listened to you and been more careful we might have stood a chance, but … I mean, we didn't even last ten seconds before I was downed. If you hadn't chased after me you might have gotten away, too."

He felt a big, meaty hand on his shoulder, giving him a sort of squeeze. "Look at it this way, kid. We rolled the dice and lost. Happens to everyone, from time to time, and it's just a matter of how big you lose. We lost big this time. It's not a matter of whose fault it is or isn't."

Opening his eyes again, Jonah turned to look at the weak but sincere grin that Abe was still wearing. "How do you do it? We're in a hopeless situation and we're gonna be dragged off to die, or have our brains sucked out, or something weird."

"I have the advantage of knowing I led a full, rich life. Full of ups and downs, full of mistakes, and full of victories. The important thing isn't what happened, though, it's where I stood at the end, it's how I went out. Fighting for what I believe is right, fighting for my friends and family. Hard to beat that, Jonah. Rolled the dice big and lost, but I still rolled 'em big."

It seemed to be some little comfort as far as Jonah was concerned, and he pulled himself up to his feet, slowly, Abe rising up next to him and helping him to his feet. "Well that's good and fine for you, but what about me? My life is full of nothing. I've never done anything important or noble or good. I get by on the bare minimum. Work just enough to pay my bills and buy a few toys. What sort of life do I have to celebrate?"

"It's like I told you," the big guy said with a soft smile. "It's not about what you've done but what you were doing. Chasing after someone you cared about, sticking your neck out for her, putting yourself on the line to try and do a good thing. It didn't pay off but that's not what's important. You went out doing something that mattered."

Once more Jonah shrugged. "I guess. I'm still not ready go go out. You sure there's no way out of here?"

Satisfied that Jonah was not going to black out again, Abe nodded and walked over to the door, giving it a little smack with the palm of his hand, letting it ring dully against its hinges. "Solid iron, three inches thick. The walls are reinforced concrete, six inches thicker. If I remember correctly this place was originally built as a sort of bomb shelter, back during the Cold War. Even the Syndicate was worried about getting nuked, so they had to build themselves a command center that would last. The walls are built to withstand a bomb, no way we're getting through.

"Worse still," he said, looking upward as he continued. "We're a ways underground. Not sure how far, fifty feet, a hundred feet, just depends on where they've stuffed us away, but in any case there's several levels we'd have to get through to escape. Watched, guarded, the whole works. Trust me, kid. I'm not ready to go out, either. I just don't see any way around it."

As if to punctuate his statement, the sound of a bolt being pulled against stone rang in the room, and Abe took a step back to look dismally at the door. "And it looks like they're coming for us now, in any case. I wish that I'd gotten to know you better, kid. It's been a pleasure working with you."

The finality of that statement made Jonah feel sick to his stomach, his mind beginning to spin once more as he came to grips with the possibility that not only was his end inevitable, but it was now only moments away.

With a slow grinding creak the door was pushed inward. On the other side was not a bull drake, but another face that Jonah did not recognize, a middle aged man with hair that was beginning to go gray around the edges, steely gray eyes that regarded them with a dispassionate gaze, and a slightly unkempt salt and pepper beard.

Abe, on the other hand, seemed to recognize the man, his countenance falling visibly as he shook his head. "Oh, Jeffress. Not you, too." Jeffress, the dragon that he and Rebekah had gone in search of, days before and kidnapped by the Syndicate. In a sad twist of fate, he would be the one to take them away to their fate.

TWENTY TWO

"Oh come on, Abraham. For being a Syndicate conspirator, you aren't very well informed." The man at the door abandoned the somewhat vacant look that he'd been wearing, a faint hint of a smile tugging at the corners of his mouth.

The reaction caught even the usually unflappable Abe off guard, the bald man staring at the doorway with his jaw slack, reaching up to smooth down his nonexistent hair. "Holy hell, Jeffress … it's you? I mean, like, the regular, real you? How?"

"It's a long story and we don't really have the time for it right now. Short version is that what the Syndicate thinks they've done to me and what they really managed to do are two different things," he said, briefly stepping inside and pulling the door partially shut behind him. "But I can't say the same for the others, and I won't be able to say the same for you two if we don't get your asses out of here, pronto."

Jonah watched the exchange with a slightly confused look, his head still throbbing a little, but the brief spark of hope once again flickering inside of him. "You're here to get us out of here?"

The man turned to look at him with a bit of a squint and then a smile. "Well, I'm not here to make pleasantries, but I suppose introductions are in order. My name's Matt Jeffress," he said, sticking his hand out.

He took the offered hand a little unsteadily, blinking. "Jonah."

"Pleased to meet you, Jonah. Yes, I'm here to bust your asses out of jail, and get myself the hell out of this place while we're at it. I'm sick of working with these Syndicate creeps and pretending to be on their side. Particularly after seeing what they've been doing to the rest of the clan."

Abe stepped in and touched the man lightly on the shoulder to get his attention. "I've heard that some were … lost."

The observation was met with a nod and a brief moment of silence.

"Yeah," Jeffress said, gnawing on his lower lip for a moment. "I'm afraid I don't have much information on what happened, I wasn't there to see it. I just know that at least two attempts have ended in failure."

"Do you know who it was?" Abe wore a grim expression but there was a real curiosity behind his eyes, a curiosity that Jonah felt as well as a bit of dread.

"Sorry. I don't know. Just that some of the attempts went badly for the subjects. They didn't make it. The rest have been, well, more successful as far as the Syndicate is concerned." He paused to look down at his watch, scowling a bit before pushing the door back open. "But we've got to move now if we're going to make sure that the two of you don't follow suit."

The space beyond their makeshift little cell was not much more inviting, matching the character of a Cold War era bomb shelter: concrete stained in places from water seepage, bare bulbs hanging from the ceiling at regular intervals, and iron doors largely too rusted to be of use. A narrow steel framed staircase spiraled upward from one end of the short, narrow hallway. Jeffress made his way straight to that stairway, grasping at the flimsy handrail and peering upward.

"Excuse my doubt, Jeffress, but how are you supposed to get us out of here? This place has got to be as as well guarded as Fort Knox," Abe murmured a little dubiously.

"Not as bad as you'd think," came the response, as Jeffress glanced down at his watch again. "They're all getting ready for something up there. I'm not sure what's going down but they're getting ready to take all of the dragons up the mountain. I think it has something to do with the elder."

While the statement didn't really carry that much meaning for Jonah he could tell by watching Abe's reaction that it must have been a big deal. The big bald guy rubbed his chin thoughtfully. "Well, still. It looks like we're at the bottom of this damned thing, you think we're gonna make it all the way out without being caught?"

Jeffress flashed a mischievous smile. "Well, I've been working on a little distraction, but I don't think the Syndicate really trusts me, either. Hard to get away without them noticing. If I only had a little more time ..."

"You? Need more time?" Abe looked at the man doubtfully.

"Wards," the man said with a dour expression.

The big guy nodded a little, his gaze suddenly looking a little distant. "Of course," he said, chewing on his lip as he seemed to be caught in thought. "Pretty good one, too. Must have learned their lesson. I might be able to help out, but it'll only be for a few seconds. Then they'd be on to us."

"Plenty of time," Jeffress said with a grin.

"All right, I'll give you what I can, but make it quick," Abe said, stepping over to a wall and resting a palm on it, closing his eyes as he worked his jaw a little. "Ah. What I wouldn't give for a cigar right about now."

Jonah looked on with a bit of confusion, first back to Jeffress, then over to Abe as he stood at the wall. "What are you doing?"

"It's a little hard to explain," the big guy said, furrowing his brow as if he were concentrating. "Thing about wards, they don't propagate through air. They need something physical. So it goes through the walls … it'll take me a minute to feel it out, figure it out."

Continuing to watch with that confused expression, Jonah nodded a little. He tried to imagine that he could feel something happening, some kind of energy coursing through the air, some taste of magic or something of the like, but for all he could tell Abe was merely mapping out the indistinct little bumps in the concrete wall. "Then what?"

Abe grinned, though kept his eyes closed. "Then I'll take it down for a few seconds and let our friend Jeffress here do his thing. If you'll be quiet a moment, that is."

Jonah almost apologized, but then bit his tongue, feeling a little chagrined. Another moment passed as Abe slid his hand lightly against the wall, his grin fading as he was now clearly deep in concentration. Finally the big man paused, his fingers splayed against the concrete as he inhaled deeply, and then nodded. "Now."

Turning to see what reaction Jeffress would offer, Jonah was surprised to see the man was simply not there. He blinked into the empty space where he had stood only seconds before, turning back to Abe with a stutter. "Where did he ..."

"Sorry," the big man said, pulling his hands back away from the wall, looking a little exhausted. "That's all I could give you. I hope it was enough."

For a moment Jonah thought he was addressing him, but before he opened his mouth he realized that the big man was looking right past him. Turning on his heel, he was again surprised to see Jeffress standing there, panting a little bit as if he too had exerted himself. "Just enough, I think. We should know in about … ahh … Three, two, one ..."

As if on cue, a distant rumble preceded a slight vibration running through the concrete, just strong enough to cause a slight layer of the looser dust and detritus to shake loose, dancing against the ground around them in a quiet little clatter. Almost immediately afterward there was the sound of shouting that echoed down from the stairs above.

Abe's face stretched into a broad smile as he nodded. "Jeffress, you son of a bitch. You did it. Just when we needed a loaded die."

Jonah blinked. "Wait. What the hell just happened?"

"I'll explain later. Let's just get the hell out of here while we have a chance." Jeffress beckoned to them both, making his way to the stairway just as another rumble began to echo through the little bunker, shaking more tiny bits of concrete loose and showering over them lightly. Abe followed shortly thereafter and Jonah finally got into motion, pulling up the rear. "Still need to be on our guard, though. They have an administrator with them."

"Terrell. Yes, I saw him."

The conversation was hard for Jonah to keep up with, their voices starting to blend in a little with the chaotic noises that were coming from further up the shaft, but he didn't want to feel totally left out. "Administrator?"

Abe looked back down in his direction, or at least he thought he saw a glance his way, but could not be certain. "Back in the day they used to call themselves arch-mages but I suppose they decided it was too old fashioned sounding. Doesn't much matter what they are called, they're very dangerous. They're very rare in the Syndicate, and very powerful. We don't want to mess with him if we can get away with it."

"What happens if we do run into this … administrator?"

The sound of Abe's chuckle was a little forced as it made its way down to him. "Fly. Fly as far away as you can, as fast as you can." Yet another rumble shook the bunker, accompanied by a loud sort of thud, with enough force to rattle the stairway that they were continuing to wind their way up. "Jeffress! I thought you said distraction, not destruction!"

"Sorry, but I had to make sure to get their attention!"

Running up the tightly wound stairway was proving more and more difficult as they went. Jonah's legs were starting to protest the climb, passing one nearly identical level in the bunker after another, concrete and rebar and dimly lit passageways. He did not know how much higher they would have to go, and to make matters worse he was starting to feel dizzy from all the turning around and around.

At last they came to a halt, Jeffress waving them off the stairs at a level that looked as unremarkable as the others, Abe protesting slightly. "Why are we stopping here? I thought you said we had to get out of here, fast."

"Backdoor," he explained simply enough, pushing one of the heavy iron doors open with his shoulder, disappearing into the space beyond with a little wave. Abe followed, ducking his head and once more Jonah was the last.

Just beyond the door was a plain concrete room, no real surprise, but in the side of the concrete was a large gash that had been hollowed out, a rough tunnel hewn right into the rock of the mountainside. Just wide enough for one person to pass and just tall enough that Jonah did not have to duck, and lit only with a string of small incandescent bulbs pinned to the rock at somewhat irregular intervals, it would have been enough to give Jonah pause if not for the urgency of their flight.

Fortunately it was not too long before they emerged from the cramped confines of the tunnel, the brilliance of the daylight enough of a contrast to the dim tunnel to render him momentarily blind. When he was able to adjust, blinking in the light, he could see that they had emerged on the mountainside somewhat lower than the bunker, the tunnel's exit nestled up against a large outcropping of rocks.

The loud report of an explosion cracked through the air, echoing across the rocks and sending a cascade of stones and pebbles skittering down toward the valley below. Obviously the source of Jeffress' distraction, it seemed to be doing the job; off to the side and somewhat behind them, a plume of smoke and dust rose upward from the explosion, and he could see a number of dragons circling overhead, likely investigating what was going on.

"We'll probably only have a few seconds head start," Abe commented as he briefly watched the scene unfold before looking eastward, back across the valley. "I'd rather we didn't get caught up in any kind of fight, this time. We're outnumbered and outmatched. We fly hard and fast and if we're lucky we stay ahead long enough for them to break off the chase; not even the Syndicate is stupid enough to follow us right over Seattle in the daytime."

With no further hesitation Abe jumped off a rock and in a writhing flash of crimson took wing. Jeffress was just behind him, his body stretching into the form of a medium sized dragon, white with a set of bluish tiger-like stripes on his sides, leaving only Jonah to sigh and leap after them, once more letting the wind carry him upward as he felt his wings cut and scoop at the air.

Almost immediately as they took to the air, a great emerald shape swooped in from above and to the side, practically cutting off their escape. It was Jenna, again, her chest already swelling as she drew in a massive breath before letting it out with a sharp crack. Not about to fall for the same thing twice, Jonah tucked his wings in and sent himself into a controlled dive, beneath the shockwave, twisting about to see where her voice slammed against the outcropping of rock like a sledge, shattering the rock into a million pieces.

The other two had flitted neatly out of the way, as well. Jeffress, smaller and more nimble, was harassing the larger green dragon, flying circles around her, zipping in closer to snap harmlessly at her sides, distracting her while Abe moved in closer, shouting in her direction. "Jenna! Do you not recognize your brothers?"

The green dragon responded only with a viscous snarl, snapping back at the smaller Jeffress that continued to nip at her sides but kept just out of range. He was too fast for her to catch, and there was no way she was going to get him with her shockwave power at such close range. Lashing out in obvious irritation she flapped her wings irregularly, bobbed and weaved through the air to try and get at him to no avail.

Abe remained close but out of the fray. "We do not wish to harm you Jenna, please, you must remember us, must know us! See us for who you are!"

"It is you who are the blind fool," a voice called out from behind them. Jonah, uncertain of how he could help and having kept back and out of the way, whipped around to see Carolus, the big ashen dragon, sneering at them almost scornfully.

Instinctively Jonah moved back, away from the big dragon, watching him cautiously though he did not make any immediately aggressive moves. Abe, unable to break off his pursuit, was forced to try and divide his attention. "Carl! What an unpleasant surprise, seeing you here."

The old dragon cackled unpleasantly. "Did you think your little ruse was actually going to pay off? We are ahead of you at every step, Ibrahim. You will not leave this place until we choose to let you. Until I choose to let you."

"Come on, Carl. You're not so caught up in this power hungry scheming of yours that you don't see what the Syndicate really wants? Can you live with the destruction of the Clan on your conscience?"

There was an angry growl at Jonah's side, and he whipped his head around once again to see Jenna trying to swat Jeffress away, still to no avail, but the smaller dragon was only proving a distraction at best. In the distance other dragons - some bull drakes, some members of the Clan who had been brainwashed - continued to circle the source of the explosions, paying them little heed. Abe split the distance between Jenna and Carolus, who was still hovering lazily on the air above the rocks.

It was proving difficult to keep track of where everyone was, what everyone was doing.

"The Clan has destroyed itself with its petty need for independence," Carolus shot back, whipping at the air with his tail. "You and those like you are the ones blinded to the truth, Ibrahim. My eyes have been opened. Open yours, or they will be opened for you."

"I will die before I serve you and the Syndicate, Carolus."

Jonah realized he had been keeping back, that he had been doing nothing to help for too long. He might have no special powers that he knew of but that did not make him powerless, did not make him useless. Tucking his wings in again, he circled around and then dove right at Carolus, just as he started to fire back, "Then you will not leave here alive . . ."

He slammed hard against the old dragon's side, his talons extended and grasping at his scales, pulling and tugging, seeking to rend. Carolus roared out in pain and confusion as he was knocked over, his wings flailing for a moment before he was able to right himself again, his thick tail whipping around in anger; Jonah managed to get out of the way just in time. "Insolent whelp," the old dragon snarled as he righted himself.

Jonah didn't respond, but tried his best to mimic what he had seen Jeffress doing. Willing his wings to work overtime he pushed himself, diving in and away, snapping his jaws at Carolus' ponderous, flapping wings, clawing at his side when he was able to get close enough, making sure to stay clear of the big dragon's jaws.

"I'll see to it you regret this," he snarled angrily again, whipping his tail about and snapping his own jaws, trying to reach out and swat Jonah out of the air but he was succeeding in keeping just out of reach.

He was smaller, weaker but faster. He knew there was no way he could hope to bring the big dragon down, but he could keep him busy, keep him away from the others. Not only that, but it felt damned good to have the upper hand for a change.

"Carolus! Enough of this nonsense! Bring them down!"

The voice had come from the direction of the outcropping of rock. Jonah caught a glimpse of a man standing there on one of the large boulders, the same man he had seen ordering Carolus about earlier. How he could speak and be heard, his voice projecting every bit as loud as one of the dragons', could only have been the work of magic.

With a loud snarl, Carolus snapped at him again, trying to pull away before responding. "Of course, administrator," he began, when another loud roar in the opposite direction once more tugged at their attention.

A great emerald dragon, head thrown back and roaring angrily was diving out of the sky, but it was not Jenna; he was, in fact, diving straight for the other dragon still busily evading Jeffress. "Jenna," he cried out angrily, desperately.

"Jason ... no, Jason no!" Abe shouted loudly at the new arrival, but when it was clear that the drake was not going to move, he simply shouted for Jeffress to get out of the way. The smaller dragon did so, flitting off to the side just as the two emerald green dragons collided in midair, grappling in a flurry of limbs and talons.

Enough of Jonah's attention had been diverted that he hadn't seen Carolus whip around and lash out, and before he could get out of the way he took a swipe right against his back. Claws raked against his scales, tore at part of his wing membrane and forced him to cry out sharply in pain. The big dragon wasn't done, however, swooping in to snatch him up.

A crimson blur crossed between them, knocking the old dragon out of the way. Jonah was barely able to roll out of the way and keep from being caught up in the tussle as Abe smashed headlong into Carolus, both of the drakes snarling as they tried to fight each other off.

Jonah looked for a way to help, some way to duck in and get a cheap shot on the old dragon but there was simply no room. He could only hang back and watch while the two dragons snapped and clawed at one another, barely able to keep themselves aloft. All the while, he could hear Jason crying and pleading in the air behind him, trying to get his sister to snap out of whatever sway she was under, but the only responses were angry snorts and growls.

Then a flicker of something bright in the corner of his eye caught his attention. The man standing on the little outcropping of rock had his hands up in the air, a sort of a spark building up in the empty space between them. "This is intolerable," he said, his voice still unnaturally amplified, when the little spark over his head suddenly burst into a sort of weird conflagration, a ball of writhing white flame that launched outward from his hands, arcing straight for the two green dragons who were locked in combat.

Jeffress, who was circling nearby, had seen it too, and cried out with unmasked urgency in his voice. "Jason! Look out!"

There was no time. It only took a second for the strange little fireball to splash against the side of one of the two green dragons - Jonah could not tell which, they were so intertwined - and immediately erupted into a brilliant firestorm that enveloped both of them in white light so bright he had to look away. It crackled angrily against the air, radiating enough heat that Jonah could feel it against his own hide from dozens of yards away, and then was snuffed out as quickly as it had burst in to life.

When he opened his eyes again to look at the aftermath, he was stunned to see that instead of a pair of grappling dragons, there was only a pair of charred, lifeless husks falling away to the ground. There was nothing he could do but gape in horrified amazement. He heard a sharp gasp from where Jeffress was circling, and even the sounds of the struggle behind him, where Abe and Carolus were grappling, suddenly went quiet.

He turned to look away before what was left of the pair crashed against the rocks and disintegrated into dust.

Both of the larger dragons had stopped fighting and were staring with openly stunned expressions. With a rough shove Carolus pushed himself away from Abe, circling around and then gaping at the administrator. "What have you done?"

"Ended one distraction," the man responded coolly, raising his hands over his head and repeating the same gesture as before, the little spark coming to life over his head. "As I shall end another."

"She was on our side," the old dragon responded a little hollowly, watching with a sort of detached horror while the mage leveled his assault against Abe, firing off another one of those balls of writhing energy. Abe, stunned as he was, was still quick enough to dodge the attack. The ball of energy exploded harmlessly in the air, basking the mountainside in unnatural heat.

The mage looked unmoved, except for the irritation at having missed. "And she was causing a distraction. We cannot waste our time on such things," he spat angrily, quickly summoning another ball of energy and lobbing it off in Abe's direction.

"Stop it … you're going to kill them all," Carolus objected, looking about in an increasingly conflicted and helpless manner as the dragons tried to scatter and avoid the attacks. "That wasn't part of the plan."

The whole scene unfolded in a kind of weird, twisted dance from Jonah's perspective. The mage was focused on attacking Abe, lobbing the writhing balls of energy one right after another. Jeffress made a rather feeble attempt to intervene at one point, diving in at the man when his back was turned, but the mage simply shrugged him off - some unseen force pushing the dragon back hard enough that he tumbled against the ground with a low groan. He began to feel sick to his stomach, realizing there was nothing he could do.

"They've proven themselves unfit for service to the Syndicate. You couldn't control them Carolus, so I am going to control them in the only way I know how," the man shouted, firing off one more fireball that exploded just in front of the crimson dragon, close enough that the drake faltered. A second fireball caught him just at the edge of the explosion, singing his wing, Abe roaring out plaintively in pain as he came down hard against the mountainside.

"Stop it," Carolus repeated, looking on with a wide eyed, wild expression.

The mage showed no interest in stopping. With Abe grounded he was no longer in a hurry, summoning up a larger, more powerful ball of energy between his hands, his eyes fixated on the crimson drake with murderous intent. For a brief heartbeat, Jonah considered diving down and attacking the mage, buy Abe enough time to get up, to carry on the fight. But he had withdrawn too far from the side of the mountain, was too far to make it. He would not be able to help. He would be unable to do anything except watch as Abe, too, was burned in front of his eyes.

When Carolus spoke again, his voice was deeper, louder, more resonant. He spoke but a single word, two syllables in a language that Jonah did not know but somehow instinctively understood their meaning : Die.

The force of the dragon's voice spilled over the mage as he stood, ruffling his hair slightly before the power of his conjured fire went out. The man's eyes widened briefly as he reached up and clutched at his throat, gagging and gasping for breath. Spinning around he shot off an intensely hateful glance in the direction where Carolus had been hovering before he keeled over, his body flapping in the breeze for the brief moment it was airborne as he tumbled off the boulder he had been perched on.

Then he was gone.

Carolus, too, had begun to tumble earthward. His strength seemed to give out as soon as he had spoken the command, his wings suddenly incapable of keeping him aloft. The big ashen dragon struggled as he fell, his head leaning back, breathing out a sort of deep, rattling sigh.

Jonah realized what he had done, and as soon as he did, he dove in after the falling dragon, as fast as he could. Before they had crashed into the ground, he reached out with his talons to snag at the old dragon, closing around flesh. He looked down to see the limp, ragged body of Carolus, the old, white haired man, dangling from his grasp. Looking for a spot to set him down, he chose a small level patch very close to where Abe had gone down, and set the old man against the dirt as gently as he possibly could.

The old man was still alive. Rolling onto his back, he looked up at Jonah with watery blue eyes and forced a sort of half smile. "Ah. You're going to have to tell Ibrahim that he was right. It wasn't worth the power."

"I hear you, Carl," the crimson dragon said, near enough that his voice carried clearly.

Carolus looked somehow immensely older as he lay there splayed out on the rock. The white hair that fell over his temples was thin and ragged, giving him a sort of wild and unkempt look. The wrinkles and creases in his face seemed to have deepened, making his eyes look sunk in, yet still he tried to smile. "Ibrahim, my brother. I was blinded by my own ambition … it wasn't until I saw what he did to the others. I didn't think he was going to kill them. I was just trying to do what was right …"

A roar in the distance caught Jonah's attention. Turning to look back over his shoulder, he could see the other dragons, the ones who had been circling over the explosions, now looked to be retreating, wheeling their way off into the distance. "They're leaving," he whispered softly.

"Listen," Carolus said, his voice growing thin in his throat. "I don't have much time to explain. The clan can be redeemed. The spell that has been placed upon them is not permanent, not yet. They are going to Olympus, they are going up the mountain. At the last light of the day their fate will be sealed. You have to help them."

Glancing back down at the old man, Jonah frowned. "I don't understand. Up the mountain?"

The old man seemed to be growing weaker by the moment, his eyes closing as he coughed. "Redeem them for me. Redeem me with them."

"Carl." It was Abe, who had pulled himself up from the ground some, speaking low and steady. "Listen to me old friend. You need to tell us how to do it. How do we redeem them? What can we do?"

"Make them remember." Carolus swallowed deeply, struggling for breath. "Remember who they are. What they are. They are not gone, only hidden … make them remember … they have the elder, going to corrupt. You must go. You must hurry."

Jonah glanced back and forth between Abe who was looming nearby and Carolus beneath him, who was quickly fading. "I still don't understand. How do we make them remember?"

The old man gasped softly then opened his eyes again, looking up at him with those watery blue irises, smiling weakly. "Go after her, Jonah. Save her. I'm sorry …" When his eyes closed one more time, breathing out a long, low gasp, Jonah did not have to be told that the old man was gone.

"Rest well, old friend," Abe said quietly, reverently, letting his head dip earthward. "The clan will know that you died a friend and not a foe. You died a hero, not a traitor."

For the next moment silence reigned, the only sound was that of nature itself: the wind winding its way through the valley, the occasional clatter of a rock or stone as it made its journey down the mountainside. Jonah felt like he ought to say something, but had no clue what to say. He didn't even know how he was supposed to feel.

"Well. We can't just stay here all day long, you heard what he said. We have until nightfall to try and undo what's been done," Abe finally spoke up, bringing himself back up to his feet and glancing up into the sky.

For some reason, he felt suddenly miserable. "I'm still not even sure what he was talking about."

"Olympus. It's a mountain peak not far from here, just a few miles. Sounds like they're going to enact some kind of ritual. I'm not sure what it is," the crimson dragon said, his voice rumbling slightly against the rocks. "But there doesn't seem to be a whole lot of time. We've probably only got an hour of daylight left."

Jonah glanced upward to the sky, as well. The sun had already hidden itself behind the mountainside that he was resting on, and he could not be sure how far it had sunk at all, but as he glanced away into the valley he could see the shadows beginning to grow long against the opposite side. "How badly hurt are you? Do you think we even have a chance?"

Abe shrugged his shoulders, stretching his wings out with a cringe. Several parts of one wing were scorched and showing signs of tearing, and as he moved them up and down he let out a little gasp of pain. "Well. I think I can at least give it a shot," he said.

"Makes two of us." Jeffress, who had fallen himself not long ago, had managed to go airborne again and was now flying circles over the both of them. "But if we're going to do this thing, let's get moving. The others are long gone and we've got our work cut out if we're going to catch up to them!"

Looking down at Carolus for a moment, Abe heaved softly. "We will return for you, old friend," he murmured, forcing his wings into motion and picking himself up into the air with no small amount of grimacing, but as soon as he was in the air he breathed a long, low sigh. "Well. What do you say, kid? I don't know about you but I'm not done pressing my luck for the day. How about we give the dice one last toss?"

Jonah breathed in deeply, taking a step back before he finally nodded. Grim as their chances might be, a chance was a chance. Rebekah might still be out there, still be alive, and if she was, she deserved at least that much. Launching himself into the air, he looked off into the distance. "Lead the way."

TWENTY THREE

Tree studded valleys gave way to barren stone, which itself slowly gave way to snow and ice as they gained altitude, soaring ever near the highest mountain peak that Jonah could see : Mount Olympus. He vaguely remembered it being the name of the home of the Greek gods in mythology, and somehow the fact seemed significant to him. He was just not certain why.

"All right, Jeffress. Tell me what we're up against."

Abe had taken the lead, the largest, oldest and presumably most powerful of the three. Jonah was content to follow slightly behind, opposite the dragon he had only recently met, a small if orderly formation cutting through the thinning mountain air. Not really knowing what they were getting into, he let himself wander a little closer to ensure he did not miss anything.

"Three more mages," Jeffress began, shouting slightly to make sure he was heard. "No administrators, but still. They'll be accompanied by three bulls, as well as whatever members of our clan that they've managed to keep under their control. They have the elder with them and I'm pretty sure they've got something in mind for him. I'm just not sure what."

"So that makes it one mage and one bull for each of us. I like those odds," the big dragon said, chuckling throatily.

Jeffress laughed in kind although he sounded somewhat less jovial about it. "Well, I know you're the betting sort so you'll be happy to know that our odds will be a little more even than that. The mages are likely to be involved in some kind of ceremony that they don't want to interrupt, so there's a good chance they'll be out of the picture at first. The clan, too, if they're going to be a part of the ritual."

"Just one bull apiece, then? Even better than I thought!"

It wasn't exactly a comforting thought to Jonah. He remembered the encounter with the bulls back in the lonely valley, where Rebekah had been taken. Between the two of them, they had been unable to best the creature, and as far as he had been able to tell, none of their clan had much luck against them in a one on one situation. Perhaps with a fearsome power like Jenna had wielded, but he didn't even know that he had one at all.

Abe seemed to have picked up on his somewhat darkening mood, chuckling a little more quietly. "You look somber over there, kid. Don't forget what I told you before. As long as there's a chance, there's hope. You are fighting for something important to you, and that gives you an advantage over a bull drake any day of the week. Stay on your toes. Don't let your guard down. You can do this."

He glanced over at the crimson dragon with a sort of frown. "Look, I appreciate what you are trying to do, but …"

"No buts," the older male interrupted, glancing ahead toward the approaching mountain peaks. "If you tell yourself you're going to lose then you've already lost. I'm sure you've heard that before somewhere, but it just goes to show that I'm not making this up. Come, now. They'll likely be expecting us, but let's see if we can get at least an idea of what we're getting into here." Diving slowly toward the nearest peak, Abe settled in on the ridge line just shy of the tallest point, Jonah and Jeffress coming in for a landing on either side of him.

Olympus rose up perhaps a few hundred yards away from them, a series of peaks that rose high enough to shed their snowy confines and bare their bald stone to the sky above. Between where they had landed and the tallest peaks was a sort of small valley filled with snow and ice. The way it spilled out down the valley to lower altitude, the little cracks and crevices in the ice, resembled something that Jonah had seen before, on some nature show.

He had never seen a glacier before in his life. In other circumstances it might have looked almost beautiful, stark white creeping along the earth so slowly that it had to be measured in inches per year.

It wasn't what really caught his attention. On a broad, flat patch of snow near where the head of the glacier - he couldn't tell if it was on the ice or on the mountainside itself - a scene was unfolding. Dragons, four of them, were standing on the surface facing in toward each other, evenly spaced and perhaps at the points of the compass. He couldn't tell, and didn't really care, either way. Even from this distance he could easily make out the sleek black figure of one of them, and at least one of his questions was answered.

Rebekah was alive.

Directly in the center of the assembled dragons was what might have been some kind of makeshift altar, a cairn of stones, atop which an unmoving figure was sprawled out. It was too far for him to know for certain simply by looking but he was confident it must have been the elder, based on what Jeffress had said.

Beyond the dragons, spaced at even intervals to form an equilateral triangle, were three more figures, their arms outstretched to their sides. There was no visible magic, no magic at all that Jonah could discern but he assumed they were the mages that had been mentioned. Beyond that there was no sign of anyone else, no hint of the three bull drakes that Jeffress had mentioned. That their whereabouts were unknown made his skin crawl.

Abe had noticed their absence, as well. "You said there were three bulls."

"There are," Jeffress mumbled a little absently, canting his head back and looking around, scanning the skies overhead. "You said it yourself, these guys are probably expecting us. They could be patrolling the area."

"Well, it looks like we've gone unnoticed so far, so we'll go ahead and say that the odds just tilted a little bit more in our favor. There's no way we're going to get down there without being seen, however, so we're going to have to make our move and make it fast. We'll take out the mages as quickly as we can. Jonah, hit the one on the left. Jeffress, the right, and I'll take the one on the far side. Do you think the clan will attack?"

Jeffress breathed out a little snort. "Sorry Abe, I have no idea. Looks like they're a part of this ritual down there so the mages will keep them in place until they absolutely cannot hold off any longer. My guess is that they'll stay put until one or more of the mages looks to be in real trouble, and then they'll come to their aid."

Grunting a little as he peered downward at the ceremony underway, Abe nodded. "Makes sense to me. All the more reason to throw everything we've got at those mages as quick as we can. Soon as we have them down we'll focus all of our efforts on the clan, try to shake them out of whatever spell they are under. Everyone got it?"

Before any of them could answer, the sound of stone bouncing against stone behind them caught their attention and all three turned their necks back simultaneously. Three men stood on the ridge where none had been before, silhouetted somewhat ominously against the clear sky beyond them. Thick, menacing, and powerful looking. Bull drakes.

Abe and Jeffress alike reacted with no need for instruction or discussion, leaping from the rocks they had perched on and throwing themselves with abandon at two of the intruders, leaving the third to stand there, staring Jonah down with an unnatural sense of confidence - or perhaps it was merely dispassionate indifference. Whichever it was it set Jonah on edge, but when he got a better look at the man staring him down, he felt his blood run cold. He had seen those dark, sinister eyes before, the raven black hair perched atop a head that seemed slightly too small for the shoulders it sat on. The small mountain of a man grunted down at him, flexing where he stood.

It shouldn't have been possible. He had seen the truck go over the edge of the bridge; he had seen the aftermath of the crash on the news the following day. Stepping backward with fear building up in his eyes, Jonah shook his head. It shouldn't have been possible, but then he, too, should have been dead. He had escaped, had lived to fight another day. So, too, had the bull drake.

As Jonah watched, the man snorted out loudly, a thin line of smoke pouring from his nostrils and wreathing his head like some kind of twisted, ethereal crown. The sounds of fighting at either side of him, snarling and roaring and the clashing of talons was heard but only just. His entire world was distilled in that moment down to nothing more than the man who was bearing down on him.

The man's image warped. His arms seemed to thicken, stretching as he dove forward, his hands swelling and twisting into wicked claws that fell to the earth, grinding into the stone beneath them and snapping it into little shards. Wings sprouted from his sides as his torso rippled and grew, thickening out from a small mountain of a man to a small mountain of a dragon. Muddy brown scales tinged with yellow covered his body, thick and calloused, looking for all the world like impenetrable armor.

Wicked looking spikes protruded from every imaginable angle. The bull's head was massive, a thick blocky shape that looked to be made of solid bone, jagged teeth sticking out much like a crocodile's. With a menacing snort the big bull took a step toward him, more of that smoke trailing out from his nostrils.

Jonah was aware that he'd been stepping backward, his talons scrabbling against the loose rock when one of them slipped out from beneath him and he briefly lost his balance. The menacing creature in front of him leaped upon the opportunity and threw himself toward him with a thunderous roar.

Almost too late, Jonah pushed himself to the side and let his momentum carry him partially along the slope, just out of reach of the bull as the big male crashed in to the rock, sending tiny little shards all over the place. Gasping, he clutched at the air with his wings, pulled himself up off the mountainside and twisted himself around.

The others were occupied fending off their own opponents. Abe managed to hold his own, nearly the size of the bull and nearly as powerful, the two large dragons circling each other over the peak of the mountain, snapping and clawing at each other. Jeffress, smaller like himself, was darting in and around his own pursuer, keeping out ahead by only the smallest of margins. It wouldn't have taken much of a misstep to spell trouble for him.

As much as he might have felt the urge to help, there was not a thing Jonah could do. The bull that had crashed into the mountainside was already recovering, righting himself among the scree and turning to face him with those deep, sinister eyes. The big jaw opened to let loose another roar, along with a jet of flame that came shooting toward Jonah with frightening speed.

Ducking the gout of flame, Jonah turned and let himself cut along down the slope of the ridge, staying just high enough off the rock that he didn't risk grounding himself as his mind spun. This bull had the benefit of fire as well as size and strength, while Jonah felt practically defenseless. He might be able to out fly the creature, might be able to stay just ahead, but there was no way he was going to be able to match him in a fight.

He didn't have to turn around to know he was being followed, the sound of wings heaving at the air behind him unnervingly close. Not the brightest, he'd heard the bulls described before. Perhaps he could out think his opponent. Perhaps he could find some advantage.

Across the valley and on to the next ridge in the mountains, he spied a small but substantial bluff in the rock, a nearly sheer face exposed in contrast to the snowy slope around it. The foot of the cliff was littered with boulders of varying sizes, victims of the slow but inexorable pull of gravity on the mountain above. Large slabs of rock still clung to the side, and even at the top there were some sizable boulders that looked like they might be encouraged to come loose. If he could only think of a way to get the bull beneath them …

Another spray of fire at his back burned close enough to singe his scales, and with a little cry Jonah let himself dip downward, deeper into the valley, rushing in toward the cliff side as it grew ever nearer. Throwing a brief glance behind him and seeing that the bull was breathing down his neck, much too close for comfort, Jonah willed his wings into action and pushed himself forward with dizzying speed.

Reaching the floor of the valley, he had to start climbing again to keep aloft, sapping some of his forward momentum, but he'd already built up quite a bit in the dive. Turning all of his attention to the cliff rushing up to meet him, Jonah tried to mentally count out the seconds, estimate the distance. He would have to time himself just right. Too soon and he'd lose his opportunity. Too late and the bull drake would be the least of his worries.

Closer. Closer. The rocks beneath him transformed into a blur as he hugged the floor of the valley, hardly daring to breathe. Closer. Closer.

"Now," he found himself shouting out loud, leaning his head back and angling his wings into the wind, cutting into them at a steep angle to force himself into a nearly vertical ascent. He could feel his weight shift, all of his insides seeming to pull down toward his legs, momentum pulling forward while he struggled to keep his wings at the right angle, struggled to keep himself moving upward, away from the rock.

A sound like a loud explosion rocked the air just beneath him, but he didn't have time to look to see what it was or what had happened. Dismayed, he realized that his timing had been just off. With the force of an enormous fist the rock pounded into his chest as he slammed hard against the side of the mountain.

For a brief second like a heartbeat all motion stopped, but gravity did not hesitate to snatch at him once again, trying to pull him back down the nearly sheer slope. His head rang from the impact, his whole body screaming in pain and stunned, but the fear of falling was just enough to keep him from going limp and giving up. Desperately he clawed at the rock, his talons scrabbling against the hard, unyielding surface, dragging against his scales as he slid for several feet.

At last his talons found a hold, snagging on some small prominence, lodging in a fortunate irregularity in the rocks, and held fast. With all the control he could muster, Jonah held on to the face of the cliff. He'd survived. Rocks the size of fists crashed against his head along with a rain of tiny little pebbles, each one conspiring to loosen him from the face of the cliff, but he was just determined enough to hold on, ride out the little cascade.

He didn't have the chance to celebrate. An angry growl and snort from somewhere beneath him caught his attention, and as soon as he'd regained enough composure to look down, he was amazed to see the bull drake in a similar position to himself, hugged against the side of the mountain, firing an almost hateful look up at him. The bull snorted once again, inhaled deeply, and opened its jaws wide in his direction.

Jonah cringed at the flame he knew was coming, the flame he knew that he could not evade this time, expecting the worst. Instead of being burned to a crisp, however, he was only subjected to a loud, grating roar. In surprise he looked back down at the bull, the big creature growling up at him in confusion as well. It tried once again, inhaling and then exhaling deeply, but no flame came.

In some stroke of luck, the impact must have rendered the bull incapable of breathing fire. He imagined Abe making some metaphor about a lucky toss of the dice, but realized that he had no idea how temporary his luck might be. He had to get out of harm's way.

To his amazement, the bull drake was the first one to start moving. Slowly but with a sort of deadly, methodical certainty it reached for another viable hold on the rock, hauling itself up the sheer face and closing the distance toward him, those spiteful dark eyes boring holes in him the entire time. The creature had one intent and one alone : to destroy him at any cost.

Jonah couldn't simply push himself away from the cliff and fly. He was too close to properly spread his wings, there would be no good way for him to turn away and fly in the opposite direction. He could try to fly straight up but it would take him too long to get himself moving, he had no way to give himself a head start. He'd tumble down to the foot of the cliff. It might not be so tall as to kill him, but the dragon practically nipping at his heels would be only too happy to finish the job.

The only way out was up. With a growing panic, Jonah scrabbled for some foothold that would allow him to pull himself up the cliff side, his talons snagging in another imperfection in the rock. It was enough to give him a foot or two of climb, enough to keep just one step ahead of the dragon that was now, in fact, literally nipping at him, close enough that he could feel the beast's breath washing against his tail as it snapped at him.

His next grasp was less successful, his talons clutching at a loose bit of rock that dislodged under his weight, throwing him off balance and nearly causing him to lose all grip on the cliff at all. The sight of the loosed rock tumbling down the mountain gave him another idea, however, and all at once he was scrabbling desperately at the stone, plucking at anything he could find that was loose and send it tumbling beneath him.

It worked, at first. Rocks the size of baseballs crashed and skidded downward, several of them smacking the bull right on the face. Most of them broke apart on impact, the drake's skull harder than rock, but it was enough to cause him to flinch back every time, swinging his head out of the way of the larger bits.

"Take that, bastard," Jonah called down to the beast, shifting himself to the side a bit to clutch at a larger piece and force it down against the drake with enough force that it briefly lost its own grip and slid down a few feet. "That one's for Sammy!"

The bull growled and snapped at the air, clearly growing angry and agitated at the cascade of rocks that was smashing against its head, but still unable to make any more forward progress. Too occupied with trying to dodge the larger rocks, all it could do was hang on.

Jonah felt himself beginning to get giddy with his newfound advantage, disassembling the cliff rock by rock, tearing it apart and sending it downward. "You like that? Screw you, bastard," he shouted downward again, digging loose a large rock the size of a basketball, shoving it downward and watching it split open against the bull's forehead, pushing it back down a bit as it hissed and snapped. "There! For Rebekah!"

His growing sense of relief, the feeling that he was gaining ground on the drake suddenly evaporated when he realized the fatal flaw in his plan. There were only so many rocks he could kick and push downward, and with each one he was making his own position on the cliff more precarious. Tugging at the rock a little too eagerly he nearly lost his grip and slipped a little, himself, gasping as panic suddenly clutched at him anew.

The cascade of rocks ceasing, the big bull saw its opportunity. With a furious snarl it sank its talons into the rock and began to scale upward even faster than before, closing the gap. Jonah could do little more than watch in horror. "Oh, shit …"

"Jonah!" He almost didn't hear the shout behind him, he was so caught up in watching the approaching maw of the murderous bull, but at the last second he turned around to see Abe grappling with another of the bulls nearby. He seemed to have gotten the upper hand, slightly, beating the foul creature around as they tumbled through the air. "Jump!"

The command made little sense to him. Despite Abe's advantage over his opponent things looked grim; there was no sign of Jeffress, and the third bull was closing in fast. There was no way that the big dragon could take on two at a time.

Still, there was a simple urgency to his voice, and, seeing no alternative, Jonah pushed himself away from the rock face, letting go of the stone, tumbling over backward as gravity took him again. He watched with an odd sense of detachment as the bull twisted against the rock, in turn watching him fall, slip past him, a fiery anger on the beasts face as if it felt cheated out of its kill.

Out of the corner of his eye he was aware of a strange, indistinct blur against the sky that was aimed in his direction. Before he could even begin to imagine what it was he felt something clutching at him, legs wrapping around him and plucking him away from the cliff side. He could see white with blue stripes.

In a slightly pained voice, Jeffress grunted to him. "Hang on."

Jonah watched with a strange sense of confusion coming over him as they rolled through the air, the sky wheeling around the edge of his vision. When he was given a view of the mountainside, something seemed very wrong.

No one was moving. Abe hung motionless in the air, stopped halfway through the motion of clutching one of the bulls by the thicker part of the tail and turning about. The one on the cliff was there as motionless as stone, frozen in a growl at the empty space where he had once been, and the third drake was stuck in mid dive.

He was struck nearly dumb at the sight. Before he could react, however, everything once again started moving, as if a switch had been flipped. The bull being grappled by Abe was flung around with a mighty shove, crashing into the cliff next to the one who had been pursuing Jonah, with enough force to cause rock to shatter and spray in every direction. At the same time Abe let loose a mighty roar, heaving himself up and out of the way of the diving drake.

Whether it was the roar, the crash of the bull into the rock wall, or some combination of both the native stone heaved. A low, grinding shudder rocked the cliff before entire boulders shook loose, tumbling downward in every direction, each loosed rock building up on the destruction until the entire mountainside seemed to be moving all at once, churned up in a mighty avalanche of earth and snow. The two bulls on the cliff vanished, the third enveloped by the plume of dust before being swallowed up in the slide.

"I won't be able to do that again," Jeffress said in a near whisper, abruptly releasing him to tumble briefly through the air. Jonah twisted and tumbled a moment before he righted himself, his wings catching at the air again and pulling him aloft.

Abe was already coming about, heading back for the ridge they had been perched upon before. "No time to celebrate, boys. Sun is getting low."

They all understood the need for haste. In a moment they were over the nearer peak, the sight of the ceremony unfolding beneath them. Though it looked exactly as it had before, Jonah could feel something unsettling emanating from the ground below as the shadows stretched further along the ice.

The mages below had seen their approach. One of them turned to face them, lifting his hands high in the air and sending a crackling spark of energy upward, aimed right for Abe. The crimson dragon twisted to the side and avoided the current, shouting out as he tucked himself in to dive. "Don't let anything stop you! Take those mages out!"

For the moment the other dragons on the ground seemed to have not noticed them, and the other two mages remained where they stood as well, evidently carrying out their task in spite of the doom that was descending upon them. The third, who had shot off the first attack, loosed another, and another, all at the big dragon, but even when one found its mark Abe seemed only slightly stunned.

They got close enough to see the terror on the man's expression before any of the others reacted, but it was too late. With a furious roar, the big crimson dragon passed right over the man, plucking him neatly off the ground and, in one fluid motion, tossed him through the air. End over end the man tumbled, wheeling through the sky like a rag doll before coming to an abrupt and fatal stop a hundred yards down the glacier.

Jonah sought to mimic the attack, but the mage that he had set his sights on was not going to fall for the same trick. The man ducked as he swooped in, flicking his arms over his head and pushing some kind of tangible force up into the air; Jonah felt himself shoved partially out of the way, as if he had skipped off some invisible barrier. Grunting, he swung himself around for another attack.

The entire group was in motion. Jeffress had actually landed next to his target and was busily trying to snap and claw his way through a crackling field of energy that the man was desperately throwing up between himself and the dragon. Abe was halfway through coming about, himself, roaring out ferociously after having disposed of the first mage. The advantage was theirs, but only for a moment; the rest of the clan was in motion.

With frightening coordination, all four rose and immediately pointed themselves in Abe's direction. Jonah realized that the big dragon would probably not stand a chance against all four, and started to adjust his turn back in that direction when Abe shouted out loudly. "No, Jonah! The mage!"

Grunting as he was forced to correct in mid turn again, Jonah pushed himself once more in the direction where the man had thrown himself to the ground. By that time the mage was standing once again, hands in front of himself, twisting through the air. Once again there was a strange sort of tangible force he could feel, as if the air itself were getting thicker, harder to move through, but it was different. It was not merely defensive; the man was attacking him.

Twisting himself to the side and changing his course, Jonah barely avoided the full brunt of the attack, a column of air collapsing in on itself with enough force that it visibly distorted everything around it and created a thunderous boom. Trying not to think of what might have happened if he had still been flying in that column of air, he changed tactics and darted about wildly, so the man couldn't predict where he was going to be next.

Frustrated, the mage pulled his hands up over his head and stretched them out. The air shifted again, thickening as it had before, a sort of shield building up between him and his target. Rather than try to push his way through it, Jonah angled himself sharply to the side and descended around it, coming to a rough but effective landing on the ground.

It had worked. He had caught the mage off guard; the man was unprepared when Jonah started to charge across the ice with furious intent. With a scream the man dove to the side, tried to gesture in the air but failed, winding up sliding along his back, helpless. Jonah dug his talons into the ice and reared back, coiling his muscles for what would be the final blow.

A flash of black at the corner of his eye made him hesitate just long enough for an enormous fireball to bloom to life in front of him, bearing down on him with dizzying speed.

TWENTY FOUR

Instinctively, Jonah threw himself to the ice. The fireball passed overhead, singing his wings and his tail with enough heat to cause him to cry out. It had done no serious damage, though, and once it passed he was able to roll himself out of the way, catching a glimpse of the scar of freshly melted snow the fireball had left in its wake.

Pulling himself back up to his feet and glancing upward, he saw exactly what he expected to see. The sinuous form of a dragon with glossy black scales and bright green eyes circling not far overhead, fresh smoke spewing from her maw. Rebekah.

He wouldn't have much time to think about what to do next. Already he could feel the air around him thickening, the distortion making his vision shift uncomfortably. Launching himself upward and scooping up as much of that air as he could with his wings, he rose up over the mage, forcing the man to resume a more defensive posture, buying him enough time to sweep around and try to get his bearings.

Abe was still trying to fend off the attack of three of his clan-mates, the big crimson dragon obviously hesitant to strike back with much force at those he had known and cared for. Instead he was trying to keep ahead of them, his tail whipping at them when they drew too close. He would be of no help. Jeffress, too, had his hands full even if he seemed to have the upper hand, having forced the other mage into a precarious position among a small outcropping of rocks.

The crackling roar of another fireball aimed at him quickly pulled him back into his own little dilemma, forcing him to whip around and twist out of the way of the attack. Rebekah was still circling over him, already swooping around to prepare herself for another volley, while the mage below looked to be preparing himself, as well.

Jonah cringed. "How the hell am I supposed to fight both," he whispered to himself, glancing around for any help, any way he might use the terrain to his advantage, and coming up empty. He couldn't afford to try and mount a direct assault upon the mage; the man's control over the air itself was an effective barrier to hitting him head on, and if he landed he would be leaving himself open to Rebekah's attack from above.

He also couldn't try to take her out all on his own. Even if he didn't suffer the same problem that Abraham was having, even if he had convinced himself that he didn't care for her and was emotionally capable of inflicting harm, he did not have any faith in himself. He had trained with her, and each and every time she had gotten the upper hand. She knew how he fought, knew his weaknesses.

There was no way Jonah could beat her in a one on one contest.

Surveying the ground beneath him, he could see the air starting to distort again. He had to pick up a little altitude, dodging another set of fireballs to keep himself out of the strange grasp of that power, when he realized he had another option. Shouting to rally himself, he whipped around and aimed himself straight at where Rebekah was flying.

The rapid change in his course had caught her off guard, briefly. He winged in close to where she was, close enough to see the frustration on her face. "Rebekah!" He called out to her as he did his best to follow her every move, keeping close. "It's me, Jonah! Please, you've got to stop fighting me!"

She did not acknowledge him. Pushing herself from one side to another, she was able to keep just out of range. He couldn't catch up to her, could not hope to take her down, but he was not trying to. There was no reason to overtake her; all he had to do was follow her, stay just behind her, match her every move.

The mage below was frustrated in his efforts to lash out at Jonah, reaching up to gesture in the air, causing some shift, some thickening and distortion near him, above him, behind him, but he was too close to Rebekah. The attacks could not harm him without harming her, either, and the man seemed unwilling to do so.

Jonah didn't know how patient the man was, how long he would hold back for fear of injuring Rebekah, and did not intend to wait and find out. It provided him with that little extra amount of time, the chance to think, the chance to try and reach out to her. "Come on Rebekah. You remember me. You've been stalking me, remember?"

With a growl of irritation she tried to shake him, dipping erratically, but he was able to keep just close enough, keep from losing her. "You said you'd watch over me. I know you can't, not now, I know this isn't your fault … but you've got to listen! We're here to help, me and Abe and Jeffress! We went to go find him, remember?"

There was an odd sort of cry off to his side, and Jonah allowed himself to look over just long enough to see one of the three dragons that was pursuing Abe had fallen back, glancing around with a look of confusion on its features. He could hear Abe shouting something over the din of the pursuing dragons. Whatever it was Jonah could not tell, but it seemed to be having an effect. He was starting to get through, at least to one of them.

It was encouraging, in its way. There had to be a way to get through to Rebekah. "Come on, Rebekah. You don't have to say anything, just listen. You know my voice, you know who I am. Now remember who you are. This isn't right, you're fighting the wrong people …"

Abruptly she spun herself around, letting momentum carry her forward while she was able to turn about and face him. It lasted but a second, just enough time for him to look into her eyes and see them burning with anger. Just long enough for her to exhale, spitting off a writhing fireball at him.

Jonah had not seen that coming. With a gasp he twisted himself, cut his wings through the air at a sharp angle and forced himself down and beneath the oncoming flames. Though he succeeded in dodging the attack, he had been thrown off, had lost the advantage. Glancing about wildly, he saw Rebekah starting to loop around, so she could come at him more directly, now with the upper hand, herself.

He also realized he was suddenly exposed to an attack from below, and cringed, expecting the air itself to come crushing down on him. When it never came, he turned to look below.

The mage seemed to have forgotten about him, given up in frustration, and turned his attention on Jeffress. The dragon, having nearly vanquished the other mage, suddenly found himself on the defensive, being assailed from both sides. Startled, Jonah let out a cry and turned himself into a dive, aiming straight for the man.

His cry had caught the mage's attention, however, the man turning to look up at him with a startled, somewhat irritated look. Once more the man's hands went up into the air, distorting the atmosphere around him, thickening it just as before. Jonah knew that he could not hope to penetrate that defense.

Just before he had to turn away he felt a blistering heat at his back. Realization washed over him, and Jonah held on to his course as long as he could, until just before smashing into the shield the mage had erected, darting off to the side, skimming right against the edge. For a brief moment the man smirked as he was once more successful in warding off the attack.

His eyes went wide with terror when he saw the fireball, intended for Jonah, tear right through the air shield without so much as slowing down. He barely had enough time to scream before he was enveloped in flame hot enough to sear him to ash.

Jonah could not help but to feel slightly disgusted at his minor victory;

there was something hollow about having killed a man, even indirectly, and even in defense of his own life. Even if he had been more inclined toward jubilation he would not have been given the chance. Rebekah was already on the move behind him, leveling her own descent, preparing yet another fireball to lob at him. She was completely unperturbed at having incinerated her own guy.

In the brief moment that he was allowed to survey the scene below him, he could see that Jeffress had redoubled his assault on the one remaining mage, the man looking haggard and desperate as he tried to rebuff the dragon, his defenses weakening and failing. Abe, halfway across the valley, had gained an ally in the one dragon that he had successfully turned, and was now essentially a one on one contest there, as well.

They had evened the odds, but that too was little consolation. Looking across the valley Jonah could see nothing but shadow filling it from one side to the other, the only hint of sunlight being the crowns of the peaks on the other side, bathed in a golden hue from the sinking sun.

He was running out of time. Carolus' dying warning echoed in his head; they only had until sunset and then whatever spell they were under would become permanent. Looking behind him he could see Rebekah still in hot pursuit, gaining slowly but surely on him.

"Rebekah!" He called out again, whipping around another outcropping of rock, his tail lashing at the air as he tried to keep far enough ahead. "Come on, it's me! I'm trying to help you out here … please just tell me you can hear me?"

Her only response was another angry roar that accompanied a plume of writhing flame tossed in his direction. Exasperated, he tried changing tactics again, turning about rather abruptly, dodging the flame but arrowing straight for her. He cringed as he realized that they were both moving rather quickly. It was going to hurt.

She plowed right into him like a freight train, knocking him briefly senseless. They both spun wildly in the air for a moment, the remnants of their forward momentum casting them in a drooping arc over the mountainside before they smashed headlong into a bank of snow. Their angle was shallow enough and the snow deep enough that he wasn't seriously hurt, and by the time the little cloud of snow they had kicked up began to settle he was able to get back on his feet, whipping around to try and see where she had fallen.

Rebekah was clawing and tearing at the snow piled around her, pushing her way back up to her feet a little clumsily while he watched. Steeling himself for how she might react, he racked his brains and tried to think of how he might snap her out of the spell. "Make them remember," the old man had gasped before giving up the ghost. Growling loudly to himself, Jonah shook his head.

"I don't know how," he complained to the chilly air, launching himself at Rebekah again before she had fully come back to her senses. He was able to latch on to her back, gripping at her sides and shoving her back to the snow, roughly, as he snapped at the air at the side of her head. "You're going to listen to me one way or another, Rebekah. Don't force me to hurt you, too."

She responded with a furious roar, thrashing wildly on the ground beneath him. He could feel her wings struggling to spread, the little claws at their joints jabbing into his underbelly and scraping at his scales, but he withstood that pain. Stray sputters of flame escaped from her jaws, licking at the ground beneath her as she tried to fight him off, digging herself against the ground and bucking backward.

Jonah had to dig his talons more firmly into her scales to keep from being completely thrown off. "Come on, dammit!" He screamed at her in frustration, knowing that his claws must have been hurting her, digging into her sides deep enough that they started to draw blood, but she wouldn't relent. He didn't want to hurt her, but if that was what it took to shake her loose from the spell …

Growling loudly, he leaned in and bit down on her wingshoulder, as hard as he dared without breaking something.

It did get a response out of her, albeit not the one that he was hoping for. Once more she roared fiercely and kicked against the ground with enough force to lift her partway off the ground, flipping her over to her back and carrying him with. Abruptly he was on his back, Rebekah's squirming and thrashing form atop him, grinding him downward into the snow and rock beneath, her tail whipping around to lash into his sides.

He lost his grip. With one mighty shove she managed to roll off of him and back into the snow, slashing at his side as she did and tearing into the hide deep enough that he howled out in sharp pain, pulled away in the other direction. Instinct served him well, reminding him that he couldn't lay there with his belly exposed, and he avoided another slash to his underside by a hair.

"Abe!" He had seen the big dragon do it, at least one of the clan had been freed. There had to be a secret, some trick to getting them to snap out of it, and he needed help. Rebekah was kicking little flurries of snow up at him, forcing him to duck back and out of the way so it didn't get in his eyes, and he was growing desperate. "Abraham! Help me!"

Help was not going to come. Abe was too far away, and even if he'd heard the plea for help there was probably only so much he could do. Rebekah was going airborne again, the snow whipping about beneath her wings as she went aloft, leaving Jonah alone and exposed on the side of the mountain.

The peaks across the valley were deepening in color, changing from gold to copper and then finally seeming to burst into flame, reds and oranges licking against the snowy peaks as the day was giving way to dusk. He was almost out of time.

Scrambling across the snow to give himself a running start, Jonah took off into the air and tried to think. His head felt like it was spinning, running circles around itself and desperately clutching for an answer, some hint of what he had to do, some hope that he might stumble upon. He needed more time, and Rebekah was coming around again to pursue him once more, this time with renewed vigor.

He needed more time. Skimming along the edge of the mountain he shifted his direction, made his way directly for the higher peaks of Olympus that rose up in front of him, jagged voids against the glowing sky beyond, as if they were the only thing that stood between himself and the sunlight beyond. His rapid ascent up the mountain meant that Rebekah was now slightly below him, angling her way upward, keeping in close pursuit.

At last he breached the shadow and was once again bathed in sunlight. Exceeding the height of the mountain itself, he looked around with a quiet gasp. There was a strange and immense sort of beauty in the scene about him; a sea of rugged mountain peaks rising up in every direction, clad snow and shadow, a mix of reflected sunlight that burned nearly blood red and shade that looked almost vivid blue in comparison. In the west the sun hung low over the wrinkled, piled earth, a tired, crimson disk seeking to find rest beyond the horizon.

He still didn't know how to save her. He needed more time. Finishing a quick little circle around the peak of the mountain, he pointed himself skyward and pulled as hard as his wings would take him.

Up he went, straight as an arrow, guided only by the deepening color of the sky around him, the tug of gravity against his tail, the heave of the air as his wings pushed against it mightily. He had no plan, no idea of what he was doing, no hope other than to keep going up, higher, as if he could delay the sunset just a little while longer, stay in its ruddy glow, buy himself just a few more moments.

Just a little more time, till he thought of the answer.

Rebekah remained in pursuit, her snarls and growls enough to let him know that she was not far beneath him, but he could not help himself. Glancing briefly downward he could see her, sleek black shape cutting through the air, gaining altitude with him. The expanse of peaks and valleys was receding beneath them, dragons becoming small shapes against the snow and then getting lost in the shifting shadows as all but the tallest mountaintops were bathed in darkness.

He still didn't know what to do. "Rebekah," he called out behind him, his voice growing desperate. "Rebekah … please, I don't know what to do, I don't know how to help you. Please, come back to us."

Still she responded only with an angry growl, and still Jonah threw himself skyward. The earth continued to slip away beneath them, the sun growing hazy and indistinct as it continued to droop toward the horizon, undeterred in its path in spite of Jonah's desperate flight upward. He had purchased a few minutes, at most, and still was coming up with nothing.

"I don't want to lose you," he cried, his voice becoming ragged. "Look ... we can forget everything that happened. Start all over. Get to know each other better ... I want to know what your favorite foods are, what you like to do for fun ... please, just give me that chance ..."

A plume of heat licking at his tail told him that he was not getting through. Shifting his path enough to keep away from the flames of her ire, he still climbed upward, ever upward, the chill in the air starting to seep into his scales, his breath growing yet more ragged as the air was becoming noticeably thinner. He knew he couldn't go much further at this rate, and the sun was losing itself in the indistinct horizon.

"What do I have to do? How can I prove myself to you?" Whipping his tail as if it would propel him a little faster, Jonah's lungs burned for oxygen, his wings seeming to slip, trying to clutch at the rarefied air.

It was too late. He'd lost all sight of the sun, vanished into the horizon, and his wings just could not keep up anymore. With one last heave and a gasp they simply folded uselessly up against his sides, and for one, brief moment he was suspended in the air, high enough to see where the earth met the sea, high enough to make out the faint curve to the horizon, high enough that the mountains were mere wrinkles beneath him.

The visions that had plagued him for the past several days came rushing back to the fore of his mind. Images of losing a loved one. Each time he was in the shoes of someone who was about to lose someone important to them, had to bid them farewell for the very last time, not knowing if they would ever see them again. He could remember the fear, poignant if muted, of knowing it might be a last goodbye.

Perhaps he would never see Rebekah again. Perhaps he had feared it all along, since before he even realized how he truly felt about her. It was a fear that he no longer remembered, but one that he felt gnawing at the deepest parts of his soul.

The wind reversed, flew past him quicker, building up to a hurricane roar in a matter of mere seconds. He could feel the membranes of his wings flapping uselessly as he tumbled earthward, could feel his tail being pulled out behind him, but somehow he didn't really care. He'd failed, when he was needed the most. They had come so close to success, so close to victory, and yet at the last moment he had stumbled.

Slowly he twisted and tumbled through the air but wound up pointed downward, as if he were diving, dropping with ever more speed and ferocity. The mountains resolved themselves from each other, the peaks and valleys moving apart as they grew nearer, close enough to see the fading light of the dusk staining the snow in blues and violets. He thought he saw the shapes of dragons there, below, as the ground rushed up to meet him.

He found himself remembering his plummet from the bridge not so long ago. The way the wind whipped past him, the way the earth rushed upward, brought the memory back so vividly that he could almost see the river undulating beneath him, unhurried in its course, preparing to embrace him in its cold, watery grasp. Just as the snow and unyielding rock would embrace him now.

Something embraced him, but it was neither water nor rock nor snow. Legs wrapped around his torso, clutched him tight and pulled, and suddenly he was not just falling straight down. His insides churned against the abrupt change in course, gravity fighting to wrench him from the grasp and complete his fall, but the limbs clutching to him were too strong and held on tight.

"Don't ever make me do this again, Jonah. I'm tired of plucking you out of the sky." He saw the little hints of glossy black, heard her voice cutting through the air. Rebekah.

His mind reeled, his whole body going a bit limp at the realization. "You remembered," was the only thing he could think to say.

Without responding, she slowed their descent through the air and pulled them around, bringing them back toward the open, flat space in the glacier. Jonah looked around a bit incoherently at the scene; Abe was on the ground, and there was another dragon next to him. There were also a small handful of people standing around, gesturing in their direction. He wondered where the other dragons had gone.

A little roughly, Rebekah deposited him on the ground, and he half sank in the snow. Coughing and flailing, Jonah sat up to realize that he had at some point reverted to human form, and suddenly felt very cold.

"Nice dive," a voice next to him chuckled. It was Jeffress, also in human form, smiling over his salt and pepper beard and reaching out to help him to his feet. "Come on, get up. We can't stay here long."

Getting to his feet a little dizzy and bewildered, Jonah glanced around and tried to make sense of what was going on. Rebekah had landed on the other side of Abe and he could only just make out her wings; tempted as he was to run over and talk to her, he decided it was not the best time. Three others, the rest of the clan who had been presumably freed from the spell as well, were busy helping an old man get to his feet from where he had been bound.

It was the elder. He looked considerably more worn than before, his eyes sunken and dim. Shaking, he breathed a little sigh. "You fools. What are you doing here?"

"Saving your hide, Nate," Abe responded, the big crimson dragon facing the other direction but turning around to grin at him.

"What have I told you about risking your necks to save me?"

Abe chuckled again, a sound that was as welcome as it was out of place. "And you really expected us to listen?"

The old man forced a weak smile, leaning heavily on the two who were currently holding him up. "Be that as it may, I am too weak to fly, Abraham. You don't look much better, yourself."

"As soon as we get you out of here we can worry about that. Help him on to my back, I will carry him; the two of you will have to stay with him to make sure that he doesn't fall," he grunted, hunching down low to the ground to let the old man climb up, assisted.

The sound of rock exploding in the distance caught Jonah's attention and he turned to look. At first he saw nothing, but there was another sound that echoed up through the valley, angry, grating roaring, and then he saw it - not one, not two, but all three bull drakes rising up from behind the opposing ridge, silhouetted against the darkening night sky.

Jeffress shook his head grimly at the sight. "Looks like our bulls finally managed to dig themselves out."

"How … I thought they were dead," Jonah complained, looking back with a worried expression, panic and dread once again forming in his chest.

"They're a bit hard to kill off. Come on, let's move!"

Once the elder was secure on Abe's back, the big crimson dragon heaved his wings and caught the air, wheeling away from the bull drakes that were now coming straight for them. Rebekah and the other dragon lifted off at either side, to guard his flanks. Jeffress, waving him on, got a running start before stretching out and shifting back into dragon form, taking to the sky.

Jonah, tired of running, tired of fighting, nonetheless worked up the energy to force himself into a sprint, leaping upward into the air and letting his wings spread one more time, catching the air and following behind the fleeing dragons.

It wasn't long before Jeffress took a look back and spoke up. "They're gaining on us Abe … we won't be able to shake them, at this rate. Don't suppose you can move any faster?"

"Afraid not," Abe said, heaving his wings a little quicker all the same. "You sure they're catching up?"

Jonah looked behind him as well, cringing to see that the bulls were not only catching up but they were doing so rather rapidly. It must have been the state of the fleeing dragons, worn down to the bone, overloaded, recovering from their injuries or worse. It was a wonder they were in much of a shape to fly, at all, and Jeffress was right. There was no way they'd outpace the bulls. "Can we fight?"

"Us? Against the three of them? Maybe," Abe said, chuckling a little grimly into the air. "But we're toast when those reinforcements get here."

Whipping his head around to ask what Abe meant, he realized that he would not have to ask the question, at all. Coming at them from the opposite direction were at least a dozen more dragons, indistinct in the distance and the failing light, but there could be no question that they were indeed headed in their direction. "Oh, my god … what do we do now?"

"Pray," Jeffress suggested.

Abe nodded. "That's about as good as it's gonna get."

It seemed like a massive injustice; they had survived against the worst of odds, taken on the bulls, the mages, even rescued their comrades and now it would come to this, on the cusp of their escape.

"Was a good run, don't you think, Jeffress?"

"Hell of a run, Abraham. Hell of a run."

Jonah was bewildered that they seemed to be so resigned to this fate, particularly after having fought so hard. He almost spoke up about it when Abe turned slightly to address him. "Glad to have had you along too, Jonah. An honor and a pleasure."

"Brother Abraham. It's not like you to give up so easily." Though the sentiment could have come from Jonah the voice did not. It was so weak and feeble that he had barely heard the elder speak up at all.

Abe laughed grimly. "You know me, Nate. A betting man knows when to hold them, but knows when to fold them, too. Sometimes the deck is stacked too heavily against you and you're outta luck. I'm sorry, Nate, but my old bones have had all they can take, today."

"Look again, Abraham. The deck might be stacked, but must it be stacked against you?"

Turning to look in front of him again, Jonah followed suit and tried to get a better look at the dragons coming in their direction. It didn't dawn on him at first, but he heard the big dragon breathe a sound like a whistle. "Well, I'll be damned …"

The dragons coming their way were not bull drakes, but dragons of various sizes and colors. A few he even recognized from the previous fight when they'd been ambushed by the Syndicate; Ryan's name he remembered, and he remembered the way the drake looked. The others he did not recognize but could immediately guess who they were.

"Ryan, you son of a bitch!" Abe shouted out jubilantly, the others flying at his sides letting loose a short little roar. "How the hell did you pull this off?"

"Not now," Ryan responded, shooting on past him almost too fast to be heard. The amassed dragons, more than a dozen strong, descended rapidly on the trio of bull drakes, descending on them in a swarm.

Jonah turned to watch the fight, but it ended almost as soon as it began. For all of their unwavering adherence to their duties, for their unerring persistence, even the bull drakes could recognize defeat when they saw it. Offering only a few obligatory swings of the tail, the three abruptly turned about and fled back the way they had come.

TWENTY FIVE

The rest of the evening passed by in a blur. Once they had been certain that the bull drakes would not be calling in any kind of reinforcements, they returned to the compound to fulfill the promise that Abe had made to Carolus. The old dragon's body lay where it had fallen, still in human form; reduced to little more than the broken and exhausted shell of an old man. Abe spoke a few words on his behalf, exonerating him in front of the rest of the clan, while some of the others constructed a makeshift pyre out of some discarded old timbers they had found.

A few breaths of dragons' fire was all it took to incinerate his body, giving him over to ash and leaving no sign that he had ever been there. A solemn prayer of sorts was offered by the aging elder Nathan, after which the dragons took to the wing and departed the scene, cloaked in the growing dark of the night and the silence of their own making.

The long flight back to the east had left the dragons exhausted. Rather than go the entire way on wing, they had set down when they had neared the first signs of civilization. A series of well-tipped cab rides brought them in to Bremerton, where they had waited for the next ferry to take them in to Seattle, eventually to head back to the hotel for some well-deserved rest and relaxation.

Once aboard the ferry, the dragons had gathered together around the elder and had begun conversing with one another in an animated, almost jubilant fashion. Jonah supposed that it, too, was well deserved; they had suffered more than their fair share of losses and hurts over the past few days, and any cause to celebrate was a welcome one. Still, he felt somehow out of place among them, unable to get into the spirit, and had detached himself from the group, eventually making his way out onto the deck of the ferry.

Night had since fallen and the moon had come out, waxing gibbous, throwing a fair bit of its silvery light upon the seascape around him. Cutting its way through a fairly narrow inlet, land rose up on both sides of the ferry, relatively steep, covered in pine trees that looked black in the night, beaches dotted with lights from houses and other buildings tucked against the water. It was serene and beautiful. As Jonah leaned up against the handrail, looking down at the wake stirring up white in the moonlight, he realized that it was the first time he had been allowed to appreciate some of the natural beauty he had seen these past several days.

It was, in fact, the first time he had been able to take a step back, breathe in deep, and relax. No longer did he feel a sense of dread about what morning was bringing. There was still a deep and lingering confusion clouding his mind, and he knew that he'd have to tackle that soon enough. For now, though, all he cared to do was breathe in the crisp night air and let it quietly fill his lungs.

"What's wrong? Not one for crowds?" He turned to look over his shoulder and see Abe standing there, looking at him with a light smile. The man had stopped at a shop back in Bremerton and bought himself a new suit, crisp and clean, and had even gotten a hold of a cigar somewhere. Clenched between his teeth and unlit - the ferry workers had forbade him to light it - he still looked rather content, himself.

Shaking his head and looking back out to sea, Jonah shrugged. "I don't know. I guess I still feel kind of out of place. Besides, I got a lot on my mind. Thought it might be nice to come out here and clear my thoughts, a little."

The big man stepped in closer and rested a big meaty hand on his shoulder. "I can only imagine, kid. I'm not gonna make you come in there and pretend to be a part of the crowd, but I want you to know that we consider you one of us. You're family to us, Jonah. We're all proud to call you one of our own. We're all proud of what you've done for us."

"Eh. It's not like I did a whole lot, anyway."

"Sure you did." Abe paused to look out over the water as well, blinking into the silvery moonlight. "None of us would be here if it weren't for you. You showed a lot of heart, kid."

Jonah let a few moments pass before he spoke up again, the words rattling around in his head as he sighed. "You know, I still don't even know what this all means. To be a dragon. Hell, I can't even believe I'm saying it," he muttered, pausing to look at his hands, holding them out over the railing. "It's like some kind of weird dream."

"I don't envy you kid, and I have to say you're handling it pretty well. None of us had to come to this realization at your age, and I can't really imagine what must be going through your head. For what it's worth, though, I'm happy to help you out however I can. If you have any questions … anything I can do for you at all …"

"I don't know, Abe. What happens now?"

Pulling the unlit cigar out of his mouth, the bald man continued to gaze out at the shoreline sliding alongside them as the ferry chugged its way through the water. "I guess that depends on what you mean."

"I mean … we're done fighting the Syndicate. So what do we do now? Go back and hang out at some big dragon hideout? What do you guys do, anyway?" Jonah shrugged again, leaning up against the railing.

"For one thing, we're not done fighting the Syndicate," Abe began, stuffing the cigar back into his mouth. "They're a big organization, Jonah. We bruised them pretty good tonight, gave them a black eye they're not going to forget for some time, but we hardly took them out. Just happened to put an end to their one little plan involving us."

Huffing a little, feeling that creeping sense of dread beginning to build up anew in the pit of his stomach, Jonah closed his eyes. "So they're still going to be after us?"

Abe chuckled softly and shrugged his broad shoulders. "Eventually, but try not to sweat it. The Syndicate is big, but they're also slow. They're nothing if not thorough and deliberate. Remember, they've been after us for thousands of years. Having to wait a few more years while they hatch their next plot is something they do not mind in the least. Yes, we'll have to be ready for it when it happens, but we can relax for a little while."

"All right," he replied, opening his eyes again and gazing once more out into the moonlight. "But what about … what about this council of yours? There aren't many of you left," he said, before he bit his tongue, fearing that it might be too soon to broach the subject.

Abe, if he thought it a tactless question, did not indicate so. He merely breathed in deeply and let out a bit of a sigh. "We took a pretty nasty hit tonight. Without Carl, Jenna and Jason we're down to six. Less than half. I don't know that we've ever been down to six before. In time others will be found, but until then … well, we'll make do."

The talk of finding others reminded Jonah that he had seen Abe pluck a small copper coin from Carolus' pocket before they had burned his remains. "I saw you take Carl's coin, his token. You left it on a counter back at the ferry terminal, didn't you?"

"You got a good eye, kid."

"Why?" He turned to look at Abe again, curious. "I mean, if you're supposed to find his successor, supposed to find the new copper dragon, why would you do that? Just leave it behind?"

The big man laughed softly at that. "It's not my job to find the next one, that's the token's job. No better way than to let it go, it'll find its way. If I kept it in a lockbox somewhere safe, well, then I'd be thwarting the process. No telling how long it'll take. Maybe a year, maybe a decade, but eventually that token will wind up in the hands of the dragon who is destined to own it."

"And the others?"

Once again Abe let out a quiet sigh. "Unfortunately I couldn't find their tokens. I'll send someone back in the morning, when it's light, when we're rested and see if we can get a hold of them, but we may not find them. They may be lost to us, and there's no telling how long it'll be before they'll find their way where they belong."

The way Abe fell quiet afterward made Jonah a little uncomfortable, and he did not have the heart to ask what would become of their tokens if they had been outright destroyed in the mage's attack. Suddenly feeling uncomfortable, he backtracked the discussion a bit. "Well, what about my other question? What do you guys do, when you aren't doing, uh, dragon stuff?"

"As far as what we all do, well, a little bit of everything. We all have our lives, things that we do. Some of us have businesses, some of us have families. We're not some kind of Dragon Justice League, if that's what you're imagining," he said with a broad, toothy grin. "Sure, we'll fight when we have to. But we don't have a Dragon Cave where we all go to live. We all do our own things."

Jonah frowned a little bit. "I guess. But what about me? What am I supposed to do now?"

Abe mocked a little frown of his own, shrugging his shoulders and tilting his head a bit. "Whatever you want to do, kid. You've got a life back in Florida, and no one here is going to stop you from going right back to where you left off."

He could not help but to cringe when he suddenly remembered the life that he had left behind. "No," he said, shaking his head. "No way I can go back there. Cops are probably looking everywhere for me. Certain that I'm guilty of Sam's murder by now … hell, my folks are probably worried to death …"

"Relax," Abe said, patting him lightly on the shoulder. "It's taken care of."

Frowning incredulously at the man, Jonah blinked. "What do you mean, it's taken care of?"

"Working for the Syndicate does have its advantages. Before our little incident, I made sure to tie up a few loose ends for you. You've been cleared of any guilt in the crime and it's all been pinned on the true killer, a man they believe carjacked his way across the country before falling to his doom in the Colorado River." Abe paused to chew on his cigar thoughtfully. "Your parents, your workplace, they've all been put under the impression you're under police protection for the time being. Maybe you should consider giving the folks a call when we get to Seattle. Let them know you're ok."

"That's all fine and good," Jonah sputtered, shaking his head. "But wouldn't the Syndicate be undoing all of that right now? I mean, what with you betraying them and all?"

The big man shook his head. "You're just a minor fish to them, Jonah. Another problem with bureaucracies like that, is that it's too easy to lose things. You, as far as they are concerned, are just some dumb kid who bought the wrong coin at the wrong time. None of them had enough interest in you as a person to put two and two together to realize you're one of us."

Jonah frowned a little at that. "They've got to know by now, though. I mean, after everything that's happened the last few days ... hell, that bull drake, the one who attacked me before. He's seen me with you guys. He fought me when I was ... well ... back there," he finished, still having trouble thinking of himself as a dragon after all that had happened.

"Don't forget, the bull drakes aren't thinkers. They just do what they're told to do. Granted, if one of his keepers specifically asked him he might say something about it," Abe said, shaking his head. "But he's not bright enough to volunteer the information. And like I said, the Syndicate is too big a bureaucracy. No one there is going to put it together. Not now, anyway. They've got other things to worry about."

"So they're not going to be coming after me? After my parents?"

Abe laughed softly. "No, Jonah, they aren't. You're free to go back to Florida and go on with your life, if that's what you want."

He didn't feel especially consoled by the explanation, but it seemed reasonable enough. Still, that lingering sense of dread was gnawing at the pit of his stomach; still there were many questions in his head. "I don't know, Abe. All this business about dragons and mages. It's a lot to sort out, and it's going to take some time. I don't know what I'm going to do ... hell, I don't really know what it means to me, to be a dragon. I never even figured out what my, er, dragon power is."

"Dragon power?" The bald man chuckled softly and shook his head. "It's really not that important, kid. Did you need any special power to do what you did? Nope. You put all your heart and soul into what you were doing and that's all that matters. You fought for someone besides yourself, you pushed yourself to the end and back for them, and that's all that matters. Hmm. Though now that I think about it, maybe your 'dragon power' is the power of love."

"Don't be stupid," Jonah scowled a little angrily as he felt hot in the cheeks.

Abe threw his head back and laughed heartily, plucking his cigar out of his mouth as he did. "Sorry, sorry. I couldn't help it. Look, don't sweat this business about special powers. We've all got one and you'll discover yours one day. Just never forget what you accomplished without it."

Still feeling a little embarrassed, Jonah turned to look back over the water. "Right. What about you, though, Abe? What are you going to do now? Surely you're on the Syndicate's most wanted list."

"You better believe it," the big man said with a broad smile. "Unfortunately there's no going back for me. By now they've seized all of my assets, or at least all of them they know about. Sure, I've got a few things tucked away for safekeeping but most of it is long gone. I suppose that's not such a bad thing though. I've been thinking that it was time to get out of the lawyering business, that it was time for Abraham Sawyer to retire.

"I hear the aerospace industry is supposed to be taking off. That might be interesting to get in to," he continued with a little grin.

Jonah couldn't help but to frown. "You can do that? Throw your life away and start over, just on a whim? No family, no roots, no connections?"

Abe shrugged a little nonchalantly. "Not really, no. Just a few friends and the like. And when you get to be my age, it's no big deal to have to start all over. You get bored with the same thing, over and over again. Kind of like a name. Been thinking about a new one, or going back to an old one. I always did like being a Ben. Ben Waring. Has a certain ring to it, no?"

"I suppose," he shrugged.

"Well. I'm going to get back inside, it's getting a little chilly out here and I have some catching up to do with the others," Abe said, clapping him lightly on the back. "Let me know if you need anything. Just try not to fret too much. It's not good for you." With that, the big man stepped back into the interior of the ferry, leaving Jonah alone with his thoughts once again.

The brief discussion had done little to settle Jonah's mind, however, and had added more questions as well. He did feel some small sense of relief to know that not only were his parents safe but that they knew he was safe, as well. He decided that he would give them a call once they were back in the city, let them know all was well, and that he hoped to see them sometime soon.

He still felt some strange lingering doubts about returning to Florida, about trying to settle back into his life. Even if the police had cleared him of all wrongdoing, there was still the violent memory of Sam's murder, there was still the memory of being attacked in his own apartment and the place being wrecked. He did not know if he could ever return to those places and feel safe, if he could ever feel whole there again.

If there were any other options, however, he could not think of any.

After only a few moments alone he heard footsteps behind him again, and wondered if Abe had decided to rejoin him when he heard a much softer, more pleasant sort of voice behind him. "Jonah. I haven't thanked you yet," Rebekah said quietly, meekly.

Jonah did not turn to look at her right away. He felt a strange lump forming in his neck, and was hesitant to turn and meet her gaze, afraid of what she might say, afraid of what he might see in her eyes. "That's ok," he croaked softly. "I was just … helping out the best I know how."

The pregnant silence seemed to sully the beauty of the night, but he remained fixed on the view of the moon against the water, waiting in silence for her to speak up again. "No, Jonah. What you did for me back there was … well, you have no idea what it was like, being under that spell. Seeing everything like it were through someone else's eyes, feeling someone else's emotions, needs, and desires. It wasn't like I was being controlled, it was like I wanted to do those things. It's … frightening, to think back on it. I'm sorry."

"It's ok," he repeated, shrugging his shoulders a little lamely. "Like I said, I was just doing what I could to help out."

"Thank you," she repeated again, more softly.

Turning his head fractionally, just enough to see the dance of moonlight against her face, he nodded. "You're welcome, then."

Another long, uncomfortable silence passed, and Jonah once more turned his gaze out to sea, resting against the handrail. He half expected her to head back inside, but out of the corner of his eye he saw her step up to the railing as well, resting her hands there and looking out in the same direction. "It's peaceful, isn't it?"

"Yeah," he agreed, mumbling.

She didn't seem to be put off by his recalcitrance, just nodding as she stood there. "I grew up near here, actually. On one of the islands up north of here. Quiet, beautiful … I miss it in a lot of ways. It's changed so much though, you'd hardly recognize the place anymore …"

He realized she was trying to make small talk, and that fact made his stomach start to flutter. She'd warmed up to him once since that awkward stay in the motel and he'd managed to foul things up once before; he feared that one slip of the tongue would result in the same. "What are you going to do, now?"

Turning to look at him curiously, she blinked. "What do you mean?"

Jonah shrugged. "You don't have to look after me anymore, so what are you going to do with all of your free time?"

"Oh," she replied, nodding with a faint smile. "Well, I'll just settle down and relax for a while, I suppose. Get back to my line of work."

"What do you do?" He turned again to look at her, slightly curious.

Shaking her head, she laughed softly. "Oh, you'll never believe it. I make wind chimes. Sell them online. It's not a lot of money but it's fun, and people seem to enjoy them, too, so, it works out."

"Wind chimes? Really?"

"Really," she said, nodding. "I can show you the website later if you want."

"Sure," he responded, managing a brief smile before he felt the awkward silence creeping up on him once more. Casting his gaze back out to sea, he felt his grip clenching on the handrail a little tighter than was necessary; his heart fluttered in his chest again as he tried to think of something else to say, something useful, something that he would not regret saying later.

He was half afraid that he'd take too long, that she'd get bored of the silence and retreat inside with the others again, but she was the one who actually spoke up first. "There's something else I wanted to tell you, Jonah."

Swallowing down a breath, he turned slightly to look at her over his shoulder again, his eyes widening some. "Yeah?"

"Seafood."

It was neither what he hoped nor feared to hear, and in fact it caught him completely off guard. He was so confused by her response that it served to disarm him, make him feel suddenly less nervous about what it was she was going to say, about what was going to happen, and he just blinked at her oddly. "Seafood?"

"Something you said. Or, at least, something that I think you said. I can't remember clearly," she said, furrowing her eyebrows as she seemed to be thinking. "My favorite food. It's seafood."

He remembered. It was one of the things he had uttered to her while he was trying to get her to break out of the spell, trying to get her to remember who she was, who he was. He had pleaded for her, said he wanted to get to know her. Wanted to know her favorite foods.

She remembered, too, it seemed, and he couldn't help but to blush a little, hidden in the moonlight. After a brief pause the ferry shifted as it rounded a corner, the lights of Seattle coming in to view from across the sound. Shifting his own weight with the boat, feeling his hand slide against the handrail and nudge up against her own, he tore his eyes away from the sight of the glimmering city and gazed at her with a little smile, letting his hand slip lightly over hers.

"I hear Seattle's got some great seafood."

ABOUT THE AUTHOR

Long a fan of all things sci-fi and fantasy, Alan finds time between work in the IT field and work in the domestic field to share that love with others through writing. When he's not dreaming up his next tale or getting his nose stuck in a great novel, you might find him indulging in a few interests such as astronomy, travel or good food.